INTO
THE LIGHT

OTHER BOOKS AND BOOKS ON CASSETTE
BY KEITH TERRY:

Out of Darkness

The Remnant

INTO
THE LIGHT

a novel

KEITH TERRY

Covenant Communications, Inc.

Cover image © PhotoDisc/GettyImages

Cover design copyrighted 2004 by Covenant Communications, Inc.

Published by Covenant Communications, Inc.
American Fork, Utah

Printed in Canada
First Printing: August 1995, January 2004

08 07 06 05 04   10 9 8 7 6 5 4 3

ISBN 1-59156-356-9

ACKNOWLEDGMENTS

My wife, Ann, who proofed, corrected, and offered her expertise in structure and content. Jerry St. Vincent for his editing skills.

The single most important group to lend scholarly support to this novel were key members of the Foundation for Ancient Research and Mormon Studies (F.A.R.M.S.). The results of their research in the past decade have opened up the exciting avenues that permeate this novel. Published studies by members of this committee opened my eyes to the possibility of focusing on this new information.

Specifically, I wish to express gratitude to John Hilton and his work on the River Sidon; Stephen D. Ricks for his insights into the Book of Mormon; Martha and Farrin Whitaker for their proofing; David Campbell, who was a great help giving concepts; Dona Max, a bright and lively scholar; Lynn McKinlay for his wealth of knowledge and understanding of scripture; and Katharina Betz for her help with the German language. Most especially to Maurice R. Tanner, who has a great talent for understanding human character and compassion.

CHARACTERS

The Convert:
Dr. Stephen Thorn—*New convert to Mormonism, faces the rejection of his wife*

The Reluctant Investigator:
Anney Thorn—*Struggles with her husband's newfound beliefs*

The Professor:
Dr. Peter Polk—*Brigham Young University Professor Emeritus, administrator of the Book of Mormon projects*

The Televangelist:
Robert Moore—*Bay Area televangelist with questionable values, Anney's father*

The Fiancée:
Katherine Latham—*Wealthy, generous, beautiful woman who loves Robert Moore*

The Assistants:
Roy Carver—*Graduate student with a focus on original American documents*
Decker Hunt—*Moore's new executive assistant*

The Discontented Heir:
Craig Kline—*Greedy, ruthless, determined to break the trust set up by his father*

The Sisters:
Delitra Kline Kimble—*Successful businesswoman, focused on saving her father's copper business from Craig's mismanagement*
Marjorie Kline Biddle—*Intimidated by Craig and Delitra; chair of the Book of Mormon Trust Board*

The Son:
Todd Thorn—*Son of Stephen and Anney, exchange student in Berlin*

The Aunt:
Elena Vluenski—*Anney's mother's sister*

The Lawyers:
William Bennett—*Attorney for the Book of Mormon Trust*
Chet Hadley—*Unscrupulous expert in breaking trusts*
Harvey Dotson—*Young attorney in Bennett's office who comes to Stephen's aid*

The Secretary:
Jolinda—*Sympathetic and competent*

The Board Member:
Markham Quail—*Curator of Southwestern Museum*

The Mission President:
William Reeves Berkeley—*President of the Prague Mission, answers Anney's questions*

The Translator:
Heinrik von Wagner III—*Moore's dramatic translator*

The Experts:
Dr. Conley Wilks—*University of Arizona professor and consultant on the Land of Bountiful*
Melvin Brookline—*Expert in ancient monetary systems*
Dr. Claus McNear—*Scripps Institute oceanographer, expert on ocean currents and ancient vessels*

Professors Helen Calmer and Doris Browning—*Lecturers on the Tree of Life in Mesoamerica*

Dr. Pierre Novue—*Surgeon and collector of metal plates*

Professor Norman Hammon—*Rutgers University archaeologist, expert in ancient civilizations in Mesoamerica*

Rabbi Elam Michale—*Oxford scholar, expert on the Urim and Thummim in Jewish tradition*

Dr. William Morrison—*Princeton geographer, theorized on the location of the Book of Mormon lands*

Dr. Marvin Johnson—*University of Missouri archaeologist and authority on Quetzalcoatl (the bearded white god)*

CONTENTS

CHAPTER 1
Stephen's Dilemma

Lafayette

Stephen slowly replaced the receiver on its base and raised his head to face his wife.

"Why? Why are you doing this to me and the children?" Anney demanded. Overhearing his conversation, she had stormed across the room with an exasperated outcry.

"Doing what?" Stephen asked, knowing full well what she was driving at.

"It's insane. You have no right to do this. You know my feelings. But you have this crazy obsession. I can hardly stand here and talk about it!"

Stephen had walked quietly into their upstairs bedroom a few minutes earlier, hands in pockets, broad shoulders slumped. In hushed tones, he had pleaded with Anney one more time not to go with her father on the tour.

Then came the phone call from Dr. Polk in Provo, Utah, to inquire of Stephen's decision to assist him in the Book of Mormon Project II. The response sparked a firestorm of fury.

Stephen's mind tried to formulate a reply to Anney's outburst. She had repeatedly refused to listen to him explain his recent acceptance of Mormonism and his desire that she learn more about the beliefs as well. He knew instinctively, as he sat dejectedly on the floral bed cover of their king-size bed, that his timing was off. He should have told Anney of his decision to assist Polk before she overheard him on the phone.

Timing. What an important factor in any human relationship. Stephen silently pondered his dilemma. *Why, oh, why is this whole thing so complex and difficult to broach? Why is Anney so unreasonable about the Mormons?*

Stephen looked away from her penetrating, deep blue eyes as she stood with her back to the mirrored closet door, hands on hips, seething with rage.

"Honey, we need the money," Stephen replied with a sigh of exasperation. "You've been on my case about bringing in money. Well, here's a chance to fill in until I get a permanent job."

"Don't twist things. I want you to get a job in your field. But how can you get a permanent job when you're gallivanting around the world working for the Mormons?"

"Anney, we've already talked about this. I told you that the agency will schedule job interviews when I'm in town. I can work it out. This project with Dr. Polk is temporary, and it won't interfere with my job search."

"It makes me furious that you accepted his offer in spite of my feelings."

Stephen sat silent, a puzzled stare on his face. Anney's blond-streaked hair swirled about as she jerked her head from side to side in dramatic rejection of his decision. "Doesn't it matter at all what I think?"

Theirs had been a strained relationship from the moment Anney had driven Stephen home from the Oakland Air Terminal at the completion of the project in Rancho Santa Fe—an odious project in Anney's mind. She had been filled with hope and resolve that their differences could be worked out. After all, Stephen had returned seemingly committed to her and their teenage children, with their welfare at heart. At first she had been convinced that his intense new faith in a religion without substance would pass. They had weathered other experiences in their twenty-two years of marriage. This time, however, they had reached an impasse.

For two months there had been a workable truce in the Thorn household, though at times Stephen would find Anney with red, tear-filled eyes when he returned from job interviews. He knew she was struggling to come to terms with her feelings; it troubled him deeply that she saw him as the cause of so much heartache.

The first major confrontation after his return had come when Stephen refused to return to work at the ministry with her father, the Reverend Robert Moore, where he had been Moore's executive assistant for the past seventeen years. He had explained to Anney that he couldn't go back to work for a person who held a totally different view of religion than the one he had come to accept. This made no sense to Anney.

It was clear to her that her father could not keep Stephen on with his new attitude toward the ministry. Maybe she was imagining it, but there seemed to be more to their stand-off than a difference in religion. To Anney, it seemed to be one of those major crises in family relationships—painful, but surely fixable. Time. Maybe time would knit the wound that had been so crudely laid open.

The whole matter of Stephen's involvement in the summer project began over money, or the lack of it. Moore had sent Stephen to that conclave as his replacement so the ministry could gain the desperately needed hundred-thousand-dollar stipend that had been offered for participation.

Anney knew that in the initial request Stephen had gone just to please his father-in-law, although the Thorns, for their part, had received twenty thousand dollars of the stipend. She had also known that it was wrong from the moment she heard he was going. *Why had they agreed to such an involvement?* Anney still could not comprehend how the ministry had allowed itself to sink to such a level that it needed financial help from that kind of source.

In spite of Stephen's boycott of the ministry, Anney refused to give up her position as a staff member in her father's ministry and insisted that she had no cause to do so. Someone in the house had to hold down a job. They needed the income. Because she worked closely with her father each day while Stephen put together his resume and began looking for a position with Bay Area public relations firms, she felt torn between the two men.

His new unemployed status had hit home for Stephen a couple of weeks after he started looking for work. The trite term "overqualified" seemed to fit his job search. When would-be employers—all the way from San Jose to San Francisco and up to the Napa Valley—saw that he had a doctorate in public relations but no experience beyond his employment with the Reverend Moore, some headhunters flatly rejected him.

Fortunately, the Executive Employment Agency of San Francisco had accepted him as a client. They took him on six weeks after Stephen began his job search and insisted in their initial interview that two months was not a great deal of time to spend looking for a position—not at his required level of income. The new agency had warned him that it could take as long as six months to land a good paying job in his field. They had suggested patience. Patience he didn't have. Anney was concerned about his ability to get a job. Fighting discouragement, he sometimes felt like it was a dead end for him.

"Perhaps," Anney had said, "you'll simply have to get training in another field." Then on second thought, she said, "But I don't see how we can afford that; we've already dipped into the money from last summer. But if it comes to that, my salary will help make some of our payments as you get training."

Stephen had exhausted his employment agency's first flush of contacts and continued sending out resumes to other public relations firms or to firms that had in-house public relations departments. But in two months' time he had turned up no serious offers.

California was undergoing an economic downturn, and jobs weren't all that plentiful, especially for a man who had held but one job in his entire life. Granted, Moore's ministry was considered successful, but it was still a ministry. His placement sources indicated that perhaps they could find him something in another ministry. In that field, he had a great track record and an outstanding resume detailing his activities. But Stephen had refused to consider such a position, which narrowed his options. Then, Anney had come home one evening to inform Stephen that her father had asked her to accompany him and his other staff members on his upcoming Eastern European tour to teach televangelism in the old Eastern Bloc nations.

The Reverend Moore had been selected as the representative of his televangelists' association to coach the rising crop of ministers in Eastern Europe, who were eager to grasp American communication skills at swaying potential converts through television sermons to a broad audience. Although publicly touting it as a benefit to those ministers struggling in the old communist satellite nations, Moore saw it as a great opportunity to gain worldwide publicity. It was scheduled as a two-month tour, ending before Christmas in St. Petersburg, Russia.

"It's a super opportunity for Daddy," Anney had interjected as she breathlessly revealed her father's plans. She had also explained to Stephen that Katherine, her father's new fiancée, was funding the entire project.

As Stephen listened to Anney tell where the funding for the tour was coming from, it crossed his mind that it had taken the Reverend Moore no time at all to sink his hooks into the wealthy socialite who seemed eager to shell out the cash. Since the death of Moore's invalid wife in late August six weeks earlier, he and Katherine Latham had fallen in love and announced their engagement.

Even though Nadia Moore, Anney's mother, had not been lucid in many years and was unable to recognize even her own family members, the Reverend Moore's position and his concern about decorum demanded that some time elapse before he marry a second time. Regardless of Stephen's reaction to the romance, Anney personally liked her father's future wife and felt that it made no difference whether they were married in a week or six weeks.

* * *

The time of Anney's departure for the European tour with her father and his entourage had arrived. It came far too quickly for Stephen, who hadn't come to grips with the fact that she was actually going. He felt insecure at the very thought of Anney leaving, especially with the group that would be part of the entourage. He had pleaded with her not to go. "Daddy needs my help. He's so excited about this tour, Stephen," Anney had reasoned. *If the truth were known, so was she. Tonight, of all times, with Anney leaving in the morning, why did we have to get into another fight?*

"I have tried, Stephen Thorn," Anney ranted on. "Believe me, I have tried. I have tried to understand this new belief you've been sucked into, but I just cannot get past my shock that you would deliberately join the Mormons. What else can I say? It is so wrong, yet you go on with this insane idea of yours that it would be right for all of us. I'm sorry. It is not right. I have an opinion, too. And now you're going to work for them? I don't care if it is temporary. I don't like it one bit! Someone has to stand up and say that you have made a big, big mistake."

Gripping the bedspread with both fists, Stephen took a breath and said, "I'm sorry, too. But I have to take the offer. Anney, we need the money. Don't you understand?"

Anney's lips tightened. She could see that he was inflexible in his decision. She turned her back on him and slammed her suitcase shut.

* * *

"You. Why you?" Dr. Peter Polk stabbed his index finger toward Stephen Thorn, who sat in a forest-green, leather swivel chair that matched the other seven around the oval table in the walnut-paneled conference room of William Bennett's suite of law offices in Phoenix. "Why were you the only one who accepted the truth of the Book of Mormon?"

The three men—Peter Polk, Bill Bennett, and Stephen Thorn: professor, attorney, and, as Stephen thought of himself, between jobs—concluded a two-hour session, wrapping up the planning strategy for the Book of Mormon Project II. As the discussion of the picky details had progressed, Polk had become as nervous as a trapped cougar, stirring around the office as Bennett formulated the legal arrangements, including disbursement of the three million dollars earmarked for the new project. Approximately twelve million dollars remained of the original endowment established by the late Thomas Kline, a wealthy associate of Polk's. Together, they had formulated a plan to excite people about the Book of Mormon. Kline had died suddenly before he could see their projects unfold, leaving Polk to carry the projects to fruition.

Dr. Peter Polk was the designated administrator and manager of the trust, working with a board of five directors. His charge was to make a success of the Book of Mormon projects, though the funds were not to be spent solely on projects; some would go for long-term endowments sponsoring further study. Project II, which was in the planning stage, would conclude with a conference in May the following year in Provo, Utah. Fifty young adult students and several guest lecturers would participate for four weeks.

"Did you hear me, Stephen? Why were you the only one?"

Stephen was having difficulty concentrating on the conversation. Important though the meeting was, his mind remained focused on his wife and their opposing views. In the days since he had watched her board the plane for Europe with her father and his staff, his fears had magnified until he was scarcely functioning. *Pull yourself together, man! This is your job. Pay attention.*

"Uh . . . well, let's think about it," he began, willing his mind to put aside personal affairs. "I have wondered myself why I was the only one of the six of us. Everybody on that project was exceptional in their own field. I don't really know, but I think maybe I had been searching for something for years. Then, too, I was representing a ministry, and I may have been more open to the familiarity and simplicity of the message. For me, it was as if the precepts were self-evident. All the fragmented truths I had learned up to the time I read the Book of Mormon came together so naturally and comfortably . . . as though they were suddenly being clearly defined for the first time. Does that make sense? Besides, the others were renowned scholars, with reputations to protect. Maybe that was a factor, too."

Stephen paused, looked down at his left thumb, and noticed that an ugly black bruise was forming under the base of the nail. He had slammed the rental car door on it at Sky Harbor two hours earlier.

He continued to ponder the first time he read the Book of Mormon and said, "It may sound a little corny, but as I read I felt like an empty bottle gradually filling up. Always before, whenever I read the Bible, it was enjoyable but not filling. I never knew there was more. I thought that I had all of God's words. Then when I read the Book of Mormon, it was like putting on a new pair of glasses for the first time.

"I saw things much clearer. I felt such a burning desire to continue reading." He squared his shoulders and spread his palms. He hesitated again, feeling the eyes of both men upon him. "I don't really know, but it seems to me that the book itself carries a certain spirit that is part of the conversion process. I read somewhere recently that the Book of Mormon has a familiar sound."

Stephen's face clouded slightly, and he shook his head. "There's no magic here, though. You still have to change your life to follow the instructions that are all through the Book of Mormon. And there are other adjustments as well." Stephen's voice dropped. "I still have a challenge with my family, you know."

"I know, Stephen," Polk said solemnly. He reached out to pat his friend's shoulder. Earlier, Stephen had related to Dr. Polk Anney's protests to his involvement in the project. "There is a saying that may fit your situation. It goes, 'I never said it would be easy; I just said it would be worth it.'"

Polk moved across the room to the wall, which was lined with bookshelves crammed with legal volumes, and wagged his round head from side to side in frustration. He knew that he didn't have the answers to his own questions—highly unusual for a scholar with his mind and experience. He was nearing seventy years of age, a professor emeritus at Brigham Young University. A determined scholar.

"Stephen, you seem willing to bite off this new project. But is the material we will examine and place before young people—who will also be paid, housed, and fed for four weeks at our conference this spring—worth the price tag? I ask you, where do we end up? Will they simply gain a bagful of knowledge and no conviction that the Book of Mormon is, above all else, a testimony of Jesus Christ, a testimony that will lead to a commitment to serve the Lord more fully? Will any of them be touched as you were, Stephen?"

With a concerned expression, Polk walked slowly across to the conference table in the center of the law office. He pulled out one of the large, leather chairs, swiveled it around, and plopped his rotund body into it.

"What are you saying?" Stephen asked. "Are you thinking about scrubbing the project?"

Bennett, the attorney, who held no deep conviction of the Book of Mormon, pulled a legal document closer to him and began to look very busy. He wanted no part of the philosophical aspects of the project. He was content to back it up with his legal expertise, ready to anticipate anything that could go wrong. He wanted to avoid being sucked into this discussion and hoped Polk would leave him out.

Polk rubbed the top of his bald head and then pressed the sides of his forehead in an effort to ease the pressure that had been building for the past half-hour. "No. No, Stephen. That is not at all what I have in mind. Nor do I think my wonderful, generous friend, Thomas Kline, bless his soul, would have wanted that either. As you know, he and I figured out this whole scheme of pulling non-members to the Book of Mormon. It's just got to work!" Polk kept his eyes fixed on Stephen for a moment and then spoke. "I must say, Stephen, you are one expensive result of our first attempt to play out our involved plans. You are pure gold to me. I hope you know that. But I want a hundred, a thousand just like you. Without incentive—in this case money—some people will probably never pick up the Book of Mormon." He paused to let the words penetrate Stephen's mind. Glancing sidelong at Bennett, he could see that his plea had not moved the attorney.

"Money alone will not make converts; we've proven that," Polk repeated. "Yet, if we spend some money to excite people about the Book of Mormon and show them at the outset what a great book it is, then they may pick it up and read it. From there, the Spirit has to take over. Are we agreed on that?" Polk's hand smacked the top of Bennett's desk with renewed resolve. "Okay, our intention is to move forward with Project II. We will highlight, mostly through scholars and other experts in a variety of fields, the external and often disputed evidence that surrounds the Book of Mormon. But in the process we have to find out what it is that will bring a person—one who has no previous knowledge of the book—to read the Book of Mormon . . . read it in humility, desiring to know if it is true." Polk's hand punctured the air with emphasis. "Do you understand what I'm saying?"

"I guess," Stephen replied with a furrowed brow. "It's a big order."

* * *

"What are you doing in London?" demanded Craig Kline, frustrated that he had to initiate the call to the Reverend Moore. "Come on, Reverend, I'm paying you good money for information, and I want it now! How are you going to be able to pin down Polk while you're running around Europe and wherever else you plan on going?"

After a two-week business trip, Craig Kline, the heir to a good part of the Thomas Kline fortune, had walked into his office at the Tower Plaza in Phoenix, expecting to find a fat report from the Reverend Robert Moore regarding the activities of Moore's son in-law, Stephen Thorn, and his dealings with a certain Peter Polk. Craig monitored Dr. Polk's activities and associates. A great deal of the family's money was slipping away because of Polk's freedom to spend the trust with little restraint. Craig wanted to stop Polk and, through court action, halt this waste. Learning that no message had been received, Craig had telephoned Moore's ministry in San Francisco, only to be told that Moore was on an extended tour of Europe. Would he like the number of the hotel in London?

Furious, Craig had called Moore at the Hyde Park Hilton, not caring that there was an eight-hour time difference. The minister had been about to leave for dinner with his fiancée when Craig Kline reached him. Kline was clearly agitated. He knew he needed hard facts now. He wanted to get to trial. If he could only seize the kind of evidence that would break his father's trust and, even better, convict Polk for fraud while he was about it. So he would have to pay as much as thirty thousand for the information; it would be worth it at twice the price. At this point, he had already forked over ten thousand dollars to this shady TV minister as a deposit for information. It was Moore's job to get convincing evidence for Craig's newly hired attorney so they could get on with the case. Either that or Moore would get no more money.

They had struck a deal: ten thousand up front, ten thousand when Moore had hard evidence they could take to court, and the balance when Craig won the case and broke the trust. Fair enough. Now that clown Moore was off in Europe for four weeks, playing the role of instructor/evangelist. What a schmuck!

Craig moaned to himself. He didn't need all this garbage tossed in on top of his worsening financial troubles. He had to get a hold of the money his father had foolishly placed in trust for that stupid project. Craig had no way of knowing how much of the original fifteen million had already been spent since his father's death. He thought of his younger sister, Marjorie. Weak-willed as she was, their father had named her chair of the trust board. *I've got to get Marj to demand an accounting of the funds. She won't like it, but I can make her do it.*

With a scowl, Craig hastily computed a few numbers on a pad. With what he had learned about the former project, he guessed a couple of million went to pay those non-Mormon scholars to complete that worthless study of the Book of Mormon in San Diego last summer. He still couldn't believe that his attempt to halt payment had failed. At least he would be able to recoup the twelve-plus million that he guessed was still in the trust. But at the rate Polk was shelling out cash, over half of the fifteen million would be depleted in a year.

What in the world was Dad thinking when he left a moron that kind of money to play with? The thought almost sent Craig into orbit.

"I told you." On the phone, Moore's dignified rebuttal held an injured tone, interrupting Kline's thoughts. "This tour was scheduled before you contacted me. And I must remind you that you are not paying *me;* rather, you are donating to the ministry."

There was a certain inflection in Moore's voice. It was not only phony, it had a touch of the Bible-Belt preacher that all the greats in old-time religion had mastered. It bugged Craig.

Robert Moore had his own plate full, and as much as he craved the thirty thousand dollars that this bully was eager to pay, he was not going to be pushed around. Still, in all, he owed Craig something.

"I have taken a couple of steps in the right direction," Moore went on defensively. "Before we left San Francisco, I had my new executive assistant fly to Provo and check out Dr. Polk. Polk was not in Provo at the time. He's been back and forth to Central America, and in a few days my son-in-law will meet him there. Precisely what they are doing I don't know, but I will find out through my daughter. You may be interested to know, however, that my assistant, Decker Hunt, learned that Polk is building a very expensive theater or amusement hall or some sort of public attraction inside a large, empty building that at one time was a supermarket there in Provo."

"With my money!"

"I presume that the project is eating up part of the trust you mentioned. The place he is renovating is fashioned after a kind of Disney ride, or so they say."

"Who says?"

"Decker, my assistant. He was told that the attraction being constructed has something to do with Dr. Polk's overall project concerning the Book of Mormon. Also, Decker discovered that it is costing upwards of two million dollars."

"Two million!" Craig screamed with rage. "How does your Decker know that?"

"He talked to a film animator who happened to be in Provo. The man came out of the building while Decker was in the parking lot trying to figure out how to get past their security. Decker took him to lunch and pumped him for all he knew. Decker told the guy that he was a contractor, that Polk wanted him to submit a bid on some lighting, and that Decker wanted to know if the project was sound. The animator told him everything he knew about the project, which wasn't a great deal, but he did tell Decker that he had a contract with Dr. Polk to create computerized drawings—you know, the kind they have on video games."

"Where was the animator from?"

"Hollywood."

"Did the animator reveal how much Polk is paying him?"

"It's a studio the guy works for. Two hundred and fifty thousand."

"A quarter of a million!" Craig choked. "For what?"

"For film drawings. I don't know any more, but I do have the fellow's name and address in North Hollywood."

"Give it to me. I'm going after Polk. He'll wish he had never heard the name Kline. He'll regret worming that money out of my father. Believe me, he will."

CHAPTER 2
Wadi Sayq

The attendant at the gas station where Stephen Thorn filled up his rental car warned him about the neighborhood when he asked for directions to Wilks's dune buggy shop.

Stephen paid for the gas, got back in the car, sped out of the gas station, took a right, and made the light at the intersection, traveling east to the industrial complex. He glanced at the flat-roofed stucco buildings as he passed through the deteriorating neighborhood. Most were boarded up, with graffiti sprayed across the walls and sidewalks. At Lancing Road, he made another right and started down the shabby industrial park street, devoid of trees or grass. As he drove along, his mind clouded with thoughts of Anney.

Never an hour passed that Stephen didn't concern himself about his family and how they were doing. He sometimes shook his head, wondering if he was doing the right thing by becoming involved in this Book of Mormon project. He wished he could get beyond these nagging second thoughts about this temporary job. It was unlike him to vacillate. He knew that if Anney were a hundred percent behind him, as she had been in most other ventures in his career, he would have no second thoughts. But she was anything but pleased with his new assignment, even though she knew that they needed the twenty-five thousand dollars he would be paid over the next three months for services rendered on the project.

At forty-five, with a wife and two nearly adult children to support, he wished his life were more settled. At a casual glance, Stephen didn't look old enough to have a daughter in her second year of college. His body was taut and athletic. The deep-set blue eyes of his mother, whom he hardly remembered, held an intense glow of intelligence, affirming that he had a brain to match his body.

The hundred-foot-long Quonset hut with its dull, corrugated, half-moon roof was war surplus from the late 1940s and was well dusted from the Tucson desert. Eight years earlier, it had served as a tractor repair shop. The current sign proclaimed that it was Wilks's Desert Vehicle Shop. Those who sought out the services of Dr. Conley Wilks had heard, more often than not, of his mechanical innovations with dune buggies. Wilks and his three mechanics were world-class in their field. Customers in search of the finest-quality dune buggies seldom complained about snaking their way through the vintage industrial complex to seek out the shop. It was located on the south side of the city in the low-rent district where, he had been warned, there had recently been a couple of drive-by shootings—by suspects in pickups and cowboy hats.

Stephen spotted the Quonset hut and knew from Polk's description that it was Wilks's shop. For one thing, it was tidier than most shops along the block; there was no trash in the parking lot or junked, rusting parts leaning against the building. Some businesses had their bay doors open, and Stephen could see Latino laborers, already sweating as they worked in tool and die, welding, laminating, and a dozen other floundering enterprises that lined the street.

He pulled the rental car next to the shop and parked. The sun was becoming intense and focused, baking the dry, dusty street. But it felt good to Stephen as he stepped from his rental car onto the gravel walk. Noticing an ordinary, unmarked door next to a large bay opening, he stood a moment, wondering if he should knock. Then, figuring that since it was a shop, it must be open to the public, he opened the door and stepped in. Three swamp coolers had been churning at full bore since morning, blowing moist air into the long Quonset hut's interior and making the crowded shop tolerable.

Gas, oil, and diesel fuel combined to emit a familiar smell that Stephen remembered from his youth, growing up on his uncle's ranch in Nevada. The odors sent a feeling of déjà vu coursing through his mind.

He had loved his uncle and aunt, his cousins, too. They had raised him after his widowed mother died a violent death on the unfinished Santa Ana freeway back in the late 1950s. It was his uncle, his mother's brother, who had left money in trust for his education. The money had even stretched into his graduate studies at Berkeley, where he received his doctoral degree in public relations. He and Anney were married while he was still in school, and by the time he moved into an executive position with Anney's father, the Reverend Robert Moore, he had a daughter of his own. Surprisingly, he had never held another job until this latest assignment with Polk, and this was only temporary.

A small engine hung from a steel beam in the shop. Stephen worked his way around it and between two framed dune buggies, stopping to admire a third buggy with elaborate black steel piping for roll bars. It was painted olive drab—strictly military, Stephen noticed. Next to it was a sand-colored Hummer, the all-terrain vehicle used in Desert Storm. It was twice the size of the dune buggy alongside it. Extending from under the Hummer, he noticed a pair of Nikes. He heard muffled swear words coming from the mechanic lying on his gurney under the vehicle. The complaint seemed to be addressed to a stubborn part that refused to come off.

Stephen chuckled, turning when he heard his name from the far end of the building. "Thorn! Hey, Thorn! How're ya doin'?"

Stephen noticed that it was Conley Wilks shouting and motioning with his hand. Wilks had emerged from his office to greet Stephen, who hurried forward to grasp the outstretched hand of the professor. Stephen had met Dr. Conley Wilks, the buggy builder and sometime professor, when Dr. Polk introduced him to the group in San Diego. He hadn't recalled the man's appearance exactly, but seeing him refreshed his memory. He was a large, blond-bearded guy between thirty-five and forty. Besides being a full professor of geography at the University of Arizona, Dr. Wilks was also an entrepreneur. Polk had talked about Conley the evening before as Stephen drove him to Sky Harbor for his flight back to Provo.

"Nice to see you again, Dr. Wilks," Stephen smiled.

Gripping Stephen's hand with a hefty paw, Wilks squinted, peering intently at his visitor. "Now I remember you," he laughed. "I know we met when I gave that spiel in San Diego last summer, but there were so many of you . . . I wasn't sure which one you were. Sorry. I remember you now."

"That's okay. I understand," Stephen said.

Wilks was deeply tanned, with premature wrinkle lines about the mouth and eyes. If he combed his hair each morning, it made no difference. His dark blond curls swirled untamed, matching his bushy beard. Beard notwithstanding, Wilks had a healthy, rugged appearance, not at all the grungy look Stephen saw these days on the streets of San Francisco. Stephen recalled that the lecture Wilks had delivered to the group last summer was on the subject of Lehi in the desert. He had covered the Lehi trek from Jerusalem to Oman and showed a video of his desert travels. Wilks was a non-Mormon, viewing the import of Lehi's trail from facts alone.

Sweeping his arm in the direction of the shop before entering the small office, Stephen asked, "So this is your place? Aren't you a full professor at the U of A as well?"

"I am. I'm also on sabbatical this year. I've been operating this struggling company for the past five years. Sometimes I wonder if I'm insane to hang onto it. I think the only good that comes out of it is the fact that those four guys out in the shop—great guys, good mechanics—can feed their families because they have a job. Lew out there is going to take over management next spring so I can spend more time on scholastic endeavors. At least that's our plan."

Wilks nudged Stephen into the office. "The only thing that has saved this underfunded venture has been the United States Army. We landed a contract just after the Gulf War to develop a desert dune buggy the Army can use in combat. It's a fast little item . . . easy to maneuver and great in sand. The jeep and the Hummer . . . they're okay, but the Army wants something faster, with better maneuverability in the desert. We have given them five prototypes in the past two years. We're still working on refitting the fifth. I think this is the baby they'll mass produce."

Wilks walked to a drawing table that stood against the upward-curving wall of his long, narrow office. On the end of the table, a three-by-five-foot map of Arabia and the Arabian sea was Scotch-taped to the slant board. Next to the map were fifty or more color photos that looked to Stephen as if they had been done by a one-hour printing service.

"Would you care for coffee this morning?"

"No. No thanks." Stephen felt that sudden urge to say yes. For the last thirty of his forty-five years, he had drunk coffee morning, mid-morning, and throughout his day. It was the hardest, most lingering residual tug of his former lifestyle and one of the vices he had to give up before joining the Mormon Church two weeks ago. He had thought it would be a piece of cake to give up coffee. Liquor was nothing for him. He had seldom tipped a glass. Beer? A tall, ice-cold glass on a hot day; well, maybe that was a little harder. But coffee . . . going through a morning without a cup steaming in his hand was tough. Man, did he love the smell of a good pot brewing!

"I've already had a cup. I don't need one either," Conley responded.

Good. I can at least work without the smell under my nose.

"Let's get down to talking about what Dr. Polk assigned me to do this time." Conley Wilks tapped the drawing board.

"That's why I'm here. I want to know what you found on your recent trip to Oman."

"Okay. Come closer, and take a look at this map."

Stephen stood shoulder to shoulder with Conley as the two leaned over the board.

Conley pointed at the coastline of the Arabian Peninsula and then pushed his index finger firmly on the small area of the village of Khor Kharfot.

"At this beach in Oman, not far from the border of Yemen, there is a spot called Wadi Sayq, 16 degrees east longitude, 44 minutes north latitude. Notice that it's spelled a little different than I pronounced it—'Sike.' Anyway, at this wadi, where I visited for a couple of days, I saw some interesting things that make even a hardened agnostic like me wonder." Conley moved his finger a fraction of an inch to the right. "See this small village? I got there by four-wheel with a guide. I had been there over a year before on my first assignment with Dr. Polk." Suddenly, Conley looked over at Stephen and said, "Hey, how is the ol' boy these days? I haven't talked to him in weeks. He faxes me something, and I fax him a reply."

"Great. He's great. I dropped him at the airport in Phoenix just last evening. He's back in Provo and will leave for southern Mexico tomorrow. He gets around."

"Good. Tell him hi for me." He turned back to the board. "The wadi—I simply filmed the area for the presentation I gave last summer to you and those other guys at that project. By the way, that was some ritzy place you were staying at!" Wilks gave a low whistle and shot his eyebrows skyward. He looked back down at his pictures and went on. "This time, Polk asked me to go to Wadi Sayq and nose around the place for a couple of days. I did that."

"What's so special about this particular wadi?" Stephen knew from last summer's lecture that a wadi in the Near East is a large ravine where rainwater pours down and makes a miniature Grand Canyon, or it could be a crevasse for a small river.

"It's the place most of the Mormons who know the region accept as the spot where Nephi built his ship." Conley moved his index finger along the coastline and said, "This particular location has been compared to all the other wadis in the region along this coastline in Oman and Yemen. It is the only place that meets all the Book of Mormon requirements for the beachfront area called Bountiful. Hands down, it *is* the one. I have this on good authority. The Astons, members of your church who live in Australia, have spent years investigating this region of the coastline. They stumbled upon Wadi Sayq quite by accident.

"They mentioned that they had roamed the southern coastline of the two Arab countries for nearly a decade, hoping to find the ideal beach that matches the description of Nephi's account. And there it was. Wadi Sayq lies in the very heart of the most underexplored section of the coastline of the entire seaboard on the western extremity of Oman. Unless it is reached by traveling from the interior desert plateau as Lehi must have done, it remains almost completely hidden from view. From the sea, the valley is concealed by the oblique angle at the point it reaches the coast. The high beach obscures this pristine area. Really it does. I was amazed."

"Then you're saying that there is a beach that fits the description in the Book of Mormon?"

"Yeah. What's interesting is the way Wadi Sayq was found only in the last couple of years. Oh, there were other wadis that the Astons had explored, before and after, just to be certain they had found the most correct. I visited those others as well. There are at least three others that roughly could be Bountiful, but they have flaws such as . . . the trees are a long distance from the water, the beach is positioned wrong to launch a large vessel, or the place lacks fruit trees, et cetera. They spent eight years researching, trying to locate the exact place that fit best." Conley smiled with a broad grin of satisfaction, as if he had helped the Astons find the location of Wadi Sayq. "They made my job easy.

"It was kind of interesting how it came about. The Astons landed at Muscat airport. They were awaiting a domestic flight to Salalah near the coast. As they milled about, they noticed a postcard on a rack in the airport gift shop depicting a lush coastal scene, which they knew from past ventures was not Salalah. A person on their flight to Salalah told them that the picture was of a coastal view at Rakhyut, a village near the beach. Believe me, they lost no time finding that village. From that point, they rented a vehicle and wound their way to the cliffs overlooking Wadi Sayq. What a discovery for Warren and Michaela. I love 'em.

"At the time they left the highway and drove over rough terrain to the cliffs above Wadi Sayq, few, if any, travelers had taken that route. It was unexplored, as I said. No group has done exploration in that remote region. It is virgin land and a marvelous outlet to the sea.

"Polk warned me that there would be no roads or even trails leading into Wadi Sayq. He had given me rough notes made from conversations he had with the Astons. They have now published a book on the subject. You see, a lot of Mormons are interested in pinpointing exactly where this prophet Lehi and his family built their ship when they set out for the Americas." Conley stretched his back, as if bending over the map caused pain.

"Let me tell ya, you can't get down to Wadi Sayq easily from the village nearby, except by boat. High cliffs prevent easy access. Oh yeah, you could hike down from the desert cliffs at the upper entrance to the wadi, but I doubt that camels could have made it to the bottom. Too steep. Maybe Lehi sold his camels and hiked in with his family. Who knows? Maybe they hired a boat back then and got to it the same way I did."

"You talk about Lehi and his family as if you actually believe he was there."

"Boy, I have no doubt that a man with the drive Lehi had to have to cross that desert could have built a ship and launched it from there. No, I've got no reason to doubt that someone once built a ship at that spot. It could have been your Lehi. Who knows? I was given an assignment to find out, and so far it looks feasible to me. Okay?"

Stephen noticed a slight edge to Conley's voice. He figured the professor did not want to be pinned down to his personal beliefs.

"So how did you get into Wadi Sayq?"

"I hired a boat and a couple of locals—by the way, they spoke no English at all. It wore me out trying to communicate with them. But they helped me find the beach I was searching for." Wilks shoved a picture under Stephen's nose. "You see, there are steep cliffs that jut right up out of the ocean on each side of the Wadi."

"But you found it okay?"

"Oh, sure. Actually, it wasn't the tough assignment I thought it would be. There were six-, seven-foot waves—that was some ride!—and I was in an eighteen-foot boat with this kid who was my guide and the captain of the boat—Arabs, of course. But I've been in tighter spots." Wilks's face melted into an infectious grin. "Those guys over there don't believe in life jackets. Anyway, it didn't take fifteen minutes to pull up on the shore where Wadi Sayq comes down to the sea. We stayed two days. The rainy season was just getting under way while I was there, but we had no problem on the beach. We hit it just right between storms. See here." Wilks tapped a spot on the map. "This area, as I explained to your group last summer, is a green belt in the Arabian Desert.

"I mean, man, I'm a desert rat, but that Arabian desert is one mother. It has to be the most devastatingly dry spot on earth, bar none, except for a few stretches of lush, tropical beaches on the tip of the Arabian peninsula." Conley shook his head, his beard waving like a floppy floor mop. "It's one of those crazy freaks of nature. It juts out here along this peninsula, and mercifully, it is barely touched by the heavy monsoons that raise so much havoc in Pakistan and India every single year.

"The beach at Wadi Sayq is about a mile wide—that is, between the two high cliffs. It's beautiful, the kind of place you would like to have tucked away when you want to shut off the world and relax." Wilks's eyes took on a faraway look. "It's sandy, green, and breathtaking. Only two rivers flow to the sea in that part of the world. One of those tiny rivers flows through Wadi Sayq. That's what made it so long and wide. I saw some dolphins playing at the river's outlet."

With excitement in his voice, Wilks continued, "The fishing is out of this world. Hey, we're talking about a real paradise—flamingos, fish, birds of all types. If you look up from the beach at this point," Conley pointed at one of the other photos next to the map, sliding his firm body to one side so Stephen could see, "you see a lot of brush and lush growth. Very tropical. Then maybe a mile inland, starting up the wadi, are forests of tall trees, maybe seventy- or eighty-foot-high hardwood trees. I took some leaf samples. They're over there." He jerked his thumb over his shoulder, indicating the table on the opposite side of the office. Stephen looked sideways and saw the dried leaves and grass, all in separate, labeled ziplocked plastic bags. "They include sycamore, boscia, and tamarindus. Something else, the place is loaded with wild honeybees. Whoa, did I find out! I stumbled into one of those natural hives and got chased off by some mad bees." Wilks's laughter filled the small room.

For the next hour, Conley described the whole experience minutely, captivating Stephen in the scenes he unfolded. The vegetation, the animal life, the fertile soil. Conley emphasized again how he had read and reread the account in the Book of Mormon and felt that, of the six possible sites in that region, Wadi Sayq was the only one that measured up to the description Nephi had written about the location where the family built their ship.

"Let me read to you from the section of the Book of Mormon that deals with my assignment." Conley reached for the book on the side stand and then had to make a comment. "I haven't read this entire book, but I have certainly digested the part I was to research, and it's interesting how the location fits.

"Listen to this from 1 Nephi chapter 17 verse 4 and on: 'And we did sojourn for the space of many years, yea, even eight years in the wilderness. And we did come to the land which we called Bountiful, because of its much fruit and also wild honey; and all these things were prepared of the Lord that we might not perish. And we beheld the sea, which we called Irreantum, which, being interpreted, is many waters. . . . We were exceedingly rejoiced when we came to the seashore; and we called the place Bountiful, because of its much fruit.'

"Isn't this graphic? I was, Thorn, I was right there. I mean, this location at Wadi Sayq fits in nearly every particular!" he exclaimed. He told of the high cliffs where the brothers could have taken Nephi when they were about to throw him into the sea. He explained how the sea along those cliffs has no shelf to speak of. It literally drops to a great depth. He mentioned that if there had been a shelf, the family would have had no way of launching a large ship into the sea, at least not the seagoing vessel Nephi built. Then he described the interesting concave stone outcropping that was still blackened by carbon from ancient fires. It looked like a giant oven to Conley's eye. "It could have been used to molten iron. By the way, that's the one thing that's missing. They have yet to find ore deposits. But, heck, ore deposits may yet turn up in the wadi further inland.

"I'm convinced that ol' Nephi and his family could have built and launched a ship at this spot. He would have needed to know how to build a ship; but if you believe the account, it says God showed him what to do. I, myself, am not a religious man, so I don't put a whole lot of stock in these things. But even so, from what I saw . . ." He nodded his head with emphasis. "Yeah, you could build a ship there."

Conley pointed toward a green vinyl swivel chair. It had seen better days. The stiff fabric was peeling at the front of the armrest. "Have a seat, Stephen." From behind his desk he pulled out another chair of the same vintage, only brown, and sat across from Stephen. Before Wilks could continue the discussion, the office door opened, and a short, young mechanic stuck his head in.

He nodded at Stephen, turned to Wilks, and said, "Hey, Con. That P-2 buggy is ready for a test. Do you want me to zip around the complex and see how she does?"

"Sorry, Stephen. I have a business to run as well as traipse around the globe," Conley said quietly, getting up and going to the doorway to talk to his mechanic. "Sure, Lew, but keep it at about ten miles an hour. After lunch, we'll put it on the trailer and go over to Sonora and try some of that back country with it, if the steering handles okay for you."

Conley closed the door as the younger man sauntered back to his task. "We're getting close to the Army's specs on that buggy," he said with just a touch of pride. "Anyway, let me tell you something that you may be interested in about the beach at Wadi Sayq. I think you guys—and you might just pass this along to Polk—need to send in a couple of seasoned archaeologists. I can recommend a couple out of Jerusalem. It isn't my field, but I know enough about the subject to know when something interesting has happened at a particular site."

Conley leaned forward with his hands on his knees and his eyes fixed on Stephen. "I know that in the book that the Astons published, there is mention of a few things that I saw firsthand, and it's these items that you need to take a good look at with some professional opinions. Polk has a copy of the book. Ask him to let you look at it. My copy is over at the university on my desk. I know that a few BYU professors are doing geological and archeological studies at the site. The experts are convinced that this is Bountiful. They also have a lead on an ore deposit."

Conley sprang from his chair, took three steps to the table, and retrieved a stack of photos. "Here, look at those. I took some pictures of what I'm telling you about." He handed Stephen the stack. "That first one is probably the best. If you look carefully in the lower center of the photo," he said eagerly, reaching over and pointing his finger to the spot, "you're looking at a stone pattern about 135 feet in length and 60 feet wide. There is a fore, middle, and aft at that site. The formation is old; I can tell that much. But you'd need some guys who know what they're doing—you know, some experts—to come up with something concrete. They need to do some carbon dating and digging, but I'll tell you this: the Astons weren't far off in my estimation. Those stones may be the very foundation rock surrounding the hull of an ancient ship built on the beach. Just thought you might be interested."

CHAPTER 3
Project II

Provo

Peter Polk was exhausted. The session in Phoenix with Bennett and Thorn had depleted his energy. Age had its ways of letting a man know when he had exceeded his limits. He had made notes on his laptop on the flight to Salt Lake City. Now, back at his home in Provo, he sat down at his desk to flesh out his notes.

Though it was late, the computer hummed. It was the most familiar sound in the house and had been for the past three years since Mary's death. Peter was alone now. He wanted to complete what he had started on the plane. It was a laundry list of details that needed attention if the project was to move along smartly—a summary of the meeting. Polk felt that Stephen would need to review on paper these important elements of the project. Of course Stephen had made copious notes during the meeting, but Polk had given him no succinct outline of the project. Peering at the monitor, he proofed what he had written:

"Stephen, here are the salient points that we talked about in Bennett's office this morning. Please review them, and make notes on any part you are fuzzy about. I will clarify them when we get together in Mexico on Thursday. I need your help to line up the presenters we want to pull in for the conference. Not all the names are listed. A couple I will give to you in Mexico because I'm not certain who the best authority is for a few of these presentations. Also, some may reject our offer. Don't worry; there are plenty of fish in this particular stream. We'll snag someone. Note that the specific topics of the external evidences of the Book of Mormon are not in any special order. We will catch as catch can. Here they are:

Game Plan

I. Pull together as many as fifty non-Mormon students (none under the age of eighteen) from a variety of religious, social, and academic backgrounds.

II. Organize a conference to be held in May of next year in Provo, Utah. Transportation, housing, and all meals will be provided.

III. Invite recognized, non-Mormon scholars to present two-hour lectures on their field of expertise related to topics of concern in the Book of Mormon.

IV. Pay each student a $7,000 stipend for full participation in the four-week study. One-third up front, the remaining two-thirds when they complete a ten-page, documented report of their conclusions.

"Stephen, the topics for discussion will include disputed points in the external evidences of the Book of Mormon. (The less the presenters know about the Book of Mormon, the better.) I have already given you a fairly comprehensive guide on each of the following subjects that we want the presenters to discuss with the students. In each of the following areas of interest, there is a counterpoint with critics of the Book of Mormon. As nearly as possible, we want an impartial presenter to give his or her point of view. This is merely a recap of information you already received in our briefing earlier today. It may help you grasp the scope of the project if you have this list in hard copy."

In some detail, Polk went on to describe the topics of presentation that would be researched by the presenters and delivered at the conference in May. Most centered on external proofs that no one could have known in the 1820s, when the Book of Mormon was translated by an unschooled farm boy. Many of these topics had been targeted by critics in an attempt to discredit the Book of Mormon.

Topics for Presentations

I.   *Geography of the Book of Mormon lands.* Did the main body of the Book of Mormon peoples migrate no farther than a thousand miles from the narrow neck of land?

II. Throughout the history of the Nephites and Lamanites, *where did the major activities take place?*

III. *Population growth.* This is a knotty problem in the Book of Mormon. How could Lehi's family have fought wars only a couple of decades after arriving in the new lands? They had to have interaction with other people, many others. Who were they?

IV. *Oceanic travel anciently.* What do we know about the ships the Jaredites sailed in? What about the ship Nephi built? How did they cross the seas?

V.   *Period classification.* Were the Preclassic Mayans actually Book of Mormon people? If so, what do we know about this era? What do the ruins tell us? Some people, not necessarily Mormons, know. Let them explain.

VI. *Tree-of-life motif.* Why is it so prevalent in Mesoamerica?

VII. *The monetary system in the Book of Mormon.* Who said they used coin? Could they have had a system of weights?

VIII. *The Urim and Thummim* that Joseph Smith claimed to use for translating. Were such instruments used anciently? How did they work? The Jews know.

IX. *The golden plates.* Is there evidence of metal plates being used for record keeping in other areas of the world?

X.   *The Land Bountiful.* Is there a lush land of milk and honey in the scorching Arabian desert?

XI. *The two Hill Cumorahs.* This is an intriguing subject.

Polk advised Stephen to study the large, spiral-bound notebook of material he had left with him containing facts about all of these topics. He listed the qualifications required for reputable scholars they would contact. "Not all must hold degrees in the field of study they would address, but all must possess extensive knowledge of their subjects. Very important."

After writing three pages filled with salient information, Polk concluded his long letter.

"Stephen, this is it. You have here a summary of what we are out to accomplish over the next three months. I do need your help. Thanks for accepting the job. Please note that I have included names and addresses of the proposed presenters and the subjects they are to address. Some I have already contacted or wish to contact myself. Some I will leave to you. They are the leading authorities in their fields of study.

"When we invite these scholars, we will offer them an honorarium for their current research and conference presentations as we did in Project I. There is no standard sum for all presenters. Some will have assistants helping in the research. Some will need to travel and present material gleaned for the project. The honorarium will range from five thousand dollars to thirty thousand dollars per presenter. Each will be paid according to the size of the task and with my approval.

"I hope I don't run out of gas before I reach the conference. I'm glad to have you on board with all your stamina. My only concern is the immediate toll this is taking on your personal life, but I have faith that things will work out for you. By the way, do you remember Roy Carver, the graduate student who was with us in San Diego? He will be joining our team in Mexico. He has been doing some research on the two Hill Cumorahs. He's a bright young guy.

"Attached is the info on two of my F.A.R.M.S. colleagues at Brigham Young University as well as Allred in Central America. Feel free to contact them if you wish.

"Best wishes, your brother in the faith, Peter."

Polk looked at the statement about Stephen's personal life and his reassurance that things would work out. It was patronizing at best. He left it in anyway.

You're in the youth of your middle age, Stephen. I thought I was still in the youth of my old age, but that just isn't so, Polk sighed ruefully and added a note to his arduous letter:

"P.S. Thanks for asking me to baptize you two weeks ago. It was a great pleasure. Stay in touch with your bishop."

Dr. Polk: professor emeritus of Brigham Young University, Book of Mormon scholar, father, grandfather, widower, project director of the privately funded study to create awareness of the Book of Mormon. Yes, he was all those things, and somehow, the day had done him in.

He printed the summary of the project for his files and faxed it to Stephen's home in San Francisco. He would see it first thing in the morning.

Mustering a bit more energy, Polk pulled up a document he had drafted the day before yesterday. At the suggestion of his attorney, Bennett, he had drafted a statement that authorized Stephen to assume jurisdiction of the project and to make decisions at his own discretion, should Polk be incapacitated. It was a long shot that it would have to be invoked, but Bennett had cautioned Polk about covering all his bases. Bennett had also reminded him that he and his wife were leaving on a much-awaited vacation to go white-water rafting in Colombia during the month of October, so he had best take care of all legal matters before they both got too far afield.

Polk punched the Print key and waited for the printer to spit out the document. A tiny red light began flashing. The monitor read REPLACE TONER CARTRIDGE. He sighed. He was too spent for one evening. He wouldn't mail the letter to Bennett until tomorrow anyway. He decided not to bother replacing the toner cartridge tonight. He shut down the printer and then the computer, turned off the light in his study, and made his way wearily to bed.

* * *

Anney was tired of the barrage of details she and Decker Hunt were arranging. She thought wistfully about her father and Katherine having a great time seeing the sights of London while she had to follow up on a myriad of tasks which had to be completed before leaving London. The Reverend Moore's staff had set up temporary headquarters in a small room adjacent to a large conference hall in the Hyde Park Hilton where they were staying. Anney didn't begrudge her father his time of relaxation, but she found prearranging lodgings and activities and meeting a host of eager, would-be televangelists more tedious than she had anticipated.

"Tell me again, Decker," she groaned. "Why are we arranging all of these details here in London and not in Prague, for example?"

"Because London is a jumping-off location, plus they speak English here," Decker replied slowly. He rubbed his eyes and spoke as though lecturing to the very young. "We can contact all the backup people we need through their representatives in London." He went on, warming to his subject. "Anney, I think you fail to see what an international city London is. I have known for some time that there are only a handful of cities in the entire world where so much can be accomplished for a multinational tour. For Eastern Europe, London is the best place to start. In the Orient, Hong Kong is the key city. In anything dealing with the Near East, Cairo is the place. You see, all of the Eastern European countries have representatives here in London that can make firm arrangements.

"I'm sure we could have accomplished the same scheduling through representatives in New York, but your father insisted that we do it here in London. He told me he loves this city, especially after the tourist season and before it gets too damp and cold in the fall. For him, it's the optimum time to take a few days to relax before the grueling tour in countries that are just now beginning to offer tourist comforts. I understand that film companies such as Spielberg's had a devil of a time with accommodations and equipment while they were in Krakow a couple of years ago to film *Schindler's List*. It is our job to smooth the way for the tour."

As she listened to Decker, who couldn't be any older than she was at forty-two, Anney heard the condescension in his voice. It was her job to assist Decker in whatever he needed to pull off the tour smoothly. She was to work with him and not against him. He could be so charming at times, and at others so deprecating. Right now, his tone was supercilious. He was certainly efficient and experienced, but it was clear that he had little regard for her feelings, especially at this time when he must know about her problems with Stephen. Apparently, his marriage had not survived. Would hers? She was startled at the unbidden question that streaked through her mind.

Anney wasn't sure what was happening in her marriage. She had received Stephen's message: he would call later in the evening. She found herself eager to hear his voice and to know how things were. It had only been a week since she left him at the airport in San Francisco, but their parting had been tense to say the least.

It was a relief that their two children were somewhat on their own and involved in their studies. With Brenda at Humboldt State University, deeply committed to good grades, and Todd in Berlin, struggling to comprehend the language and culture, she felt that her mothering duties were on hold. Nevertheless her thoughts and concerns were frequently focused on the children. Anney now realized what generations of mothers had learned before her: mothering instincts do not diminish just because the children grow up.

Anney looked at the ornate clock on the wall. "I have to get to the Russian embassy within an hour, Decker," she said. "I still need to have them stamp my visa. I understand it's not too far from here, somewhere over in Grosvenor Square. Have any of you guys been there?" Two of the other staff members looked up from their monitors, shook their heads, and returned to their computers. Anney's brow furrowed. "I don't want to get lost."

"I'm sorry, Anney," Decker replied briskly. "You've asked the wrong people. Why don't you check with the concierge in the lobby? I'm sure he can direct you."

She got up, waved to the staff, and moved quickly to the main hall and down the wine-colored carpet to the lobby. She could see through the large glass windows at the front of the lobby that it was a warm, very pleasant, fall day. She loved walking along the quaint streets of London. After obtaining directions from the concierge, she stopped at the main desk to inquire about the two books she had left for Dr. Frederick Shaw, a professor here in London. Following Stephen's instructions, Anney had called the University of London to let Freddy's secretary know that she had left his books at the hotel desk. Stephen had borrowed the books from Freddy last summer when they were together in San Diego. He felt that Anney would be the best courier to see that they got safely back to Freddy.

Anney had met Freddy during the troubled weekend she and the children had visited Stephen in San Diego. She and the others who were guests at the Hotel Del Coronado for that weekend of relaxation had lunched together, but there had been so many new faces among the group that she was hard pressed to recall what he looked like.

Stephen had described him as rotund, with a zest for life and people. But it didn't matter; she would not see him again. She needed just to make sure he got his books.

"Anney! Anney Thorn!" a voice shouted. Anney turned. The bulky man walking in her direction seemed to know her. Puzzled for a moment, at last it occurred to her that the Englishman must be Stephen's friend Freddy.

"You're Dr. Shaw," Anney said with an outward smile and an inner groan. She wished she had cleared the lobby before he spotted her.

"Yes, yes. I thought I recognized you." Freddy extended his hand, and Anney took it graciously.

"My, I didn't expect that you would come in person to pick up your books. I thought perhaps your secretary would drop by, or one of your graduate students."

"Thank you ever so much for transporting these books. I told Stephen that I would be back in California over the holidays and would pick them up at that time. But, thank you all the same." Freddy shifted the packaged books from under his arm to his large hand, holding them in a vice-like grip. "I understand from the letter I received from your husband that you are accompanying your father on one of his . . ." Freddy wasn't sure what term to use for whatever her evangelical father/minister was about.

"His instructional tour on televangelism to Eastern Europe and St. Petersburg, Russia," Anney finished for him.

"How delightful!" Freddy's face was a study in tact. "I suppose the poor devils in those countries are starved for the kind of professionalism your father can offer them."

"Yes, I suppose," Anney said vaguely. The last thing she wanted to do was prolong a conversation with this man. Besides, she really needed to get to the embassy offices before they closed. "I hope I'm not too abrupt," she said sweetly, "but I really am running behind schedule. I have to get my visa for Russia, or I'll not be part of the tour. We are leaving for Prague in the morning, so . . ."

"Of course. I understand. Would it be presumptuous of me to offer to drive you to their embassy? I have my motorcar just out front and would be delighted to take you, if that would help. I know precisely where the Russian embassy is located here in the West End."

"Well . . . I was going to walk. I have directions from the concierge."

"Please allow me. That is, if you trust British drivers."

Aware that she was not going to get rid of this fellow easily, Anney admitted to herself that it would speed things along if she took him up on the offer. "Okay," she replied. "If you don't mind, and it won't take you too far out of your way."

"Not a'tall," Freddy beamed. "I would love to do some small favor for the wife of my good friend Stephen. By the way, where is Stephen? I tried to call him a couple of times at your home in California. I wanted to let him know of my plans to visit there. I got no response when I rang him up."

Anney felt an odd little stab of concern. Freddy wasn't the only one who would like to know exactly where Stephen was and what he was really involved in.

* * *

The legal strategy of putting Dr. Peter Polk and associates out of business rested with one of Phoenix's most competent and expensive attorneys. In the past five years, Chet Hadley had slithered up to a high-rise suite of offices, carefully weaving his own law firm into a bulwark of guarding or destroying wills and family trusts. The allocation of family fortunes was his specialty. After fifteen years as an associate with two of the trade's craftiest practitioners, the Martin twins, he had struck out on his own.

The aging twins, until recent years, had practiced law in the fast lane. They represented large state and federal funding projects for freeways, dams, airports, military bases, and the like. They also maintained a department dealing with trusts and wills that Chet had developed into big business for them. Chet's keen nose for legal loopholes seemed to point the way through tight situations in sacred trusts and wills that, by all means, for his clients' interests, needed busting. It was Hadley who had won back twenty-five million of the old Pencock estate that had been entrusted to an environmental group. Hadley had cleverly demonstrated in court that The Society for the Preservation of the Desert had (though ignorantly) mismanaged the funds. They lost the right to administer the trust and eventually lost it outright, whereupon it reverted back to the family. It took two years, but the Pencock family, a sister and a brother, got back what they referred to as "their rightful estate." In Chet's devious mind, those two heirs were ruthless subhumans that he hoped never to represent again.

With a passel of professionals on the payroll—attorneys, paralegals, clerks, and secretaries—Chet and his staff stretched across the entire fourth floor of the twenty-five story Phoenix Towers. Lawyercraft was big business in the Towers, and Chet was well within his league. His new client, Craig Kline, and his recently inherited copper corporation executive offices sprawled above between the twentieth and twenty-second floors of the Towers. Though neighbors in the Tower, there had been no connection between Craig Kline and Chet Hadley until last week. Craig learned of Hadley's legal track record after the Pencock settlement and wanted him at nearly any price.

Chet Hadley knew how to vault the legal hurdles when it came to trusts and wills. His firm had won the last five cases they had challenged. He felt confident he could size up the trust situation that was irritating Craig. Kline's father had left a good deal of money in the wake of his recent death. The problem rested in the disbursement of that fortune. It was Chet's massive job to bust the trust.

Chet regularly worked a sixty-hour week. No one faulted his appetite for work. It was his ambition and drive—and, at times, his amoral behavior—that took its toll on his character rating. He had consumed the Kline legal documents, which bequeathed a great deal of cash to projects dealing with the Book of Mormon. Mormons—Chet knew a covey of Mormons in Scottsdale. He had no quarrel with them. They seemed like savvy businessmen who pretty much stayed to themselves. Something about them reminded him of the Jews—a closed religious society that was more a way of life than a simple Christian faith. That was the only thing that annoyed Chet about the Mormons.

Chet had done his homework on his new client. He learned that Craig's father had become a devout Mormon late in life. The whole Kline clan had been Mormon since Brigham Young whipped his people into shape and spread them across the Mountain West. Craig, on the other hand, had a mother of some generic Christian faith who didn't think much of the Mormons and went out of her way to see that her children had nothing to do with their father's legacy. She had done all right along those lines. As near as Chet could tell, Craig Kline was a hard-drinking, tough-fisted businessman who knew exactly what he wanted and how to get it, even if he had to walk on the shady side of the street from time to time. The talk among the old-timers had it that the old man Kline had been a bit rowdy himself until he got religion. But his brand of religion meant that the word of God was in the Mormon Bible, the Book of Mormon. Once he discovered it, he changed his life and his business practices and never wavered from his commitment.

Over the weekend, while relaxing at his White Mountain cabin with his wife and two teenaged sons, Chet had familiarized himself with the details of what Craig Kline referred to as "the Book of Mormon Project Trust." It was a four-page document that, in effect, left fifteen million dollars . . . *fifteen million!* No wonder Craig was inflamed about the trust and determined to get it safely back into the family coffers.

Craig had explained to Chet that over two million dollars of the trust had already been spent on a frivolous project in San Diego. It had funded a study group of eight non-Mormon scholars from reputable universities whose assignment was to attend a seven-week confab in the plush surroundings of northern San Diego's locked community of Fairbanks Ranch. On the estate, the professors—two women, Chet noted, and six men—were to take apart the Book of Mormon to see, among other things, if it held up as an ancient document with roots in the Near East. Who knows what all they discovered about the Book of Mormon? They compiled a collective report, but according to Craig no one had seen it as yet. For their seven weeks of round-the-clock confinement—except to fly off to a couple of locations in New York and Israel for research in an expensive chartered Gulf Stream jet—they were paid handsomely. Chet reviewed the terms of the participants. Each was paid one hundred thousand smackers. That kind of money for seven weeks of research! *Even I would have participated for that kind of money!* Then Chet smiled as he remembered that his fee for legal services for Craig would amount to over two hundred thousand dollars.

Of the original eight scholars who signed on for the romp through the Book of Mormon, one remained to assist Dr. Polk in his second Book of Mormon project, called Project II. What was his name? Chet flipped through his notes to find the name. Ah, yes . . . Stephen Thorn. Chet noted that Thorn had fallen out of favor with his televangelist father-in-law—a preacher who could be bought. Craig had already demonstrated that little tidbit. Word was that Thorn was a different animal, however.

Chet hunched forward over his cluttered desk, lightly drumming his fingertips across his chin, a subconscious habit he slipped into whenever he was deep in thought. But Thorn could be the bait that would hook Polk. He had spent the entire weekend examining the documents from every angle, hoping to see a tiny crack in the trust. Now back in his plush office, he was beginning to feel that his game plan was falling into place. It would come.

The trust itself was a bear. Craig's former attorney had tried to break it during Project I. No luck. But Chet refused to look at it in any light but success. *Luck is with me, baby. I intend to bust this thing wide open. How could one doddering old man control that kind of money and not slip up? He was bound to.* The only real problem for Chet was time. Kline wanted the trust busted within the next two months. That was pressure even for Chet. It would be possible if they had some hard evidence of fraud. Again he tapped his chin with his fingers. He had to get something on Polk or Thorn. Either one would do.

He already had a couple of ideas that might get a court order restraining Polk from progressing with the current project. For one thing, he may be in violation of paragraph five, line six: "All monies expended for the two projects are subject to review by the disbursement committee." Chet could see no evidence that Polk had ever reported to the board. He scanned the report, saw that Craig's sister Marjorie was chair of the board, and made a note to contact her.

Chet pushed his chair back and sighed. So much to do in a short period of time. His thoughts raced, never veering from the case at hand. He just might develop a criminal case against Polk for willful misuse of funds without board approval. *I must advise Craig to keep his sister from holding a board meeting or attempting any sort of communication with this Polk. We'll just ease out the rope and let him hang himself.*

In his line of work, which often consisted of molding the law to suit his needs, Chet had learned to operate as a pro. He had won accolades by moving into voids and tossing up roadblocks to foil numerous would-be recipients. Chet knew he was just beginning to get a handle on this case. He was ready to take on the pious Polk. Craig seemed to detest the man.

Oh no! Chet shot his left wrist out of his cuff and looked at his watch. Speaking of Craig, he must be downstairs in the parking terrace, waiting for him to drive out to the Paradise Valley Country Club for a round of golf. A twosome. Chet flung down the folder loosely labeled "The Mormon Project," jumped up from his black leather chair, and was out the door without giving a word of instruction to his staff. He would be ten minutes late. No problem; he would say he had an urgent call that put him ten minutes overtime.

The golf course was greener in early fall than it had been in early summer. The monsoons had helped. Phoenix got in on the tail end of the monsoons, but they came and transformed the desert into lush green growth. Craig had played golf since he was ten. He was good. On the tee off, he eyed the ball, studied the fairway, and then struck the ball with his driver, hurtling it like a small sparrow through the eighty-degree air to the dogleg two hundred and fifty yards away. He then turned to Chet. He was still irritated with the man.

"When I say meet me at four o'clock, I don't mean four fifteen. If you want to be my attorney, then keep a tight schedule. I hate to wait for anyone, especially those who are on my time clock."

Chet was chagrined that he had been late. He knew what was expected. He had lived with enough cranky clients to know how to kiss up to them. Sometimes, for all the money he made, he realized that he was just a lackey for the Craig Klines of the world. He shrugged, not dignifying Craig's reprimand with a response.

Craig moved back from the tee and let Chet step up. "By the way, I have some useful information. I want you to act on it as soon as you get back to the office."

The office would be closed at five-thirty or six. They would be back in Phoenix after nine holes at about six-thirty. Kline demanded the whole mind and body of his legal advisor. Chet felt himself sliding into the old grind of licking the boots. It went with the territory.

"Moore, the preacher I told you about . . . the guy, if you can believe it, is on his way to teach old commies how to preach on television in some of those old Eastern Bloc nations of Europe. He promised me he would feed us good, indictable information about Polk and his former assistant. That's Thorn, who is also his son-in-law. I finally caught up with Moore in London a few hours ago, and he told me that Polk is building some type of Book of Mormon show along the lines of a Disneyland ride or something. All he knew was that the thing is costing over two million bucks as a starter. I tell you, we've got to get that Polk, or he'll have the whole trust blown in a year."

Chet narrowed his eyes as Craig spoke. He turned his physical attention to his drive, but his mind was locked onto Craig's words. *We'll get Polk. No fear, Craig, my friend. I'll find a way to get him, all right.*

CHAPTER 4
Complex Individuals

London

The chairs were oversize for Anney, and the tea and biscuits were very British. Freddy had taken her to the Russian embassy, waited while she secured her visa, and returned her to the hotel. During the drive together, Freddy spoke of his seven weeks cloistered on the estate in San Diego with Stephen and the other five remaining participants and the close relationship he and Stephen had developed, particularly since they were roommates. Freddy had worked the conversation around to Stephen's seemingly sudden commitment to the doctrine and beliefs expressed in the Book of Mormon. He mentioned how impressionable he thought Stephen had been last summer and how he had become concerned that Mormonism comprised such a different set of beliefs than any Stephen had studied in his mature life.

Anney found what Freddy had to say intriguing. She wanted to hear more. She tentatively asked if he would like to park his car and join her for tea. "That is the customary thing to do at four o'clock in London, is it not?"

Freddy had laughed. "Yes, I suppose, only I hate to disappoint you Americans who have such indelible impressions of the British. The custom is still in force, but nothing like it was at the turn of the century or, for that matter, fifty years ago. The purists look upon the younger generation as twits."

"Well, all I know is, here at the Hilton they remind us that tea is served from four to five each day. So if you have the time, I would love to repay you for your courtesy in driving me to the Russian embassy by inviting you to have tea with me." What she really wanted to say was, "Tell me more about your relationship with Stephen last summer and what on earth came over him."

"They perform an admirable service of tea here at the Hilton, I must say," Freddy commented as he sat in his large chair opposite Anney, surveying the delectable food on the silver tray in front of them.

At last, Anney could wait no longer. "Tell me more about your experience with Stephen last summer," she urged. "What really happened to cause my husband to accept the Book of Mormon whole cloth?"

"Ah, yes, you are troubled. I can tell . . . and rightly so. I warned Stephen not to get emotionally involved in the study we were about. You know we had a . . . what is the term they use in America?" Freddy set down his cup of tea and patted his lips with his linen napkin. "Ah, a buddy-buddy relationship. That's it. I felt for the first little while that he had come to participate for the money, as had I, and indeed as had all of the others as well. Then he began to get serious about the subject matter. We all noticed it. He was no longer the slightly bored, slightly detached participant that some of us were—at least the way I was. He would ask me very pointedly what I thought of the concepts we were examining in the Book of Mormon."

"And what did you think of what you were studying?" Anney asked, pressing to know Freddy's thoughts.

"Strange that you ask. I must be candid with you, Anney. The Book of Mormon is not a book to set aside. It has kept coming back to me these past several months like a bright halfpenny. I frankly have difficulty getting it out of my thoughts. Though, mind you, I did not let the experience of that seven weeks turn my head about as it did Stephen's." In a spontaneous, intimate gesture, Freddy reached across the small table and placed his hand on Anney's. He patted it gently as if he had been a lifetime friend of the family. "This whole thing has upset the routine in your home, has it not?"

Anney struggled to hold back the tears. "You know it . . . What can I say? It has upset our whole lives. I'm here with my father and the others, and Stephen went with Dr. Polk to Central America to help with the next phase of his project." Anney pressed her napkin to her trembling mouth, trying to regain her composure. "Please forgive me," she said at last. "I never intended to get emotional about this matter, but it has been such a burden for me, and I'm sure my attitude has been hard on Stephen, too. I simply don't know where this thing will lead." She caught the next surge of emotion, took a deep breath, and stifled her tears. Surely she could control herself better than this, seated in a public tearoom with a dozen people about, and *especially* speaking to a person she hardly knew.

"The next phase of the project," Freddy repeated, a perplexed frown creasing his brow. "I knew that Polk planned further studies, but I did not realize that Stephen would be involved."

"Well, you see . . . Stephen can't seem to find a job. It's been terrible!" Freddy watched helplessly as she struggled to regain control. "So," Anney began tremulously, "when Dr. Polk offered him a temporary job helping him set up the project, he accepted it . . . over my objections. We do need the money, that's for sure. But I'm so worried that it will pull him even further away from us."

"I am so very sorry. I wish I had more concrete advice to offer you, Anney. I simply do not," Freddy responded sympathetically. "My heart goes out to you. I like Stephen very much, but I feel that he has made a mistake in this matter." Freddy adjusted his large frame and leaned forward in the chair. "May I ask you a question?"

"Certainly."

"I feel that I know very little about Stephen's background. Though we roomed together at that opulent estate for seven weeks, I don't think Stephen ever told me about his youth or how the two of you met. Tell me, what was Stephen's family like?"

Anney rearranged the silverware in front of her, picked up her cup, and sipped her tea. She sighed. "Well, Stephen had no real family when we met. He was an only child whose father died in the military while he was an infant, and his mother was killed in an auto accident when he was about ten years old. Actually, he was raised on a cattle ranch in eastern Nevada by an uncle and aunt who had children roughly the same age as Stephen. When Stephen was a senior in high school, his uncle and aunt and a cousin were all killed in a small plane crash. As far as any serious religious training went, Stephen told me that his family had no particular beliefs other than that they considered themselves Christians."

"Then where did Stephen tie into your father's religion? I do know that he spoke about both you and your father. It appeared to me, at least in the beginning, that he had a great deal of admiration for your father. He is a popular preacher on television in San Francisco, is he not?"

"Stephen was already committed to Christ when we met at Biola College in Southern California. He had been left enough funds from his uncle's estate to get a college degree. He had been so troubled by all that had happened to rob him of his family that he turned inward and wanted deep answers about life and spiritual commitment, so he enrolled in a conservative Christian college. I happened to be there because my father and the administrator were old friends. We met and fell in love. He went on to Berkeley for graduate school. We were married by my father in the little chapel on campus, and Stephen earned a doctoral degree in public relations and media. Then he went to work for my father. We have two children: Brenda, the oldest, who now attends Humboldt State in California; and Todd, our high school senior, who happens to be in Berlin as an exchange student. And you know the rest."

"How did you receive Stephen when he returned home? I know that this troubled Stephen immensely. He spoke to me more than once about you and your reaction to his newly found beliefs. I warned him about this new commitment to the Mormon faith. I told him it would not go over well with his family."

"It didn't. From the day he left for San Diego, things have not been the same. He never went back to work for my father at the ministry, not that he really could have with his change of attitude about what Daddy is doing. It was a mess. I've tried, believe me, Freddy. I am still trying. If I weren't, I would not be here speaking to you. What am I to do?" Tears welled up in Anney's eyes once more.

Anney didn't expect an answer. She wiped the tears from the corners of her eyes with a tissue retrieved from her purse; then, with clear vision, she looked at Freddy and asked, "Why did the study only affect Stephen? Why were you immune to the influence of the book?"

Freddy looked down at his cup and took a long breath, then said as if he were a man condemned before a judge, "Anney, I was not. I was frankly overwhelmed by what we had seen and heard. The book is a masterpiece in its particular field. I would be a hypocrite to sit here and tell you that it did not have an impact on my mind. There is something so uncanny, so persuasive, so authentic about the Book of Mormon that I have to tell you it *did* affect my thinking."

"Then why haven't you taken the steps that Stephen has?"

"That is a very good question. I have pondered it for the past two months, and still it haunts me. I must confess that I lack the perseverance and courage that your husband possesses. I simply turned my back on what I know is a book that not even a *well-educated* man in *contemporary* times could possibly have fabricated. I wish it were otherwise; that I were more staunch in character. Believe me, I do. But I would have to give up so much to do as Stephen is doing that I have elected to block it from my mind. You may never understand what I am telling you, particularly if you never read or study the book. But should you gather the courage to take a serious look at it, I must advise you that you will have many of the same feelings I do. I know this is not comforting to you, but I am expressing what is in my heart."

"Then you are saying that this Dr. Polk got through to Stephen, while you were able to resist? Were there others in your group who fell for Mormonism?"

"No, no, no," Freddy said, reaching for another tart and setting his cup of tea on the tray in front of him. "You misunderstand. Dr. Polk never convinced Stephen of anything. I was there all the time. I know the influences that may have been exerted, and believe me when I say they did not come from Polk. He was quite reticent to communicate his great love of the Book of Mormon. At times throughout the seven weeks we were together in the study of the book, I felt as if Dr. Polk was biting his tongue and straining at his reserve. No. It was the book, Anney, clear and simple. The Book of Mormon captured Stephen. Perhaps it has something to do with his naive, trusting nature.

"You do realize, don't you, that among those of us who were deeply involved in the analysis of the Book of Mormon, Stephen was the only non-academician? I think this accounts for some of what transpired. None of the rest of us made any moves toward the religion of Mormonism itself." Freddy paused. His double chin curved like a flesh-toned balloon, but his eyes sparkled as if he were discussing the crown jewels.

"At the risk of repeating myself, I must also tell you that none of us took the Book of Mormon lightly by the time we were four weeks into the project of searching it for authenticity. Every last one of us—to the person, mind you—had a growing respect for that book. It was a document that rang so convincingly. I can't express what it was, but it could never have been written by Joseph Smith; you have our committee report to verify my statement.

"It is a highly complex, detailed religious history of a people who lived at the time of Christ in the Americas. But it definitely has roots in the Near East. I know. I listened intently and came away from that study with a good deal of respect for the mind of Joseph Smith, though I don't for a moment believe he penned that book." Freddy paused and studied his hands.

"Nor do I accept the idea that some other person in the nineteenth century wrote it. We had it proven to us, by some very astute scholars from Virginia Tech, who didn't even know they were working from the Book of Mormon. They showed us, through a fascinating new method called 'word prints,' that the Book of Mormon was written by at least twenty-two writers."

"And you believed it?"

"But of course."

* * *

"Katherine," Bob said in his velvet-smooth tone, "how can I possibly express to you my gratitude for what you have so generously done for the success of this tour? Do you have any idea how you have smoothed the way for us to do a grand and glorious work for the ministry? You're a great lady, and I love you for it."

"Have you ever been at a loss for charming words?" Katherine teased. "I hope you don't keep bringing up the subject of my participation. I came as a tiny mouse in the corner; please don't put the spotlight on me. Besides, the funds I contributed are not only tax deductible, they were earned by my hard-working late husband, whose name I have vowed to keep out of our relationship." Katherine gracefully lifted her champagne glass and touched it to Moore's. The soft music at the Café Realto blended perfectly with the mood Katherine felt. She loved London, always had. Only this time, she was in love and nothing, but nothing could compare to being with the one person most dear.

Moore had known Katherine Latham for the past three years. Katherine had accepted Christ in her life shortly after the death of her husband, Charles E. Latham, formerly chairman of the board and CEO of Chemcon Corporation in Baltimore, Maryland. The international corporation had supplied the U.S. Army with defoliating chemicals during the Vietnam War and had since been a major supplier of a line of insecticide chemicals and other products that had made Katherine Latham one of the wealthiest widows in Baltimore. A native of the Bay Area, she left Baltimore after the funeral of her husband and resettled in San Francisco.

One Sunday morning, not long after moving into her new high-rise penthouse apartment, while channel cruising, she caught a glimpse of the silver-haired televangelist. She quickly flipped back to his channel. His resonant voice, his square jaw, and his penetrating eyes matched the strength of his Christian commitment. From that moment, Katherine planned her strategy to snare the Reverend Robert Moore.

Bob Moore and Katherine had seen a great deal of one another before Anney's mother died, but all contacts had been related to the ministry. As though part of Katherine's plan, Nadia Moore had passed away sitting upright in her hospital bed at the nursing home on a hot August day two months earlier. With his wife laid to rest in the mausoleum in Walnut Creek, Bob felt that he had enough latitude to allow himself to be drawn into a more meaningful relationship with Katherine. He sincerely liked her, and her money was a welcome amenity for Bob Moore, whose lifestyle was continually beyond his ministry's ability to fund.

Katherine was a stunning woman who had taken advantage of surgical body sculpting and facial contouring to whittle away at least ten of her natural sixty years. She exuded an international look of elegance and wealth that fit so naturally with the soft leather and sleek lines of her Silver Shadow as she wheeled through the steep inclines of San Francisco on Sunday mornings—to be enchanted by the one man she desired. He could be found at his ministry on the lower south side of the city, and for the past three years, Katherine could be found there as well.

Katherine and Bob had announced their engagement just three evenings before at a small dinner party at Cerrenets near Nob Hill in San Francisco. Besides the invited guests at the small announcement dinner, diners in the restaurant had recognized the striking couple and had nodded as Katherine and Bob passed their tables. At the proper time, they told everyone present that they would be wed on New Year's Eve.

"Thank you," Bob had said, as the waiter held his seat following the announcement. Bob's silver mane and tall frame hinted at his former athletic prowess. At sixty-eight, he still had the look of a carefully groomed top executive. Katherine, seated next to him, blushed charmingly as she accepted the felicitations of their guests. She had the enduring beauty of a lady of means, impeccable upbringing, and grace. Her Armani gown of cream silk spoke of her exquisite taste in clothing. Some insisted that they, too, could have her figure and regal looks, given the money she had at her disposal. Not even Bob guessed that her real value was within.

Moore had to admit that for a kid born in a tar-paper shack in Waco, Texas, he had come a long way. He had no memory of his mother. She had died at the birth of his younger sister when he was two. His father's mother, Granny Lee, came to live with them. She seemed to Bob to be a hundred years old. She was a dyed-in-the-wool, toe-tapping born-again Christian who took Bob with her to the Waco Community Church where they listened to a fiery preacher whose magnetism kept the members coming to hear his hellfire-and-segregation preaching. Later, Bob learned that the preacher had been a Klansman in Tennessee prior to his stint in Waco.

Bob's father had no time for his only son. He was a field hand who liked to operate tractors whenever the foreman would let him. He did keep a job, even during the Depression, because he was handy with machinery and willing to work fifteen hours a day. The most vivid memory Bob had of his father was one Sunday when Bob was eight years old. He had gone to Sunday School without his Granny, who was too laid up to get out of bed that day.

A bully in the Sunday School class had followed Bob home, tagging along, making fun of the way Bob walked and the overalls he was wearing. Bob was not a fighter by nature, but he was large for his age. The bully was about the same size but two years older. Bob had hurried along the dusty street on the edge of Waco to the four-room frame house that his father had rented when they moved into town.

He reached the porch, then leaped the three steps to the top and lunged for the door. His father had watched him run across the street and corner the bare front yard a mere ten yards in front of the bully. It took but a second for the senior Moore to size up the situation. He moved quickly to the door and locked it from the inside, moments before the boy grabbed the scratched brass doorknob. Bob was locked out.

The bully caught Bob by the shoulder and swung him around, and the two rolled off the porch like tomcats. Dust flew up from the dry ground surrounding the run-down house. Fear and panic had caused the adrenaline to flow through Bob's young body. He pounded on the bully with a frenzy that brought tears to the older boy's eyes before letting him retreat to the street. All the way across the hard-packed dirt yard, the bully cursed Bob, warning him that one day he would catch him when he wasn't looking and beat the tar out of him.

Slowly the shabby front door opened, and his father walked out onto the porch and peered at his son, who was covered with dust, hair grimy with bits of sandy soil and scratches across his right cheek. "Well, boy," he said, "thought you oughta take care of your own problems. Y'all did good." Then he stepped back into the house and closed the door.

Bob remained on the ground, staring at the peeling paint on the front door. The sun glared in his face and hampered his vision—but not his thinking. He reaffirmed his hatred for his father.

At sixteen, Bob had joined a traveling gospel tent. The week his granny died, he left home and followed the show. Three days before her death, in frail condition, she had begged Bob to take her to a tent revival that was in Waco for the week. At the gospel show, a portly evangelist, the Reverend Tally, had delivered an awe-inspiring gospel message about Christ and his goodness. Bob was electrified. He had never heard such a dynamic, powerful speaker. The man got cripples to *walk* down and confess Christ at the far end of the tent.

Even Granny made it to the canvas-covered bench that served as an altar, where she pleaded for the reverend to lay his hands on her head. She hoped for a cure to her consumption, as she called it. It never came. After the show, Bob begged his granny to allow him to stay behind while his sister helped her home. He needed to talk to this astounding evangelist.

With all the finesse Bob could muster, he asked an assistant leaning against the small trailer house that stood at the rear of the tent if he could please speak to the preacher Tally and tell him how much he enjoyed his sermon. Tally heard the request from inside the trailer and welcomed Bob in. That was the beginning of a near father-son relationship. A week later, as the evangelist's crew was striking the tent, Bob walked from his granny's open grave and caught up with the traveling gospel show. His father never spent a day looking for him.

America had entered World War II by the time Bob was working the crowds and striking the tent in town after town on the leather lining of the Bible Belt in Texas, Arkansas, and Oklahoma. Tally saw immediately that Bob had talent as a speaker. Until he dropped out of high school in Waco, Bob had been a strong B student and loved history and the Bible. Tally tutored the youth in a variety of subjects up to the time Bob was inducted into the Army in 1944. He particularly schooled his young protégé in the mastery of working a congregation into a fever pitch of "amens" and "glory hallelujahs." "At that point, you know that they are with you, and my boy, when the congregation is really with you they come forward and confess Christ. They also dig into their pockets."

After basic training at Camp Roberts, California, Bob became well acquainted with one of the fundamentalist chaplains who initiated Bob's transfer to his unit and took him along to Europe as an assistant. He was with the chaplain when the allies took Germany. During the joint occupation of Berlin by, among others, the American forces, he was at the chaplain's elbow.

People were starving on the streets of Berlin when Bob arrived and saw the devastation of war. At a refugee camp in Bonludenburg, the chaplain offered assistance to all who passed through the line, giving their names and hometowns. Bob had watched the hordes of refugees: old, young, tired, crippled. All had the weight of the world pressing down on their feeble bodies. Late one afternoon, a girl of not more than eighteen or nineteen stepped up to the desk. She had taken the time to curl and brush her hair. Makeup was rare on the faces of most of the refugees, but Bob was certain he detected lipstick on her soft lips. She was thin, but there was a clearness to her light complexion. Her fine, even features appealed to Bob. She was, by far, the most attractive girl he had seen all day. It was a relief to see someone with alert eyes and a beautiful face.

"Your name?" The chaplain asked in high-school German.

"Nadia, Nadia Vluenski."

"Spell it, please."

She did.

"Nationality?"

"Russian."

That startled the chaplain. He questioned her further and learned that she had been born in Ukraine, spent part of her teens in Czechoslovakia, where her parents lived, but had spent the war years in Berlin, living with her older sister and her sister's husband's family. All of her sisters-in-law had been killed at Brennsohn when the entire block was destroyed by fire bombs. Her mother had died early in the war, and she was not sure whether or not her father was still living. She was certain that she wanted to go to America and live in peace.

Bob wrote down her name and that evening, during the mealtime of soup and bread, when dozens of refugees filed by to receive their rations, he saw her again. He sidled up to her and smiled hello. The English language was a mystery to Nadia. She begged off in German, but Bob persisted. In desperation, he enlisted the help of a young American private who spoke some German to interpret for him.

It began there. Bob took special pains to accommodate Nadia. Everything about her pleased him. With the encouragement of the chaplain, he returned to school in Oklahoma on the G.I. Bill, and Nadia followed six weeks later as his war bride.

They had only one child, Anney. She arrived after a long series of miscarriages. Nadia learned English before Bob graduated from the University of Oklahoma, but when Anney was born, she spoke only Ukrainian to her beloved, blond, blue-eyed daughter. She often wrote letters in Ukrainian to her older sister who had left Berlin and returned to Prague to nurse their ailing father, who died soon after the war ended.

Though Bob Moore became a well-known evangelist in the Bay Area by the late 1970s, his wife Nadia never realized he had achieved his dream. In 1972, shortly after Anney's marriage, Nadia had undergone surgery for a hysterectomy to remove benign fibroid tumors. During the procedure, her heart had stopped. And in spite of a frantic effort by the medical team, who were finally able to revive her, too many brain cells had been deprived of precious oxygen. The mind of Bob's light-hearted wife, Anney's tender mama, was gone. Nadia lived on for the next twenty-plus years, a frail shadow of the woman she had once been, but she never returned home. Anney was living in Berkeley with Stephen when they placed her mother in a convalescent home in Pleasant Hill, where she remained until she succumbed.

Bob had been virtually without a wife for twenty years. He was able to build his ministry to the point that, with his charisma and long hours, plus an excellent staff, he was able to reach out to the entire region as the most astounding voice for Christ that televangelism had yet seen in the Bay Area. Now he was ready to go national. All he needed was money— and Katherine had lots of that. All in due time. It would happen after the tour in Eastern Europe. There was time. He felt robust and certainly as vibrant as the Reverend Schuller in Orange County.

* * *

Katherine, caught up in her own thoughts, sipped the champagne and mused a moment with Bob as the waiter removed the remains of their escargot appetizer. "You remember when we were introduced at the dedication of the new Spreckles Gardens?" Katherine's pretty mouth drew into a coquettish little smile. "I'll bet you didn't know that I bribed a man on the committee with a large contribution, just to get him to tell you that I was one of your most loyal fans. The only reason I attended was that I heard you would be there. I had to meet you." Katherine lowered her voice to a soft purr. "What a disappointment when I learned that you were married!"

Reluctantly, Bob put aside his dreams of fame and turned his attention to his fiancée. Katherine snuggled closer to him and continued: "And you said, in your smooth, masculine voice, 'I'm sure we have met. But I must tell you that the term *fan* is hardly the correct word to describe your enthusiasm for my work.' And I said, 'I disagree. You are on television, and you do put on a superb performance. When I enjoy a performer, I have every right to describe myself as a fan. What would you call me?' Then our eyes met, and I knew that I wanted you more than anything in this life, but you were married. I'm so proud of myself for being a patient woman. I knew that one day you would be free and able to marry me."

Bob chuckled, and with a glint in his gray-blue eyes, he teased her gently, "How did you know you would marry me? That doesn't sound proper for a lady of your breeding."

"Forget what a lady of my breeding does or does not do." Katherine tossed her head and laughed. Then looking deeply into Bob's eyes, she said in a serious tone, "Your wife was not really a wife those last years, so I felt that I was not violating some Christian standard of morality by waiting for you. After all, our relationship was purely platonic. I have had my eyes on you, Reverend Moore, since I first saw you up close, and nothing has diverted me from my goal. I do love you." Katherine's voice became husky with emotion. "I adore you, and more than that, I want you to love me."

The fervor of Katherine's declaration of love failed to penetrate Bob's personal thoughts. "Oh, Katherine, Katherine, I wanted to do this tour in the worst way. Think, if you will, of all the future sermons I can create from this one trip. There will be moments in these countries when people will pour out their souls to me. I will capture every splendid moment and use each one to build a meaningful insight. This tour needs to be done right. By that, I mean I need my full staff and the means to command television time. You've made it possible. Thank you, Katherine, thank you."

Katherine sat immobile as Bob continued to enlarge upon his plans, painfully aware of the real love in his life. Finally, she shifted slightly in her seat and glanced at the curved glass dessert cart that the waiter had left beside them.

She placed her long-stemmed glass on the table, and then turned back to face Bob. Her earnest demeanor had been replaced by a carefree look. "Now then, what do you think would be appropriate for dessert, since you are the master of appropriateness?"

"Ah, dessert."

Shaking off a twinge of disappointment, Katherine smiled as she watched Bob eat a large wedge of carrot cake. "Thank you for bringing me along with you and your staff. I'm glad that Anney is with us. You know how some of these old gossips would have talked about us off in some foreign land together. I'm not one to care what they say, but for the sake of your reputation, this is better. But I wish Stephen were along, too. I really like him. Well, I have only seen him from a distance, but he's a doll."

Bob sighed and looked down. "Stephen needs to follow up on job leads."

Katherine watched Bob's face and decided to pursue the issue. "Why can't the two of you get past your differences?"

Bob shook his head slowly, a frown deepening the lines across his forehead. "Stephen has chosen his own path."

"You haven't told me why he left the ministry. I always thought he was your right-hand man."

"I'm afraid that he is something of a lost sheep, but the issue is much too involved to discuss on this evening of celebration. Let's just say that my son-in-law wants a new challenge that I can't provide. Will that answer suffice?"

"Certainly." Katherine observed the muscle along Bob's jaw tighten and decided to leave it alone.

"Oh, Bob, I have heard some horror stories lately about travel in some of the Eastern European countries, especially Russia. I understand from a friend of mine that she was unable to find a decent place to eat in Moscow."

"Well, we're not going to Moscow." Bob responded. "St. Petersburg is as far into the country as we'll go. They say it's not too bad there. Things have improved since the Summer Games were held there."

Bob lifted Katherine's left hand and looked at the eight-carat diamond sparkling on her finger, wishing that he had the kind of money it would take to purchase such a ring. He gently placed his lips on the back of the slender, manicured hand; then pulling away, he brushed the ring lightly with his lips and whispered, "I love you, Katherine Latham. Indeed I do."

Bob's tour had materialized for one simple reason: Katherine had money and the proclivity to lavish part of it on the man she loved. She had made arrangements to place three million dollars into the ministry: half a million for the evangelical tour of Eastern Europe, the remainder to pay off any debts of the ministry and to underwrite an ad campaign. Bob was quietly gleeful that at last he had funds to prime the pump of publicity and secure more air time. He would tape his European sessions for the next two weeks, make a quick trip back home, tape two sessions in the Bay Area, return to his seminars in Eastern Europe, and there, in some of the most culturally rich places of the world, complete four more tapes. He would arrange for his evangelical friend, the Reverend Cottum, to take his place during the two weeks before Christmas, and be home in time to present his special Christmas broadcast, which he would never assign to anyone else.

Bob felt an inner glow of satisfaction as he contemplated his plans. At least he had removed his son-in-law without a family feud and replaced him with a real professional who, Bob was convinced, had the skills to help elevate him nationally. A little smile played about his lips. *Too bad, Stephen. You made the perfect move. Now I can make a fundamental change. What's more, you will help me earn a little bonus from that Kline fellow. Thank you, my boy. I do thank you.*

CHAPTER 5
Todd

Berlin

Todd finished his shower and rubbed the towel over his firm, young body. Steam clouded the mirror over the washstand, obscuring his reflection. He felt his chin with his left hand. His new goatee was doing just fine. His mother would not be exactly thrilled with the new hair above his lips and along his chin, but she was far away and didn't need to know. Besides, the girls liked it. At the moment, that was all that mattered to him. He decided that he didn't need to shave this morning; most of the guys, even here in Berlin, showed a three-day growth before they shaved. At six feet two, he wished at times that he had bulked up more. His best buddy, Kane, in California, had filled out last summer and didn't miss a chance to let Todd know it. Todd knew that his muscle growth was simply slower. Not to worry. By the time he returned home in the spring, he would buff up great, especially if he continued to work with weights at the club three blocks from his apartment. He had decided to work out at least four times a week. Besides, his body already had great definition, just a little on the lean side. When he strained the muscles in his abdomen region, he could see the framework of a six-pack. All in all, he felt that his body was certainly semi-buff.

"Get off this," he said aloud to himself. "You're no stud. Don't kid yourself. There are a couple of flaws. The nose could be a tad smaller and perhaps the eyebrows darker."

As Todd pondered the essentials in his life, he slipped on a fresh pair of jockey shorts and a tee shirt, rubbed the fog from the mirror with the bath towel, and brushed his blond hair. Then he took out his toothbrush from his travel kit on the basin counter, piled on the toothpaste, and brushed.

As he brushed, he wondered about this year away from home. Germany seemed so far away. There it was again—that weird feeling inside. Todd had heard about others getting homesick, but he had scorned them as wimps. No way was he a sissy. Still, the strangeness of Germany and the difficulty he was experiencing with the language—boy, two years of high-school German had not made him fluent. He had not expected to yearn for his family, the easy lifestyle at home, even his school. But always one to tough out a situation, he wasn't about to reveal his true feelings. With a flicker of excitement, Todd remembered that by tomorrow, his mother and grandfather would be just a few hours away in Warsaw. Even having them that much closer was comforting to him.

The Gutenbergs, his temporary family, were nice enough. Günter seemed like a successful engineer, and Greta, his wife, was a college economics professor—a very bright lady. They had been friendly and were trying to ease Todd's adjustment to life in Berlin. Todd had to continually remind himself that he was, in fact, gaining a marvelous experience in a changing, interesting part of the world. The Gutenbergs' only child, a son, was in Munich in his first year of college. As a matter of fact, Todd had Erik's room with all of its electronic sound equipment and CDs. It had surprised Todd that the kids here liked many of the same groups the kids in California did.

The apartment the Gutenbergs owned was certainly comfortable, convenient to the local high school where Todd was enrolled, and part of a complex of upscale residences. He had expected it to be this way. By German standards, the Gutenbergs were thoroughly middle class.

Todd spit into the commode and then flushed it. He didn't care for the waterless, porcelain-bottom toilet. When it flushed, the water appeared, only to disappear again after everything had been whisked away. Strange contraption, he thought.

As he pulled on his jeans and buttoned his Polo shirt, Todd thought of his father. His forehead drew into a frown. He had real concern about his father. His mother had not been able to hide her distress from the children. The two did not seem happy together. Perhaps when he was a small child they could have concealed it from him, but no more. A senior in high school, after all, is observant. Maybe his parents didn't realize how perceptive he was. He knew that it had all started, or at least his awareness of something amiss in the family, began at that fabulous old hotel in San Diego. *Oh, joy, San Diego. Was that a bust, or what? Mom was so upset with Dad. Dad must have said something about that seven-week confab he was attending—something about the Mormons. Why did he, of all people, get tied up with this Mormon stuff?* Todd didn't pretend to know why his mother had been rude and weepy on that flight home from San Diego, leaving his father to finish his work on that strange, high-paying assignment last summer.

Maybe it was just as well he was in the student exchange program. Why worry? By the time he returned in the spring, things would be smoothed over. Still he worried.

Well, he wasn't going to think about their problems, not now. His thoughts shifted to Hilda, one of the real pluses of this whole trip. She was one fine girl. It had taken Todd all of his first week at school to spot her. He had covertly kept his eye on her for the next few days, finally mustering up the nerve to speak to her. She spoke some English and had agreed to help him get a handle on German. *Good ploy, Todd, old man. You landed, mind you, one of the best-looking, hottest chicks in school—at least as a tutor, even if she hasn't accepted a date yet.* Todd wished Hilda had said yes to going with him to a movie tonight. Nevertheless, he looked forward to the evening. His new friend, Hans, was taking him with his buddies to the Ku-damm, a hot spot in the center of Berlin. He had heard about the bright lights, fun, and free spirits in town. Underage or not, Hans had boasted that they could see the sights. So what if they got kicked out of a bar or two? Hans insisted that they would have no problem. He would have no problem with the Gutenbergs either— though he had not told them exactly where he was headed with a couple of the guys from school. They didn't ask. So long as he was in by midnight, that was their rule. Hey, Germany wasn't going to be half bad.

Todd slipped on his shoes in the final stages of dressing. He couldn't stop his mind from slipping back to his father. In a way, he wished he were home, just to toss a ball with his dad, to be sure he was all right. It would be great to be with him. A worried expression flashed across his face. Home. *Don't think about it.*

* * *

Freddy had left after tea. Anney, too depressed to budge, had sat thinking over their conversation, her mind winding from one dead end to the next as she tried to devise a way to reach Stephen. No solution popped up as her mind struggled to traverse the maze.

"There you are," Decker said abruptly, cutting into her thoughts. The executive assistant was pleasant enough, but at this moment she was hardly in the mood to carry on a conversation with anyone. Decker must have sensed it. Still he barged ahead. "I'm wondering if you could spare a moment with me in the conference room. We have a problem with our setup at the studio in Prague." He took out a small itinerary chart and tapped it against his palm. Anney sighed with a twinge of irritation, wishing instead for a hot shower and the heavenly goose-down pillow on her bed. But she arose and followed him through the lobby to the ministry headquarters. Anney resigned herself to another couple of hours of scheduling before she would have that shower and ease her head onto the feather pillow.

She knew it was Decker's responsibility to see that the Reverend Moore had media coverage, a sound stage, an audience, adequate technical assistance in the various studios they would visit, and a skilled interpreter in every city. He had hurriedly put together the tour, realizing that his lead time was insufficient to do the kind of job he had hoped to accomplish, but the tour did not have the luxury of half a year's advance planning.

Decker had already made one trip to the designated countries and cities, but that five-day tour had not only left him exhausted, it had taxed his patience, smoothing out the complexities of studio scheduling, participants, hotels, officials, and a host of minor things that could evolve into major crises if not properly coordinated. At least he had been pleased with the interpreters he had hired so far. They seemed competent and had agreed to remain with the entourage throughout their designated country or through countries where they spoke the language.

He had spent three days in London, coordinating the entire itinerary with the interpreters and religious directors who were already there, laying their plans. Decker smiled smugly to himself, convinced that his predecessor, Stephen Thorn, would have been out of his element had he been in charge of this tour. Anney's father had privately assured him of that fact.

Decker liked the Reverend Moore. He was man of decision and charm—a contrast to the contemptible Bobby Sharp, who had been almost unbearable at the last. Chicago. If he never returned, he would count it a blessing from heaven. All the blame could not be laid on Bobby Sharp and his giant ego, though. The head accountant for the Sharp ministry ranked even above Bobby in utter hatred in Decker's mind.

Perhaps it had started with Decker's divorce and the cost of maintaining an ex-wife with an expensive lifestyle, plus his own considerable needs, that caused Decker to make side deals. As executive assistant to the Reverend Bobby Sharp, with complete control of all funds gathered and processed though the various fund raisers, it seemed so easy to siphon off a small percentage. He had first targeted the outright donations that crossed his desk on Sundays and weekdays. Many of those funds were cash contributions, so he began to tap the till.

"We can't prove anything at this point, Decker," the Reverend Bobby Sharp admitted, as he and his accountant confronted his executive assistant, "but there is enough suspicion that I no longer feel comfortable with you on my staff. After our investigation, Frank agrees with me. I will expect your resignation within an hour. For the sake of your own eternal soul, I beg you, clear this up with me and get it out into the open."

Decker's eyes narrowed, and his mouth twitched on one side. But he stood erect, completely composed, and said firmly, "May I speak with you alone?"

Bobby nodded to his accountant, and Frank left the room.

A tense silence followed, Decker immobile in front of Bobby's desk as Bobby fiddled with a gold-plated pen between his thumb and index finger. Suddenly, Decker placed both fists on the edge of the desk and leaned over the minister.

"I'll have that resignation ready for you in an hour, *Reverend Sharp*," Decker spat out the words in fury. "But you hear this: you will guarantee me a high-mark reference, both written and oral, when anyone calls. I have busted my butt around here for the past ten years.

You know and I know that it cost me my marriage. I've helped your ministry take the number-one spot in this region in television ratings. If this reaches the press, you will have a lot of explaining to do. If you don't smooth over this whole issue, I will make life miserable around here." Decker removed his fists from the desk and slowly rose to his full height, never taking his eyes from Bobby Sharp. His voice became deceptively soft. "Personally, I like you, Bobby. You've been fair with me but I suggest that you remember that I covered for you with Jan two years ago. I wish that mess had never happened, because I think you are basically a moral man, just human."

Bobby's ruddy, Irish skin flared a bright pink. "I don't know what you're talking about," he blustered.

Decker got the high-mark reference letter he requested, and when the Reverend Robert Moore called Bobby Sharp about Decker becoming his executive assistant, Bobby gushed with praise and told Moore that Decker wanted a change from the environment where his former wife and her family lived, and besides, he was most anxious to work with San Francisco's greatest evangelist.

* * *

"There, that should do it, Decker," Anney said wearily. "At least, that's all we can do tonight." Decker slipped his arm gently around Anney's shoulders and smiled. "You've been terrific, Anney. Your solution worked out just right. No wonder your dad insisted that you come with us. Let me buy you some dinner, okay? You must be famished."

Anney hesitated and bent over, ostensibly to pick up a pen that had fallen to the floor but actually to ease away from Decker. He was just a friendly person; he couldn't be suggesting that she might be interested in him or, for that matter, *any* other man except Stephen. She whirled around and brushed her hair away from her face. "Oh, Decker, honestly, I'm still stuffed from that marvelous tea I had this afternoon, not to mention being in the throes of jet lag. That goose-down pillow is calling my name. Besides, Stephen is supposed to phone me tonight. But thanks, just the same. You go find the others and explore some of these great restaurants. I saw an Armenian place just around the corner."

CHAPTER 6
Monetary System

New York City

Roy Carver was a strange duck. He kept to himself. When he made a friend, however, he kept the friendship alive through frequent contact. He almost worshiped Dr. Peter Polk. He could remain at a computer for up to twenty hours to work through a seemingly unsolvable problem for the professor.

He had come from a New England family of agnostics and intellectuals. His two older brothers were surgeons, one neuro, and the other cardiovascular. His father was a physics instructor at MIT, his mother an editor at the *Boston Globe*. His youth was sheltered and introverted. Roy never played sports. He was tall enough for basketball but poorly coordinated. He tried to get involved in tennis but dropped it his freshman year at Harvard. Girls tended to intimidate him, beginning with his mother. When he completed his undergraduate work and, through a strange quirk of events, decided to apply for entrance to the Brigham Young University graduate school, they accepted him posthaste.

The family had a fit. He carefully explained to them that Utah Valley was becoming in the 1990s what Silicon Valley had been in the 1970s. It had become the incubator for savvy computer entrepreneurs whom Roy wanted to learn from. He had soft-pedaled the other reason he was anxious to study at Brigham Young—he wanted further enlightenment on the original translation of the Book of Mormon. The family really had no choice but to acquiesce in the matter—they were great advocates of free choice. He had arrived in Provo the year before to work toward a doctoral degree in original American documents. He met Polk, and his plans to move west and finish his studies at the University of Southern California were placed on hold.

His parents were stymied by his commitment to Dr. Polk and his reluctance to get on with his pursuit of a higher degree in Southern California. They failed to see the challenge awaiting their son under the careful tutelage of Dr. Polk, who encouraged him to work on the Book of Mormon project for eighteen months. Roy accepted the offer.

It had all come about when Roy met Dr. Polk in the Lee library while searching for an article on insights into the civilization of the Maya. Seeing Roy's obvious computer skills, Polk asked him if he would care to interview for a very special job he had in mind. Little by little, Roy postponed his doctoral program and did more and more assignments for Polk. He had gone to the estate in San Diego and helped Polk set up the final stages of the gathering. He then stayed on to lend support to the task of orienting and directing renowned scholars in their quest to unravel the Book of Mormon.

Roy had by now spent two and a half years in a thorough study of the Book of Mormon. After six months of delving into the material for the cloistered scholars at San Diego, he realized that he was fond of his mentor and sympathetic to what he was trying to accomplish.

Roy would frequently drive Dr. Polk to the airport in Salt Lake City, and the good professor would fill Roy's thoughts with enticements to join the Mormon Church. Always Roy offered the same old responses—he was not ready, or he was not religious in any way.

This morning, Roy was in a high-rise, eighty stories into the sky above Wall Street. He brought along his friend from the prior summer project, Dr. Bernard Stein. True to his promise, he had contacted Bernie when he arrived in the Big Apple. Bernie was on sabbatical from New York City College and had not yet departed for his extended research in Cyprus on Middle Eastern warfare. Roy promised him lunch if Bernie would go with him to the scheduled interview, the purpose of Roy's trip to New York. Bernie would lend confidence to the young man. He explained that Polk was setting up a second Book of Mormon project, and this time the focus was on physical and external evidences of antiquity in the Book of Mormon.

Among a handful of scholars on ancient monetary systems, one of those at the top had to be Melvin Brookline. He looked more like a quiet, backroom CPA, with thick glasses and a slight nervous twitch to his left eyelid, than a hard-hitting stock market investor. Everyone noticed that Brookline combed the few strands of hair he could salvage from the right side of his scalp to the center and beyond. The light brown hair was parted an inch above his ears and pulled to the left in a flatter-than-a-pancake, greased-down look. Regardless of his looks—or lack thereof—he was Jewish and savvy in the field of financial investments. He appreciated his own worth and wasn't shy about declaring it.

Bernie sat to one side of the desk, hoping not to interfere with Roy's interview, a big order for a man who liked to comment on almost any subject. Roy sat in an oversize chair in front of Brookline's massive walnut desk. He could not help wondering why a man so physically insignificant would want to surround himself with a large desk, high bookshelves, large overstuffed chairs, and the like. It all dwarfed Brookline. It was as if the man dared his environment to try to overpower him.

There was one entire wall of glass-enclosed shelves filled with a host of monetary objects going all the way back to the Egyptians and the rise of the Roman Empire. What impressed Roy as he glanced at the illuminated shelves were the varied forms of currency, ranging from tiny flat pieces of gold and silver to copper slices, even weights and measures. The latter interested Roy most.

Deferring to Bernie as the elder of the pair, Brookline asked, "So, Dr. Stein, what do you teach at the college, if I may ask?"

"Ancient warfare, at least that is my interest, though I teach courses in ancient history."

"Well, if you teach ancient warfare in the Middle East, you must know that one of the principle methods of payment to the common soldier was with blocks of salt, which could be traded in the market-places of a thousand cities. It was a means of bartering."

"Yes, I'm very much aware of that method of payment." Bernie nodded toward Roy and said, "Please, I'm sure Roy here has questions to ask. I'll sit by and remain silent."

"As you wish. Well then, Mr. Carver, ask away."

Roy came directly to the issue of ancient monetary systems in Israel. "Did Israel always use the shekel, and if so, in what form?"

Roy was not the type to ask a question that he had not already explored through the magic of computer software. He knew the answer. He had consulted all existing CD catalogs and half a dozen other online helps that plugged him into the entire world of information. He knew that the Lydians invented coinage in the eighth century B.C.E.

"If you mean the shekel as coin, then, of course, there were other forms of currency transactions. Prior to the coin as currency, the shekel was in the form of weights and measures."

"Would you mind explaining that to me?"

"Prior to the sixth century B.C.E., actually up to the time the Babylonians sacked Jerusalem in 587 B.C.E., the predominant method of exchange was through a system still practiced in parts of the world—China, areas of India, even in Central America—called weights and measures. It is a simple system and requires little mathematics to compute. Step over here, and I'll show you a few samples that I have collected from around the world. The system is as uniform as coins, but the value for each weight may differ from country to country. Notice this one . . . Come, Dr. Stein. Join us."

Bernie arose from his chair and followed Roy and Brookline to the shelf lined with antique objects. The entire wall was thirty feet in length, one giant display case of ancient treasures.

"In case you're wondering, we have excellent security in this building." What he didn't mention to Roy was the security check he had run on him the day before, anticipating this visit. Bernard Stein was a surprise, but he appeared to be what he claimed. He would have building security check out his background as well. At the right auction, his collection was worth in the neighborhood of two million dollars. He took no chances with casual visitors.

"On this shelf here, do you see those gold cups?" Brookline pointed at the object directly in front of him. Nesting in the object were three additional small cups, one inside the other in diminishing size. The one in the center was as small as a tiny thimble. They looked like small measuring cups. "You mentioned to me that you were interested in Near Eastern and Central American monetary objects. On the shelf second to the bottom, you will see weights and measures from Guatemala and El Salvador. Notice that they too are formed much like tiny measuring cups. The one beside it has the lid latched down. Of course, all of the tiny cups weigh varying amounts. Those you are looking at came from ruins just outside of Guatemala City. I had a devil of a time getting them out of the country. I did, however, and they are legal. They are also gold." Brookline moved to his right, and Roy and Bernie followed. "These weights and measures are from China. I bought them at an auction in London. I'll not tell you how much they cost."

Roy probed, "Do these pieces have names? Are they all made of precious metals?"

"The system is little different than coins. Some coins are precious metal, and many are made of iron or steel. It depends. You asked about the shekel. When it was spent on the narrow streets of Jerusalem anciently, six or seven hundred years B.C.E., it was in the form of weights. The Jews did not mint coins until later, and then they stopped using the weights and measures, especially under the Persian rule of Jerusalem. They even let the shekel go by the wayside when the dominant, more valuable, more reliable Roman coin came into play in Jerusalem over a hundred years B.C.E."

When Roy concluded his questions with Brookline, he asked the stockbroker if he would care to share his findings, for a fee and lodging, with a group of students in the spring. He could read from lecture notes if he cared to. Brookline replied that it sounded intriguing but that he would have to check his schedule and get back with Roy. Roy had a feel about presenters. This Brookline would be there. His ego would force him to make the journey.

He and Bernie graciously said good-bye to Brookline and wandered out of the eighty-story building onto Wall Street with all its frenetic activity. It was early for lunch. The sky was blue and the air refreshing, even for lower Manhattan, so the two men decided to walk toward central Manhattan.

"What is your object in having that money genius attend one of your sessions and give his spiel?" Bernie asked as he side-stepped two hard-hats working from a manhole in the center of the sidewalk.

"You're a student of the Book of Mormon. Do you remember the monetary system they had going among the Nephites?"

"Are you nuts? If we had discussed money, I would remember. I have a lot of things still in my head rolling around about certain aspects of the Book of Mormon and the fun we had tearing things apart, but I don't recall a discussion on money."

"It wasn't a topic of discussion, and it had more to do with grains marketed in the Nephite lands. In the Book of Mormon, Alma mentions that a senum of silver was equal to a senine of gold—gold being worth more—and for a measure of types of grain. In other words, the Nephites used the original form of exchange. Alma described a system of mathematical sophistication: the number of weights required for a purchase.

"To my knowledge coins did not enter into the monetary system for many years to come. They had their system of weights in gold and silver, and everyone seemed to know the value. For example when Alma talks about the monetary system of silver, for example, he said that an amnor of silver was as great as two senums. And an ezrom of silver was as great as four senums. And an onti was as great as all of them.

"It seems logical that these tiny, thimble-like precious metals fit one inside the other, like tiny measuring cups. Alma clearly said that this was the way they named their different pieces of gold and silver."

"So what are you saying? That critics cry foul, claiming that Joseph Smith cited the use of coins when no coins have been found?"

"Right! But no one ever mentioned *coins* in the Book of Mormon. I know. I did a computer search of the Book of Mormon. I doubt that there were any coins in the usual sense. Maybe they came from the Near East with the Phoenicians, but the Nephites had no locally minted coins of their own. They bought and sold with weights and measures. The critics of the Book of Mormon are way out in left field on this one. As you suggested, they have jumped all over Joseph Smith for setting up a monetary system in the Book of Mormon when there were no coins to be found in Central America. No one ever mentioned that the Nephite monetary system was based on coins. Why don't they wake up?"

Bernie reached up and patted Roy on the shoulder. Roy was a foot taller than Bernie. "Hey man, take it easy. Has Polk got you on some kind of pill? You sound like an addict. Tell me, have you joined the Mormon Church yet?" Bernie's face contorted into his famous, wicked grin.

"No, of course not," Roy protested hotly. "It's just that I see so much every time I delve into the book. You know I'm not the religious type. I just like a serious challenge to staid ideas. This has become a challenge to me, and it's rewarding in itself. You were so laid back that you never got that far into it last summer."

"No, and I don't intend to."

"By the way, I'm leaving from here to fly to Veracruz, Mexico. Two professors from the University of Texas will be about ready to leave a conference that started yesterday and will conclude tomorrow. Dr. Polk called me early this morning and wants me to meet with them before they take off. Later Polk and his new assistant arrive in Veracruz. Remember Thorn? Polk hired him to help out. We're going to tour the ruins in Central America. My original plan was to pick up a new Land Rover that is waiting at the dealer in Veracruz. I speak a little Spanish, you know."

Bernie stopped suddenly, causing the person close behind him on the busy street to run right into him. He raised his hand in disregard as the irritated pedestrian swore at him and hurried past. "You mean Stephen got back into this Book of Mormon business? I can't believe that, with all the trouble he had with his old lady. How are they getting along?"

"I haven't asked. Actually, I haven't seen Stephen since San Diego. Maybe they split up. The way things were going . . . from what I heard it didn't look good. Anyway, it should be an interesting adventure. I've done my homework."

"I'm sure you have," Bernie smirked. "Roy, weren't you supposed to take me to lunch or somethin'? Don't get cheap on me."

"It's your city. You tell me where you want to go. I hear they have some great delis in this city."

"Yeah. I go to one over near the East River. They serve killer corned beef sandwiches and pseudo-kosher pickles. Let's catch a cab, okay?"

* * *

Todd surrounded himself with friends who, if not totally committed to the academic scene, at least maintained socially acceptable grades. Good grades had never been hard for Todd to achieve. He knew he was no genius, but he could hold his own in school with a strong A-minus or a B-plus. That would get him into most any college. He wanted to go to Berkeley, and he felt sure he would be accepted next year. A great score on the SAT, and he would be in.

"Todd! Here, we get off here," Hans shouted from his seat three rows back on the U-Bahn. The car came to a halt, and the doors opened under great air pressure with a hiss. Hans and his two friends stepped out onto the platform. Todd pushed his way to the doors and leaped out.

"Wir sind da," Todd said in German. He had no trouble with slang. Hans and others had taught him the key words and were now in the process of teaching him some dirty words in German. It went with the territory, Todd rationalized. He was eighteen. What the heck.

The guys had talked about Ku-damm. It was *the* hot spot in Berlin. No one asked your age; no one cared as long as you could fork over the cash. Todd felt his wallet in the right, rear pocket of his loose jeans and was glad he had fifty marks to blow.

The students rushed to the escalator and bounded up the moving stairs two at a time to the main level. The U-Bahn, Todd thought, was really little different from the Bay Area Rapid Transit system—BART to the locals. He had traveled on BART lots of times.

Because it had been in the former western sector, the Kurfürst-endamm and the surrounding street comprised the center of Berlin nightlife—theaters, nightclubs, and drinking spots, not to mention the dives and porno shows on the fringes. Todd and the boys surfaced on the club side of Kurfürstendamm near Joachimstalerstrasse. Where those two streets converged, the fun began.

Hans, who looked older than eighteen, had been to a couple of the clubs. He had no problem buying drinks. Beer, of course, was plentiful to youth in Berlin, but hard liquor was monitored more carefully. The club Hans wanted Todd to see featured live, hard rock music and served drinks. Todd was reluctant to drink, but he loved the idea of live music by a hot group.

Two men stood at the padded double doors to the Club Rock entrance. They nodded as Hans pulled Todd into the club. The two other youths, both of whom had been with Hans on previous visits, trailed behind. The sounds were loud and raucous, the same beat Todd had enjoyed since sixth grade—familiar, alive, and pulsating.

"Das ist heiss," Hans shouted to the others.

Todd understood that he had said, "Stay close."

Strobe lighting freeze-framed the shifting, fragmented crowd. Hans and his friends snaked slowly toward the stage, hoping to find a table; if not, at least a waiter cruising the scene, taking orders for drinks. Noise was king. It was nearly impossible to make out what they were saying to one another.

Hans grabbed a waiter, ordered drinks for all, and screamed at the waiter that they would be standing against the pillar four feet away. The waiter must have understood; he was sucked into the sea of rockers and lost from sight.

Two hours of deadly sound and five drinks later, the four sought fresh air and peace. They made it to the sidewalk, though they were all swaying slightly from so much unaccustomed alcohol.

"Kommt," Hans shouted.

Off they trudged, crossing Joachimstalersstrasse at the intersection of Kurfürstendamm. Todd didn't see the fast-moving VW Golf swerve to the left. The German driver shouted words that Todd had not yet been taught.

"Ach, nein. You don't want to know what he said. I'll educate you later." Hans laughed and lunged slightly to his left, trying to catch his balance. He led the group toward a more sedate biergarten.

Todd had drunk a few beers with his friends at home and even tipped a couple of glasses after the prom last year, but he had never downed this much booze in his life. He could tell it was bordering on too much for one so unused to drinking. His thoughts swam from random sections of his consciousness. He felt queasy. Oh, that he had gone with Hilda to the movies! Why was she shutting him out? *It must be her parents. They probably hate Americans. Who wouldn't? We beat the tar out of 'em fifty years ago.*

The biergarten was an enormous hall with an open second floor and lines of tables where whole families enjoyed the loud but traditional Bavarian music. As Todd moved toward the rest room, he shouted at Hans in English that he had about twenty-nine seconds to make it before he let it all flow right into the center of the biergarten. The waiter pointed to the side of the hall, and Todd swayed in that direction. He saw the sign hanging above the door and giggled. A little fat wooden man in lederhosen held the men's room sign.

Todd proceeded into the lavatory and relieved himself, while two men stood on either side of him. Todd paid no attention to them. After trying several times to zip up his fly, he looked down and turned around, using both hands to hold and pull the zipper. At that moment, the two men turned and bumped him from opposite sides and then squeezed in close, forcing Todd forward, causing him to catch his step to keep from falling. Silently, the two men stepped aside and moved around him out the rest room door.

Todd instinctively felt for his hip pocket. The strangeness of the men pushing so hard signaled his foggy brain that perhaps . . . He looked up, startled. His wallet was gone. Near drunk or not, he had presence of mind to rush through the rest room door in pursuit of the men who had taken his wallet.

As he stumbled into the main hall of the biergarten, Todd spotted one of the thieves in a dark blue jacket. He was slithering his way among the tables through the crowd of drinkers. Todd ran after the blue jacket. The man was on the far side of a long table of gaily singing Germans who were celebrating an anniversary.

Todd suddenly felt sober. Perhaps the adrenaline had washed out his blood. He could see that if he had to go around the end of the table, he would lose his prey. In one fast move, he grabbed two hefty Germans by the shoulders and leaped onto the table between them. With one foot on the table and another in Wiener schnitzel, he vaulted over the equally stout women on the opposite side and literally flew through the air, catching the blue jacket by the collar

Todd wrestled the man to the floor, shouting in English, "You took my wallet! Dang it, you took my wallet!" Todd began reaching into the blue jacket pocket. The man, four inches shorter than Todd and no more than a hundred and thirty pounds, shook his head, "Nein, nein!"

The women who were seated on the bench closest to Todd turned around and reached down, lifting Todd by his belt. They pulled him away from the smaller man in the blue jacket. All the while, they were saying rapidly in German, "He's gone crazy! He's crazy! Call the police. He's crazy!"

The burly boys from the other side of the table had come around from the opposite side, and with hands the size of bear paws, they yanked Todd to his feet. He whirled around and hit one of the burliest in the face. Outraged, the man landed a left jab to Todd's cheek and nose and it was all over. Todd lay in a pint of spurting blood on the sawdust floor. By the time the police arrived, the blue jacket was gone and the two robust ladies were pouring a pitcher of beer across Todd's face in an effort to revive him.

Hans and his friends were nowhere to be found. Todd was out only a moment, but was so dazed and weakened that as the police were helping him to his feet, ready to cuff him, in one shuddering convulsion Todd vomited across their boots. It was mostly liquid, dark and foaming, but so smelly. Todd remembered nothing more until he revived in the tank at the main downtown police station, booked for drinking, disturbance in a public establishment, and assault, though his victim—the man in the blue jacket—had disappeared, and no one knew just who he was.

CHAPTER 7
The Mormons

En route to Prague

"Decker, do you know anything about the Mormons?" Anney asked, seated next to Decker on the European Airbus. It was a two-hour flight from London to Prague. They had left Heathrow twenty minutes earlier and were now over France. Near silence prevailed in the front section of the cabin. Anney hoped that her voice had not carried to the row in front of her where her father and Katherine were seated. She did not want to involve them in the discussion, especially her father, who had a short fuse for such conversation. Anney felt troubled knowing so little about the Mormons, so she had decided that perhaps Decker Hunt might give her some insights. He seemed like a knowledgeable person.

Decker turned his head slowly to scrutinize his seat companion. "I know some," he replied. "I attended a couple of conferences where evangelists spoke about the Mormons. I personally have had nothing to do with them, but those who have encountered them have mentioned how different they are. What do you want to know?"

"Different, how?" Anney asked. "Do the Mormons believe in Jesus Christ?" After knowing for three months that Stephen was involved in Mormonism, she had not yet bothered to study the religion to determine for herself what its tenets were. She guessed that was because the very thought of Stephen joining that church was repugnant to her sense of right.

"Why haven't you gone to your father with such questions?" Decker asked with raised eyebrows. "From what he has told me, he has lectured on the Mormons." As he spoke, Decker nodded toward the Reverend Moore, seated in front of them.

"I'm asking *you*," Anney said pointedly, with no further explanation. Of course she was not going to discuss the matter with her father; it was already a sore spot with him. So why should she aggravate the problem?

Decker looked at Anney keenly. She was virtually holding her breath for his answer. He leaned his head back and formulated the precise phrasing for his views. At last, in a confidential tone of voice, he launched into his version of whether or not the Mormons believe in Christ. "It is my understanding that the Mormons claim the very name of Christ in the official title of their religion. You see, their name is something like 'Christ's Church of the Latter-day Saints.' What mockery," Decker scoffed, his lip curling as he spoke. "Officially, they are not the 'Mormon Church'; that is a common nickname that has stuck. No, they have the very name of Christ in the official title of their church."

Decker turned in his seat to face Anney. He let his eyes drift slowly over her features. She was attractive . . . very attractive. He had been struck by her blond, shoulder-length hair that framed an oval face with creamy skin and high cheekbones. Her large blue eyes, focused directly on him, were clear and alert. No doubt about it, one of the perks of this trip was the opportunity to work so closely with Anney. He loved being near beautiful women. Always had.

With some effort, Decker pulled his thoughts back to the subject. "So to begin with," he continued, "I was told that the Mormons have usurped the name of Christ to give their church some sort of official sanction from heaven. It's all a sham. The Mormons have created their own Christ who is not the Christian Christ at all. They worship a Christ who they claim has a body . . . a body like we have. They maintain that he is a man who ascended into heaven with a body after the resurrection."

"You know . . ." Anney interrupted, a quizzical look on her face. "Oh, nothing."

"He is a spirit, Anney. That is my point." Decker leaned closer to Anney. He found the scent of her perfume enticing. "What the Mormons have done is attribute to Christ the form of a man in heaven. He is not a spirit to them. He is a living man with all the characteristics of a man. It is here that they veer from the accepted understanding of the Christian world, and it is this fact, more than any other, that has caused such a rejection of these people." Decker could see that he held Anney's full attention.

"Oh, there is more," he said with consternation. "Their very doctrine is screwed up. They teach that man is not born with original sin. I heard a detailed lecture on the evils of Mormonism just three months ago at a Southern Christian gathering in Memphis where the speaker was, by the way, an ordained minister. He said that they teach that little children are innocent before God until they are old enough to commit sin, at which time they must be baptized. They have turned around the whole concept of original sin."

Decker patted Anney's hand, which rested on the armrest between them, and said emphatically, "The Mormons are not Christians. They are a group unto themselves, but they are growing rapidly all over the world. I'm afraid in time they will become a rather large group, influencing thousands of gullible people for no good."

Anney felt Decker pat her hand. She knew it was a friendly gesture, but her first reaction was to withdraw it from the chair's arm and pull it into her lap. "What is the attraction of the Mormons? I . . . I find them to be anything but appealing. Why are they able to convince so many decent people like . . ." Anney wanted to say, "like Stephen," but she held back.

"Another thing, they are as close a community as the Jews. They separate into their own group in any community. And they insist that they are the only true church of Christ. This elitism separates them from all Christians."

"Don't the Catholics feel that they have the true church built up by Peter, who was given his charge by Christ while He was on earth?"

"We're not talking about the Catholics. They have their own problems. That isn't all. You might be interested to learn that the Mormons also preach something that appeals to base instincts."

"What do you mean?"

"They tell their people that if they follow the dictates of Mormonism, somewhere in the eternal scope of things they will become gods."

"Gods?" Anney asked perplexed. She had never heard such audacity.

"Yeah, gods. They believe that if they keep all of God's commandments while they are here on the earth, and perform certain rituals, one day they will be just like God and create worlds as gods. It is blasphemous, I tell you. The Mormons appeal to the greed in man. They promise people that as gods they will actually own a piece of the universe. Can you believe it? Gods!"

Anney didn't want to hear any more about the Mormons. What Decker had just told her confused the issue even more. She wanted to get up and move down the aisle—anything to allow her thoughts to reshuffle and return to calm. "Decker, would you excuse me? I'll be right back."

"Sure. I only hope I've been able to clarify a couple of things for you."

Anney unbuckled her seat belt and stood up. "You have, Decker. Thanks."

Walking the few steps to the rest room, Anney was overwhelmed by the feeling that she had lost Stephen. Somehow, he had been dragged into the maze of a new religion that seemed to affect his power of reasoning. He had bought the whole concept of Mormon salvation, and there seemed no way in the world for Anney to convince him of the wrong he was committing. Her conversation with Decker only served to convince her that she and Stephen had lost the common ground they shared. He had gone over to the other side. She had heard of such things in her life but had never in the world imagined that it would happen right in her own family.

She tried to push open the rest room door and then noticed that its little sign said "Occupied." Glancing around, she could see that the others were likewise occupied. She moved back a few steps to the exit alcove and waited.

"Would you like some coffee?" a voice asked with the kindness of one trained to comfort and serve passengers.

"Oh . . ." Anney turned to see a smiling young flight attendant awaiting her reply. "Yes, if you please."

Soon the cup appeared, and Anney thanked the slim attendant. Leaning dejectedly against the partition, she cuddled the cup with both hands, savoring the warmth. *Have I reached the end of the line with Stephen? What possible alternatives do we have in our marriage? The deeper he goes into this Mormon thing, the less chance we have of rebuilding our relationship. Why? What on earth did I do to deserve this turn of events? Why me, God? Why have I been victimized by such evil?*

Anney felt as violated as she had a year ago when a teenage hoodlum had sprung from a theater crowd and snatched her pearl necklace, instantly darting back into the crowd on the streets of San Francisco. Stephen had tried to catch the kid, but it was hopeless.

Anney had that same sick feeling of being robbed of something beautiful and precious to her. She felt as if someone had reached out and snatched Stephen, too, right in front of her face. How could this be? Where could she turn for help?

* * *

He looked like an old salt—the deep lines in the tanned face, the grizzled beard, and the bony body. Dr. Claus Reynolds McNear looked for all the world like a shipwrecked sailor. The image dissolved into respect after Stephen had sat with the oceanographer for half an hour. The man had a vast knowledge of the sea.

They were seated on a small bench at Scripps Institute of Oceanography, twelve miles north of San Diego on the cliffs overlooking the Pacific. Stephen had caught the very busy McNear as the instructor concluded a briefing of four young Navy Seals who were spending the day away from their post at Coronado to study under the leading oceanographers in San Diego. The session split up, and McNear graciously explained to Stephen the purpose and overall objectives of Scripps Institute and what it was doing to promote an environmentally safe and clean ocean.

"I was told by several authorities that you have had extensive experience studying ocean currents of the world."

Dr. McNear looked down at the gray planks under the bench and shuffled his feet in canvas shoes without socks. "I think that is a rather large order. Let's just say I've spent a good deal of my career studying ocean currents of the Pacific and related seas. I understand you are here to ask if it is possible to sail a ship—a crude ship, to be exact—from the southern coastline of Arabia across the Indian Ocean, across the Pacific, and end up on the shores of Central America. First off, of course it's possible; it has been done. But there are certain conditions that have to be met in order to succeed in such a wild venture."

"I'm interested in your opinion as to what those conditions would be. It's a long way, and there are those who think it would be impossible for a family—an inexperienced family—to set out and make it." Stephen leaned to one side, picked up his worn leather briefcase, and pulled out some notes. "I sent you a fax of questions that I would like to discuss."

"Yes, I have them in my office on the second floor." McNear tossed his thumb upwards over his shoulder, pointing to the wide-glassed office at the top of the stairs. "Why don't we go on up? I'd like to show you some maps that indicate ocean currents."

The two men arose, climbed the outside stairs to the landing, and entered McNear's office.

* * *

Stephen had been traveling for several days since leaving Polk at Bennett's office. From Tucson, he had taken a flight to Oakland and arrived at his home in Lafayette by late afternoon. The house was empty and quiet when he walked into the kitchen from the garage. He had called his daughter Brenda at her dorm at Humboldt State for a ten-minute visit. Brenda told him that her mom had called her to see how things were going. "Daddy, she said she would be leaving London for Prague. Boy, the rest of you get around, while all I do is sit here with my face in a book."

The next morning, after reading the fax from Dr. Polk and booking a Mexicana flight out of Tijuana International for Mexico City, Stephen had caught the early commuter flight to San Diego and arrived at Scripps.

It was now mid-morning as he stepped into McNear's cluttered office. It may have appeared to be chaos, with stacks of papers, maps, and drawings in every corner and along the walls, but it was McNear's version of a filing system. He knew where every document was located. Standing by the window was an interesting object. Noticing that it had caught Stephen's eye, McNear volunteered, "That's a little antique I picked up some years ago. It's the helm off the S.S. Dakota. It's solid brass. I need to shine it, but I can assure you that it's the genuine article."

Stephen walked over to the freestanding brass helm and touched the wheel, which turned freely.

"Go ahead. Sit down right there." McNear pointed to a dark-stained wooden chair next to his desk.

Stephen explained in more detail that his assignment on the Book of Mormon project was to find a leading authority on ocean currents and sailing ships of the sixth century B.C.E. That was the extent of his current concern on this particular matter. He also mentioned that he was doing research for a private group concerning ancient sea travel of a family described in the Book of Mormon.

McNear assured Stephen that he had no problem with that, though he cautioned him not to misquote him on what he would present. Besides, there were two men at Scripps who were Mormon and knew a great deal about oceanography and current patterns of the Pacific. "Perhaps you would rather speak with them."

"No, I want someone with no apparent bias. Do you know what I mean?"

"I think so, though I can assure you that the men I speak of have great credentials.

"I'm sure."

"Now let me get this straight. You want to know about ancient sailing vessels, vessels that might have been constructed during the period you mentioned, between 1000 and 500 B.C.E. In preparation for this meeting, I did a little reading up on early sailing vessels. You do understand that my so-called expertise does not extend to vessels of that period? I checked out what historians had to say, such as Potts's *Arabian Gulf in Antiquity,* Hourani's *Arab Seafaring in the Indian Ocean,* and Finney's great work titled *El Niño.* We have these books right here in our library. Of course, if I were to do a presentation on the subject, as you've asked, I would do a great deal more research. You did say that the stipend is five thousand and that you want me to take up to two hours in a lecture next spring? That is, if I meet your scholarly requirements." The weather-beaten face smiled broadly.

"That's right." Stephen smiled back. He wasn't too concerned that McNear would fail to meet the requirements. But there was nothing wrong with leaving the back door open on final commitments. He knew he needed to keep that in mind during future interviews with other possible lecturers as well.

The preliminaries settled, McNear waxed long and detailed on the subject of oceanic crossings in ancient times. "From my research, I find that Arabian ships, until relatively recent times, were what they called *sewn ships*. They stitched together fitted planks with cords. Leather was the most common cord. The ships they built contained no metal hinges, screws—no metal at all. Rather ingenious, though the ancients out of Egypt had the reed boat strapped together with rope. It sailed like a bobbing cork on the sea.

"In the last decade, an Irishman and his crew followed the concept and design of the sewn ships and actually built one—an eighty footer—and to prove a point they sailed it from Oman across the Indian Ocean to Canton, China. So we know it was possible anciently, at least to China. They made a number of stops along the way, but they made it in about seven months. Not too bad.

"Building the ship may have been the easy part for your Book of Mormon family. Catching the right winds and currents is a whole other matter."

"Wait a minute," Stephen said. "Before you leave the ship construction, did you find out anything about sails? What would the sails have been made of in that region?"

"Camel hide or woven camel hair. That was in my readings. They could have spun wool, but hides were far less trouble."

"Back to winds and currents." McNear cleared his throat and asked Stephen if he would care for something to drink. Stephen begged off. McNear continued, "Winds carried ancient seamen from the shores of southern Arabia across the Indian Ocean as far as China. They called them the monsoons. That actually means to set sail from one region to another shore, or a close interpretation thereof. Today it means the storms at certain times of the year. Oman, by the way, has always been a major sea-trading region, with goods being shipped as far away as Indonesia. Trade went on for centuries. When vessels reached that part of the Pacific, things got tricky. You see, at that point the winds discontinue blowing toward the east and reverse themselves. It's tough going east with the wind blowing west." McNear had a slight smirk on his face.

For a moment Stephen wondered if there was a hitch in the Book of Mormon account, and then McNear explained the solution to the wind problem.

"Fear not. There is a way to sail east. I merely said it was tricky, not impossible. Here we get into my area of expertise, the Pacific. Have you ever heard of the term *El Niño*?"

Stephen nodded that he had. He knew that it periodically brought unusually wet weather to California.

"The term we use is the ENSO effect. *El Niño* begins to blow every two to ten years around late December, early January. It is a southern oscillation, referring to the wind changes and climate patterns over most of the Pacific basin. *El Niño* expands the narrow east-moving equatorial countercurrents—aptly called the doldrums—for as much as a year's duration, and sailing ships travel on that current across the Pacific. This accounts for so many groups of people leaving the Asian continent and settling the Pacific Rim over the past three or four thousand years. There is no reason to dispute the fact that this ENSO has been around for thousands of years.

"Now, duration of time for such a voyage anciently is purely speculation. Those attempting such a risky voyage would have to make port after port for water, food, and repairs. I would guess that the voyage would take at least two, maybe three years to make it to the west coast of Central America. If they were lucky, the currents would bring them ashore somewhere along the northern coast of South America, or Central America as far north as the west coast of Mexico.

"From the Far East, the currents sweep southeast, move up the outer coastal regions of South America, and come close to the outer regions of present-day countries like Costa Rica and Guatemala, even southwestern Mexico's shoreline."

"So, you're saying, if my notes are correct," Stephen said to recap the one-on-one mini-lecture from McNear, "that the sailing party in the Book of Mormon could have left with the monsoon winds from the coast of Arabia and traveled to the islands of Indonesia, where the winds blow in the opposite direction—meaning west. There they would have to time it right or wait to catch *El Niño* to sail eastward, and then they could ride the currents all the way to the Western Hemisphere and ultimately reach the shores of Central America."

"Essentially, you have it. Though they could also reach the shores of South America, as did Thor Heyerdahl back in the 1950s with his reed boat. There is a lot more that I can add to the discussion, but basically that's it." McNear shifted in his chair, which Stephen felt was a signal that the lecture was over. Then he turned back and made another comment, "You asked me about the ancient ships that were common in the time of the empires of Assyria and Babylonia and earlier. I'm sorry to disappoint you, but I know nothing about the ships of that period."

"I knew it was a long shot. As I wrote you in the fax, the Book of Mormon depicts a body of people called the Jaredites who sailed, perhaps from a port along the Pacific, or at least from the Far East somewhere, in eight ships that were sealed tight. Anyway, I wanted to know if there was any ship in ancient oceanic travel that resembled that kind of vessel."

"I can't be of much help, but I called a Navy man in Washington, D.C., about your request, and he put me in touch with a historian at Annapolis. The instructor at Annapolis said he would be glad to talk to you by phone, if you don't mind calling him during academy hours—8:00 A.M. to 4:00 P.M.—at his office. I think he could give you some direction."

* * *

Stephen slipped his card into the phone slot and dialed the historian at Annapolis. He had half an hour before catching a Tijuana taxi across the border at San Diego on the way to Tijuana International. Since he was going to be in San Diego anyway, he figured he might as well save a few hundred dollars by flying to Mexico City from Tijuana. He had never flown on Mexicana, but so what? He had been told that it was an easy check-in—much like any other airport. If so, he would be able to make the late-morning flight on a DC-10.

"Kellerman," declared a voice on the other end of the line. Momentarily startled, Stephen found his voice and introduced himself to Frank Kellerman, the historian, and explained that he was searching for information about seagoing vessels in ancient times in the Assyrian and Babylonian empires. Kellerman recalled his conversation with McNear and said he was glad to share what he had researched.

"You know," Stephen qualified his assignment, "I am making a study of an account recorded in the Book of Mormon. Have you heard of the Book of Mormon?"

"Oh, sure. I have a neighbor who's Mormon. Not that I know a great deal about their book."

"In the Book of Mormon it says that a group of people left the Middle East—perhaps at the time of the Tower of Babel—and eventually ended up on a seashore where they were instructed by the Lord to build eight relatively small, tight vessels that were quote, 'like unto a dish.' You know, covered with a tight lid." Stephen was reading the quote from his note pad. "The ships were peaked at the ends and as long as a tree, whatever size that would be. Also, they were designed with doors. On each ship there was a door at the top and one at the bottom to keep out the water should they flip over or become submerged for a short time. Kind of like a crude submarine, I guess. It also states in the Book of Ether, which is one of the books within the Book of Mormon, that 'they were tight like unto the ark of Noah.'

"Can you shed any light on this fragment of information concerning vessels they might have used?" Stephen asked, wishing he were there in person rather than on a telephone near a noisy McDonalds. He pressed his Panasonic micro-recorder to the receiver and listened with part of his ear touching the lower, circular part of the receiver.

"Oh, yes. You are speaking of what they referred to as a Sumer *magur* boat. I have lectured about these ancient ships. Take down this name: Hermann Hilprecht. He wrote years ago about the magur boats. If you will wait a minute I'll get the quote for you."

It took two minutes for Kellerman to find the quote and get back to the telephone. "I have the place marked. Here it is: 'The magur boat had a solid lower part, strong enough to carry heavy freight and to resist the force of the waves and the storm. . . . The boat is called a house . . . which has a door to be shut during the storm flood . . . and at least one air hole or window.'"

Kellerman spoke louder when he heard noises coming from Stephen's end of the connection. He said, "The term *houseboat* is from an Egyptian loanword *ark*. Apparently the magur boat had a cover or a lid because further study of the word *houseboat* in Sumerian was associated with a box or chest. In other words, I think the magur boat was a sealed craft that could be submerged for a brief time in a violent storm—a very durable craft that was used for freighting goods. It was also specially designed to be driven by the wind. Seen from the side, the ship resembled a crescent moon. In other words, it had peaked ends and a box-like hull as I understand the description."

"That's amazing," Stephen breathed. *Like following a pirate map and finding a buried treasure chest. Wait until I tell Dr. Polk about this!*

* * *

Kline and Hadley, client and attorney, had flown together to Los Angeles for the day. They rented a Lincoln Town Car and drove to the graphics studio office of Melrose Green, not far from Universal Studios in the southern hills of the San Fernando Valley. Chet Hadley approached a receptionist and asked to see Mr. Weinberger, an illustrator. The receptionist picked up her telephone and pressed a button. After a short wait, she handed the receiver to Hadley. Weinberger spoke from somewhere deep in the creative caves of the animator's world. Hadley introduced himself as an attorney handling the Kline trust. Then, pulling a card from his wallet, he read: "I represent the trust interests that are part of the Book of Mormon Project II." He had gleaned the title from Bennett's secretary, who had divulged it to Hadley, assuming he was a Utah attorney associated with the trust. Bennett being out of town made the deception much easier.

"I know Mr. Bennett, but no one has mentioned your name."

"May we have ten minutes with you on how to secure the animations you're doing under current copyright law?" Hadley knew he was risking exposure, but it was worth a try. Weinberger sighed and agreed to come to the reception desk.

When Kline and Hadley introduced themselves, Kline posed as Hadley's associate. Mr. Weinberger was a man in his middle years who wore glasses with thick lenses and was as wide as he was tall. He invited the two to step into a side conference room where they could talk.

The room was furnished with one round table and six formed plastic chairs. A telephone was nearby on a stand in the corner, within reach of any person at the far end of the table. They sat.

Hadley lied profusely as he unraveled his story about copyrights and wound his verbal path to the key issue of what was going on in that building in Provo. Hadley told him that he had recently been hired to look into the trust and copyrights, but he was not familiar with the project within the building. He wanted to know how Weinberger's group fit in and what would be the final creation in that building.

Weinberger quickly apprised the inquirers that he had an agreement with Dr. Polk not to reveal anything concerning the design or construction of things in the building. Also, he was not to broadcast the fact that he and his assistant were creating drawings and helping to coordinate sound for the television presentations.

"Really, fellows, I don't know who you are. Your names have never come up in any discussions I've had with Mr. Bennett or Dr. Polk. I think I would have to get some sort of verification by one or the other of these men."

"If either one were available," Hadley agreed, "we would put in a call, but Dr. Polk is somewhere in Mexico and Bennett is in the wilds of South America." Hadley decided to go for broke. "Why don't you call Mr. Bennett's office and ask to speak to his secretary? She knows about our involvement. I'm sure her verification would be all that is needed." Hadley glanced quickly at Bennett's number in the address book that had been inside his briefcase and read it off to Weinberger.

Weinberger shifted his hefty frame and reached back for the phone. He punched the number nine and then stopped abruptly. "What am I doing? We have a new phone policy around here. I have to have my supervisor's approval to make long-distance calls. This line is only set up for local calls." He replaced the receiver, turned back to the two men, and considered the issue, tapping all ten stubby fingers against each other in teepee fashion. "You have to be who you say you are, or you wouldn't have me calling Mr. Bennett's office."

Kline and Hadley both sighed within, hoping Weinberger didn't detect their relief.

Before Weinberger finished talking about how beautifully things were shaping up in the building in Provo, Kline and Hadley had a fairly accurate view of what Polk was building. Kline hated the very thought of so much of his family's money being sunk into such a worthless project. Weinberger mentioned that he thought the animation and sound alone would eat up hundreds of thousands of dollars. The project was scheduled to be completed by next April.

Kline sat in the plastic chair, fuming on one hand and cheering on the other. At least they were doing something so expensive that they would hang themselves and maybe end up in jail.

CHAPTER 8
The Tree of Life

Veracruz

Roy slipped into a padded chair in the great hall. He had checked into the Mar Vista Hotel in Veracruz, Mexico, at three in the afternoon, after his flight from New York via Mexico City. The Mayan Studies Symposium at the Mar Vista was in its final session, scheduled to conclude in an hour.

Among scholars from all over the globe, Roy listened to Professor Helen Calmer describe some recent archaeological finds, mosaic symbols in La Venta that dealt with a representation of the tree-of-life motif. Her colleague, Doris Browning, who had finished speaking, sat on the stage beside the symposium sponsors, listening attentively. Roy wrote a note to the speakers and slipped it to a young Mexican usher, along with a wad of pesos equivalent to three dollars.

While most of the conference attendees got up and moved out of the hall, Roy remained seated and watched the two women step down from the platform and walk directly to him, smiles on their faces. His note, requesting a few minutes of their time, had said, "Look for the tallest, thinnest young guy in the hall; I'll be in the back."

Roy stood up as they approached, extending his hand. The two professors from the University of Texas introduced themselves. Roy thought of them as free and easy, like two sisters on a lark. Neither was married; they were decidedly beyond the childbearing years and dressed somewhat alike in skirts and blouses. They were only slightly different in their builds—both thin. Roy knew he would never remember which name went with which woman.

"So you are here representing Dr. Peter Polk?" Professor Doris Browning inquired. "And you want to know if we will lecture on the tree-of-life concept in ancient times, next spring in Provo?"

"That's right." Roy nodded, unaccustomed to such directness from would-be presenters.

"Sure, we'll go. On one condition."

"What's that?"

"That we don't have to say anything about the Book of Mormon and the tree-of-life dream that is recorded in it."

"That's fair. We're just asking you to explain the many aspects of the tree-of-life traditions. We need experts in certain topics for our conference, and one subject is the Tree of Life."

"That shouldn't be too hard. We lecture on the subject all the time," Helen Calmer said.

"Good. I don't know what your schedule is, but I have some questions about what you would cover in your lecture. Do you mind if we discuss it a minute?"

The two women looked at each other, and Helen Calmer said, "No. But first let's get some coffee or tea. I hope it's still hot." She glanced at the refreshment table where a young waiter was picking up the used coffee cups and piling them on a tray. Browning had tea, as did Roy; Calmer had coffee. They pulled three chairs in a circle and began conversing.

"Would you mind giving me the high points of what you would explain about the Tree of Life to a group of college kids who know nothing about the subject? By the way, none of them will be Mormons." Roy addressed his question to either of the women. Browning responded.

"We would begin by explaining what the Tree of Life is and then give background information on the subject. That's how I would approach it. I do it all the time."

"I do, too," Calmer chimed in.

Roy already knew a good deal about the concept, but he was interested in probing their findings and insights. "For a starter, what is the earliest record of this famous legend?"

"Oh, it's more than legend," Browning cautioned. "It's interwoven into several cultures in the world. The tree-of-life tradition extends from the Near East all the way to India, and of course is known throughout Central America. It's so embedded in these cultures that its symbolism pops up everywhere."

"I know that this may sound elementary on my part," Roy interjected, "but would you mind telling me, briefly, what your understanding is of the tree-of-life tradition?"

This led to an animated discussion of the salient points of the tree-of-life concepts in half a dozen civilizations. The professors, alternately speaking and listening, amicably interrupting each other to make their points, detailed the key elements of the representation of the Tree of Life in those cultures. Then Calmer explained the imagery.

"The images include a tree, often white or with white fruit, springs or a pool of water, a path leading to the tree, and sometimes people under the tree. The Egyptian tree-of-life literature—that is perhaps the earliest example of the theme—is part of their redemption ritual. The tree represents something divine, with a spring nearby as the living waters, while the murky water off in the distance represents evil.

"Then, if you move into the Greek inscriptions of the Tree of Life, the Orphic gold plates give a good, detailed account of the tree-of-life elements. All the symbols are there. The water, the tree, the images of good and evil."

"What gold plates?" Roy asked, startled by the professor's comment.

"The Orphic gold plates were probably discovered in the eighteenth century, but the first writings appear in the mid-1830s in Europe. Orphism was a religion that flourished in the sixth century B.C.E. On these plates are inscribed writings of that religion. Anciently the plates were buried in the ground and discovered, as I said, in the eighteenth or nineteenth century.

"They present an elaborate work of poetry dealing with, among other things, the Tree of Life. The message of the gold plates is that a dead man is given portions of sacred literature that will instruct him as to how to behave when he finds himself on the road to the lower world. They indicate the way to go and the words he is to say."

"Then, of course, there is Dura Orpheus that Goodenough writes about," Calmer added. "In 1932 they discovered the Dura Europos synagogue that dated back to the third century C.E. In the ancient synagogue, they uncovered remarkably well-preserved, impressive murals. After they cleared off centuries of dust built up on the central composition that crowns the Torah shrine, which was the ritual center of the synagogue, they discovered a depiction of the Tree of Life. It is elaborate to say the least. It shows the twelve sons of Jacob on one side of the tree and on the other, Joseph blessing his sons Ephraim and Manasseh. The tree is an olive tree with vines intertwined in the branches.

"As we said, the Egyptians had an elaborate literature on the Tree of Life. This Tree of Life, often known as a miraculous tree, is represented down through the history of man in the form of different specie: a cypress tree, a white poplar, a silver cypress, and a silver apple tree among the Celts. It represents a type of divine love. But not only is the tree significant, but the spring of water that is mentioned is important. At times it is referred to as *living water.*"

Roy listened intently to their discussion. *Then there is a compatibility with the ancient Near Eastern origins of the tree-of-life concepts in the Book of Mormon.* He reasoned also, as he sat listening to the two professors explain the concept historically, that the tree-of-life story that Lehi claimed to have had was a universal scene in Lehi's time in the Near East. *Very interesting. Then Lehi's dream is similar to the writings of the Egyptians, literature that Lehi may have been familiar with. Could Lehi have been thinking or reading about the literature of the Tree of Life and had a dream from God that enlarged on this common account of his time? Certainly there were no scholars piecing together the tree-of-life motif in the 1820s, when the Book of Mormon was translated.*

"One question. You two have spent most of your academic life researching this subject of the Tree of Life and its various forms throughout the world. When do you think serious research began in recent times on the subject?"

"That's a fairly simple question," Calmer responded. "I would have to say that scholars sat up and took notice with the discovery of the Orphic gold plates. When the first published writings appeared in Europe, as we said, in 1836, it was the first real light on the ancient subject."

"I agree. We have not found anything on the subject—period— before that date," Browning said. "At least I haven't. Face it. Very little was done on the subject, at least in the western world, until this century."

"Then are you saying that for someone to write about the essential elements of the tree-of-life concept, it would have to have been written after 1836? That is, to give the usual elements of the account such as the white tree, the living water, the path, et cetera?"

"Oh, definitely. Wouldn't you say so, Helen?"

"Since you are here at this Mayan Studies Symposium," Roy interrupted, "how do you feel the ancient Central Americans developed the theme of the Tree of Life that you claim is everywhere?"

"We have no clear picture of how it was transmitted from the Old World—that it did come from the Near East we are pretty much settled on—but science is finding more evidence that there was periodic contact between the ancient cultures of the Mediterranean and the Western Hemisphere. They picked it up from the Near East during some sort of cultural exchange. The Thor Heyerdahl voyage proved that a ship made of papyrus reeds could cross the Atlantic anciently. He did it in *Ra II*. Maybe you don't remember. That was back in the late sixties or early seventies."

"You're right. But I have heard of his voyage in *Ra II*."

Roy started to ask another question when Calmer interrupted him. "I know what you are going to ask us: 'How does this fit in with the account in the Book of Mormon?' Sorry, you will have to seek out some other researcher for that answer. I know little about the Mormon research on the subject."

"Hey, I didn't intend to ask you that. And for your information, I'm not a Mormon. I happen to be working with a project dealing with disputed topics in the Book of Mormon, but that's all. You brought up the subject. Now let me tell you that by your own admission, Joseph Smith, the translator of the Book of Mormon, could not have had access to documents to write about the tree-of-life dream that is in the Book of Mormon. The Book of Mormon isn't far off the mark. Really, it isn't. Obviously, there is historical compatibility with the Book of Mormon. I'll say no more."

Roy surprised himself that he had been so assertive with the renowned professors. Then he very kindly said, "Nevertheless, you have certainly given me some new insights. I appreciate the information and your time. We will get back to you."

* * *

The two men sat hunched over the mosaic-topped table. Their seats were black vinyl. They would have been hot and sticky were it not for the air conditioning blowing across the lounge area of the Veracruz air terminal. It was morning in the tropical city. The hazy sun that streamed through the glass wall on the east, casting faint rays on the scratch pad in front of Dr. Polk, was already heating up the day. Stephen Thorn had flown in from California the evening before, while Polk had been in the city for two days. And now Polk was set to enlarge upon some of the perplexities of the Book of Mormon regarding population growth.

"We'll have further research to do with population growth in the Book of Mormon," he said thoughtfully. He shifted his bulk to the left and loosened his belt. "Anyone who really analyzes Lehi's family's growth in the promised land will see some possible discrepancies." Dr. Polk rubbed the eraser end of his pencil behind his ear. "You see, after living in the land for only twenty-five years, Lehi's family had already gone to war. If any of the few adult men had been killed in this first feud, then there must have been a population decrease from the original party rather than an increase, which would make the whole group little more than a handful of people."

Dr. Polk stretched his arms above his head and shifted in the chair again. He was tired. Traveling at his age was a strain on the body—the bed, the food, the time. All strange. But he pressed on.

"So what are you suggesting?" Stephen asked, unaware of his own physical self. His smooth features and slightly receding strawberry-blond hair contrasted with the dark, handsome features of the Mexican businessman seated next to him who was engrossed in *La Prensa,* the local newspaper.

"Well, we have to take a good look at this situation and lay it out in a logical pattern of presentation. There are several issues we must address. Were there other people already living in the Mesoamerican region where evidence indicates Lehi and his family landed in 590 B.C.E.? If so, how many? And did they have immediate contact with Lehi and his family? Let's find someone—a scholar, of course, and someone outside the Church—who can take this matter in hand and resolve it to our satisfaction. I have several leads in mind. I may need your help interviewing these people. If we can find someone with strong experience in demographics and can somehow piece together the population growth of Lehi's family over a one- to two-hundred-year period, we will have a whole new perspective of the early years of the family. First, however, you need a little background on the problem."

"That's good," Stephen said with relief. "Don't ever assume that I know what you are talking about."

Dr. Polk leaned over the table once more and tapped his Book of Mormon. "There is clear evidence of the presence of others in the Americas when Lehi came ashore—besides those we already know about. It is clear that the Jaredites were here, but there must have been others. I think that there were tribes or communities of people nearby when Lehi and his family set up their tents near the seashore." He turned the worn, dog-eared pages of his book. "Look at this declaration in 2 Nephi 5:26–34. Only thirty years had passed from the time they arrived in the promised land. After another ten years, they had experienced 'wars and contentions' with their relatives, the Lamanites. Forty years into their settlement in the new land, Jacob is concerned that the men began wanting wives and concubines.

"So I have to ask myself, what is going on here? How many descendants would there be after just forty years? Think about it. If you look at childbirth and population increase under the most favorable conditions—go ahead and assume the birthrate to be double what it is today in the most undeveloped nations. Assume that there were no deaths besides Lehi and Sariah. Allow for all possible growth. By the time you reach fifty years in the land, the population would be roughly 300 to 325. Among those would be perhaps sixty-five adult males and the same number of adult females. This, of course, is an absurd figure because they had already experienced a war and some deaths must have occurred. Then you have to figure that not all the females were fertile, or at least not able to bear many children. In reality, perhaps there were thirty-five to forty adult females and thirty adult males. Experts on population growth would put the figure smaller than that. The traditional concept that the family of Lehi made up the entire population until they meet the Mulekites doesn't hold up. I'm convinced there were many groups of people when Lehi arrived. It makes sense. And who said that there weren't?

"You have to factor in death and fertility in any projection of population growth. If the males were interested in wives and concubines, then those women had to have come from some other area. The original group could not have sustained 'many wives and concubines.'" Dr. Polk reached for another book in his well-worn brown leather briefcase and quickly flipped through the pages.

Stephen opened his mouth to ask a question, but Dr. Polk went on without glancing up. "Look at this statement from a critic of the Book of Mormon. It points up what I have been saying. 'Less specific information from the scriptures also produces some startling results when viewed in the light of date. For example, Nephites and Lamanites had already waged wars against one another by 560 B.C.E. Even if the original colonists had been multiplying at the unheard-of rate of two percent annually, the total number of reproductive-age Nephite and Lamanite men and women alive in 560 B.C.E. would have been a mere fifty-five. If half of those fifty-five people were women and some of the males were too old, too young, or too infirm to fight or were occupied with agriculture or other tasks, then the total number of combatants on both sides in these "wars" must have been fewer than twenty.

"'Some have suggested the problem is solved by considering the actual descendants of the Lehi and Mulek groups as only a tiny fraction of the total population described in the Book of Mormon.'" Polk held a hand over his paper, looked up at Stephen, and said, "If you ask most members of the Church if there were numerous other tribes of people in the Book of Mormon lands when Lehi landed, they will shake their heads and tell you there were not. As a people, we are deeply imbued with the idea that, except for the Mulek group out of Jerusalem that the Book of Mormon explicitly explains, there were no other tribes here. I think that is nonsense.

"Let me quote Kunich further in his studies. 'Nephites and Lamanites may have interacted with indigenous native groups, becoming their religious and/or political leaders by virtue of their more advanced culture. The authors of the Book of Mormon may have chosen not to mention these aboriginal peoples out of an ethnocentric penchant to focus only on the chosen people. The others might have been important only as extras in the grand drama orchestrated by the

Hebraic elite. In this way, the enormous populations described in the scriptures may be accurate, but not as direct biological progeny from those two tiny clusters of immigrants.'"

Polk stopped reading once again. "Kunich makes it appear as if the Nephites felt superior to other tribes. That may not have been the case at all. They likely absorbed the others into their group with little mention because it was not significant for Mormon to explain this matter in any detail when he compiled the record. There are places where, in some cities governed by the Nephites, the writer of the Book of Mormon text indicates that so-and-so was a Nephite as opposed to most of the others of the city. I think there were many groups inhabiting these lands at the time Lehi came ashore with his family at the start of the family's religious history.

"By the time the younger brother of Nephi, the prophet Jacob, encountered Sherem, there would only have been a small settlement of Nephites at best. But look what Jacob records when Sherem meets with him: 'Brother Jacob, I have sought much opportunity that I might speak unto you; for I have heard . . . that thou goest about much, preaching.' This is a ridiculous statement for Sherem to make if he were one of less than fifty adult members of the settlement. He seemed to have come to Jacob after seeking him out. Where did this Sherem come from? Was he a relative of Jacob's? If so, why did he have to seek much opportunity to speak with Jacob?

"Where is the fighting force coming from to launch wars in these first few decades the family was in the land? Natural demographic increase does not allow for that. Doesn't it seem logical to you that there were others in the land? There may have been many others who joined with the Nephites during the first fifty years of settlement.

"Sorenson further tells us that 'archaeology, linguistics, and related areas of study have established beyond doubt that a variety of peoples inhabited virtually every place in the Western Hemisphere a long time ago.' When Europeans arrived in the Americas, they found dozens of major groups of people, speaking nearly fifteen hundred different languages. This can be explained only by supposing that speakers of these ancestral tongues had been in America for thousands of years. The notion that the 'Indians' constituted a single ethnic entity is totally outdated. No one believes that nowadays."

Stephen looked intently at his friend. There was no doubt that Dr. Polk was engrossed with the subject at hand. His brow was furrowed, his face flushed, and he orally punctuated each sentence with an exclamation point. He seemed to be striving to convince the scholars of the world, and not just Stephen, who barely grasped the implications of his premise.

"There are references in the Book of Mormon that indicate that not all of the peoples in all the Nephite cities sprang from Lehi and his family." Polk scarcely paused for breath. "Alma indicates that the Zoramites were perhaps a mixture when he prayed to the Lord for them: 'O Lord, their souls are precious, and many of them are our brethren.' Turn that statement around and it indicates that some were *not* their 'brethren.' The text always indicates those who were their brethren—Nephites or Lamanites. So who were the others among the Zoramites?

"When you look carefully at the history recorded in the Book of Mormon, it's evident the Nephites were the governing religious family—not that there weren't other religions in the land. They kept the key records and were always in the minority."

Dr. Polk paused, pulled a handkerchief out of his pocket, and wiped his face and glossy forehead. He suddenly seemed aware of Stephen watching him. He stopped and grinned at the younger man.

"Okay, so I'm interested in the subject. I have only hit some of the more salient points. There is so much more in the text that indicates there were others in the land. I have tried to elucidate for you some of the findings; now, we need to work this into our presentation. Look for those who were different in the culture. Find out all you can about various ethnic and racial groups among the Nephites. It is amazing how much information indicates that the Nephites were but a small part of the population at any one time. Granted, they were an important part but not large in numbers compared to all the others who were present in the land. I think the problem most Mormons have in this regard has to do with simplification. It is much easier to categorize all of the people in the Western hemisphere into two groups—Lamanites and Nephites—without accounting for all of the others that have contributed to the numbers of those two groups. The Mormons hate to admit that there were numerous other tribes besides those that are well known in the account, but it has to be. There seems to be no other explanation for such numbers of people. Of course the critics have had a heyday with this one."

A voice over the PA system—first in Spanish and then in English—indicated that those passengers bound for La Ciudad de Mexico—Mexico City—and on to the Caribbean, were to begin boarding immediately. Stephen tried to disguise his relief.

"I've got to go. That's my call."

"Yeah," Dr. Polk agreed and began picking up his papers and books from the table, stuffing them under his arm. "Sorry you came to Veracruz for nothing. As I said, I learned that this was Novue's last day in Guadalupe after your plane took off. You'll like this fellow, Dr. Novue. He's one of the foremost collectors of engraved metal plates. But he also travels nonstop, teaching some specialized surgical technique. It's hard to catch him. But I appreciate you going in my place. Tell Dr. Novue that I regret not being able to come, but I do have to meet with the archaeologists in La Venta."

"Are you sure I can handle it?" Stephen asked dubiously. "I'm afraid I might nix it for you. I don't know much about ancient writings of any sort, let alone on metal plates."

"Don't worry a minute. You can handle this discussion just fine. Wait, I meant to give you . . ." Polk shuffled through his briefcase and pulled out a few rumpled photocopies. "All you have to do is read these articles on the plane and you will know as much as I do. Remember, I haven't done much homework on the plates either, so it's all new stuff for the both of us.

"You'll have to meet us in Oaxaca, as I explained. Roy's driving me down in the Land Rover, but we'll wait and tour the ruins together after you arrive. We have plenty to do until you catch up to us. Okay?"

Polk shook hands with Stephen, turned, and started toward the front entrance of the terminal. Suddenly, he turned around, reaching into his pants pocket for his wallet. "Oh, Stephen. I almost forgot. Your American Express gold card arrived in the mail at my place. Use it, and you won't have to wait for reimbursement when you pay for your travel and lodging."

Stephen remembered that he had cosigned on the project bank account in Bennett's office. "Thanks. It may come in handy."

* * *

Stephen scanned the large room as he rushed from the tarmac and headed towards the customs counter. He hoped to clear customs ahead of the crowd. His plane had arrived in the French possession of Guadalupe two hours late from Mexico City. The passengers, including Stephen, were antsy all the way. The Caribbean island fun spot known as the French Department—the capital city of Basse-Terre—was pumping up its tourist trade to peak season, and the passengers were impatient to get in on the fun. Stephen was no tourist, but he was frustrated just the same.

At the first of five stalls, he shoved his completed declaration card and passport under the half-moon opening in the glass, behind which sat a uniformed clerk. The African-French customs clerk gripped a rubber stamp in his right fist and opened Stephen's passport with his left hand with the dexterity of a Vegas dealer. He took the requisite time to study the passport, unmoved by Stephen's anxiety. Delays were nothing new to him. He compared the photo to the face and nodded approval, perused the declaration card, and then with a practiced flair and red ink he stamped a blank square on a clean page in the visa section of the passport.

Stephen grabbed the passport and whirled around. He moved swiftly to the baggage inspection station and went straight to the empty counter on the far right. He could hear the hordes of tourists from the plane stampeding behind him. The pleasant, aging baggage inspector smiled and waved him through the stall. It may have been Stephen's sheer willpower that prompted the inspector to overlook his lone, black, carry-on bag, stuffed so tightly it had stretch marks. He never checked his bag, preferring to carry it on board; he detested waiting in baggage claim areas. With a smile of relief, he shouldered his heavy bag and dashed past Duty Free, ticket counters, and a snack bar to the electronic front doors. He was jogging by the time he reached the terminal exit.

Lush tropical plants, exotic flowers, and hanging vines created a canopy over the entrance. Stephen was jostled by an arriving tour group. He elbowed his way to the taxi stand at the curb. A large, boisterous American with a briefcase beat him to the first waiting cab. Stephen swung open the door of the second Peugeot and dived into the back seat, dragging his flight bag behind him. "You speak English?" he asked the driver.

"Yes, a little," the African-French cab driver said with the same cloned smile of the customs agent.

"I need you to take me, as quickly as possible, to the French Hospital. I understand it is about three miles—or rather about five kilometers from here."

The cab driver was already pulling away from the curb, heading toward the circling thoroughfare to the main highway that led northeast to the high ground where the French Hospital was located. The highway belted downtown Basse-Terre and cut the distance to the hill where the government-run hospital stood surrounded by groomed jungle growth. Stephen leaned back in the cab and inhaled. Suddenly, he became aware that he was indeed in the lush Caribbean islands. The tropical air held the same fragrance as Maui, where Stephen and Anney and their two nearly grown children had vacationed a year earlier.

* * *

Stephen bounded for the front door of the hospital and came to a sudden halt at the reception desk. He guessed the hospital to be at least thirty years old, but it was well maintained. He gave his name and indicated that Dr. Pierre Novue was expecting him.

The receptionist informed him that Dr. Novue had left instructions that an orderly was to accompany Dr. Thorn to the scrub room, where he was to wash his hands and dress in a surgical gown. Then he was to go with the orderly to the O.R. where Dr. Novue was already performing a liposuction procedure.

"Into the operating room?" Stephen asked, stunned at the thought of observing an operation. "Isn't this a little unusual?"

"No, you're a doctor. So?"

Stephen began to explain that he was not a medical doctor but a Ph.D. and then decided against it. *If the receptionist thinks I'm a doctor . . .*

From locker room to O.R. was five meters through an inner hallway. Stephen traversed the distance behind a husky young black orderly who wore hospital green trousers and a white tee shirt with CHICAGO BULLS in large black lettering across the back.

Stephen wondered if the young man even knew who the Bulls were. The orderly stopped at the double doors to the surgical suite and peered through an observation glass. He turned and said in a richly West Indian-French accent, with a touch of Belafonte, "Sir, you see through the glass? That is Dr. Novue on the left. I cannot enter. Just go in, and tell him you are here."

Stephen thanked the would-be Bulls fan and stepped quietly into the operating room. Suddenly he experienced the sensation he had once felt when he walked into a women's rest room by mistake.

The room was tiled in white. The light from the lamps immediately over the heads of the five people gowned in green was brilliant. Those surrounding the operating table were intent on the surgical task before them. No one looked up as Stephen slipped silently into the room. Between the elbows of the surgeon and a nurse, Stephen could see a female patient lying supine on the table.

So far, Dr. Novue was oblivious to his presence. Novue was extracting fat from the patient's abdomen with a syringe. Stephen stood without moving for the next five minutes, fascinated with the procedure he was witnessing.

Novue said something in French to the nurse beside him and looked up. He turned his head as if he had known that Stephen had been standing there all the while. He must have asked the nurse to position his half glasses closer to the front of his very thin, angular nose to enable him to see Stephen above the glasses.

"Ah, you must be Dr. Thorn."

"Yes, nice to meet you, Dr. Novue."

"Come closer. Stay about a meter away." The small surgeon had a deep, resonant voice and a charming French accent. He beckoned to Stephen with his right hand, waving the syringe as if it were a baton. "So you have made it. Pardon us, but we had to begin the surgery fifteen minutes ago."

"My flight from Mexico was held up for two hours. Sorry to be late."

"It is nothing. We can talk while I suture this patient." Dr. Novue then turned back to the team and spoke rapidly in French, answering questions, instructing, demonstrating as they watched. Turning to speak to Stephen, he said, "We will only be another few minutes. Come closer still."

Stephen stood as close as he felt proper, then paused.

"Is it okay for me to be in this O.R. unit? I mean . . ."

"You are a doctor, aren't you, Dr. Thorn?"

"I'm a Ph.D., not a medical doctor."

"My dear Dr. Thorn, simply refrain from making a distinction. No one here cares. But if it worries you, then don't explain what type of degree you have. I already told these people here that you are a doctor. Who cares?" Novue's lower lip protruded as he lifted his shoulders and spread his hands in that characteristic French "it-doesn't-matter" look.

"Have you ever seen liposuction surgery?"

"I'm afraid not." *No, and I've never seen a leg amputated or a cataract removed either.* "I've always understood it was performed with some type of suction machine."

"It is, as a rule. Yes, but I am touring the world, instructing surgeons in my method of syringe liposuction. It is the wave of the future. I can go anywhere in the world and perform liposuction with a hand syringe. For me, it has become that simple."

Stephen had already been briefed about Dr. Pierre Novue, considered by many to be the father of liposuction surgery. But he had been sent to ask the doctor about his second highly respected expertise: antique metal plates.

"So, mon ami, you have come all this way to speak with me about metal plates."

"Yes. As Dr. Polk explained to you yesterday, he would have come, but he had to meet with some archaeologists in the Yucatan. I hope you don't mind. I am his assistant and will conduct the same interview with you that he would have done. No, let me rephrase that. I will take his place and conduct an interview; I can hardly class myself with a man who is as knowledgeable as Dr. Polk. I understand you two met in San Francisco a month ago."

"Yes, yes. It is true. We have tried many times to find an opportunity when our schedules would allow us to meet for a discussion. Apparently, it is not to be. But he tells me that you will represent him well."

"As you know," Stephen said, nervous about how well he would represent the erudite Polk, "we are interested in learning all we can about the various collections of metal plates in existence, and since you're an authority in the world on the subject, we've come to you for information." Stephen spoke in a rush of words, hoping he could convey his respect for this surgeon and his avocation of collecting and studying about metal plates. He had crammed on the plane, hoping to sound intelligent enough to converse with Novue about the subject. He was uneasy about the time wasted by his delayed flight because he knew that Dr. Novue was scheduled to leave Guadalupe in a couple of hours.

"So you have come to ask me questions about ancient metal plates. Good. Ask me."

"Yes . . . okay." Stephen's mind whirled, trying to stabilize and lock onto the information he had absorbed on the plane. "Let's see . . . specifically, I want to know if any plates have shown up in the Americas, and I am particularly interested in metal plates used to record wars, religious happenings, whatever. Then I would like to know about any Near Eastern plates." Stephen's words came faster and faster. "I understand that some interesting metal plates have come to light in nations of the Middle and Far East in the last twenty years. I guess you might say I've come to find out everything I can." Stephen stopped, embarrassed that he had blurted out everything he knew about plates in twenty short seconds.

Stephen could not see the smile hidden by Dr. Novue's surgical mask. "Tell me why you are interested again," Novue said while he sutured the incision below the patient's navel. One of the other surgeons simultaneously sutured the other small incision that had been made on her side, watching Novue carefully as he worked.

"We are involved in a private project. It concerns a study of the Book of Mormon. Have you heard of the book?"

"Oh, but of course."

"Joseph Smith claimed to have translated the book from a set of gold plates that he was loaned in the 1820s in upstate New York." Stephen was aware that he was slicing to the heart of Joseph Smith's work of translation, but in the interest of time, he could only give the gist of it.

"Yes, yes. Interesting project this translator undertook to accomplish. I would surely like to have met this man—what is his name again?"

"Joseph Smith."

"Of course, Smith. He seems like a fascinating fellow. My only objection to the account he gave was that he claimed that he received the gold plates from an angel. I have reasoned that he must have taken them from an Indian. None of the North American tribes have been known to have written records, and certainly none recorded on metal plates, but who knows what will yet come to light? The visionary nature of the man demanded that he would say that an angel loaned them to him. After all, was he not the founder of the Mormon religion? He was seeking a following."

"Yes, he was." Stephen was uncomfortable, wanting to defend the Prophet Joseph Smith, yet reticent to get into a debate.

"And what happened to this Smith of yours?"

"He was martyred on the frontier of America."

"Pity, such a gifted mind. Prophets do practice a most dangerous profession and must live in expectation of martyrdom. It has always been thus."

Stephen leaned on one leg, then the other, spending the next few minutes hesitantly discussing what he could remember about the plates that Joseph Smith translated. At first he feared that Dr. Novue might be mocking him. Finally, daring to look into Novue's eyes, he saw that they expressed something entirely different. They revealed a keen interest in what Stephen was relating about the gold plates. There was no doubt in those eyes. He believed that Joseph Smith really had in his possession a set of gold plates. Encouraged, Stephen also brought up the instruments of translation—the Urim and Thummim, the convenient codex plates, and the reformed Egyptian characters that Joseph Smith claimed were inscribed on the plates.

As Novue checked the incision, he listened intently, then said, "Excuse me a moment." He held up his gloved hand to Stephen as if he were a traffic cop. "I must speak to my associates in French. We must discuss the procedure. Pardon."

Stephen waited. Muffled comments streamed between the doctors as Novue explained techniques to those surrounding him. Stephen could see that the procedure had pleased the surgeons. Dr. Novue patted the patient's shoulder and declared in French that the surgery was a success, and then stepping back from the table he began pulling off his right glove. Then with his bare hand, he released the tie of the surgical mask. Stephen saw for the first time the hawk-like nose, which emphasized the large, deep-set eyes, revealing a man of sixty or more. Alert, profound, and in control.

"Now, then, Dr. Thorn—tell me your first name, please. I have forgotten it."

"Stephen, with a ph."

"Yes, Stephen. I have heard of this Book of Mormon. I believe it is translated into French from English. Am I correct?"

"Yes, I think so."

"Do you have a copy in French?"

"No, but I'm sure I can have one sent to you Fed Ex."

"Thank you, I would like that. The reason I am interested in your explanation of the Book of Mormon as an ancient writing, originally composed on metal plates, is because of my own activities with gold plates. You did say they were of gold. Right?"

"Yes."

"I have come across some gold plates myself. It is an interesting account of what happened to me and . . . but another time, perhaps."

"Do you mean you have actually seen a set of gold plates?"

"I didn't say that. At any rate, I have a collection of photos and some plates at my home in Paris. I would like to show you my collection when you are in Paris sometime. Will you be visiting Paris in the near future?"

"It is not on my scheduled itinerary, but if you have something interesting to show me, I will be more than happy to work it in when I go to Sweden to view the Kontiki. I'll be there in a couple of weeks."

"Pity," Dr. Novue said, shaking his head. Stephen surmised by his accent that Dr. Novue had been instructed in English by a British tutor. "You know, I travel all over the world, and I would have to check with my secretary to know when I might be back in Paris after this weekend. However, I would like very much for you to see my collection. I am returning home to Paris on a flight this evening." He glanced at the wall where a large round Westclock indicated four-thirty. "Ah, it is two hours from now that my plane leaves. I'll be at my home in Paris for three days only, then who knows? I believe I'm scheduled to instruct in Tokyo, then I have a full calendar for perhaps the next month."

Stephen quickly evaluated his own timetable, wondering if Dr. Polk would want him to travel to Paris and take a look at Novue's collection. Maybe Dr. Polk and Roy could delay the tour of the ruins one more day. "I don't suppose you would be available to show me your collection tomorrow if I can arrange it, would you?"

"But of course!" The doctor grinned with delight. "Would you like to accompany me to Paris? Does your schedule allow this? I can request the administrator here at the hospital to make flight arrangements for you. I'm sure the airlines will reschedule your itinerary. I really think you should see what I have in Paris and hear me tell of my experience with some gold plates some six months ago. You will find it intriguing."

Stephen knew that there was a contingency fund in the line of credit on his new American Express card. It was rather novel to move about so randomly. He was sure that Dr. Polk would urge him to go. If he couldn't reach him now, he would call him from Paris.

"Okay!" Stephen grinned. "I'll go if someone will help with flight arrangements."

CHAPTER 9
The Gold Plates

Prague

He was fat and jolly. He was also fluent in six European languages. After meeting Heinrik von Wagner III, Katherine found a chance to whisper to Bob that he looked like the Pillsbury Doughboy.

The doughboy moved rapidly along the hall to room 456, the Reverend Moore's suite at the Hotel Atrium in Prague, the finest. It was a new four-star hotel. The wide halls and spacious vistas on each floor sparkled with white, bright blues, and pink. Decker had selected it on his earlier trip for two reasons: it was close to the city center, and it was western in service and accommodations.

Decker had also hired Heinrik in London two days earlier. He came with outstanding credentials and a deep love of the arts. Evangelism was a new twist in the life of Heinrik. He had been raised by theatrical parents who, throughout his life, had lived in some of the finest hotels in Europe as well as some of the seediest. He had been tutored to be associated with the arts. When the opportunity surfaced in London for a translator to assist a celebrated evangelist, Heinrik reminded himself that religion is a vital part of the arts. Evangelism. He was not exactly certain just what a televangelist did within the Christian faiths, but it had to do with some type of drama on television, and that was certainly within the venue of the arts. Heinrik informed his parents that he was to interpret for a great American dramatist, who happened to be promoting a sort of religion. He needed Heinrik's linguistic services. His parents agreed that he should accept the job offer. They currently resided in the seedy part of east London.

Heinrik felt uneasy about the message he was on his way to deliver to the Reverend Moore. A call had come in from Berlin. A young man sounded desperate to speak to Anney Thorn or Robert Moore. Unfortunately, he had called before the Reverend and his party had arrived to check in. Since Heinrik was in the conference room that would act as a command center for Moore's staff, he had taken the call and promised to deliver the message as soon as Moore's group arrived at the hotel. Now, an hour after their arrival, Heinrik was delivering the message and wished that he had remembered it sooner. He certainly did not want to lose his job.

Moore was in his room unpacking when Heinrik knocked.

"Heinrik. I see you have already been busy arranging interviews with the press and others," Moore said, characteristically launching into a spontaneous conversation. "Come in, my lad."

"Before we discuss those important matters, sir, I must tell you that a young man called from Berlin over an hour ago. I have been so involved downstairs helping arrange the conference room that the message has gone undelivered until now." A cardinal rule with Heinrik was never to admit error. The implication was that Heinrik may not have been the staff person who took the message.

"It's my grandson. I'll call him as soon as I finish unpacking. In the meantime, would you call this man?" Moore walked to the petite desk in the suite where he retrieved an invitation to a special musical presentation in Prague to be held that evening. Handing the card to Heinrik he said, "I understand that this fellow has charge of all musical productions scheduled at the Lucerna Hall. He would be a great contact. Ask him if we can have lunch tomorrow. If he agrees, I will need you to join us. He speaks not a word of English—only Polish and Czech."

Heinrik took the card and studied the name and number. "I'll attend to it immediately."

"You'll need to make the call from the conference room. I will be calling my grandson from this phone."

"Oh, here is the number in Berlin." Heinrik pulled a scrap of paper from his shirt pocket with the number scribbled on it. "I'll return in half an hour. Is that suitable?"

"Certainly." Bob Moore looked at the number as he closed the door and stepped back into the suite.

Katherine finished applying her lipstick while glancing in the large bathroom mirror. "Who was that, darling?"

"One of the young men Decker hired in London. You met him, the kid who speaks all those languages. He's so eager to please, though he did forget to give me this message from Todd, which came in just before we arrived."

"Oh, the Pillsbury Doughboy. He's sweet."

"I hope he didn't see you. It would not look good to have a lady in my room, even though we're engaged."

"Oh, Bob, I'm hardly sleeping in your room. I'm simply helping you unpack. What is so risqué about that?" Katherine arched her eyebrows. She dropped the tube of lipstick into her handbag, snapped the bag shut, and then walked over to Bob and very boldly kissed him squarely on the lips.

She moved back, and, taking a paper tissue from the bedside dispenser, she wiped Bob's red lips. "I love doing that to you, Robert Moore, my handsome man. But we have no time for such little games. You'd better call your grandson."

"You're right, though the message was for me or his mother. Do you think Anney is in her room?" Bob wavered a moment, undecided. "Oh, I'll go ahead and call Todd first. He's probably a little homesick and just wants to talk. This is his first time out of the country and away from home. I think he feels like we're so close here in Prague." Bob picked up the phone and requested that the hotel operator place the call and ring him back. In three minutes the call was through.

* * *

They stood before the brightly lit glass enclosure. The entire hall had been designed to create the appearance of the highly polished interior of a Greek temple. The glass display cases were at least comparable to any in the Louvre. This was the inner sanctum for Dr. Novue, his holy of holies. In all of his life, Stephen had never known a true idol worshiper, but here in this miniature museum, tucked away not four full blocks from the Arc de Triomphe, were housed Dr. Novue's most precious art objects, which he adored. They were glistening, bathed in refracted light, like facets on a diamond. The gold and brass plates—rather fragments of various sizes, some no larger than a stamp—were as refined and pure as any objects Stephen had seen at Tiffany's in downtown San Francisco.

"These are my most rare and treasured plates. They may be fragments, but they are artifacts of the first order. They cost me a fortune, but I do enjoy having them." Novue's face was alight with pride of ownership. "I must show you two sheets of Darius. Look to your left. Do you see the card that says, 'The encounter in the plains of Noaman'? Those two plates contain a partial history of the famous Persian King Darius. He commanded his scribes or imprinters to engrave an account of his military campaign on the plates. It is now two thousand four hundred years since the scribes imprinted those for the King."

"How did you get them?" Stephen asked, expecting to receive a straightforward answer.

Novue seemed taken aback by the question. "Ah, I cannot divulge my source. Surely you understand such things. This work of art came from the East, but the story of how it became mine I will take to my grave. I dare not risk revealing my source," Dr. Novue replied, standing aside. Stephen viewed the two plates displayed side by side on an exquisite royal blue velvet drape that enhanced the brilliance of the gold.

"I will tell you this much. There are people who make a handsome living trading in such items. Here in Paris one of our famous families secures objects of tremendous value and sells them for a great deal of money. You know—vases, headgear, gold belts, clay and stone documents. I have no interest in such things, but I am acquainted with a host of people who dabble in them."

"You mean plates and scrolls, too?"

"No, no, no! I mean artifacts only. Most of the material that this Persian family traffics in is contraband. Gray market, you know." Novue pushed out his lower lip, raised both arms, and pointed his open palms in his gesture of acceptance. "We all do it. There are serious patrons of the arts . . . arts that are not for public viewing."

"Are you saying that there are reputable people who buy and sell this type of thing?" Stephen pointed at one of the gold plates.

"They do, but very cautiously. Not many buy plates, but some do. I'm talking about people who buy all types of artifacts that have value. Many specialize in one form of art or another. Some of my associates buy only vases from the Near East, some strictly Egyptian art. It's whatever they choose to invest in."

"Do they do it for investments?"

"Not strictly. We are speaking of individuals—and there are over two hundred in the world that I know of—who have personal wealth in excess of a hundred million dollars. Men and women of wealth must do *something* with their money. Some love race horses, classic cars, great works of art; some even collect military relics. The group I associate with buys only antiquities such as scrolls, plates, vases, rare carvings on stone, and original documents on papyri. We are a very select body. We buy and sell from each other, and we do even that . . . how would you say? . . . *very* privately. We have trusted liaisons."

"How do you buy from one another? Is there some sort of auction?"

"Never. That would be much too crude and, of course, risky. Most of the material is gray market. It has been taken from the country of origin without permits. I'll not tell you how that is possible, but it is all very carefully transacted." Dr. Novue picked up a piece of stone small enough to fit into his palm. It was inscribed with faint but discernible engravings. "This piece, for example, should by law have remained in the nation of Syria, but I chose to keep it in my collection. I bought it through photographs sent to me."

"Photographs?"

"Oh, yes. Our group has several excellent, bonded photographers who take photos of items we wish to exchange. The pictures are sent to the party wishing to buy, and if the item and price are agreeable to the buyer, he responds with the right amount of money. Then a bargain is struck. Usually we contract through an agent who arranges for the object of art to pass through international borders. That can be a messy business that none of us who buy and sell wish to get into. Of course, the agent arranges for a courier, and the item is transported without any interference from members of my group. It is all arranged and carried out professionally, you understand. It is not unlike the diamond trade. There is never a contract in writing. It is all done as a gentleman's agreement." Dr. Novue grinned as he quipped, "As you say in your country . . . 'the old-fashioned way.'"

"All very legal, of course," Stephen said quietly.

Dr. Novue moved his thin lips into a knowing smile.

"Why would you tell me this? I might go to the authorities with the information you have given me," Stephen warned.

"Go," Novue shrugged. "The authorities already know that we are a group, a sort of federation—and they know that we have contraband. So?"

"Why don't they pick up the stuff? Your collection, for example?"

"Why should they? I'm one of the better taxpayers in this country. I know very influential political people. Each situation is administered by the country in which the relic resides. France is no different than Germany or the United States, for that matter. You see, those who are part of my association are among the wealthiest and most respected persons in their countries. What authorities are going to invade my home and take my most precious possessions? My dear Dr. Thorn, be realistic. It would be political suicide for a person to do such a thing in almost any country. Of course, we don't place these materials on public display, but we do allow private viewings. As you can see, I'm giving you a private viewing."

The two men walked to one side of the hall. Directly in front of Dr. Novue stood a large, darkened glass case. He flipped a switch on the wall behind the case, and it was instantly illuminated. Inside, Stephen could see four gold plates, two on the first shelf and two on the second.

"These are my most prized objects. By the way, the glass is almost bombproof. Notice its thickness. The plates are genuine gold plates that I obtained near the headwaters of the Amazon River. This is why I am interested in your tale about Joseph Smith. He was onto something unique in America. It is my personal opinion that there were many gold plates of this type in the Americas when the Spaniards conquered the western world. They simply melted them down and took the precious metal to Spain in blocks. What desecration!" Gesturing at his collection of gold plates, he finished, "These escaped their greedy grasp."

"How did you get them?"

"I bought them. They do have their own story, however. I am told by several experts in the field that these four plates date back to no more than a hundred years after the birth of Christ. The Indians who once possessed them held them in great esteem as religious objects."

Dr. Novue pointed to one of the plates on the top shelf and said, "That plate was torn from the grip of a medicine man in the jungle who desperately tried to hold onto it. I bought it from the man who wrested it away."

"Who was the man who took it from him?"

"An American. You know him. Yes, but of course. You would recognize the name. He ran a helicopter expedition near the Indian village to the cave where the plates were stored. They lowered this man down to the cave in a basket attached to a cable that ran off of a—what do you call it? a . . ."

"A winch?"

"Yes, yes. A winch. He grabbed the plates that were resting on a pedestal. They were bound together with a wire-like ring, like a binder. This American started back to his basket with the plates in hand when the medicine man came at him and grabbed for the plates. In the scuffle, he ripped off the top sheet and bent the corners. The American leaped into the basket, while the pilot reversed the winch, lifting the American out of reach of the medicine man who remained on the ground, yelling for his tribesmen to come out of hiding and fight the monsters who came from the sky. They got away with the plates."

"That's robbery," Stephen felt compelled to say.

Novue shrugged.

"In time, I saw photos of the set and bought four. They were split up among five of us."

The account jolted Stephen's sense of fair play. Not only had the plates been stolen from the Indians, who held them in high esteem, they had also been split up and sold off to whoever had the cash to pay the highest price, thereby diminishing their historical value.

"As a collector, surely you are aware that it is . . ." Stephen paused for a moment, trying to think of words to express his feelings without offense. He was not there to accuse his host of wrongdoing. His assignment was to commit Dr. Novue to participate in the conference next spring. These plates behind the bulletproof glass were of the type that Joseph Smith claimed to have translated. They were a witness that such plates, in fact, did exist in the Americas. Stephen reminded himself to tread lightly on this man's personal actions, but his own integrity demanded that he take a stand.

He smiled to soften his words. "You, of all people, Pierre, realize that a document, to be of greatest academic value, must be as complete as possible. If you have four of the original plates and another person has a few and a third person a few more, the document can never be translated and verified as to the authenticity of the plates." Stephen shoved his hands into his pockets still peering into the glass case at the incredible plates.

"Not so," Dr. Novue reassured him. "We have already taken care of that matter. All of the plates have been filmed, carbon tested, and completely documented. We merely have the residue of scholarship, the actual gold plates, without the requisite expertise to translate them. That remains for men of a higher order, such as your Smith. You have to admit, Dr. Thorn, that our preservation is a bit better than your Joseph Smith's. He claimed that he only had the plates on loan. Did you ever wonder if he sold his set? You don't even have the original reproduction of the Book of Mormon characters. We have been more careful with our plates."

Dr. Novue smiled and placed his hand lightly on Stephen's shoulder. "I perceive that what I have told you has made you uncomfortable. You are incensed that such duplicity exists. Many who view these precious treasures share your views at first. Please do not worry about my feelings. I have a clear conscience. As for the natives the plates were taken from, well, upon our insistence, part of the money my associates and I paid for the plates has been spent on their tribe—for housing, food, and a reserve fund to help them with medications and to improve village life. We are not savages, you know."

Novue looked at his Rolex and said, "As I told you, my curator will be coming along. Before he arrives, let me show you some photographs." He turned toward a grouping of enlarged photos along the wall on the far end of the gallery, each illuminated by a photo lamp. "Look over here, Stephen. What do we know about metal plates as a method of recording data anciently? I'll give you a little insight. Come, I'll show you." Stephen followed Novue to stand before the photographs. "Here are pictures of a few of the latest finds of metal plates in the world."

The first photograph was a magnificent, poster-size, color photo of the gold and silver plates of Darius I. "This is the most prized of all the discoveries of metal plates that I am aware of. By the way, they are on display in Tehran, Iran, in their National Archaeological Museum. These have not been polished and detailed. Not at all. These plates are as shiny and bright as the day they were deposited in a stone box over two thousand five hundred years ago. That is the beauty of preserving one's records on gold. Gold does not tarnish, rust, or crumble. They are of equal quality today as they were the day they were engraved. It was little different with the mask of King Tut of Egypt. When they uncovered his tomb, except for the dust, the gold mask was brilliant." Novue's eyes were alight and his voice held a note of excitement.

"Notice the engravings. The words are written in three types of cuneiform: Persian, Babylonian, and Elamite. These engravings describe the boundaries of the kingdom of Darius—which brings up another aspect of writing on plates." Novue reached up and pointed his stick-like index finger to the edge of the photo. "Notice that two of the metal plates are silver. Gold and silver are among several types of metal used—gold, silver, copper, bronze, even iron and steel—though anciently engraved plates would tend to be copper or bronze, maybe silver, but very rarely gold.

"Your man Smith specifically said that the plates he used were gold. Isn't that correct? That would be very rare. They did use gold—witness Darius. He had at least two of his plates engraved on gold to commemorate the building of his great palace at Perspolis. He placed these tablets in a stone box. Did you notice the stone box?" Again he tapped the photo with his finger.

Stephen studied the gray stone box in the picture and saw that recessed inside were the gold plates. He could see the cracks that ran through parts of the box.

"Darius wanted this little treasure to survive the ages because after engraving the plates and placing them in a stone box—which, by the way, is characteristic of Near Eastern hiding receptacles for treasure—he had them buried in the foundation of his palace. He wanted them in gold because it befitted his stature as a king. You see, only the most important documents were engraved on gold plates. It made a statement to do so. Perhaps the person commissioning the work was wealthy or powerful, or both. Or it might be that the subject matter was of such importance that it was only fitting that it be written on the finest metal available. Oh, and by the way, zinc was also used. The most common method of preserving records in the Near East was, of course, on clay tablets. Hundreds of them have come down to us over the past two hundred years."

Dr. Novue continued to point out other plates engraved on gold in the exhibit of carefully mounted photographs that extended across the breadth of the hall. He pointed out the photos of the silver plates of India that many believed contained Buddha's first sermon. There was an enlarged photo of the plates of Sargon taken from the Assyrian palace of Khorsabad, engraved a hundred years before Lehi left Jerusalem. "The originals are not more than five kilometers from this very room in the Louvre. The nineteen gold plates of Buddhist scripture are in the National Museum in Seoul, Korea."

All in all, Stephen counted over fifty photos of metal plates found in the world: the Orphic gold plates; the small gold plate found at Amphipolis that was one-inch long; the unearthed plates found at Gallep; silver and bronze plates. Novue even mentioned that there was a gold plate at the J. Paul Getty Museum in Los Angeles.

The last photo was of the famous copper scroll from Qumran, near the Dead Sea, that currently resided in the National Museum in Amman, Jordan. "By the way, I do not subscribe to the theory that Qumran was some sort of monastery for Essenes before the birth of Christ. I side with the more enlightened scholars of the Dead Sea scrolls—Golb, for example—who maintain that the Dead Sea scrolls were deposited in those caves at Qumran before the Romans sacked the temple at Jerusalem in C.E. 71. As far as I'm concerned, Qumran was nothing more than a military outpost."

Novue had lost his guest. Stephen was certainly not familiar with the Dead Sea scrolls and could hardly be expected to have any sort of opinion on the scrolls. But he listened with interest.

"Before your curator arrives, let me ask you one more important question," Stephen said. "Did American scholars know of metal plates as a means of recording very significant events at the time Joseph Smith began translating from gold plates back in the early part of the nineteenth century? He was ridiculed by almost everyone for stating that the record he translated was inscribed on gold plates."

Novue fixed Stephen with his piercing eyes. "Ah . . . you are thinking, I see. Well, let me enlighten you. There *were* no reputable American scholars in the time of Joseph Smith. Besides, in the 1820s, Champolion had only just begun to crack the Egyptian code on the Rosetta stone. The first in-depth writings published about such things came out of Europe, Paris, and Oxford almost a century later. Of course those ignorant people in America would accuse Joseph Smith of not knowing his facts. No one had heard of such things, so what could they do but take issue with him? You are more familiar with the time and people in the life of Smith than I.

"At the present time, only the most ignorant of scholars would dare say that there were no engravings on gold plates. There is far too much proof in the world for such narrow thinking. Even the Bible speaks of brass plates as a means for keeping records. I know from personal experience that the Central Americans used gold plates in ancient times. According to traditions, a complete history of the Mayan culture was recorded in the *Golden Book of the Maya* in Central America and hidden from the Spaniards, who were going about melting down gold objects and plates and hauling the gold back to Spain. I have spoken to natives who still carry on the tradition of searching for their ancestors' records that were written on metal plates."

Stephen was about to explode with excitement. This guy would be perfect as a presenter for Dr. Polk's project. He certainly had the expertise. This was exactly the kind of evidence he was sent to find. He scrutinized Dr. Novue out of the corner of his eye and mentally crossed his fingers. "My next question is," Stephen said, holding his breath, "will you attend our conference in Provo, Utah, next spring . . . the one I explained to you on the plane? As I said earlier, we are prepared to pay you five thousand dollars for a two- or three-hour lecture before the group concerning metal plates in the ancient world."

Novue smiled warmly at his guest, sensing his discomfiture. "If my schedule fits, of course I will come. You have my word on that. But I think you will prefer my director to me. If he is available, I suggest you invite him. You will not offend me if you do. I would like him to have the exposure."

Right on cue, Mullineaux came striding through the concourse of the small private museum and extended both hands to Dr. Novue. He took Novue's right hand in both of his and patted it. Stephen judged Mullineaux to be somewhere between fifty and fifty-five with a small toad-like body, wide cheeks, little hair. His eyes were alive. Stephen was immediately attracted to the director. His face beamed with discovery and excitement. After a lengthy welcome, Dr. Novue turned to Stephen and introduced him to Mullineaux. All was spoken in French. It was apparent to Stephen that Mullineaux spoke little, if any, English. Through Novue, Mullineaux asked Stephen how he could be of service to him.

Stephen observed that Novue was very good at his new role as interpreter. He cleared his throat and asked, "According to Dr. Novue, I understand that you are the leading authority on ancient metal plates." The director spoke to Novue with modest protestations and then continued to listen to Stephen's relayed words. Stephen explained his assignment from Dr. Polk and frankly told Mullineaux that he was a Mormon and that the Mormons had a great stake in learning as much as possible about metal plates, especially records written anciently on gold plates.

Mullineaux told him that he had heard about Mormon claims to the translation of their sacred book from a set of plates. He again asked how he could be of immediate assistance.

Stephen had a list of questions. At the top of the list was the subject of the Byblos Syllabic inscriptions on bronze plates that were receiving some attention in the scholarly world.

"Of course I am acquainted with the Byblos Syllabic inscriptions," Mullineaux responded in French. "I personally know Professor Walter Burkert, who is one of the leading authorities on the subject. Perhaps you would do well to speak with him."

Stephen agreed but still probed Mullineaux's understanding of the ancient engravings, of the earliest known surviving examples of writing on copper plates. Stephen had read the documentation Polk had given him along with other articles and knew that Byblos was a city on the Phoenician coast not too far from Jerusalem. He also knew, from doing his homework, that the Syllabic inscriptions were written in "reformed Egyptian characters" that were inspired by the Egyptian hieroglyphic system.

"Yes, yes. Burkert makes a point of the Phoenicians writing to the Greeks on bronze plates in the seventh and sixth century B.C.E."

Stephen said nothing about the fact that this was precisely the time and general area when Lehi asked his sons to return to Jerusalem from the wilderness to secure the brass plates that would be the single greatest link between the culture and religion at Jerusalem and the New World where Lehi was fleeing with his family.

"What do you know about subscriptio, practiced by the Greeks and transmitted from the Near Eastern regions?" Stephen knew that Joseph Smith had taken a lot of flak from critics when he wrote after translating the Book of Mormon, "The title page of the Book of Mormon is a literal translation, taken from the very last leaf, on the left hand side of the collection or book of plates, which contained the record which has been translated." In other words, the title and author were written anciently on bronze plates on the last page of the records and not, as is the practice today, on the first page. Why did Joseph Smith mention that fact? He didn't have to. Stephen already knew the answer before he asked the question, but he wanted to hear Mullineaux's opinion on the subject.

"Today," Mullineaux began in French, "scholars in the field know that subscription was a common practice anciently in the Middle East. Subscriptio—the practice of placing the title page at the end of the document—has come to light only in this generation. Contemporary scholars are in agreement that it was the standard form of titling a work. Always the last page. Always."

CHAPTER 10
A Moment Together

Prague

"Oh, Daddy. What is happening to my family?" Anney lamented as she stood looking out of her hotel window onto the crowded street below. People were rushing in all directions. It was hard to believe that they could have their own set of problems.

"I just don't know. Did Todd tell you why he was in a beer hall in downtown Berlin? What was he doing there? And why did the Gutenbergs ask him to move his things out? He is usually a responsible person. Really he is. You know that," Anney said.

"I know that, but whatever you're thinking right now, you need to catch a plane this afternoon and get over to Berlin. I'll have this Heinrik we hired escort you to the terminal. The language could be a problem."

It was the old take-charge father that Anney had known all of her life. "Daddy, I wish you could put my whole life back into shape as easily as you arrange other things for me. Do you realize that I don't even know how to reach Stephen? I think he's somewhere in Central America between hotels. He left a message while we were in London that he would be in Oaxaca, Mexico, tomorrow or the next day. We're down to that kind of communication. Now that I need to talk to him about his own son, I can't reach him. Oh, Daddy, Daddy."

"Stephen has really let you down, hasn't he, honey?" Moore could see that Stephen's behavior bothered Anney more than Todd's. A little fight in a beer hall at age eighteen wasn't all that alarming—not to Bob Moore, who had tramped across the Bible Belt at eighteen, running into every type of lowlife known to man. Stephen, on the other hand, as he saw it, had real problems. "If only I could help. Really help."

That was all it took for a flood of tears to erupt. Anney wished she were alone so her father wouldn't have to see her in this troubled state.

Bob moved to the window, put his arm around Anney, and drew her close to him. She let go and sobbed aloud.

"Honey, let it all come out. You've kept this inside far too long. Just let it go." Bob patted the back of Anney's head, touching the blond hair that was clasped fashionably in a knot.

Moore rocked slowly from side to side as he comforted her. At last Anney got control of her emotions and looked around the room, trying to decide which suitcase to take with her. She would not be gone more than a couple of days. She knew to travel light. Bob sat on the bed, wanting to help but unable to. He hoped that merely being in the room was help in itself. When the telephone rang, Anney grabbed it, wondering if it was Todd. "Hello?"

"Anney, how are you?"

"Stephen?" Anney went limp with relief. Just hearing his voice unleashed another torrent of tears.

"Anney? Honey, are you crying? What's wrong? Has something happened? Sweetheart, relax . . . tell me what's wrong." Stephen gripped the receiver and held his breath. He could hear his wife struggling to speak. Stephen tried to calm her with soothing words.

Finally, Anney managed to gain control. "Stephen . . . where are you?"

"I'm in Paris with a collector of sorts. I just wanted to talk to you. What's happening?"

"In Paris?"

"Yeah, I had a change of plans. What's wrong? Is your dad okay?"

"No . . . I mean, yes . . . it's Todd . . . a fight." Anney was convulsed in sobs once more.

"A fight? Where? Is he hurt?"

Anney haltingly told Stephen the few facts she had been able to learn about Todd and what had happened the night before in Berlin. Stephen listened carefully without comment, his thoughts whirling.

"So I'm flying to Berlin. I think the next flight is this afternoon," she finished.

There was a pause on the other end, and then Stephen said reassuringly, "I'll meet you there, Anney. Everything will be all right. Where will you be? Is Todd still at the police station? Where, then?" Anney explained, then gave the phone number and address of the Gutenbergs' apartment.

"I'll get a seat on the next plane out of Paris. I'll clear it with Dr. Polk, but I'm sure he will understand." *He and Roy may have to go on that tour without me . . . but my family needs me now.*

"Good," Anney gulped. She slowly replaced the receiver, slightly puzzled by the conversation. Something was different about Stephen. Was his voice deeper? Surely not; it was the connection, of course. But he was so confident, even in his concern for Todd. He seemed . . . what? He sounded like her father. He had taken charge of the situation.

* * *

For all the years that Stephen had followed the news coming out of Berlin, he had formed in his mind a grim vision of the city. It was the place where Hitler had ruled and committed suicide. He had seen pictures of bombed-out buildings, starving people, and the bleak Berlin Wall. His uncle had told him tales about the city and his experience as an Army MP immediately after the fall of Berlin in 1945 and '46. Stephen remembered the horror stories Uncle Ned had told and retold about Berlin while they were out riding on the ranch.

There was no longer such a place. Stephen understood that Berlin had changed. Rationally, he knew that it had become highly commercial—one of the great centers of Europe—but he was not prepared for the sights before him. He was mesmerized by the beauty of Berlin in all of its fall colors and busy streets. The cars shone; the streets were spic and span. The tall buildings on Bismarckstrasse were as modern and functional as any in San Francisco, if not superior.

The cab driver pulled the Mercedes to the curb and told Stephen in accented English that the apartment building to the right was 51 Dudenstrasse, the destination he had given when he hired the cab at Tempelhof.

* * *

Todd sat in the darkness of his room, waiting for his mother. Frau Gutenberg, who was cool toward Todd, had told him that his mother was flying to Berlin and would arrive from the airport about seven this evening. Todd looked at his watch again. It was past six. There was a certain gloom about his whole person, not just his black eye and cut brow, but his ill feelings as well.

He had left jail with the Gutenbergs at ten that morning. The police had released him into their custody with the understanding that he would be required to appear in court in two days. Things were uncertain at best. Would it be a surprise to be sent home? Not at all. He had blown it, and he knew it. It was his own fault. The German kids had been raised on beer. What was drinking to Hans? But whether the cops believed him or not, those guys in the biergarten had stolen his wallet.

A light knock pierced the silence of Todd's deep concerns. "Todd, may I come in?"

Todd's head jerked up. It was an unexpected voice. "Dad?"

Todd lunged for the door. Black eye or not, he was elated to hear that familiar, reassuring voice. Todd swung open the door and grabbed for his father. "Dad! Dad! I didn't know you were coming."

"Hi, son." Stephen smiled and rubbed the back of Todd's head, and then brought both hands together on his cheeks and kissed him. "Todd, whatever has happened, it can be fixed. Believe me, I'm here to help fix it."

"Oh, you look so great, Dad." Todd threw his arms around his father one more time and squeezed. "So great, so great."

* * *

Anney's flight was delayed an hour and a half in Prague, and then customs took several frustrating minutes more. Todd and Stephen were at the gate as she came through the international section. It had been but a few short days since she had seen Stephen off in San Francisco. But right now, it seemed like years since they had been together. Amid smiles and laughter, Anney held them both as if she would never let go. Stephen kissed her over and over on the right cheek. Todd hugged her on the left. Anney responded with joy. She had craved such a moment with the two men she loved most.

"Let me look at you." Anney pushed Todd's hair—hair exactly the color of his father's—gently away from his brow and was startled by the wound she uncovered. She scrutinized the bruises and the exposed stitches, finally let go of his head, and put both hands on her hips. "Todd Moore Thorn. You in a fight! I can't believe it."

"Believe it, Mom." The boy slouched and folded his arms dejectedly. "I may get kicked out of the country. But like I told Dad, those guys I went after stole my wallet."

"That may be, but the word I got was that you'd been drinking."

Todd scrunched up his face and looked away. Finally he nodded and said, "Yeah. You got that right. I'm . . . Mom, really, you don't have to worry about it happening again. It's behind me. You can take my word on that."

"I guess we really ought to go back to the Gutenbergs' and discuss the situation," Stephen volunteered. "But they told me when I picked up Todd that they stay up pretty late. So what do you say we go somewhere and have dinner?"

"Not downtown, okay?" Todd cautioned.

Anney smiled, taking Stephen's arm and snuggling up beside him. "Going to dinner with two of the best-looking men in the world. Wow, this is living! You know, the one thing I enjoy about having semi-adult children is conversing on a more mature level. Don't you?" With her other hand, she reached out for Todd, who smiled with relief that she was not going to rail on him further, at least not now.

They found a small, intimate restaurant a block from the Hotel Resoone, where Stephen and Anney checked in and dropped their bags.

An unspoken agreement prevailed—they would talk about home, family, and each other, and not get into uneasy topics: Stephen off on his project, Anney with her father's tour, and Todd perhaps expelled from the exchange student program. This evening they would bask in each other's presence.

Two hours after leaving Todd and the Gutenbergs, who had relented and allowed Todd to stay, Anney lay staring off into the darkness of the hotel room. The lined drapes blocked out all street light. Stephen breathed heavily at her side, but sleep refused to come for Anney. In the darkness, she mulled over a dozen irritating problems and resolved none. The most recent, Todd's fight, seemed to be the simplest to solve.

The Gutenbergs had raised a son and were understanding, not really concerned that Todd would repeat such behavior. They stipulated that Todd must clear all extracurricular activities with them and reassured the Thorns that they would be a little more attentive insofar as Todd's social life was concerned. Stephen indicated that he intended to call his friend Brad Miller, Rotary president back home, and explain what had happened. He didn't want his friends and the officers in Rotary to hear about the incident through some other source. Stephen felt certain Brad Miller would understand and not push to expel Todd from the program. It wasn't a given, but Stephen assured Todd that he would do everything he could to save him. Todd thought his dad could do absolutely anything. That was crystal clear in the adoring, grateful look he shot his father as Stephen and Anney left for their hotel room.

Oh, to have the trust Todd has, Anney reflected in the dark. *What was it about Stephen that seemed so . . . so confident and strong?* Maybe she had just missed him. But he seemed so much more assertive or something.

Anney moved closer to Stephen and laid her cheek against his back, as she had done nearly every night for twenty-two years. She sighed and slipped her arm over his chest, aching to remove all barriers between them. In spite of herself, her thoughts turned to the deeper, much more difficult problems: Stephen's new religion and this ridiculous project. They would not go away.

Anney had determined that tonight, with Stephen, she would not bring it up. She knew that nothing could be resolved in twenty-four hours. Stephen would fly out to Central America by late tomorrow; she would be back in Prague. Why complicate things? The evening had been wonderful—like a vacation together. She smiled, thinking back. Stephen had bought Todd a new wallet at the gift shop in the hotel. She wanted little more in life than her family. For a few hours, she had managed to feel like the wife she had always been. And she was so glad to be near him; nothing else had seemed worth worrying about, until now, awake in the dark.

In spite of it all, she reasoned, Todd dearly loved his father and seemed not to be affected by all that had happened with the family since Stephen had returned from San Diego.

Is it me? Am I taking this entirely too seriously? Does it really matter? Anney forced herself to look at the situation from a different perspective. Did it really matter that a couple of weeks ago Stephen had become a Mormon? She had politely declined the invitation to attend his service. She was glad that both of the children had been away the evening Stephen had been baptized at a Mormon church near them in Lafayette. He probably would have asked them to attend, and they would have gone. That, in its own strange way, would have been a show of condoning what she so fiercely opposed—her husband becoming a Mormon. It was official now, and what could she do about it? Nothing.

Even so, it irritated her to think that he had gone ahead with baptism despite her objections. And he even had the nerve to plead with her to study the Mormon doctrines and be baptized, too. Anney shifted her position, her head tight with tension. Would sleep ever come this night?

Yet Stephen had a right to his own beliefs and feelings. She just disagreed with the whole issue. How would they ever be able to be a family again? Could there be unconditional love between them again? Home had always been so special. It was Christmas. Kids bounding in after school. All of them chattering around the dining table. Neighbors coming and going. Lots of warmth that they both provided. Love that abounded, for each other and for their children—even for her father. Would true love still be a part of her relationship with Stephen if he remained a Mormon? Did she still want him?

Stephen turned and sleepily enfolded her into his arms, those strong, protective, masculine arms. Oh, yes, she wanted him all right.

* * *

"There have been studies done on the Urim and Thummim. I have written about these stones of light," the youthful, bearded Rabbi Michale said, speaking in clear but heavily accented English. Hebrew was his native tongue. He had learned English as a student at Oxford. He was now an instructor of ancient studies programs at the Synagogue Berlin.

Stephen studied the eyes of Rabbi Michale. They were deep brown and alert. He asked, "Would you tell me what you understand to be the nature and purpose of the Urim and Thummim mentioned in the Old Testament?" He nodded to Stephen that he would. Then he slowly stood up, turned to the book-lined wall, and slid his finger along the books in a caressing manner. Finding what he was looking for, he took down a rather large book and began thumbing through it.

Both men were silent as the rabbi searched for specific documentation to share with Stephen. He paused to push his heavy glasses up on his nose and then continued his search. Stephen could hear the traffic swishing by in the light morning rain. The office window was slightly open, and the fresh fall air felt good. There was a stuffy odor in the office. It smelled of old books.

It had begun sprinkling half an hour ago when he helped Anney into the taxi that would take her to pick up Todd and on to meet with the school director. She would then return to Prague after the meeting. Stephen's schedule required that he go directly from his meeting with the rabbi to the Tempelhof terminal for his flight to Mexico.

When Stephen and Anney had arrived back at the hotel the night before, he had called Dr. Polk to let him know his updated itinerary. Polk had informed Stephen that a Rabbi Elam Michale lived and taught in Berlin. He often lectured in Europe and occasionally in the United States on the sacred Urim and Thummim. Since Stephen was in Berlin anyway, Dr. Polk requested that he call Rabbi Michale at an institute in Berlin to see if the Jewish professor would squeeze Stephen in for a half-hour discussion—an opportunity to invite him to the May conference. Stephen made the call, and the rabbi agreed to disrupt his schedule to meet him in his office at ten-thirty this morning.

Not too shabby. Stephen prided himself on his quick arrangements, although he was a bit uneasy about Anney. He now wished that he had scheduled his meeting with the rabbi for later in the afternoon and had gone with Anney to face the school administrator instead. He could have taken a red-eye and arrived in Mexico City later the next day. As it was, he would not meet Dr. Polk and Roy until morning anyway.

His eyes watched the man finger page after page, scanning the words to find the material he sought, but his mind returned to Anney.

He had kissed her good-bye in their hotel room before settling her in the taxi. There was no doubting the coolness in her touch, and a sick uneasiness had swept over Stephen. She was uncharacteristically silent. What thoughts were going through her mind? She had not slept well, that much he knew. Her eyes were dark and troubled. In the brief hours they had spent together, she had not once mentioned anything about his project, nor had he about hers.

It was the first time in their marriage that there was an obvious barrier between them—a strange arrangement for two people who had always been able to discuss anything at all. Stephen was puzzled by her silence, considering all the verbal volleys he had taken from Anney since returning from San Diego two months earlier. At least they had a truce; that was something. But was it an improvement? Her unnatural reticence worried him. *What can she be considering?*

"Ah . . . this is what I was searching for." Stephen's mind was jolted back to the rabbi. "Forgive me for taking so much time. I know you have but a short while before you must go to your airplane. You may find this interesting, however." The rabbi turned another page, found the paragraph he was searching for, and said, "This is a description of the interpreters. I will read it, then I will explain further." He read: "'Certain objects, the nature of which is not known, were worn in or upon the breastplate of the Jewish high priest, by means of which the will of Jehovah was held to be declared. The term often used to identify the Urim and Thummim was light and perfection.'"

The rabbi closed the book and placed it reverently upon his desk. "If you were to walk out on the street and ask any person of normal intelligence to tell you what the Urim and Thummim are, you would, in all likelihood, receive a blank stare. The same thing would be true among the faculty of any of thousands of campuses. The instruments are little known, and their function is not completely understood. There are references to them in both the Old and New Testament. I have written a paper concerning the loss of the instruments among the Israelites, which occurred either before or at the time of the destruction of the temple at Jerusalem in the year 586 B.C.E."

"What do you think they were used for in ancient times?" Stephen asked, seeking to gain insight into the man's scholarship, though he realized that Dr. Polk must have felt that he was qualified. "Can you tell me more specifically what the Urim and Thummim were used for?"

"I can give you only limited information on the instruments. There is so little known about their design and exactly how they were used. But there is always legend."

"Perhaps you could explain to me what is known about them," Stephen probed gently. He had the urge to move his chair closer to Professor Michale's in an effort to hear every word the quiet man had to say. He was grateful that the rabbi's command of the English language was excellent.

Excitement heightened Stephen's breathing. The world needed to know that Joseph Smith did have special instruments to aid in the translation of the Book of Mormon—the Urim and Thummim. He knew from reviewing Polk's notes on the instruments that the ancient prophets explained that they had relied on the instruments for receiving the word of God in Old Testament times. In the brief time he had to spend with the rabbi, Stephen desired to absorb all this Biblical scholar knew about the fascinating instruments.

"From my study of these interpreters, this is what I have come to understand." The rabbi leaned over to one side of his desk, opened the upper right-hand desk drawer, and withdrew a yellow note pad. He placed the pad on the desk in front of him and jabbed his right index finger on some handwritten notes before he continued.

"I hurriedly reviewed some of my own research on this subject before you arrived. Let me read to you from things I have listed about the Urim and Thummim. May I?"

"Certainly," Stephen said, anxious to know but impatient with the rabbi's slow, deliberate speech.

"To begin to understand the instruments, I have researched their Biblical history since finishing my studies at Oxford. The Old Testament refers to the Urim and Thummim as instruments worn upon the high priest's breast when he went into the holy precincts of the temple. There is a reference to this in Leviticus 8:8. They are described as denoting the two essential parts of the sacred oracle by which, in early times, the Hebrews sought to ascertain the will of God. As I mentioned, one translation renders them as interpreters, 'light and perfection.' This source further states that the Urim and Thummim were two stones closely connected, in some fashion no longer intelligible to us, with the equally mysterious ephod. There is speculation among scholars as to their shape and size, but I know of no indications in historical text that offer a clear, graphic description.

"Ideas have been put forth that this instrument consisted of clear, flat stones. One commentary has this to say: 'The Urim and Thummim were two small, oracular images similar to the Teraphim, personifying revelation and truth, which were placed in the cavity or pouch formed by the folds of the breastplate, and which uttered oracles by voice.'"

Stephen held up his hand. "Rabbi Michale, would you mind clarifying that? What do you think was meant by two small, oracular images? Do you have a visual concept in your mind as to what those two small images were like?"

"I guess I think of them as two clear stones. I also think they were like . . . say, the lens of a microscope, though probably thicker. They functioned together as one instrument, only in the case of these sacred stones, they overlapped each other. They required that the user be a man of God. I can only think of a prophet. The person using the instruments had to have a great deal of spiritual insight and knowledge. Some use the term faith, but I'm not sure that means faith as the Christians use the term—more knowledge and desire, rather than simple acceptance."

"This is fascinating," Stephen replied. "Were they like thick lenses in a pair of glasses? Or clear flat stones like large diamonds or crystals? What do you envision them to be like?" Stephen continued to press for specifics.

"Yes, yes," the rabbi's voice rose with zeal, caught up in Stephen's interest. "Perhaps any one of these descriptions could be correct. I have come across writings that depict them as flat, crystal-like objects, something like a large lens in an expensive camera. However, I have never heard anyone describe their appearance to my satisfaction."

"I have come across one description of the instruments," Stephen said, recalling Roy's in-depth presentation to the group in San Diego the summer before. "The person telling about the instruments said they consisted of two smooth, three-cornered diamonds, set in glass, and the glasses were set in silver bows which were connected with each other in much the same way as old-fashioned spectacles, only much larger. Does such a description make any sense to you?"

The rabbi sat up, piercing Stephen with his intense eyes. "Well," he replied cautiously, "I have not before heard such a specific description of what they appeared to be like, but certainly it was some type of instrument that could be used to see through. I repeat, to my knowledge, none of the ancient Hebrews left a detailed description of the exact appearance of the instruments, probably because they were so sacred. They were used in the Holy of Holies in the Tabernacle and later in Solomon's Temple, you see. There is, of course, mention that the instruments were somehow fitted on a breastplate and that men of God, who wore the breastplate, looked through the objects to interpret the will of God."

The rabbi paused, deep in thought. "I really know very little about the instruments," he repeated. He was a modest man. "They were instruments of divine origin used for sacred purposes. I think this is the key concept to concentrate on. The ancients were in possession of instruments we know very little about, but the instruments offered great insight to those who used them. In some way, the Israelites in the wilderness used the Urim and Thummim to inquire of the Lord."

Stephen was moved by the rabbi's deep reverence for the prophets of old. *I am beginning to see that Joseph Smith was up there right along with Abraham and the other prophets. Wow! Why can't the world see the truth?*

Deep, resonant chimes startled both men. Stephen followed the sound to a stately grandfather clock towering in the corner of the room. He verified the time with his watch.

"I'm going to have to hurry to the airport," he apologized, "but I have one more question. Do you see any correlation between the Urim and Thummim and the Star of David?"

The rabbi sat immobile.

"I mean . . . do you know the origin of the Star of David? Do you see it as two triangles overlapping one another?"

The rabbi searched Stephen's face intently, surprised that this Christian would know the origin of the Star of David. "It is pretty well understood that the Star of David is a figure consisting of a six-pointed star formed by placing two equilateral triangles one upon the other, such that the base of each triangle bisects two sides of the other, and it is used as a symbol of Judaism."

"I would say that is a pretty concise description," Stephen smiled. "Then is it part of your traditions that the Star of David is a symbol of the Urim and Thummim?"

"Oh, yes. It is sometimes called Magen David, Mogen David, or even Shield of David. There have been entire books written on the subject. As you said, the Jews understand the Star of David to be symbolic of the Interpreters. I use the term Interpreters rather than Urim and Thummim simply because of my training. Both are acceptable definitions of the same objects."

"And what other purposes were they used for?" Stephen asked, drawing closer to the desk with his head and shoulders, his body language declaring to any observer that he was keenly interested in what the youthful rabbi had to say.

"As I said, to interpret the will of the Lord."

"Then, in summary, would you say that the prophets of old used the Urim and Thummim to receive revelation in the temple and also adopted it as the very symbol or logo of their religion?"

The rabbi slowly answered, "I think that is perhaps a fair summation of their purposes. Yes, from my studies, the Interpreters were certainly used to receive revelation, but exactly how that revelation was manifested through the instruments I'm afraid I don't know."

Stephen slid back in his chair and pulled out one of the business cards he had ordered in San Francisco a couple of weeks ago. He handed the card to the rabbi and said, "Would you kindly consider a proposal? I would like you to give a brief lecture to a group of young scholars on the nature and uses of the Urim and Thummim. It is to be held in the United States in mid-May of next year. We will pay all your expenses, as well as an honorarium in advance. The group will be a mixture of youth from various faiths, including Jewish.

"We do not wish to reveal exactly the nature of the conference to preclude a bias on your part as well as the students. I will be happy to call you and explain as much as possible about this conference and the nature of its sponsorship, but at this time, I would like to know if you would be at all interested in giving a two-hour presentation.

"We will not broadcast or publish anything you present without your written consent. My attorney will be in touch with you—his name is Bill Bennett—and you will have the opportunity to discuss the matter with him." Stephen was out of breath; he had spoken rapidly. He felt as if he were doing one of his five-mile jogs. He also wondered who would accept such a vague invitation. The next remark from the rabbi caught him off guard.

"How much is the honorarium?" he asked with interest.

"I am authorized to offer you five thousand dollars. Plus, as I said, we will pay all expenses for the trip and lodging."

"I would be interested," the rabbi replied without hesitation

* * *

The studio was small, too small to seat even a tiny congregation. Bob Moore's studio in San Francisco held two hundred worshipers at each Sunday taping, many of whom belonged to local churches. His staff made tickets available to local ministers to distribute among their parishioners. Bob frowned in disappointment at the size of the studio. He always played to his congregation.

In minutes, Moore was scheduled to begin taping his sermon. In frustration, he sat at a mirrored table, protesting the grotesque makeup on his face. His discontent was directed at Heinrik, his interpreter, though the makeup technician who smiled with pride in her creation was clearly the object. He was not about to go before the camera wearing so much rouge and lipstick. He looked like a mime by the time she finished. He had sat in enough makeup chairs in his career on television to know the right shade of reds and blues needed to give him the lively, yet masculine, appearance he desired. He instructed Heinrik, who stood nearby, to tell the young lady, who understood no English, that today he would do his own makeup. "Don't offend her, Heinrik," Moore cautioned, reaching for a box of tissues. "Tell her that I have experience in this and know what skin tones and shades appeal to my audience in America. Also, tell her that I'm sorry, but perhaps next time she can do me if she would like. But for the American show, no."

Heinrik leaped into his translation, and Moore saw instantly that he had offended her, all right. Although Heinrik was merely the messenger, the girl aimed her raging insults directly at him. She could not understand how Americans could be that different in makeup. Who did he think he was, wanting to do his own? Maybe the Americans needed to see a real artist at work. Heinrik listened but refused to interpret the barrage. He shrugged his shoulders and turned his back on the irate girl. Besides, the Reverend Moore had already dismissed the girl and was moving toward the sound booth to speak with Decker, wiping off the garish makeup as he walked.

Inside the booth, the two men leaned against a white wooden counter on the opposite side of the instrument panel. "Decker, we need to communicate with that fellow in Phoenix—you know the one I told you about, Craig Kline—who wants to break the foundation trust that my son-in-law is involved in."

"Oh, yeah. You mean that guy who called you the other day in London," Decker acknowledged, setting aside Bob's script, which he had been reviewing for the show. He had been studying the text for the past hour, fine-tuning the fifteen-minute sermon that would be canned in video and rushed to San Francisco by UPS. Decker had checked out the connections and the facilities of CNN, hoping to transmit from studio to studio. Finding that it would be far too expensive to tie up a satellite, he settled for videotaping the service, sending it by two-day express, and airing the sermon after a week's delay.

He was confident that his programs from Eastern Europe, via video, would be a hit in the Bay Area. It was a fresh approach and one that would keep him in touch with his television congregation—Decker's suggestion. Bob had lined up his good friend and fellow televangelist, Larry Stockton from Los Angeles, to do the remainder of the shows in San Francisco. The live broadcast set to follow the taping would be in conjunction with one of the more popular televangelists in Prague. Bob would deliver a ten-minute sermon that would consist mostly of praising the people for opening their hearts and minds to the gospel in this fresh new land of opportunity.

"I haven't really gone over this Kline situation with you," Bob explained to Decker with frustration. Decker could read all the signs of stress in his employer. "This tour . . . keeping my fiancée happy . . . public appearances, not to mention instructing these hopeless evangelists, is sapping me of every ounce of energy I have."

Bob's eyes narrowed, regarding Decker shrewdly. "I may need you to help me with Kline."

Bob hesitated, wondering if he should divulge how much Kline was willing to pay for helping to dissolve the trust. Naw. It would only stir him up inside to know the amount. Some things ought not be shared with the hired help.

"Decker," Bob began in a conspiratorial voice. "Well, it's . . . I haven't told you the whole skinny on this matter. I've made a financial arrangement with Kline to help him stop the Mormon project my son-in-law is involved in. It isn't so much that Kline is going after anyone on criminal charges. He just wants to cut off the funding. I frankly agree with him. Stephen and that group are pouring out millions of dollars on a worthless project. The money is part of a grant or a trust that Kline's father left in his estate. Kline is convinced that his father was hoodwinked into turning that kind of money over to the Mormon group just before he died. I have to agree with Kline. He says his father was not himself when he signed the papers. So—"

"Reverend," Heinrik interrupted from a discreet distance. The booth door was partly open. "Please forgive the intrusion. The director wonders if you are ready to begin shooting. He says the crew is in place." Heinrik hesitated and then reminded Bob politely, "Did you still want to redo your makeup?"

"Yes, yes," Bob was instantly the warm, confident minister. "Tell him I'll be along in five minutes. Oh, and by the way, tell him that I want to tape the ten-minute sermon for the Prague audience as well. So, Heinrik, you will have to apply some makeup yourself, at least a powdering, because you will be on camera, interpreting for me."

Heinrik's thespian blood surged. "Oh, thank you for having me beside you on national television," he beamed. "I have a few friends here in Prague who may be watching."

"You might want to look at the script over there on the table. I won't adhere to it exactly, so you may have to improvise a bit here and there. I'm sure you'll do fine."

Heinrik whirled around, spoke to the director, and then headed for the script to brush up on key words that he would need to translate.

Moore motioned for Decker to follow him to the dressing table where the jars of cosmetics lay in disarray, exactly as the dismissed makeup artist had left them. Shifting personalities again, in a low voice, he picked up their conversation exactly where he left off. "I have agreed to help stop Kline's financial drain by finding out all I can about what my son-in-law and Polk are up to. Now, you and I have to fly back to the States next week. While we're there, I want you to fly over to Provo, Utah, and get inside that building. Think of some way you can present yourself without it being obvious what you are about."

Decker was nodding, a gleam in his eye. What a sweet deal! Couldn't have set it up better if he had tried. Helping Bob Moore in a tight situation suited his plans perfectly. Bob would be in his debt. It was sort of an insurance policy in his hip pocket; he could smell money and, even more vital, job security. There might be a hidden picture here, too. It couldn't hurt his case with Anney if it should be discovered that Stephen was involved in something shady. She was already wavering. If there was one thing he could sense, it was a woman about to run.

CHAPTER 11
The Sisters

Phoenix

Delitra Kline Kimble was the oldest of the three Kline children. She had attended a finishing school at her mother's insistence, something rare in the social circles of Phoenix in the mid-1960s. Like her father, she possessed a keen intellect; from her mother's example, she developed a tenacious will to pursue an independent course in life regardless of the prevailing winds. She had married, had borne two daughters, and was widowed at thirty-two when her husband was killed on one of the many narrow roads in Paradise Valley, where he had been trying to market real estate in the then-developing region northeast of downtown Phoenix. The death interrupted her personal life but never interfered with her ability to run the growing real-estate firm she and her husband had established in the more posh area of Phoenix-Scottsdale.

In two decades she had latched onto the franchise concept. She had opened five offices in Phoenix as well as three in Tucson. The astonishing savvy she brought to real estate had given her father a sense of pride. Since leaving college, Delitra had needed none of her father's money to maintain her own lavish lifestyle, which included a beachfront home in Malibu and a sleek apartment in Manhattan.

With two daughters in college and a fast-paced life of her own, Delitra had little time to bird-dog her brother's activities as he ran the family business that her father, Thomas Kline, had left to the three children: Delitra; her younger brother, Craig; and their sister, Marjorie.

Lately, her brother's lack of business acumen troubled her. She had little confidence that Craig could maintain the level of management and growth the company had experienced for more than a quarter of a century under her father's able direction. If she had acquired no other assets than the inheritance her father left her, she would have taken a more direct hand than she had up to this point in supervising her brother. Heaven only knew that her sister Marjorie had no interest in anything but receiving her quarterly income. Now it was time to place a few demands on her arrogant brother.

Delitra had politely invited Craig to her Paradise Valley real estate office. It was a low, southwestern-design building with the look of money. She had hired a Santa Fe, New Mexico, architectural firm to design the exterior and interior of the office building with an Indian motif. The office exuded that well-manicured look of quality material, right down to the wide front doormat that welcomed clients. Even the rustic clay tile floor had been designed and created by Maria Amada, who kept a fashionable southwestern interior design shop in Scottsdale.

Craig was on time. He strode through the tasteful lobby, past the receptionist without so much as a nod of recognition, directly to his sister's office off the central section of the suite at the rear of the building. He heard the girl ask if he had an appointment with Mrs. Kimble but feigned deafness as he reached for the doorknob to his sister's office.

"Well, come in, Craig," Delitra said, looking up from her desk. It was the focal point in the large, plush room, a kidney-shaped glass top on a massive driftwood base. She wore heavy eyeliner, her lipstick too dark to suggest feminine innocence. The plain white blouse and dark brown skirt bespoke all business.

"Hi, sis," Craig said, lowering his overweight body into one of three leather sling chairs in front of his sister's desk.

Delitra asked about his wife and children, the business, Craig's cabin in the White Mountains. He answered all questions quickly, not lingering on any one item. He knew she had called him in for an update, a chewing out, and a lecture on the finesse of running a winning organization. He had heard it all before and knew that he would hear it five hundred times again. It went with the territory of taking over the family copper business. As he reported on the failed copper deal in Graham County, he could see that he would never measure up to her standards.

Delitra was seething inside. She started dishing out orders on what Craig should do to secure the Little Rock Mountain copper lease. He listened while she briefed him on what she had learned of the deal and the key people to meet with. It amazed him how she knew so much about the copper business yet never set a foot inside the family office complex. She concluded with her final salvo: "Craig, try to remember that you represent Marj and me when you start making deals, and remember also that the three of us have equal shares in the company. You are employed by us to make money. We would like to have reports more often and know that you are making no side deals." She looked at a stack of printout sheets that had been delivered to her desk that morning. It was a monthly report on the projects and expenditures of the Kline business.

"I see from the report here that you've retained Hadley as legal counsel." She looked down at a financial printout of expenditures. "I know him. He's at best regarded as a less-than-honest man. Word has it that he's crooked. Why?"

"Why what?" Craig asked sharply as he shifted his body and sat erect in the sling chair—not an easy maneuver.

"Why hire him?"

"I'm going after the trust Dad gave away. I thought we agreed that I would break it and get the money back."

Delitra sighed. "Yeah, we did, but I don't know how you ever got Marj to go along with it. She's such a twit about people."

She pulled the printouts to one side of the clear desktop and in a very matter-of-fact voice said, "Go easy on the expenditures for legal action; they can get costly. The last time you got an injunction, it soured. Those kinds of actions make all of us look bad. Either get the money, or drop the matter altogether!"

"Listen, I was hired to make the most money I can and to do it the best way I can. I happen to think we have this Polk on the run, and I plan to get back what I think is money Father didn't intend to be spent the way those clowns are going through the millions. Okay?"

Delitra could see that she had touched a sensitive nerve and decided to back off. She personally didn't want to get involved in any

sort of litigation, and for the moment she was too involved in a land
swap in Mesa to worry.

"You're a little testy about this whole thing."

"You're darned right I am." Craig hauled himself out of the chair.
"Don't worry about court action. It will resolve itself when I get
through compiling a fat folder on Polk and his cohorts. You see if it
doesn't."

As far as Delitra was concerned, she had listened to her brother
long enough. She had no more time. Craig sensed it and left, feeling
like a hired hand. His big sister had always been able to make him feel
that way. Too bad she hadn't bowed out in the same accident that took
her husband years ago. Things would be less complicated without her.

* * *

"Frail" hardly described the five-foot-tall lady dressed in black. Elena
weighed less than ninety pounds but sat erect on her worn sofa, waiting
for her friend to come. She had dressed in her best, ready to go with her.
The only flesh visible was the part of her face not covered by her shawl
and her spindly hands. Her withered skin was almost transparent it was
so thin, with purple veins visible as it draped across the back of those
pale hands. The hands were folded, the knees close together.

A block down the Street, the Metro would take them to Svermuv
station, and from there it was a two-block walk to the new chapel
Elena attended. She looked forward to Sundays the way a kid who is
into rock music anticipates a live concert. She was ready for church
fifteen minutes early, but that was her pattern of punctuality—never
late for anything.

Her husband had been a prompt person up to the time he was
killed on the Russian front. Promptness must have been part of his
German upbringing. Elena had wept at his funeral. It happened so
many years ago that she sometimes had difficulty recalling his face.
He had been a foot taller than Elena was. She remembered that
clearly. He was also a military officer. She remembered him best in
the Third Reich uniform that he proudly wore.

He was gone so suddenly. It happened during those last days of the
Russian invasion of Berlin. Elena had watched as the city crumbled

under the Allied air attacks. The army brought his body home to Schloss, a suburb of Berlin, for the family to bury. There were no coffins nor any morticians to prepare the body for burial. Elena did it all. She had wept as she washed his blood-covered body and placed him in a large storage chest that had remained unscathed in the basement of his parents' stately home. By that time, her husband's childhood home was in its last stages of survival.

A powerful bomb had exploded two houses away on the once elegant, tree-lined street. Bomb fragments had ripped through the house, shattering the skull of Elena's sister-in-law, killing her instantly. Her parents had died two years earlier in the country. It was a double funeral—a large cardboard furniture box, also found in the basement, served as her sister-in-law's coffin.

Elena's younger sister, Nadia, helped with the burial as well. It was the end of an era, not a happy memory of family life in Berlin.

A year before, Elena, with her sister in tow, had fled from Prague to her parents-in-law in Berlin, where they were welcomed, but with very real misgivings. A Russian-Czech married to a German officer, Elena was considered a traitor by both sides.

The week of the siege of Berlin was a frightful time for the sisters. They hid in the basement and kept secret the fact that they had been born in the Ukraine.

While the concealed sisters ate the last of the canned food they had squirreled away, the Russians pushed into the heart of Berlin. They brought in their heavy tanks and guns and leveled parts of the city. They raped the women and plundered the homes, though mercifully they did not destroy the suburbs. Miraculously, the girls escaped discovery by the Russian troops. The house was so badly damaged that once the Russians had taken the remaining good furniture, they never returned. Then, within weeks, the British and American troops arrived to help with the occupation.

The sisters waited, huddled and starving, in the basement. The Allies brought food that was distributed by international agencies. It helped the Berliners through part of the summer; then by July, feeling more secure with the American presence, the sisters entered a refugee camp set up in Berlin. At the camp, things quickly improved for the two young women. Nadia met a tall American soldier and went to

America to marry him. Elena decided to return to Prague to find her father and pick up her life again. It was difficult for the sisters to part. When Nadia left Germany for the United States, Elena was happy for her. They would see each other again. That was their hope. "At least you will always have food in America," Elena assured her sister as they clung to each other before Nadia climbed on the train for Bremerhaven, where she would board a passenger ship for America.

Elena had not had any communication with her father for eight months. She was not at all sure what she would find in Prague. She left the refugee camp three weeks after Nadia boarded the train. Elena trekked across Berlin on foot, winding her way through heaps of brick and huge chunks of concrete. She held tight to a pillowcase stuffed with clothes and a meager amount of food that she had stashed away at the refugee center. She had tied two blankets in a roll and strapped them to her back.

Elena was amazed at how clean and repaired some of Berlin's streets appeared such a short time after the massive air and ground strikes that had disrupted the city's infrastructure. When Elena got to Wilhelm and Gitschiner, in the southeastern section of Berlin, a girl approached her to ask if she knew where the Bundastrasse Hofhaus was located. Elena had never been in this section of Berlin. She shook her head. She knew only that Prague was southeast of Berlin a few hundred miles and that sooner or later, if she withstood the hike and found enough food, she would arrive home. The corner was crowded with whole families pushing carts and carrying tattered baggage. Why the girl had singled her out she didn't know. Just chance.

Elena asked why she inquired about the Hofhaus. The girl explained that some church group from America was handing out food and bedding. Wasting no time talking to Elena, she turned and asked directions of another stranger. Elena overheard the man say that the Hofhaus was in the next block to the south. He pointed through the afternoon haze to one of the few standing buildings on the street. The sun had almost disappeared from the sky, and the rubble began to cast long shadows. Night would soon be crowding in. Elena dreaded the night. She had never been alone in her life, least of all with little food and no way to travel except by foot. She had already decided to huddle near a group of families on the side of the street near a wall and bed down for the night as best she could.

But free food up the block? If the girl was right, that was enticing. She quickened her pace behind the girl who was walking rapidly. The Hofhaus was a large building, scarred but not destroyed by the bombs that had erupted over the city three months earlier. Most of the streets for the next ten blocks were nothing but rubble. The massive cleanup had not yet reached this sector.

Inside the open building, people were crowded against a back wall and crammed into the main hall. Elena sidled in behind the girl. Those who came early had plank seats; others had makeshift seats of their own baggage or bedrolls. Elena preferred to stand with the crowd against the wall. Fortunately, those in front of her were seated, so she had a view of the man at the front of the hall.

The speaker was tall, slightly balding, but nice-looking. He wore frameless glasses and had a broad smile across his face. A German stood next to him and loudly translated every word he uttered. The tall man was an American—Elena could tell by his fine suit and immaculate white shirt and tie. She listened for the next half hour as the man spoke words that sounded familiar to her heart. The translator did his best to capture every phrase. The speaker told of a prophet in America; he also spoke of a religion that Christ had brought back to the earth. He welcomed the people and reminded them to read the small tracts that would be distributed with the food. Assuring them that God loved them and was very much aware of their hardships, he then ended his speech, using the words "Jesus Christ" and "Amen."

She had heard nothing religious since her family had lived in Russia, and even then, many had been afraid to attend church openly, so Elena's family had removed God from their lives. Thoughts of God were strange to her. Now, suddenly, something inside her began to stir. She felt so warm and comforted just knowing that there were kind and caring people in the world. Was there really a God?

Much to Elena's delight, two lines began forming in front of her, and surprisingly, she was close to the head. Four young men in army uniforms motioned for the people in line to step forward and receive the offered goods. The translator had left the tall man and was standing near the soldiers, interpreting for them and shouting out instructions and reassurances that every person in need would receive their portion. A young American soldier handed her two cans each of peaches, pears, tomatoes, and beans, plus four cans of corned beef and a can of milk. All of the labels were in English.

Elena held the cans and studied the words printed on the labels: D-e-s-e-r-e-t I-n-d-u-s-t-r-i-e-s, whatever that meant. She had never seen them before. She quickly slipped the gift of food into her pillowcase, along with the religious tract the young men handed her. She surmised that if she were careful, these goods, combined with the cans she already had stashed away in her pillowcase, would last ten days. Wonderful. If she rationed it carefully, it could last two weeks. She must save the peaches for her father. He loved peaches, she remembered. At least she would not starve if she could hike fifty kilometers a day.

Elena lingered near the table where a soldier handed out the cans and said, "May I ask you a question?"

He held up both hands in a helpless gesture of no comprehension and replied, "No spreckense Deutsche." He took hold of her arm and pointed in the direction of the man who interpreted the words of the tall speaker. She made her way through the crowd to the interpreter. He was German, beyond middle age, with a slight stoop to his shoulders. Elena felt she could talk to him.

"Sir, can you tell me who the man is who just spoke to us?"

"Bitte?"

Elena pointed to the tall man.

"Yes," the interpreter said, studying Elena, whose clothes were soiled and torn. His manner was kind. "That is Elder Ezra Taft Benson. He is an apostle of the Lord. Do you know what an apostle is?"

"Thank you," Elena replied. "Would you thank him for me, for the words and the food?" Elena turned and pushed her way back towards the open doors. Suddenly, she was anxious to leave and find a place to sleep before it was pitch black. The interpreter shouted after her, "Why don't you go over and shake his hand and tell him yourself? He doesn't speak German, but he will understand 'Thank you.'"

Elena, peering between the shoulders of two short men, could see that there was a crowd around the tall man. She shook her head no to the interpreter. Her only thought was to find an alcove or a sheltered wall near a family where she could sleep through the night. As much as she would like to, she had no time to speak to him. Yes, he deserved a personal thank-you, but Elena needed rest. She was exhausted from walking across the city and felt stifled by the crowd pushing against her in the stuffy room. In spite of her fatigue, she felt part of her burden lift, as if someone had taken hold of the pillowcase and held it up while she struggled to the outside and fresh air. It was a marvelous feeling that she had not expected.

* * *

"Elena, Elena. Turn on your television. I want you to see the preacher on television this morning. He may be your brother-in-law!" The excited shout came from the front door of the flat. Elena's neighbor remembered that she had mentioned a television priest who would be visiting Prague—her brother-in-law, she had said. It had been in the papers. And, sure enough, she had seen him moments before. He was here in Prague, just as Elena had said, and on television.

Elena was too slow rising from the couch, so the friend switched on the television for her and found the channel. It wasn't difficult; there were only three of them.

The Reverend Moore came into focus, speaking live from the studio downtown. He spoke a couple of lines, then waited. The camera shifted and Heinrik looked straight at the lens and translated Moore's words.

Elena stared at the screen for a full two minutes. She studied the man's gestures, his appearance. Yes, it was Nadia's husband. This was her brother-in-law. It was so thrilling. Was Nadia nearby? Had she come with him? Was she healthy again?

"Freda, that's him. That's him. Do you know how to call him on your telephone?" Elena urged. Personal telephones were a great luxury. She had never had one of her own. She was grateful to have a three-room apartment to herself. She had lived for years with a young family who just last month had moved into their own place. With the new government policy, she would not have to report that they had moved. Everything was changing. And now, here was her family in Prague. She must contact them!

Other neighbors came to the door when they heard the stirrings in Elena's apartment. Instantly caught up in the excitement, one rushed back to her own apartment to call the television station and confirm the identity of the speaker. She breathlessly left a message that the man on television was brother-in-law to Elena Musser and that he must call her. And he must bring her sister, Nadia, to visit.

* * *

Stephen's flight from Berlin to Central America made a stopover in Miami. He placed his phone call from the international section of the air terminal where he awaited his connecting flight. It was late afternoon in Miami and midnight in Prague, but he had promised Anney that he would call her to see that she arrived back safely. He was concerned about how things went at the school where she had gone to speak with the director about Todd's status.

He had half an hour to catch his flight from here to Mexico City . . . time enough to make the call. He heard the phone buzz in Prague. It never ceased to amaze him how easy it was now to place international calls and how clear the voices sounded. He asked for Anney's room extension at the Hotel Karlova.

Anney came on the line. She was aloof and cool. Stephen knew at once that something was troubling her. He asked how things had gone at the school.

The question touched off a megabomb. In the days to come, he would try to remember the way he had phrased the question—the exact words he had used—that had seemingly blown things apart. It seemed so phenomenally fast, a reaction that defied his comprehension. Anney's dissatisfaction with his Mormon project. Of course, that had to be at the core of her anger.

"I am so upset . . . I can hardly speak to you! What right do you have to lay all of this distress on your family?" She hardly took a breath, spitting out the words in rapid fire. "Answer me that one question, and I will stop hounding you about your involvement in this . . . whole thing."

Stephen was confused at the response. That morning Anney may not have been her old self—all bubbly and bright—but at least she had been civil. She had kissed him good-bye. But he had to admit, three or four times since he returned from San Diego after the confab, she had released her pent-up fury and let him know of her displeasure with his new religion.

Stephen drew in a slow breath, grasping for words to soothe his wife. "What distress, darling? At least we are a family and have a home. I'm here trying to keep us from going broke while I look for a job."

"Yeah, about that job." Anney's voice held a biting, sarcastic tone. "How can you be looking for a job and be traveling all over the world? Who are you fooling?"

"I'm not trying to fool anyone. I will be back in the Bay Area a week from tomorrow, the day the employment agent I've been working with scheduled me for some interviews. He couldn't get any appointments before then anyhow," Stephen replied in hot defense.

"Maybe not, but at least you would be in the area so he could call if something came up." There was silence on both ends of the international connection. Then Anney spoke. "It's not only the job . . . it's you, Stephen. I want my old Stephen back. I want the man who was content with his life and doing a great job at the ministry. If I can't have that, at least I want you to have a respectable job. What sort of legacy will be left for our children if you're hauled into court? Stephen, what's really going on with this Mormon project?"

"Court! What are you talking about?"

"Decker Hunt told me in confidence this evening that you and Dr. Polk are being investigated for fraud."

"What?" Stephen shouted. "Anney, how could you believe that I would do anything illegal?"

"Stephen," Anney said. Anger was still shaking her voice. "Mormonism is a cult. Decker told me so. He has told me several unsettling things about your church. How could you sink to that?"

"Anney . . ." Stephen's heart was leaden. How could she reject the precious truths he had found? "Look . . . I'm perfectly willing to piece things together and cement our relationship, but I will not turn my back on my beliefs." Stephen gripped the receiver fiercely. "I cannot do that, Anney. I simply can't. And Decker is wrong! This church is definitely not a cult. It is the true church of Christ. How can you listen to him instead of me?" Stephen was nearly hyperventilating. "What's more, if you knew Dr. Polk, you would know how ludicrous it is to accuse him of fraud."

Once again, there was no response from Anney. There was a tense and unsettled quiet in Miami, with only the background noise of international fight announcements. Silence prevailed in Prague as well.

At length Anney spoke. "Stephen, if things don't improve—I mean *change* on your part—I'm going to ask for a legal separation."

The words streaked through the satellite system like cosmic rays of destruction. Stephen's mind was doing a fast-forward, then play . . . pause and replay. There seemed to be no way for him to utter any kind of response. Maybe he was naive, but he had never really considered that this could happen. The very thought of losing Anney was a strange invader to his mind, like a computer virus that erased all normal functions. There must be some code that he could punch into his brain to call up words to smooth over this catastrophic moment in their relationship, but he was mentally paralyzed.

Why was she so distraught? What had he done to cause her to be so angry? It had to be that Decker Hunt. Up to no good. What could he possibly know about the Book of Mormon project . . . or Dr. Polk, for that matter? Suddenly Stephen gripped the receiver tighter. *Bob Moore! That's who is behind this. Decker must be his messenger boy. I'll bet he is siphoning money from that Kline fellow again. It would suit him only too well to be rid of me. And I guess no method is too dirty for him.* His head was bursting. In any scenario he could imagine, the roadway ahead would be strewn with obstacles that could end his relationship with Anney. Reality seemed to be bombarding him from all sides. *How can I get her to see reason when I'm not there to counteract Bob's undermining tactics?* Stephen had a realization of one thing: the whole issue was at a stalemate. His wife was inflexible, but so was he.

When Stephen failed to respond, she spoke again. "Face it, Stephen. We are presently incompatible. You do realize what that means, don't you?"

Stephen still had no ready answer. All he could say was, "Anney . . . please, Anney." If only they were not a quarter of the world apart. He longed for time. He *needed* time to pull his family back together, time to explain to Anney what the gospel was all about. He yearned above all to have his family in the Church. Would that be impossible now?

Stephen sensed that anything he said to Anney in her present state of mind would come back to him like a double-edged Wilkinson sword. His mind continued to whirl, trying to say something that might reconcile their differences. He was unable to make the grade. The silence between them seemed to pound like a huge boulder rushing down a mountain, destroying all in its path.

"Anney, Hunt is deceiving you. I don't know what he wants, but don't believe him. *Please* don't believe him."

Anney sighed. "Stephen, I'm too exhausted to carry on this heavy conversation. It is all up to you whether or not we even have a home together when this tour is over. Don't call me unless you have decided to clear up this mess you have created. I'm sorry. I have loved you all these years. I'm sure you loved me, too. But now . . . I don't know what to think. Everything is different. Good-bye, Stephen."

Stunned, Stephen slumped against the side of the phone booth, the receiver pressed against his forehead. Gradually, he became aware of the indifferent buzz of the dial tone and the irritating flight announcements over the intercom. The volume of ordinary sounds swelled until they seemed deafening. He wanted to shut out the entire world and find some peace. Peace and love. Love and family. Wife and husband. Home and joy. He stood there in the middle of a circle of six phone booths and wept for all he was losing.

* * *

They had tramped about the ruins of Cuello in Belize, the small country that at one time had been British Honduras. It stretched along the Caribbean coast, facing east. Norman Hammon took charge, showing Dr. Polk and Roy the ruins of the once-thriving Mayan settlement. Norman had met them at the site where he had been for the past two weeks with a crew from Rutgers University. Conversation flowed between the three at an accelerated pace, as if Polk and Roy would be at the site for half an hour, never to return again, when, in fact, they planned to spend two days in the area.

Hammon's current fieldwork had the advantage of funding by the trust Polk administered. It was all part of the "grand tour of Book of Mormon lands" that Polk had promised Stephen they would take in the new Land Rover that Roy had picked up in Veracruz, Mexico. Since Stephen was still in Berlin, Polk had commenced the tour. Stephen would have to join them in Guatemala City the next day.

Dr. Hammon, a stout man in his fifties, of Irish heritage, had jumped from university to university over the years in his quest of the best campus for Mesoamerican research. Currently, he was at Rutgers. He had been eager to accept Polk's offer six months before when asked to research the concept of a vast Preclassic Mayan period in Mesoamerica. The two men agreed that there had been a great civilization in the Mayan lands prior to the so-called "Classic period."

Polk told Hammon further that he had selected him because of his fine work showing the scholars of New World archaeology that there were dynamic civilizations before the Mayas of the Classic period (between C.E. 300 and C.E. 900). Polk felt it was significant that a respected non-Mormon scholar present his findings at the spring conference. Hammon accepted the challenge. It was time for scholars to begin thinking along the lines that a lot of things had happened eight hundred years before the Classic period. *Good heavens, the whole Nephite civilization rose and fell before the Mayan "Classic period." Wake up, world!* Polk chafed at the title "Classic" period. If anything, the civilization of the so-called Mayans had dipped by the year 300 C.E. What a title to give to that era of post-Book of Mormon writing—Classic. It should be labeled Postclassic. The Classic period, to Polk's way of thinking, encompassed the period of 600 B.C.E. to C.E. 400. Right on the mark so far as Book of Mormon civilization was concerned.

Hammon had published an article for *Scientific American* that thoroughly discredited the old-school theory of the Classic period and caught Polk's attention. In the article, Hammon had stated:

"It has long been clear that the Maya, who occupied the Yucatan peninsula along with parts of Belize, Guatemala, El Salvador, and Honduras, created one of the most sophisticated of all native American cultures. At its height in the Classic period, Maya society was highly stratified, with a ruler at the apex of six or seven clearly defined social classes. A complex cosmology held places for gods, natural forces, and ancestors.

"An elaborate calendar provided the framework for ritual and historical events. The rituals were enacted at ceremonial centers that formed the core of great cities. This superstructure rested on the cultivation of maize, and techniques had been developed for making steep hillsides and swamps cultivable.

"A decade ago it was thought that the Classic Maya civilization sprang into being quite suddenly during the third century C.E. The preceding period, called Preclassic or Formative, was believed to have been an age of humble village farming societies. Since 1975, many discoveries and reassessments of known evidence have radically changed the accepted picture of Preclassic culture. It has been found that intensive agriculture above the slash-and-burn level was developed far earlier than had been dated to Preclassic times, implying substantial social and economic organization. Recent excavations show that standardized tools were made in large-scale workshops and traded over great distances."

Then Hammon had made a crucial statement about a sudden change in the civilization about the time that Nephi had taken over as leader of the family. Hammon wrote in his article: "Yet what happened near the end of the Middle Preclassic period poses some of the most significant questions in New World archaeology, because by the beginning of the Late Preclassic period in 450 B.C.E., a society quite different from that of the village farmers had emerged. Indeed, during the six or seven centuries of the Late Preclassic period, true civilization appeared."

That statement alone stirred the juices in Polk and drove him to meet with Dr. Hammon at Rutgers, where the restless scholar enjoyed the position of professor of archaeology, anthropology, and classics as well as being director of the university's archaeological research program. Polk and Hammon cut a deal. He accepted Polk's offer to do an independent study for Project II and to give a lecture during the spring conference.

Polk had told him, "I am fascinated by your comment that around 450 B.C.E. a wooden temple had been burned." Polk knew that among the ruins in the heavily wooded regions of Central America, temples had already been constructed of wood. Nephi's brother Jacob presided at such a temple that had been constructed along the lines of the famous temple of Solomon in Jerusalem. Hammon had mentioned that in their digs in that region of the Cuello ruins, a broad open platform capable of holding a large audience or congregation had been uncovered. It had been built on rubble.

Hammon stopped at the base of a stone-and-concrete platform that measured one hundred by one hundred and fifty meters. Surrounding the platform were large round holes that were filled with debris. The holes extended down at least thirty feet and must have been the footings for large wooden pillars that had supported some type of roof, or perhaps a wooden building for public gatherings.

Hammon's red, hairy arm shot into the air, signaling the two others to stop. It was midday, and sweat poured down his temples. He turned to Dr. Polk, who was sweating just as profusely, and commented, "You know, a growing number of findings suggest that midway through the Late Preclassic period—not long before the birth of Christ—a real political power had been forged in this region. And before that, our sites indicate that about 450 B.C.E. a sharp demographic growth—at least fourfold—took place in the region. I published those findings of our group over a decade ago. Our study was conducted with careful supervision. We were operating under the auspices of the British Museum and the Corozal Project of the University of Cambridge—very stuffy, conservative, respectable bosses in the field. I'll include this information in my lecture to your group next spring.

"I'll show that most of the early structures were built of wood. It's the burned and rotted remains of the wood that gives our carbon testing an advantage. We can certainly make a point that most of the structures were of wood. It is, in part, this fact that has thrown off so many of the early excavations and caused the diggers to overlook the fact that there may have been a mightier civilization than the Classic Maya."

"Not maybe. There *was* a more creative civilization than we have been told," Polk corrected.

"Does your Book of Mormon mention wood construction?"

"It doesn't make a distinction as to what materials were used. However, the prophets in the Book of Mormon say they constructed the temples of the finest materials and along the same architectural lines as Solomon's temple. I think most Mormons assume that the structures were stone and cement. It may be that we will have to rethink that concept now that we know so much wood was used and certainly available in these jungle regions and over in the mountains."

"Well, of course, some of the temples were constructed of stone and cement, but not all, and certainly not the major public buildings in the Late Preclassic period."

CHAPTER 12
The Call

Prague

The neighbor's call came into the studio as Moore concluded his quasi-sermon to the "Christians and all others" of Prague. Bob didn't mean for it to sound that way, but Heinrik's translation gave the impression that all others were inferior. Even the cameraman, who was jaded to public figures, thought the remark was a tad too condescending to the unbaptized of the city, which was probably two-thirds of the population. Since it was Sunday morning, the drinkers and swingers of Prague who had been out late the night before could not be expected to stir until nearly twelve noon, and even then it would be to watch two favorite soccer teams clash at the stadium. No need to worry. Those who would have been offended were not watching the religious program.

There were loyal Christians who enjoyed their new freedom of public worship, but religion had not been as readily accepted as the Bible societies had hoped it would be. There were a few fresh believers, but not many. Most figured they had better things to do with their Sundays. It was enough to make the would-be televangelists want the God of the Old Testament to rain down fire from heaven and consume the wicked. That didn't happen either.

Elena's neighbor tried to speak to the Reverend Moore without luck. She was forced to leave a message with the soundman, who had grabbed the phone and listened impatiently. Would the man be so kind as to tell Reverend Moore that his sister-in-law wanted to speak to him? In her excitement, Elena's neighbor forgot to give the technician her number so Bob could return the call.

* * *

"What are we looking for among the ruins?" Stephen casually asked Dr. Polk as they drove along one of the main highways out of Guatemala City in the direction of the highlands of Guatemala in the north. The dusty Land Rover purred with all the smoothness that the ads touted, while Roy adroitly negotiated the turns and the overloaded natives burdened with wares or produce strapped to shoulders and back. The streets of Guatemala's early morning traders bustled with commotion. Strident merchants were determined to be in street stalls set for bartering by the time the households of the city began gathering for the day's purchases. Some of the hawkers had been up since four in the morning preparing their produce and wares for the market. It was a daily ritual that Dr. Polk assured Stephen had been going on for centuries, going all the way back to the Preclassic Maya.

"We are here to illuminate the Book of Mormon, Stephen. You are about to receive the premier guided tour of all guided tours by the one and only Professor Peter Polk. How does that sound?"

"Great. I'm all for the best. How many tours have you directed in your career?"

"I lost count a few years back, but I would guess at least thirty and perhaps more like forty. I'll have to admit, though, I've never gone in style like this. It is usually done in buses, a jeep, or whatever, but never so private and so plush as this little Rover has proven to be."

Dr. Polk sat propped up in the rear seat, glancing about like a child on a trip to Disneyland with his parents. Stephen and Roy detected the lilt in Polk's manner. "Our project this time goes beyond the doctrine and internal aspects of the Book of Mormon. There are those among Church members who feel that the doctrine of the Book of Mormon is really the only relevant part of the document. I agree that it is the primary purpose of the book. After all, it is a spiritual account of a people. But there are important matters in addition to the doctrine. The book was written with a cultural and geographical setting. Mormon must have felt that those aspects of the book were important, or he would not have taken the time to record so many. By uncovering the cultural and geographical aspects of the book, we lead people to respect and read the work. In the process they touch upon the central theme of the book, which is a testimony of Jesus Christ.

"There are some key topics to consider as we tromp through this land. What was going on in this region during the Book of Mormon period? Up to twenty years ago, the scholars were telling us that those who settled this area of Central America in the Preclassic Mayan period—keep in mind that Preclassic means 500 B.C.E. to C.E. 350—were slash-and-burn farmers. Now we are watching the whole of scholarship on the Maya make a complete turn toward the Preclassic Maya being the more intellectual, refined, and interesting segment of the entire history. What a change. I have seen it firsthand.

"When I first started bringing groups, usually BYU tours, into this region, for every study done on the Preclassic civilization of the Maya, there were fifty to a hundred done on the Classic period. That is changing like you can't believe. They are digging into the ruins and discovering that the Classic Maya built their structures—you know, the huge temples—atop the Preclassic structures. A great example is the ruins of Cholula up in Puebla, on the way to Mexico City. There are three very distinct, very large structures built atop each other. First the massive ruins that date back to 300 B.C.E. and then the major structure built sometime during the Classic period, C.E. 700. Then in the sixteenth or seventeenth century the Catholics came along and built a magnificent cathedral on the very large mound that looked like a hill out on the plains. If we could remove the cathedral and lay bare all the buried structures beneath, the world would very graphically see that the most extensive structure was built during Book of Mormon times. It's very simple. All the Classic Mayan civilization did was use the Preclassic structures, many of them temples, as foundations to their buildings. In many building projects, the Classic Maya sort of renovated, rather than erected, original structures.

"But ruins are just part of what we are looking for. We want to see mountain ranges. We'll see what I consider to be the Narrow Strip of Wilderness that divided the Nephites of the northern regions from the Lamanites in the southern. It is that range of very high mountains on the map in the highlands of this country.

"Rivers are important. The River Sidon in the Book of Mormon was a major waterway. We'll visit the Grijalva River that I feel is the Book of Mormon River Sidon in the Land of Many Waters. We have done careful research on that as well. You'll see the primary candidate for the Central American Hill Cumorah. Oh, there is so much we are looking for. You'll really learn about Book of Mormon lands from this private tour. Believe me, you will."

Roy had done most of the driving in the grimy Land Rover. They had covered a good deal of terrain in the past three days, and the vehicle that could climb like a Billy goat showed it. There was a fresh, deep scratch on the right front fender, but that was to be expected. The roads over the pass going north out of Guatemala wound through high mountain passes that served as a natural barrier between Mexico on the north and Guatemala on the south. According to Polk, it had also served the same purpose for the Nephites and the Lamanites. The road was paved, or almost. The entire landscape of high, tree-covered mountains was verdant. The rainy season was all but over, and Mother Nature was everywhere her most radiant self. The air out of Guatemala City was heady with fragrant blossoms of every kind of tropical growth known. The rains hadn't completely ended. A downpour had caught the three travelers off guard and forced them to stay at the pueblo of Santa Cruz del Quiche on the Guatemala side of the border. They had hoped to take a side trip to the ruins at Coban, but time wouldn't allow it now.

Stephen had joined them in Guatemala City. He had slept intermittently as they traveled toward Mexico. He wondered how pilots endure so many changes in time zones as they fly intercontinental routes. He was tired from his recent trip to Europe and back. Even on the rough, disintegrating stretch of road, his mind had finally, mercifully found oblivion. The rapid change of continents via both day and night flights plus his concern over his marriage had left him almost too weary to function. His body had simply demanded some healing rest. He began to appreciate what the Secretary of State must go through on his many jaunts around the world.

Guatemala City epitomized third-world hygiene. Stephen knew at once that he would have to be careful of the food and drink. The city had its own unique scents of urine, aromatic flowers, rotting garbage, and sweaty humans. It was also one of the most beautiful cities he had ever seen, laced with tropical plants everywhere. The day before, Polk had given him the Cook's tour of Guatemala City. They trudged across the ruins of Kaminaljuyu on the outskirts of Guatemala City and hiked over its several dirt mounds that archaeologists had not as yet uncovered. Polk reminded Stephen that here was the proposed site of the city and land of Nephi—the area where the Nephites had settled for a few hundred years before the Lamanites overpowered them and the Nephite nation fled permanently.

That same day, they had driven northwest to Lake Atitlin, a body of water that Dr. Polk insisted was the Waters of Mormon. It was dotted with small islands and green vegetation that swept to the water's edge. Clouds shrouded the lake, and the tropical air was misty and warm. There were flowers everywhere. Stephen could appreciate Alma's delight in bringing converts to the shore and baptizing them in the warm, clear lake. His brow furrowed as his desire surfaced. *Oh, to bring my family to the waters of baptism.*

Today, as they moved along in the Land Rover, the lake was glorious and clear, with the freshness of a thousand springs. Stephen struggled to pull his thoughts to the present and the task at hand. Now, refreshed from sleep, he was taking his turn at the wheel. Thinking about Dr. Polk's running discussion of the history of the area, he mused, "You know, Roy, I still have a hard time using the politically correct terms for denoting before and after Christ."

Roy glanced over at Stephen and grinned. "Well, I learned it early. Actually, I'm in total favor of the change. Have you ever considered the percentage of people in the world who are not Christians?"

"Maybe so, but the initials B.C.E., which indicate 'Before the Common Era,' and C.E. for 'Common Era' just don't have the same impact for me as 'Before Christ' and 'Anno Domini.' It's amazing how the new terms roll off of Dr. Polk's tongue. He is a true scholar. By the way, how many miles do you think you've covered in the past three days, Roy?" he asked the reclusive graduate student who sat in the passenger seat, studying the regional map showing northern Guatemala where it bisected the border of Mexico.

"Do you really want to know?" Roy asked lazily. "I'm trying to locate that other pass Dr. Polk told us about." He grinned and jerked his head over his shoulder, motioning toward Dr. Polk, asleep in the rear seat. Roy was amazed at the older man's ability to sleep through bumps and twists in the road.

"Naw, just give me your best guess. I'm curious."

"Well . . . we started out in Villahermosa. We made the great loop through Guatemala, and now we're heading north into Mexico." Roy paused, computing distance in his mind. "I'd say over five hundred miles. What do you think?"

"You're probably right." Stephen looked to the west at two-hundred-foot-high cliffs. Beyond the cliffs he could see ranges of mountain peaks unfolding, one range higher than the other with the highest at ten thousand feet, straight up from the sea. "These mountains seem to go on forever. How wide does the map show they are?"

"I think they stretch about twenty miles across once you get into the foothills, maybe more, then they cascade to the lowlands in Mexico. We're not too far from the headwaters of the Grijalva River. One of the tributaries should be less than two miles from here. Mormon scholars say it's the river mentioned in the Book of Mormon as the Sidon. At least that's what the Nephites called it. You know, this main river today, the Grijalva, has several tributaries which now have individual names. Yet in the Book of Mormon, the entire river drainage system was called Sidon. It's simpler that way, don't you think?"

"Well, yeah, sure. It saves having to pronounce all those Spanish names." Stephen took his eyes from the road for a split second to look at Roy. "You know, for a Gentile, you really have your facts down on the Book of Mormon." Stephen stole another side-glance at Roy. He looked uncomfortable. "Yep, you spit it out just like you really believe it. I suppose that's possible. I had a literature teacher who spoke of Hamlet as if he had been an actual historical figure in Denmark. It's possible."

Roy feigned concentration on the map. He gave no reply to Stephen's comment. Then he glanced through the windshield and offered another fact with the same detached though authoritative insight that caused Stephen to wonder how the guy could remain an agnostic. "Do you know that some of the early Mormon leaders insisted that the inhabitants of the Book of Mormon actually traveled from Peru on the south to Canada on the north, and that they traipsed around the two continents with little thought as to climate, major waterways, or the great American desert?

"I don't mean Joseph Smith," Roy lectured, as if he were instructing a class. "There are no original statements from him about the actual location of these people. Others have said he believed that, but their understanding is a long way from having him personally state it for the record. Those who came after him espoused the idea that the prophet Mormon moved the plates—an entire library of records engraved on gold—from the Hill Shim to the Hill Cumorah, which would have been from the narrow neck of land here in Central America to what has become known as upstate New York. That is, if we logically pinpoint the narrow neck of land to be along here in Central America. He supposedly did this, including transporting all his people and his army—we're talking hundreds of thousands of people—all in a matter of weeks, or at most, a few months. It's absurd." Roy spat out the word "absurd."

"Here we are, tooling around in this brand-spanking-new Rover, and we have to be careful we don't get too far off the beaten path or we may get bogged down. They had to walk—walk, mind you—and herd their animals and trudge along with their women and children. A crazy concept. Impossible for me to accept.

"Do you know that it took the Lewis and Clark Expedition, in the early 1800s, over a year and a half to go from Independence, Missouri, to the Pacific Ocean at the mouth of the Columbia River? Granted, they packed it in for the dead of winter and stayed with the Indians, but they were on the move much of the time. Those guys were in top shape. They were probably as fit as Swedish cross-country skiers training for the Olympics. I'm serious. Even with that kind of strength and endurance, it was still a struggle to make it. Think about it. It would have taken Mormon at least two years to go from here to there." Roy jabbed his finger on the map and then jerked his thumb in a northeast direction.

"I think they would have lost as many people in the process as the Cherokee nation did when President Jackson ordered the military to move the Indians from the deep south to the Oklahoma Territory. Their casualty rate was sixty percent. Then to top that off, the Lamanites were on the tail of the Nephites all the way. Remember, those guys with their supply lines had to make the trek. It's amazing that they were in such great shape, ready to launch the final battle at the foot of the Hill Cumorah.

"By the way, the Hill Cumorah in New York is not really much of a hill compared to anything in the western United States. Hey, if there had been over a million people in battle at that hill, they would have had to bring with them wagon loads of supplies. There is no mention of wagons in the Book of Mormon. Can you imagine the caravan of goods it would have taken to sustain that many people for an extended period of time? Who knows how they transported their supplies? Anything short of horse and wagon would have been impossible for that many people.

"And what about crossing the Mississippi, the Wabash, the Ohio River, and all the terrain in between? Once they got there, they would have had only a short season to clear the forests, till the soil, and raise crops, providing they arrived by late spring.

"Where does Mormon mention the deep snows that hit that area year after year? We took photos of the Hill Cumorah in the winter. Sometimes the snow is three- and four-feet deep on the hill. Somebody needs to wake up and smell the coffee. Not even George Washington fought battles during five months of the winter along the eastern seacoast. Besides all that, Mormon clearly says that the Hill Cumorah was near the narrow neck of land and the land of many waters.

"Did you know that Moroni never once mentioned the name of the hill during all those night visions when he showed Joseph where the plates were hidden—you know, when he came in 1823 to Joseph's bedroom?

"Come on . . . something is not clicking right for those who insist that New York was the scene of the last great battle. Moroni simply said that the plates were in a stone box. You know what I think?"

"No. What?" Stephen asked, caught up in what Roy had researched and was pouring out for Stephen to grasp.

"He never said the word Cumorah; at least, that's what the record shows. Joseph Smith called the hill where he uncovered the plates the Hill Cumorah but not until after he had translated and studied the writing. Do you know the word Cumorah has another meaning?"

Stephen looked over at Roy again. *Listen to him! Wow, there's a boiler about to blow inside this quiet intellectual. He has it all figured out, the whole puzzle of the Book of Mormon location.*

"I think Moroni took the abridgment of the plates, the copy bound with rings, hoisted it onto his back, and wandered northward to the hill in present-day New York," Roy continued. "He was gone for nineteen years. I think he buried the plates in a stone box and left them there for the next sixteen hundred years. Naw, I don't buy the idea that Moroni's Hill Cumorah, mentioned in the Book of Mormon, is the same hill where Joseph Smith found the plates. If I were a critic of the Book of Mormon, which I'm not, I would zero in on that one piece of muddy thinking and drive my point home. Boy, would I!"

"So would I," Dr. Polk said from the back seat, struggling to sit upright.

"Well, you decided to join the living," Stephen grinned, without taking his eyes from the road. "We think we're very close to the headwaters."

Dr. Polk glanced to both sides of the road and looked off into the mountainous region. There were no guardrails on the side of the winding road that took them higher and higher into the mountain range. "Gentleman, you are now going through one of the passes that the ancient Lamanites used with their armies in full march. They were hoping to defeat the Nephites in the outpost city of Manti. If you will turn left up here, after we reach the plateau, you'll come to a dirt and gravel road. That's the road we will take to Frontera Comalapa and on over to Motozintla."

"Man, I'm glad you woke up. We probably would have gone right past it," Stephen sighed.

"I'm glad, too." Polk was unruffled. "Just outside of Motozintla, we will meet our boys who are involved in a field study. What time is it now?"

"Three. How long will it take us to get there?"

"Not more than half an hour. We have to check through the Mexican border, but that's no problem. Isn't this fun, you guys?" Polk said, with a lilt in his voice and a bright smile on his face. "I've been here maybe thirty times. It's always exciting to see it again."

Dr. Polk leaned his hands on the headrests of the bucket seats in front of him and said to Stephen, "Now that we have a few minutes, while we're all awake to talk, tell me all about your encounter with Novue and the Jewish scholar in Berlin . . . what's his name?"

"Michale."

"Yeah. Did Novue show you his private museum? I haven't seen it, but he told me about it when we met in San Francisco a while back. He's one of the elite of the globe. He's living his fantasies. Nice guy, though."

Stephen told of his visits in Europe for the next twenty minutes. He cut it short when they pulled into Frontera Comalapa at the border checkpoint. They all got out of the Rover and stretched their legs.

* * *

"You know what they're doing up there! Now, how do we stop them?" Craig asked in frustration as he looked across the table at his attorney. They had gone to Tony's for drinks and the dark, private atmosphere of the lounge where they could plan their next moves against Polk and company.

"Let 'em hang themselves," Hadley advised, wiping foam from his upper lip. "I've explained the legal aspects of the trust agreement. So let it ride until the injunction kicks in. That ought to happen in a few days. I explained the situation to the judge, and she seemed to be in agreement, though those people are never ones to let on to their real opinions until a decision has to be made, especially a woman judge. We've come downhill since I started practicing law. You've got so many oddballs in the judicial system."

At Hadley's prodding, Craig had managed to get his sister Marj to get him a copy of the provisions of the trust that William Bennett, his father's personal attorney, had drawn up before his father's death. The provisions were straightforward and clear. Polk was to have control of the arrangements and funds for all Book of Mormon projects. The money was to be used for the projects, plus follow-up studies over the next ten years. If some untoward event happened so that Polk, for any reason, was unable to carry out his duties as administrator of the trust, then he had full authority to designate an interim administrator until such a time as the board could meet and appoint a new administrator. The designated administrator would function until Polk resumed full administrative duties or a new administrator was appointed.

There were other vital stipulations in the trust agreement, and it was here that Hadley knew he had Polk where it would hurt. The board of directors appointed to oversee the actions of the administrator was to meet quarterly at his invitation and review all matters pertaining to the progress and administration of the trust. The board had never met.

Polk had assumed the role of administrator in January of this year; now, ten months later, he had not called one meeting. He might have placed conference calls to legally satisfy the requirements of the trust, but he had not. A quorum would consist of three members of the five-member board. However, since completing Book of Mormon Project I, Polk had kept up a constant correspondence with all members of the board, informing them in detail of the progress of projects and, each time, including in the information letters a standard copy of Thomas Kline's approval of all projects, to keep the board apprised of current activities.

"Why hasn't your sister Delitra blown the whistle on this project, since she must know that quarterly board meetings are to be held?"

"She's too involved in her own bailiwick to concern herself with such technicalities. Remember, she sits at the head of a twenty-five-million-dollar organization that she has built largely since the death of her husband. In the beginning, my dad helped her out and gave her financial advice, but she has pretty much done this on her own. She's a natural-born salesperson. Some people have that talent. Frankly, she doesn't care about what direction this thing goes. In her opinion, the money has been allocated to a foundation, and she sees nothing in it for her."

"But there is! She would share in the remaining millions to the tune of one-third. That kind of money ought to cause her to wake up and help you more vigorously than she has to date."

"You don't know my sister," Craig said with scorn. "She hopes I fail. She doesn't want me to have one-third of anything. But it sure would boost my position in some business ventures I have my eye on."

What Craig didn't share with Hadley was the sharp decline of the family corporation in the past three months. Nor did he tell him that if he didn't find some new cash, the copper business his father had left would soon be without cash reserves, and he would be out of a job. Lately, Craig was depending on his annual salary of $160,000 to keep up with his personal debts. His wife and sons had no comprehension of the meaning of money. Around the Kline estate, dollars flowed like beer at Oktoberfest. He failed to tell his attorney that he was in deeper than he ever dreamed he would be so soon after his father's death. He also felt anxious about his sisters and their attitude toward him and his mismanagement of the family business. There were a host of stresses Craig shared with no one, not even his wife—especially not his spendthrift wife.

CHAPTER 13
Katherine and Anney

Prague

"Thanks for coming with me, Katherine. Oh, I wish Dad could be here to meet her, too," Anney lamented as she and Katherine wound through Prague's old quarter. The labyrinthine streets held a certain charm, but the cobblestones were hard on the women's feet. Heinrik had left them among the tenements in Mala Strana, while he searched for a parking spot. It was a courtyard arrangement, with aged balconies all facing the center court.

Katherine looked about her as she walked, fascinated by the appeal of Prague. She wondered why she had never come east of Berlin to visit the Old World capital. In all of her travels with her late husband, she had never desired to visit the old Eastern Bloc countries. She had painted herself a mental picture of them—black and white and bleak—because of communism. Granted, communism had fallen, but still the cities remained the same. They were charming, and this section of Prague held the sort of quaint beauty she never dreamed she would discover.

"That woman said it was on the first floor, meaning the second floor to us. Right?" Elena's neighbor had realized her mistake and had called again, this time giving Elena's address to Heinrik, who relayed it to Robert Moore. To Anney's regret, Bob's schedule was too tight to allow him to visit his wife's sister.

No apartment numbers were visible, as though everyone who visited already knew the location of the apartment. "Does this look right, Katherine?" Anney asked, as the two well-dressed women came to the landing on the first-floor balcony.

"Ah, I suppose . . . look!" Katherine nudged Anney's elbow. "I think that door over there may be her apartment. Did they say the second or third door from the landing?"

"Second."

"Then that's it."

"You knock, Katherine," Anney said nervously. "I'm feeling strange, almost as if someone from the dead is going to open that door. If this really is my mother's sister after all these years, then it's going to be weird. I'm afraid I won't be able to understand her. It's been years since Mother was able to talk to me." The fact that Anney had slept little since her angry threat to Stephen added to her emotional state.

"Relax! Heinrik will be along in a minute," Katherine replied with sympathy. "I have some of the same feelings, and I'm not nearly as emotionally involved as you are."

Katherine knocked. She cast a sideways glance at Anney, who was clearly tense with anticipation. She knocked a second time. Still they waited in silence. Then the door to the aged apartment creaked open. The sunlight cast its early afternoon rays across the door and captured the lined face of the tiny woman who opened it.

Anney stood back, her heart beating rapidly, barely aware that Heinrik had caught up with them, bounding up the stairs just as the door opened. He, too, stood back until the old lady was fully visible. She wore a black shawl and cupped her right hand over her eyes to shield them from the bright sun, straining to see the three people who had come to her door.

Heinrik spoke in Czech, asking if Elena Musser lived in this apartment. "Are you Elena Musser?" he asked, taking a half step forward to indicate that he was in command. The old lady nodded guardedly. She asked Heinrik who he was and what he wanted.

Heinrik turned to Anney and said, "This is Anney Moore Thorn. Her mother is your sister. She is your niece."

Elena studied Anney carefully, watching emotion alter the expression on the younger woman's face. Slowly the wrinkles along her mouth doubled in length. Her face came alive and her hands flew to her mouth, tears gathering in her eyes.

Heinrik turned to Anney and said, "I told her who you are and . . ."

"I know," Anney whispered. "I know." Her eyes were transfixed on the tiny woman's face. She resembled Anney's mother.

"She is Elena Musser," Heinrik assured Anney unnecessarily. Katherine, watching the two women, reached for her handkerchief.

Elena stepped forward, opening her arms to Anney. She exclaimed, "You are Nadia's baby!" Anney understood only her mother's name, but that was enough to fill her soul with joy. She reached out to her tiny aunt, her body reacting to the release of anxiety with wracking sobs. "You have your mother's smile and her hair," Elena continued in a fevered pitch, switching to Ukrainian. "You are Nadia's baby. I would know it anywhere. You are family. You are family!" Her face glowing with warmth, she reached up and embraced her niece with the tender love that Anney had always known in her mother. It felt so familiar—surely a family trait to embrace in this special way.

Heinrik, earnest in his assignment, pressed close to the two women, loudly interpreting every word Elena shouted. Katherine took him by the arm and gently pulled him back, putting her finger to her lips to hush him. "They know," she said in English, tears streaming down her lovely, chiseled face.

* * *

Katherine insisted that Bob and Decker stay at her penthouse in San Francisco during their short visit. Bob's home was in Concord, but his studio was in San Francisco, and her apartment was much more convenient. What Katherine didn't know when she invited them to stay there was Decker's itinerary. From Chicago, where the two men landed from Prague, Bob boarded a flight for San Francisco International, while Decker, at Bob's direction, caught a flight to Salt Lake City.

They arrived at their separate destinations, where both took care of pressing matters: Bob taped two shows; Decker spied on the Provo project. By noon Sunday, the two men met at San Francisco International.

The Faith and Values Television Company was on hand to tape Moore's departure at the terminal. The crew had pulled him to one side of the international departure gate, camera rolling and lights glaring off the makeup Bob still had on his cheeks from his earlier taping. The Faith and Values reporter had been interviewing Moore for ten minutes when Decker moved into the curious crowd that had gathered to see what the commotion was all about.

Decker had arrived a half-hour earlier from Salt Lake City. He had rechecked his luggage and headed for the international gate to join Moore for the return flight to Prague. Moore spied Decker as he spoke to the interviewer about the great work that televangelism had in store in the old Eastern Bloc nations. He waxed dramatic about the spiritually starved in those countries and how he and others would bring the gospel to their screens. Two minutes more were spent detailing who he intended to instruct in those capital cities, then the floodlights went dead and the interviewer shook Bob's hand. It was a wrap. As Bob moved toward Decker, three spectators reached out to shake his hand and to tell him how much they enjoyed his Sunday sermons. Bob glowed amidst the adulation.

Excusing himself from the group, he took Decker by the elbow and picked up his briefcase, and the two men moved through the electronic security gate to the counter, all set to return to Prague. Bob was feeling the strain of travel, dreading the return flight to Eastern Europe. Though he flew first class, even the wide seat failed to replace a bed, and the plane's constant motion disturbed his sleep. He kept telling himself that in just a few more weeks he could relax on the next journey home with Katherine. The thought buoyed his spirits.

He turned to Decker and asked, "What did you find out in Utah?"

"I got in."

"You what?"

"I saw inside that fancy layout they have created in that super-market building. You won't believe what I saw there."

"How did you get in?" Moore was suddenly alive with interest.

"I did as you said. I called Kline in Phoenix to let him know I was investigating things in Provo. He told me to tell the security people in Provo that I worked for Melrose Studios and was an assistant to the art director, Weinberger, in North Hollywood. It worked. Not a soul checked me out. I simply told them to call Hollywood if there was a question. They merely assumed I was real and let me walk through the front door. Terrible security. It was a piece of cake."

Bob looked up at a monitor when he heard the boarding call over the intercom. He held up his hand and interrupted Decker. "Wait, they're ready for us to board. Tell me as soon as we get seated. I'm curious." Bob let Decker pass in front of him as the attendant at the gate took their boarding passes. "What's more, at our stopover in Chicago, I want you to call Kline back and report on what you found out. Okay?"

"Yeah, sure thing."

* * *

"By the way, Stephen, did I ever tell you about Dr. Sammi Hannia? He's a Middle Eastern Scholar of the first water. Brilliant man."

"No, I don't recall that you did." Stephen replied, seated on the stoop, drinking a warm Orange Crush. It was midday in San Juan, and on the dusty street, except for a mangy stray dog and a *campesino* with a bundle of sticks tied on his back, nothing else moved. The proprietor explained to Dr. Polk in Spanish that his refrigeration unit was broken and hoped the repairman would come *mañana*. In the meantime, warm soda pop. They had pulled up to the small corner store in what had to be the most isolated village in the Chiapas region. At the southern end of the village flowed the Grijalva River, less than a kilometer away. Mostly the inhabitants of the area farmed tobacco and mangos. Stephen noticed a cattle ranch or two, but the majority of the Mexicans were field laborers. It was as good as any spot to take a break from exploring the currents of the Grijalva that Polk insisted was the Sidon River described in the Book of Mormon where an army had made a crossing anciently.

"Listen, and I'll tell you about my Sammi, who told me about his experience with the Book of Mormon. Roy, I know you've heard this before, but maybe you'll see a new angle."

Roy nodded without enthusiasm.

"Sammi's Egyptian—Sammi Hannia. He has taught at several universities in the States as well as in the Middle East where he grew up. Smart man. He was at the University of Chicago when he got an offer to teach at the University of Utah.

"He had only been at the U of U for a year when, in the mid-1970s, the First Presidency of the Mormon Church decided to translate the Book of Mormon into a Near Eastern language, a Semitic language. The Brethren were undecided as to whether to translate the Book of Mormon into Hebrew or Arabic, both being Semitic languages. They ultimately decided that since so few Semitic people read and write Hebrew and so many hundreds of millions read and write Arabic, they would seek out an authority, a scholar on Arabic. They wanted someone who could take the English version of the Book of Mormon and translate it into Arabic. Nowadays, of course, we have it in Hebrew, too, but at the time it was in neither tongue."

Dr. Polk shooed two large blowflies away from his face and then continued his account of the professor. "In the course of things, Church officials contacted the department chairman of Middle Eastern studies at the University of Utah and asked for a qualified scholar to do the translation. The department chairman suggested they approach my friend Sammi Hannia. At first, Sammi was skeptical about accepting the assignment. The only thing he knew about the Book of Mormon was the misinformation he was being fed by those enlightened scholars at the U of U. They told him it was a messed-up bit of nineteenth-century writing that was, in part, lifted from the Old and New Testaments. And, of course, when Sammi did a little background study on Joseph Smith and learned that he claimed that he had translated the Book of Mormon from gold plates, which were lent to him by an angel, you can imagine his delight to have the opportunity to translate the book into Arabic," Dr. Polk said sarcastically.

"Sammi also noted Joseph Smith's written comments that the book had originally been written in what Joseph termed Reformed Egyptian. The whole thing smacked of something that could only have originated on the frontier of America in the early nineteenth century.

"Naturally, he was not impressed with Joseph Smith's third-grade education. Basically, he was a little taken aback by the assignment to say the least. I mean, Dr. Hannia prides himself on being a man of letters and integrity. But I guess the grant the Church offered him to make the translation was sufficient for Dr. Hannia to at least take a look at the Book of Mormon and make a better judgment as to how he would proceed."

Dr. Polk smiled and added, "My old friend Thomas Kline, the deceased benefactor of our current project, understood that if you offer scholars enough money, most will take on any task, regardless of their own personal convictions. I don't know that this was the case, but it seems that Dr. Hannia accepted the challenge to translate the Book of Mormon because they had hired him for a fair amount of money. Hard to resist for most of us. Wait a second." Polk began to ease himself off the porch.

"I have a copy of his lecture on this experience, which he gave at Brigham Young University during a symposium there. I brought it and a couple of other things I want to share with you while we have a few minutes in our travels. Let me get it out of the Rover and read parts of it to you."

Polk groaned as he finally got to his feet, stiff from traveling. Then he moved smartly to the rear door of the Land Rover parked in front of the store. He returned with his wide briefcase in hand, kicking up dust as he walked. He stood in the narrow strip of shade cast by the porch roof, and laying his briefcase on the porch, he fished through a ream of paper to find the notes. At length, he pulled out the sought-after paper and pushed his reading glasses snugly against the bridge of his nose.

"You know, Dr. Polk," Roy said, finishing off his disgustingly warm Coke with a grimace, "you are the only person I've ever known who carries a portable library in a briefcase. There must be some kind of award for your type of performance in scholarship. You know, a sort of Academy Award for Instant Scholarship Retrieval."

Polk looked over the top of his reading glasses and smiled. "Young man, I take that as a compliment. Anyhow, here's Sammi's statement. Listen to this: 'When I began reading the Book of Mormon to acquaint myself with the book, I expected to find a very poorly written volume. I had been told by critics of the unschooled nature of the youthful Joseph Smith, who was purported to have translated the book.

"'What I found, however, was not a book of poor English; to the contrary, I found myself reading the most beautiful Semitic word structure I have ever read in English. I took pleasure in translating this book. Naturally, it wasn't long before I knew that I must join The Church of Jesus Christ of Latter-day Saints. This I did, and I now hold the office of elder in the Church.'" Stephen's thoughts flew to his own conversion and Anney's embittered response.

"Interesting, isn't it, Stephen," Polk went on, "how, if a true scholar comes along and really studies the Book of Mormon, one of two things usually happens? He either accepts it as the authentic book that it is and joins the Church, or he becomes confused and tries to find some way to reject the claims of its origin. Dr. Hannia saw the book for what it was.

"Sammi goes on to say this: 'There are some basic characteristics of the Semitic family of languages that Joseph Smith had to understand and use effectively to convince me that the Book of Mormon was a translation from words written by persons who originated in my native region of the world. In the 1820s, it was virtually an impossibility for anyone in the Americas to accomplish such a task. Why? Because there were no texts, schools of thought, or instructors to teach these important points that we will look at: First, Semitic writing is from right to left, not as the Indo-European writing which is left to right. Joseph Smith had not been told of this when he began translating the documents.

"'Second, in my language there are no capital letters. It is evident from my research that this was a puzzling problem for the scribes who sat at the elbow of Joseph Smith. The scribes simply had no guidance in how to transfer non-capitalized words in Semitic into a western style of writing. For example, Oliver Cowdery, one of the scribes, wrote Jerusalem *ger-Asulem*. The scribes made errors in the transcription due to this confusion.'"

Roy smiled as he fondly watched Polk reading aloud. It was the old professor-before-a-group-of-eager-students tone that crept into Polk's voice as he delivered the facts, totally oblivious to the heat and the flies.

"'Third, the written Semitic languages contain no paragraphing or punctuation. This became a problem for the printers who were confused and felt to advise Joseph Smith and his assistants that they needed to decide on paragraphing or punctuation to smooth out the wording. E. B. Grandin, the printer, who had nothing to do with the translation of the Book of Mormon, hired John H. Gilbert to spend a couple of weeks helping to edit the Book of Mormon manuscript. He liked adding commas, periods, and paragraphs. Joseph Smith and his assistants went along with Gilbert's editing suggestions.

"'Fourth, there are but two verb tenses in the Semitic languages—past and present. As Joseph Smith translated, he kept the original form of two tenses. This highlights the Semitic background of the book. And he also maintained the highly unusual form of compound verb usage such as *did eat, did fight, did shout.* Poor English grammar, excellent Semitic usage.'

"There are numerous examples of this in the Book of Mormon," Polk said emphatically as he looked up from his notes. "Here Dr. Hannia shows the necessity of using the word *and* in the proper sequence. If those 'ands' had been left out, it would have altered the meaning in many parts of the Book of Mormon."

Dr. Polk resumed reading Sammi's lecture notes: "'And what about the numbering system? Notice that when there is numbering of years or even places and things, it reads: And it came to pass that the *fifty and second* year ended in peace. All through the book this strange word construction in numbering appears. In English it would read, *fifty-second* year. No educated writer or translator would insert *and* between each digit.'

"Shall I go on?" Polk again glanced up from his notes. Noting that both of his companions were listening closely, he continued, "According to Sammi, the idioms are pure Semitic. He explains, 'Suffixes and prefixes are crucial to sentence development. Take a look and make an in-depth study as I have, and what do you find? I find a book more Semitic in language structure than Indo-European.'

"Dr. Hannia concluded that there was no way, not even today with all that is known by translators, that even a highly educated, Western writer-translator could have produced such a Semitic book in English. What is more, Joseph and his scribes maintained that the whole translation had been accomplished in less than seventy days.

"Impossible!" Polk exclaimed, letting his voice rise. The store owner, who leaned against the doorjamb, flipped his dirty, wet cloth at insects flying about. He wondered what the old man was reading to his young listeners. It was all in English.

"One could not in a hundred days get through thirty pages of original translating with all the tools that are available today without stumbling badly in the process. No, surely you fellows know that Joseph Smith lacked the scholarly skills needed to translate such a model of Semitic language usage into English. It wasn't just Joseph Smith who lacked the scholarship required at that time to complete such an ambitious undertaking. There was no one in America with that ability. Believe me." Polk sat down once again on the stoop and replaced the sheet of paper in his briefcase.

Roy looked over at Polk with a wide grin across his thin face and teased, "Do I detect a slight bias? You don't have to convince us that Joseph Smith lacked the skills to complete such a translation. But I'm too hot to get into a verbal battle about who did or how it was accomplished, short of an angel coming down and handing it to Joseph complete. You know, there may have been some other way to accomplish what Smith did. Give researchers enough time and they may surprise you."

"Roy, Roy, Roy. Thou art forever the questioning student who will not operate by anything except empirical evidence. Oh, Roy." Polk shook his head in exasperation while Stephen watched the interplay between the two highly accomplished scholars. He decided to remain silent and finish his Crush.

"By the way, Dr. Polk," Roy asked inquisitively, "what became of your friend Sammi?"

"Oh, he joined the Church, as I quoted in the beginning of the paper, of course."

"I mean, where is he now?"

"He lives in the Northwest, retired."

"And?" Roy already knew the answer to the question.

Dr. Polk shot Roy a look. He was silent for a long moment. Finally, he sighed and answered the question. "And he's alone. His wife was not pleased. As a matter of fact, she divorced him. He's a troubled man but still insists that joining the Church was the right move."

It came like a punch. A wave of the now-familiar nausea hit Stephen. Thoughts of his own situation and his dear family swept through his mind. The sickeningly sweet soda began churning in his stomach. He wasn't sure he could hold it down. Dr. Polk's reluctant comment brought back the turmoil he had endured with Anney for the past few months. The piercing thought that Anney and he might not make it seemed to rocket to the surface of his skull.

Dr. Polk watched Stephen with concern. He saw him flush and then turn deathly white, finally leaning his head down between his legs. *Why does this seem to happen to some who join the Church? They find the Lord only to lose their families. No wonder the Brethren discourage teaching and baptizing one spouse without the other. It just isn't fair. It isn't . . . Dear God, please help my friend Stephen.*

* * *

Katherine encouraged Heinrik to return to the hotel without them. She explained that she and Anney wanted to window shop in the old city, and that Reverend Moore needed him more than they did.

It had been a warm, wholesome visit with Anney's Aunt Elena. Katherine felt that it was just what Anney needed—to feel her roots and have someone she could mother, at least while they were in Prague. She had noticed a gradual change in Anney. She had seemed downcast for some time, but lately she had been even more withdrawn and depressed. She knew from Bob that Anney was thinking of leaving Stephen. *How could someone let a little thing like religious denomination destroy a marriage? Give up a person like Stephen? Unthinkable. I must talk to Anney about this.*

Heinrik dropped them at Wenceslas Square, where shops and vendors cluttered the streets. They would find a taxi to take them back to the hotel. The two started up Vladislavsky, stopping now and then to look at clothing or unusual crafts.

The aroma of freshly baked pastries wafted from the open door of a bakery and quickened their appetites.

Katherine stopped at the entrance to the tiny shop and looked at the pastry display in the window. Anney smiled and asked, "Shall we?"

They carried their small, waxed sacks of feather-light pastries down the street. Neither was interested in serious shopping. They casually strolled past the hordes of street vendors who blocked parts of the sidewalk with their small display tables and portable shops. Most of the merchandise was tacky but expensive. At the far end of Vladislavsky Street, Katherine spotted a park. The leaves were thick on the paths, and sunlight streamed through the almost bare branches. Fall had taken its glorious toll on the maple trees. Anney, always the Californian, hoped they would end the tour before severe winter weather made its blustery entrance.

"Do you mind if we sit here and talk for a few minutes?" Katherine asked, lowering herself onto a badly peeling, green wooden bench.

"Gladly," Anney agreed with a sigh. She pulled off one boot and wiggled her toes. "Ooh, why did I wear these boots? I knew they meant trouble."

"I think the hardest thing about being a tourist is the walking," Katherine said. "Funny, too, because I walk almost every morning on Nob Hill, down and up again. I think I walk perhaps two miles a day. But when I'm out like this, I get so weary. Maybe it's the shoes." Katherine pulled her collar tighter about her neck.

Then she looked over at Anney and smiled. "Can we talk?"

"Sure."

"I need to confide in you." Katherine rocked slightly as she spoke. It was a nervous habit that manifested itself when weighty problems arose in her life. She had tried since childhood to overcome it. "Your father is very dear to me, and I can't bear the thought of losing him."

"Losing him? What on earth are you talking about?"

"I'm talking about a getting-older lady who is deeply in love with a handsome, strikingly charming, popular man. I don't want to risk losing him."

"I don't see any danger of that happening. Has Dad said anything to cause you to be concerned? He certainly hasn't told me anything."

"No. You don't understand." Katherine rubbed her hands together and then pushed them deep into the pockets of her fur coat. "Your father is about to become a national televangelist. Oh, he doesn't know it, but tomorrow a film crew is scheduled to arrive from Los Angeles and record the Reverend Moore in action. I'm springing this on him. I have made arrangements through a public relations firm to promote your father and all that he is doing here, really promote him—nationally. It's expensive, but well worth it for a man with his talent and experience to become known throughout America. I will sponsor him on affiliated stations across the country."

"Wow!" Anney never seemed conscious of Katherine's wealth because she never flaunted her money. Understatement was her style. "Dad ought to be thrilled with such a plan!"

"I think he will be. I am also sure that he will be in great demand in a few months. In short, women will throw themselves at the great preacher. Mark my words, they will."

"So, you're afraid that he will lose interest in you? I don't think so. You don't need—"

"I need to marry your father now," Katherine interrupted tensely. "I mean in the next few days, or at most, in a week."

"You mean here, in Prague?"

"Well, I mean somewhere. I think we'll be in Krakow in a few days. Wherever. I don't care about the location. I want to marry him on this tour." Katherine pulled her right hand out of her pocket and reached over, took Anney's hand, and squeezed it. "Does this sound foolish?"

Anney felt a fondness for Katherine. She liked her humanness. She had felt a kinship since that day at the studio when Katherine had gone out of her way to meet "the daughter of the great Reverend Moore." There was a refreshing frankness about a lady who could have whatever she wanted and went after it like a heat-seeking missile launched from an F-16.

"What can I say?" Anney shrugged. "Are you asking my permission? I've already given you both my blessing. If you want to do it as soon as Dad gets back from San Francisco, that's fine with me."

"Anney . . . I guess I still haven't made myself clear on this whole thing."

"What do you mean?"

"I want *you* to ask your father for me. I want you to take him aside and tell him you want him to marry me—now. I know I sound like a ninny asking you to do this favor for me." Katherine suddenly had a concerned look on her cold cheeks. "You see . . . what if he says no? It is a real possibility. If he does say no, I can't handle the rejection. I know I can't. How well I know."

182
KEITH C. TERRY

A smile crossed Anney's wan face; her deep blue eyes, the color of glazed-blue porcelain, were suddenly alive. In spite of her own problems, she felt like a thirteen-year-old, plotting with her best friend. "Sure, I'll talk to him," she agreed. "As soon as he gets back."

Anney eased her miserable toes back into her boot and prepared to resume their stroll, when Katherine reached for her arm and held her back. She remained silent for a moment longer, then she said, "Thank you, sweetheart. I think I'm going to enjoy being your mother." Anney could see that Katherine had more on her mind.

There was a long pause; Katherine's body was rocking again. Finally, she began, "I want to say something else. This is not about me. Forgive me, I . . . since we are practically family, I hope you won't mind me asking you about Stephen."

Anney's lips quivered and she ducked her head down. *I can't talk about Stephen . . . I just can't.*

Katherine could see Anney struggling with her emotions, but she gathered her courage. Anney might not realize it, but she needed help from someone. "Do you know I have only seen him at a distance a couple of times at your father's studio, and those times were only while your father was delivering his sermons? But I was so impressed with him. I look forward to getting to know him."

Anney drew a deep breath. "I . . . really, I don't think there is a lot to talk about. You surely know that Stephen and I . . . well . . . we're not getting along, and I'm sure you know why." There was a defensiveness to Anney's tone that was not lost on Katherine.

"Tell me anyway," Katherine said gently. "I want you to tell me. I don't want to be left out of the loop. I know you may think me pushy, but I do care about you and your family."

There was something compelling about Katherine. She expected people to respond to her requests. Anney studied her future mother for a minute and then looked off in the distance, seeing nothing. Slowly, bit-by-bit, she found herself pouring out her anguished thoughts to Katherine. She rehearsed all the troubling months of summer and fall that she had endured with Stephen and his obsession with Mormonism. She covered the latest, down to her last, bitter phone conversation with him. It was all out, though Anney had a feeling Katherine already knew most of what she related. But even her father had not been privy to the depths of her anger. Anney had been too distraught to confide in anyone about her blowup with Stephen the night before last.

"The phone call was . . . terrible. Earlier, in Berlin, I felt such a surge of goodwill and love toward my husband and son that I decided not to bring up the subject. Stephen probably thought I had given in to his new religion.

"Then, right after I got back from Berlin, Decker warned me that there is legal action pending against the group Stephen works for . . . and maybe against Stephen himself. I guess I just saw red. When he called me from Miami that evening, I had turned into my witchiest self. I was hateful and resentful of what he was doing to our family. My anger was out of control, so I let him have it." Anney was shivering, wiping her uncontrollable tears with a napkin from the bakery.

Katherine's eyes narrowed as Anney mentioned Decker's shared information. The man was altogether too smooth in her estimation. And what connections did he have that would provide him with inside information about Stephen's activities? Even if it were true, why would he tell Anney so coldly?

She slid her hand under Anney's arm and squeezed it affectionately. Anney was not looking for sympathy. "When I pretended to be cheerful in Berlin," she continued haltingly, "I felt that I had been untrue to myself and to what was right. I guess I thought I could get around the problem by remaining silent. Then when Stephen called, I somehow had to be ruthlessly honest and let him know I was upset. At that very minute, I was angry to the point of wanting him out of my life. That's where this whole mess is right now."

Anney stared down at the tall boots she had worn against the drizzle that had crept across Prague earlier in the day. There was stillness in the fresh fall air, though people scurried by, carrying leather and plastic bags stuffed with breads and cheeses, cheap clothing, and produce.

The two women sat contemplating the words Anney had just spoken. Then Katherine leaned toward Anney and sighed with the experience born of a few added years. "Okay, so maybe this is exactly how it goes down in real life. You've certainly confirmed my fears—but nothing in life is worth sacrificing a good man." Katherine's head shook as she spoke. "I'm just not plugged into some of the murky things that happen in relationships."

"I didn't say that our relationship is murky," Anney protested.

"No, but it is. I'm old-fashioned and I know it. Let me say this much. Then, if you wish, I'll drop the subject from here on out." Katherine's red lips were pressed tightly together as she mustered up the necessary nerve to advise someone who was seemingly unwilling to take advice. "Anney, you may have to change your mind-set. This is a fact of life. Many women have done it before you. Whatever you do in your relationship with Stephen, I beg you to deal gracefully with the problem. You can, you know. You certainly can. Make up your mind to one very important fact: It will be up to you and not Stephen to resolve this issue between you."

Startled, Anney peered keenly at Katherine's face, which glowed with a luminous quality. In spite of herself, she considered what Katherine had said. She let the words sift through her burdensome thoughts and realized that perhaps there was wisdom in Katherine's advice.

"This morning when I awoke," Katherine went on, "and knew your father was returning from San Francisco, chills spread over my body. I shivered like a young bride-to-be. Anney, you have to get back that kind of feeling about Stephen. You have to. And what's more, you can, honey. You can."

"I don't know . . . I hurt deep inside and the thing just keeps on raging. I feel like Stephen made a conscious choice. He weighed his family against his new beliefs, and he chose the religion. I guess that is what hurts the most. I feel rejected. He even said as much . . . that he couldn't give up the truths he has accepted, not even for me." Anney's shoulders shook with silent sobs; she bit down on her lip to keep from crying aloud. Katherine hugged her close, her heart breaking for this troubled young woman.

Finally, Anney pushed out the words, "Oh, I still feel a desire for Stephen. I'm so anxious for real life to begin again. I'm so anxious that it hurts. Do you realize that sometimes the reality of life is so cruel? It just bites and bites and bites. There is no letup. That's why I couldn't keep from being ruthlessly honest with Stephen and letting him know that he has to pay the consequences for the way he has walked out on his family."

"Walked out?"

"Well, not literally . . . but he might as well have."

"Anney, it's time to begin to put this whole thing in perspective. Stephen loves you. Even I can see that from my vantage point. Wake up, honey, and figure out a solution. As far as Decker's revelation goes, I don't see how he could know anything like that. I wouldn't give it another thought.

"Anney, the price of your pride is too high if it means losing the love of your life. As I said, it's up to you, not Stephen."

CHAPTER 14
Book of Mormon Lands

Oaxaca

"Over here, Dr. Thorn!"

Stephen was standing at the curb on the corner of the magnificently shaded plaza with bougainvillea and hibiscus flowering in a canopy of jungle-like vegetation among low-limbed breadnut trees. He could hear the sound of wild parakeets in the trees above the din of taxis and buses.

Stephen turned about when he heard Dr. Polk's voice behind him. Looking in the direction of a sidewalk café, he saw his friend seated at a round table with three men Stephen had not yet met. One was at least fifty years of age; the other two looked to be students. These must be the guys Dr. Polk wanted him to meet. Stephen made long strides toward the group. *Yep, these have got to be the Princeton geographers.* Stephen chuckled to himself, sure that Dr. Polk had addressed him as "doctor" just to impress the men at the table.

"Dr. Thorn, come over here and take a seat. I want you to meet these gentlemen."

Stephen reached out and shook hands with each of the three men as Dr. Polk introduced them. "This is Dr. William Morrison, full professor of geography at Princeton." Gesturing to the younger men, he went on, "And meet his two assistants, Ephraim Johnson and Doug Turner, who are currently working on their doctoral degrees at Princeton. Be seated, everyone. At last we meet."

Stephen appraised the scholars as he pulled out his chair and sat down. He was curious about what sort of fellows could be fired up about geography, particularly in their youth. Doug was about twenty-three, of average height, with muscular shoulders and a deep tan. *Looks more like a lifeguard than a scientist.* Ephraim looked to be a little older. He was a tall, thin African-American, with piercing black eyes and an all-business demeanor.

"Dr. Thorn," the Princeton professor said, "it is a pleasure to meet you. Dr. Polk here has been telling us that you are also working with him on this project." Stephen could hear a slight Bostonian accent.

"That's right. This is my first trip down here to see the area and the ruins and, of course, to meet with you gentlemen. I'm full of questions, so I hope you don't find me too naive in these matters. My training is not in this field of study at all."

"Oh," Professor Morrison responded with surprise. "Where did you do your graduate work and in what field?"

"I got my doctorate at Berkeley in the 1970s, after all the demonstrations on campus. I majored in a field that seems to have no bearing on my present assignment—public relations. I have been working in an entirely different field of—"

"It's much too long a story for Stephen to explain at the present time." Dr. Polk cut him off in a warm, friendly way, but Stephen could sense that he did not want the men to know about his recent work in televangelism. Stephen smiled amiably and nodded in agreement.

"What I'm here for now," Stephen asserted, "is to get some sort of handle on the Book of Mormon geography, and I understand from Dr. Polk that you fellows have—"

"Café, señor?" a voice interrupted at Stephen's back. Stephen looked over his shoulder and smiled, and then waved away the waiter.

"Un momento. Cinco minutos. Está bien?" Dr. Polk answered. In the years he had been traveling in Mexico, he had learned enough Spanish to enable him to get around easily.

The dark, youthful waiter bowed and backed away.

"It is my understanding," Stephen said, "that the three of you have been at this study for nearly six months, along with your normal duties. Is that right?"

"Yes, we have," the dark-eyed Ephraim answered with quiet self-assurance. "We have been with Dr. Morrison on this project from the beginning."

"As I explained to you, Stephen," Polk interjected, "these researchers have made some interesting inroads on the geography of the Book of Mormon." Turning to Morrison, he suggested, "Why don't you give Stephen here a quick overview of what your assignment was and what you have accomplished so far. You'll like this, Dr. Thorn."

Dr. Morrison began explaining to Stephen what Polk had already learned in earlier telephone briefings. Polk had hired Morrison to research and attempt to locate the lands of a people in a document that Polk had disguised. With some alterations in names and sentence structure, Polk had printed sections of the Book of Mormon with no reference to indicate the identity of the material. It was similar to the unmarked manuscripts the presenters had worked from last summer at the estate when Stephen and his group were searching for internal evidences of the Book of Mormon.

For anyone not familiar with the Book of Mormon, it was difficult to know the origin of the document. Morrison had accepted the assignment and stipend. He, in turn, had employed his two assistants to help with the task. Morrison paused, took a sip of his amber-colored wine, and then launched into a twenty-minute recital of the methods and results of his search for the location described in the history he had received in manuscript form.

"It's interesting what we did with the assignment we had. You see, Dr. Polk was rather cagey about the people in the account he gave us. At first, I felt that the manuscript was a bit jumbled. We spent two months, as time allowed, highlighting every facet of geography and movement of the people and armies in the manuscript. In time, we narrowed our ponderous search strictly to specific topographical features mentioned in the document. Dr. Polk had told us that the location was somewhere in the western hemisphere. That narrowed it down some."

Morrison revealed how they had created a model on a large three-by-five-foot transparent sheet and charted names and places in relationship to one another.

"Needless to say, it was not easy," grumbled Doug, the tan fellow.

"No, it certainly was not," Dr. Morrison agreed. "We had to refer constantly to the document. We soon decided that the best approach would be to devise some logical system of charting settlements, rivers, and other bodies of water, landmarks that were indicated, hills, and where possible, mountains. We assumed that the directions indicated in the manuscript were true to the compass. In arriving at a system, we began to write terms that showed geographical relationships.

"In other words, we would give a detailed description of each city. We went on like this for weeks, making our commentaries and beginning to create on paper a model of just how extensive the terrain would need to be to accommodate the distances described in the manuscript.

"It amazed us that we were about to confine most of the geographical features we had to work with into an area the size of Southern California, from Santa Barbara on the north to San Diego on the south. In fact, we even considered our mystery location to be Southern California. That didn't pan out. There was no east or north sea, and a few other topographical features were missing, such as a north-flowing river.

"We discovered that whoever wrote the text we had been given, which we now know to be the Book of Mormon, had a first-hand knowledge of events and places. In some cases, the writers were observers, or persons who had received reports or found records. All of this was carefully compiled into our database. For example, when the text referred to 'up,' 'down,' 'over,' and such, these were indications of elevation. That was important. Some things did appear to be ambiguous, but for the most part we soon had a working knowledge of terms to use in our model.

"I'll cut this short by simply saying that one of our major problems was establishing distance. How far was it from the narrow neck of land to the Hill Shim? There was no textual reference to 'miles.' We knew that they traveled on foot. Therefore, unless the army moved at route step, they likely traveled at say, three miles an hour. We assigned a slower speed when they traveled from one point to another with women and children along. A messenger would travel at perhaps twice the speed of a large company of people. The environment and terrain would have influenced travel as well—things such as forests, swamps, mountains, and so forth. All of this we had to compute.

"We came up with an amazing systems model of the general configuration of the region we were looking for. Give or take a few high miles, we felt certain, after five months of study and entering pertinent information into the computer, that our entire region could not encompass more than a thousand miles from end to end, and two hundred to four hundred miles from side to side. We already knew that the side-to-side configuration had to have an east sea and a north sea. That really restricted our location.

"So we had specialists in graphics design us three transparent models indicating settlements, passes, hills, a river, many waters, and wilderness. We came up with a startling definition. We had a misshapen hourglass configuration that had to fit somewhere in the western hemisphere.

"We began sliding our model across a mockup map." The professor's face contorted in an unaccustomed grin. He lowered his voice conspiratorially. "We thought about renting a small warehouse to lay out a huge map of the western hemisphere, but we refined it to scale."

"We already knew that there were few areas with a narrow neck of land," Ephraim explained. "Because of its configuration, Central America became a prime target. We moved our transparency along the region of southern Mexico and Guatemala where it seemed nearly a perfect match. But to be sure that we had covered all possibilities, we tried it on every square inch of the Western Hemisphere.

"Again we moved our pattern back to Central America. It looked better and better, but what proofs did we have? We decided to select one landmark that was perhaps unique to the area because of its description. We focused on the one river the document mentioned, the River Sidon. We assumed it had tributaries, but that the tributaries either had the same name as the main river or were simply not mentioned. Our study narrowed to the hydrology of the document."

Dr. Morrison cleared his throat, signaling that he had charge of this report. With a deep, confident tone, he continued the tale. "We knew from the text that the single river flowed from a mountain region in a northerly path to the sea. The current had to be strong enough to carry dead soldiers who were dumped into the river to the sea, yet not so deep and swift that armies could not ford it. We discovered that in all the western hemisphere, there are only two rivers that flow in a northerly direction with the proper water flow to meet our needs. Both were located in southern Mexico. On assumption that one of these two rivers was the only plausible, actual, physical match, we felt sure that we had found the primary site we were searching for. We noted that there are extensive geographical descriptions, interrelated references, and physical details recognizable on modern topographical maps that fit the description of our manuscript's location.

"After due consideration for other likely locations, failing to find anything as revealing as the one we had settled on, we now hypothesize that the physical location of our river lies in the southernmost part of the Mexico-Guatemala frontier, northward from the Continental Divide to the upper end of the Chiapas Central Depression, which flows into the delta region located along the coast of the Gulf of Mexico. We firmly stand by this discovery. We are prepared to demonstrate our findings with charts, maps, and video recordings of the topographical features to show conclusively that we know approximately the location of the principal cities, nations, and confines of the document we were given."

* * *

It had been one of those restless nights that Anney had come to dread. This time, Stephen was not the focus of concern. It was her Aunt Elena who dominated her thoughts. She had longed for morning to come quickly. When it finally did, she dressed and was in a cab headed for her aunt's apartment, where she arrived by eight o'clock.

Anney felt uneasy about arriving too early. Then she remembered that older people tend to rise early, so maybe it would be okay to get there at this hour. She couldn't wait. There was something compelling about Aunt Elena. Anney needed to talk. She wanted to talk without anyone else around. Of course, she could have continued a long conversation with her aunt in Ukrainian the day before with Katherine and Heinrik present, but somehow it was not the same as being completely alone with her aunt. Besides, Anney wanted to take her shopping and buy her a few things, as long as the items weren't too expensive. She had noticed that there was little food in her aunt's cupboards. Aunt Elena's apartment was sparsely furnished with a few well-worn pieces of furniture. When the young family had moved out, she had been generous in sharing her belongings with them. She had scrimped for years to buy her treasured television set.

Elena was up and dressed, hair in braids and knotted at the back of her head, when she answered Anney's knock. The two hugged for a long while, and once again Elena cried, repeating over and over that she thought she had been dreaming the day before when Anney had come. She kept repeating how beautiful Anney looked, and how wonderful it was that they could talk to each other in their family tongue.

Fresh tears flowed as Elena spoke of her sister being dead. "Ah, all the night I thought of Nadia. We thought when we parted that we would one day be together again. We were young. The war was over, and we were so full of hope. Now my dear Nadia is gone." Anney held her aunt close, her own emotions tender as she shared the forlorn little woman's grief.

Later, Anney sat at the small dining table as Elena poured tea through a strainer into the small porcelain cup decorated with tiny pink flowers. "I drink only herbal tea now. You know the real tea is bad for you. That's what President Winder has told all of us who had bad habits drinking tea."

Anney patted Elena's hand as Elena placed the teapot on the table pad and sat down in the straight-backed, hardwood chair, ready to converse. "Do you know, Daddy and I have not cleaned out my mother's closet?" Anney said, hoping her aunt would not begin crying again. The language seemed to flow much smoother than the day before. "Her clothes have been hanging there for years." Elena now knew that her sister had been in a convalescent home for years. "You two are the same size. I know the clothes are old, but they are still in good repair. I called my father, who is in San Francisco this week, and asked him to pack the nicer things and bring them back here when he returns today. He said he would."

"Oh, oh. I would love to wear Nadia's clothes. What a kind thing for you to do."

Anney did not mention how her father had grumbled about leaving downtown San Francisco, driving out to Concord, and then packing things into two large suitcases, plus the extra cost for excess luggage on the flight. Anney had suggested that between his ticket and Decker's, perhaps the weight would not be considered excess. "It will be," he said before hanging up. Though he did tell Anney how pleased he was that she had found her mother's sister.

"How did you survive all these years? And who were you talking about just now when you said President someone?"

"I worked. When I returned from Berlin—on foot, mind you—your grandfather was still alive, but barely. He died six months after I arrived here at this apartment He died in that bedroom." Elena pointed toward the open door to the only bedroom leading off the small living room. "I got a job in a bakery. In time, I worked up to counter lady, and then I became cashier. I worked there until a few years ago. Now I live off my small pension. Oh, but it is not much. You know with the new government, it is not the same. We had more benefits for the old people under the communists. The hospitals, bread, and milk were practically free." She shook her head slightly as she spoke. "But I would not want to go back. Other things are better now. What did you ask me a moment ago?"

"Oh, about someone you called 'president.' It's not important. How is life better now?"

"Ah . . . that is easy to answer. I can be a good church member. I can go to my church over in Svermuv on the Metro every Sunday and be with those wonderful people. My neighbor, Banska, goes with me every Sunday, even though she is not a Mormon."

Mormon! The shock of what Elena had uttered was so startling that she could not form proper words in Ukrainian to ask if she meant she was a Mormon. The language completely escaped her grasp for a moment. *This can't be.* She knew that she had clearly heard the word "Mormon" . . . that Elena was a Mormon, but response failed her.

Elena looked puzzled at her niece's reaction. "What did I say to startle you?" She thought for a moment, then said, "Is it that I'm a Mormon? Does this trouble you? It is true. Also, it is the reason I do not want communism to return."

Anney was finally able to reorder her process of speech. At length, she responded to the startling news. "You are a Mormon?"

"Yes, I have been a member of the Church since 1948. I wrote your mother and told her. Did she not tell you?"

"I wasn't born until 1954," Anney said gently. "I do remember my mother telling me about some of the things in your letters when I was a teenager, but nothing specific."

"Yes, I joined the Mormons. Two very handsome young missionaries came right to this door and spoke with me. I was on my way home from work and was about to open my front door when they came up and told me that they would like to tell me about a prophet and that they had apostles, just as they did in the time of Christ. I sensed that there was something familiar about them. Then I asked them if they knew whether their church had given away food at the end of World War II. They didn't know. I asked them if they knew the name Benson. They said that Ezra Taft Benson was an apostle. I somehow knew that those young men were part of the same good people that helped the starving Berliners after the war. I told them to come in and get warm, even though I was tired after working all day. I told them, as I let them into the apartment, that I had my own church, but they were welcome to come in and have a cup of tea and get warm."

Elena's voice softened with the memory, "Maybe it was the cold. I don't know. Those two young men were nearly blue from being out all day. Oh, they had overcoats, but it was late January and I felt sorry for them being out in the cold, so I invited them in for tea—real tea. They refused my tea but said they would enjoy a hot cup of water. I fed them hot milk and rolls that I had brought home from the bakery. I always had day-old rolls in the house. They ate all of my rolls." Elena smiled at the memory flashing through her mind.

"When they finished the rolls and hot milk, one of them, Elder Tingey, had already explained to me as fast as he could about the Prophet Joseph Smith. He just bubbled as he told me about the Church. Then his companion, Elder Winder—such fine, fine-looking young men. Oh, my. I was young too, but not so young as they. Elder Winder asked me if they could return and tell me more about their church. I liked them, so I said yes."

"So, what happened?" Anney asked, having gained her speech and composure, still unable to fathom how the Mormons could reach so far from Utah and prick her very life in a distant foreign land. She was eager to know if her Aunt Elena's reaction to Mormonism had been similar to Stephen's.

"It took me six months before I consented to be baptized in the Vleta River. It was summer, and the water was pleasant. Then the communists came and drove those young men out of Czechoslovakia. For over forty years, I heard very little of the Church. Then, after the communists fled, the missionaries came back. Elder Winder had become head of the mission, and he came to see me. He was still a handsome man. Older, but handsome. He had a lovely wife who could not speak the language, but so sweet and pretty. They came right here to my apartment and met with me and invited me to come out to a church meeting. Now we have a wonderful building. At one time, it was a hotel, but they have completely repaired and built more rooms onto it. It's a wonderful place where I go for church meetings." Elena's eyes started to water and her thin lips quivered as she fought back the emotions. "I went to the temple in Germany with other members. I'm so pleased to have the Church. They are all so good to me . . . to be sure I have enough food and fuel."

Anney forgot about taking her aunt shopping. She was still stunned and tense, trying to follow the meaning of her aunt's words. She probed her for more information about her conversion. The thought that she should tell Aunt Elena that Stephen was also a Mormon kept hounding her, but she refused to divulge the information. *If I tell Aunt Elena about Stephen, she will want to know why I am not a member, too.* Anney was not prepared to voice her objections about a religion that was obviously precious to this dear little person. Not yet, at least.

CHAPTER 15
The Mission President

Prague

"We leave for Krakow tomorrow morning," Decker announced with everyone seated in the conference room of the Hotel Karlova. "I dread the production glitches I'm sure we will find. Oh, well. Everybody needs to cooperate and give it your best. Krakow is an ancient city with lots of charm . . . and lots of bureaucracy, too."

Decker looked directly into the camera's lens as he spoke to the crew operating the equipment. "I'm sure you boys will be able to make the most of filming, especially since you have all of your own equipment. Be sure to update your equipment inventory now. Immigration will ask for all kinds of information at the border. You can be sure of that." Decker looked into the blinding lights at the silhouettes of the camera crew who had arrived that morning from Hollywood, courtesy of Katherine, who was beaming from the edge of the group.

They had set up their equipment immediately and were filming the briefing session, which was the start of the documentary they would record throughout the remainder of the tour. There were five people in the crew, all American.

Katherine had taken charge of supervising the continuous recording of all events and activities. She wanted it to be ongoing, morning, noon, and night. They could always edit out unsuitable material. As she had told Anney, Katherine had arranged to sponsor the special that would be telecast in early January across America on dozens of affiliated Christian stations.

When she and Bob met at the airport the day before, she had sprung her little public-relations surprise on him. Bob was elated with the gift—a rather expensive gift, he thought. Decker, who was filled in later about the surprise documentary crew, had some reservations. He had told Bob in the men's room at the Jiri restaurant, where the entire entourage went for lunch, that he must insist on complete control of everything on film or sound. "We have to be able to edit this thing so you look good."

"Decker," Bob said with a smile and a raised eyebrow, wiping his hands on the warm terry-cloth towel a female rest room attendant had handed to him, "I always look good on camera. And, my good man, don't forget that." Decker felt the barb. He was uneasy at the increasing position Katherine was assuming—not only in Bob's personal life, but in his business as well. Decker had shrugged. He had more immediate problems with the staff, and he knew he had to stay in the good graces of Katherine, as much as he hated it.

In the briefing room, Heinrik had gone into overload under the frenetic challenge of interpreting for everyone at the same time. The other interpreter had quit. He had walked out under the stress of working with such "demanding Americans." Heinrik's round face and popping eyes were outward manifestations of a frustrated man. When he protested the impossibility of being the sole interpreter, Katherine overheard his outburst and advised him to find another young man or woman to help him with the translating. She would pay the going price, but since they were headed for Krakow in the morning, could he survive for one more day? He wished that he could clone himself. One good Polish interpreter was all he needed in Krakow. He would find another, perhaps, in Warsaw the following week.

Decker continued his briefing to the entire entourage. Even the Reverend Moore sat front and center, providing excellent shots of an attentive minister. The crew could see the guy manning the Ikegami camera as it cranked out long segments of taping. They knew that this latest equipment enhanced skin-tone detail, that it was a sort of electronic airbrushing camera that removed undesirable blemishes, imperfections, and even age lines for a more youthful and healthier television appearance. Presto! Bob looked even greater than real life.

Bob did allow his assistant to lead out—something rare to witness for those who had known him for years. "Now then," Decker concluded, "this gives us this evening free for a little relaxation. Actually, I'm going to bed. And from the looks of you camera people, you may want to rest up as well. The jet lag must be getting to you."

A bearded, ponytailed, thirty-year-old from Hollywood shouted from behind the camera, "Don't worry about us, sir. We want to go wherever you'll let us while you're relaxing. We'd like to get the whole thing on film. Our job is to keep the cameras rolling."

Decker shrugged nonchalantly. "Suit yourself."

As the group broke up, Anney pulled her father aside and, in a coy manner, asked him if he had time to go for a short walk with her. The air would do them good. Bob knew this was Anney's way of getting alone with him. He also realized that Anney did not want Katherine along. As a matter of fact, he had watched Katherine slip out a moment earlier. He knew she had little interest in the details of travel and thought nothing of it. Anney knew that Katherine had left so that she and her father could, in fact, be alone together to have a little chat.

Bob wondered if Anney's request had to do with Stephen. He hoped not. He was not in a frame of mind to discuss the decline of their marriage.

Out on the street the sun was growing hazy in the late afternoon sky, making red-orange slices through the tall trees along the busy street. Taxis and buses and a few private cars, honking and screeching, sped by on their way up the avenue. The noise level forced Anney to speak louder than usual, and even though she spoke in English, she looked around uncomfortably at those passing by to see if anyone was paying attention to their conversation. As they walked, she presented to her father Katherine's wish to be married immediately.

"When?" Bob blurted out as if he had indigestion.

"Well, maybe when we get to Krakow. Is that okay? Oh, and Daddy, she wants a church wedding, not some civil quickie. She wants to feel like a young bride all over again." Anney held her father's right arm with both of her gloved hands and leaned against him as she had as a child when he sometimes took her shopping. Her mother had never enjoyed shopping in downtown San Francisco.

Anney gradually came to realize that her mother was embarrassed by her poor grasp of English. She never really mastered the language and was uncomfortable confronting what, to her, amounted to a foreign environment.

Bob responded, "I'm flattered that she wants to get married right now, but sweetheart, I'm booked every hour of every day we will be in Krakow. Do you have any idea how many people want to see me? There are ministers coming up from Hungary and over from the Ukraine. Some will come down from St. Petersburg to get an early orientation to what they need to do to prepare for my coming. By the way, when those people from the Ukraine come, I'll need you to help with translating."

"I know, and believe me, I don't mind working. It's just that I think we can squeeze in a few hours for a wedding. I'll help with all the arrangements."

"Uhmm . . . I don't know. Heaven only knows I love Katherine, but we have this thing all set for New Year's Eve back in San Francisco. All of our friends will be there. We'll even have the governor of California at the wedding. That would be a real complement to the service."

"Daddy, come on. This is your personal life. You're not marrying the governor. Who cares? It can be a very private wedding in a large cathedral. And, of course, we'll want to film it. With your influence, I'm sure there is a church that will allow a private wedding. Besides, Katherine will pay to use the building. She told me she would. We talked about how it can all be pulled off in Krakow this weekend."

"Are you insane? This weekend!" Bob pulled away from Anney long enough to look at her before she snuggled back to his upper arm. "Besides, why isn't Katherine talking to me about this wedding deal? Are you suddenly some kind of matchmaker?"

"I don't care what you call me. I think you two should get married, and the sooner you do, the happier you'll make your bride."

"I've gotta think about this." Moore considered the situation.

"Daddy, it's simple. Do you love Katherine?"

"Sure."

"Then marry her. Please. I told her I could talk you into it. If I go back to the hotel and tell her that you said no, I swear she will pack up and be on the first flight to Paris."

"Why Paris?"

"Because she will be so upset, she will spend a week buying clothes and drowning herself in expensive French perfume."

"You really think she would leave if I simply said, 'Let's wait until we get back home—as we both agreed to do—and plan the wedding for New Year's Eve?' What is so unreasonable about that?"

"You're not a woman, Daddy. Boy, are you not a woman."

Bob furrowed his brow. He knew well that if he let Katherine slip through the cracks simply because he was too busy to marry her, he was certain to lose in both the short and the long run. He would be back to the struggling televangelist he had been for the past thirty years, trying to make enough each month to pay the cost of expensive productions and his own chosen lifestyle. Marriage to Katherine would be his insurance against a repeat of the good ol' lean days. He was ready for marriage, especially to one so rich.

"Film it, huh? Mmmm . . . that might add a nice touch to the television special." *Then . . . not only our friends in San Francisco, but millions will view the wedding.*

They had reached the end of the block, and Bob took Anney by the waist as if he were waltzing with her and turned her back toward the hotel. Then he stopped, pulled Anney around in front of him, and throwing back his head, letting his gray mane sweep to the rear, he laughed out loud. Then he said in clear English for anyone within ten feet to hear, "Tell me, why am I fighting this? If you two can come up with a church that suits the occasion—and it has to look good on camera—I'm game. That's what you want me to say, isn't it?" Bob was game, all right.

* * *

Kline and Hadley had made their move in court the day before—filing criminal charges against Dr. Peter Polk and Dr. Stephen Thorn. Hadley was confident. He blamed the failure of last summer's injunction on Kline's former attorney, of course. Having scrutinized the trust, line by line, and with solid dope on Polk's careless, from-the-hip methods of authorizing expenditures, he was sure he had them on mismanagement of funds, if not outright fraud.

The key to the charges was a provision requiring board approval of expenditures. Craig's sister Marjorie had confirmed that Dr. Polk had not called a meeting of the trust foundation that had been set up. One of the provisions of the trust was a quarterly meeting of the trustees: Dr. Peter Polk, Marjorie Kline Biddle, William Bennett, Markham Quail, and Delitra Kline Kimble. As chair of the foundation, Marj had reluctantly agreed to do whatever Craig wanted.

"Well, Polk played it by the seat of his pants and he got caught," Craig laughed. "The old boy is in trouble now. What will happen next, Chet?"

"Well, if the court agrees in the next few days, we can shut this thing down. I don't mean we will simply put a clamp on the spending; we will take over these projects and bring them to a halt," Hadley declared.

"When they get back from Mexico, they're going to be in for a real surprise," Kline grinned maliciously. "If all goes as planned, they will be arrested. There's nothing like a little charge of fraud to get a guy's attention."

"Well, let's not celebrate yet," Hadley cautioned. "Just make sure your sister Marj doesn't back out on the deal. It won't fly unless the chair of the board presses charges, and the majority backs her up."

"Don't worry about Marj. I've always been able to get her to sign things and go along with me on just about everything."

"What about your sister Delitra? You mentioned to me the other day that she didn't want the family name dragged through the courts. How are you going to get her to go along with it? It's already headed for the courtroom."

"That's okay. We'll have the board dismiss Polk or face court proceedings. Marj and Delitra will be on our side; Bennett will be on Polk's; and the other fellow, Quail, will vote with my side of the family. He's Marj's godfather, after all. He'll do what I recommend through Marj." Craig slapped his hands together with a loud pop. "We've got him this time."

"I'm a little curious," Hadley looked pensive. "Why didn't your father put you on the board along with your sisters?"

Craig's face darkened with anger. He knew the answer but was not about to reveal it to Hadley. His father hated him, that's why. He knew his father had been fearful of what he would do if he were a member of the board. He had always been frank with his father about the waste of money the Book of Mormon projects would be. Of course he would have tied the thing up in knots at the outset if he had been named to the board. Craig turned from meeting Hadley's questioning eyes and glowered at the city from his vantage point twenty stories in the sky. "I'll tell you why. Dad and I didn't see eye to eye. He didn't want me there. That's it."

* * *

Reluctance permeated every cell in Anney's being as she trudged alongside her aunt Elena. She would never have come on her own. They had taken the Metro because Elena had insisted that she must travel as the people in her station in life travel. "Only the rich ride in taxies," she explained to Anney.

They had been able to communicate very well, on the whole. Since Anney had been taught Ukrainian as an infant and always spoke in Ukrainian to her mother while growing up, she was able to hold her own. It was easier to understand her aunt if she spoke slowly. Anney had difficulty conjugating her verbs because it had been so many years since she had spoken the language, but she found herself understanding almost everything Elena uttered. Aunt Elena's voice and inflection were nearly identical to her mother's.

She had finally revealed to her aunt that her husband, Stephen, had joined the Mormon Church and that she was troubled by his actions. When she asked her aunt to enlarge on several points of doctrine, the little woman had protested with all her might. "No, no, no," she had exclaimed. "I could never tell it the right way. I would only confuse you. You must speak to the mission president. He will answer all of your questions."

Aunt Elena had held Anney's hands and peered into her eyes for a long moment. "Dear Anney," she began with a husky voice, "for me, the Mormons are like family. I love the Church. Without the Church, I would not have been able to endure these many years without family." She had paused again, considering her niece's concerns. "Why do you dislike the Mormons? Have you been wronged by someone of my church?"

A memory of Chip streaked through Anney's mind. Chip was the only Mormon she had ever really known personally. Had he wronged her? She had loved him, she remembered, at least she thought so when she was in college . . . until he tried to interest her in his church. Really, his attitude was pretty much the same as Stephen's, that his beliefs were the most important thing in his life. He had told her that her father's television ministry was basically an ego trip for him . . . that what he preached was a "feel-good" religion. How angry she had been!

Anney began to feel something akin to terror as they walked toward the Mormon mission headquarters. *Why did I agree to come here? I can't just confront this man with his false doctrines. I should have kept quiet about Stephen's baptism. I'll tell Aunt Elena that I don't feel well. It's absolutely true . . . I don't feel well at all.*

Anney was suddenly aware that Aunt Elena had stopped and was tugging at her arm. "We are here, dear. This is the mission home where you will see our good president. Come inside, and you will see how kind he is." Aunt Elena beamed as she gently pushed Anney up the stairs to a wide front door.

The reed-like receptionist had golden-blond curls. Her complexion was creamy white, startlingly clear, her cheeks naturally rosy.

"Hi, I'm Sister Brighton," she said with a warmth and sincerity that took Anney off guard. She was obviously American. Anney wondered if most of the people here in the building were American. Sister Brighton also welcomed Elena in Czech.

"The president is expecting you, Mrs. Thorn."

"Do you mind if my aunt waits out here? I would like to talk with him alone."

"Of course not," the girl smiled. "I know your aunt. She comes to church here. We'll have a nice visit."

Sister Brighton, sensing that Mrs. Thorn was ill at ease and wanting to make her feel welcome, chatted with Anney for a moment longer. She asked where in the States she was from and if she was staying with her aunt here in Prague?

While the receptionist conversed with them, the dark mahogany door opened from within and a very tall, graying man of not more than fifty stepped out. He recognized Elena and spoke with her in

Czech. Sister Brighton introduced Anney to the president, who greeted her in English.

As soon as the small talk ended, President Berkeley excused himself to Elena and invited Anney into his office. Elena touched the man's arm and looked anxiously at Anney. "President Berkeley, my niece is not Mormon. She has come to ask you some questions. Her heart is heavy and troubled. She will explain it to you in English. I will let her tell you . . . then maybe we can talk. Okay?"

Berkeley nodded. He stepped into his office behind Anney and asked her to be seated at a table near a glowing fireplace.

Regardless of the warm reception of Sister Brighton, Anney reminded herself that she had passed over into the enemy camp. As a child, she had gone to a house of horror with friends. She felt that same anxiety now. She chided herself mentally. Why was she not more rational in this matter? These were normal, friendly people. Why did she feel as if something would seize her very thoughts? It made no sense.

The room was large and well heated. There was a decidedly American atmosphere to the arrangement of the furnishings. Beyond the table and chairs, there was a wall of books. Anney felt certain that all of them, in some way, pertained to Mormonism.

She sat down and took a second look at the man she had come to talk with. He was a large man with an intelligent face and nice hair who wore a suit jacket. His smile was friendly, but there was a no-nonsense air about him—the type who would get the job done, the lawyer type, she judged. But he was strangely rather warm in his manner—on second thought, more like a surgeon who is skilled and concerned, but reserved.

President William Reeves Berkeley was, in fact, an attorney. He had grown up in Arlington, Virginia. His father had been a Washington attorney with strong Republican ties to the White House, regardless of which party had been in office. He followed in his father's political/legal path, and after a mission to Germany, college, and law school, he married an Ogden, Utah, girl whom he met while she worked one summer at the Capitol. They had five children over ten years. Berkeley settled into law and worked under the able assistance of the late Robert Barker, becoming, in time, a partner in his law firm.

Without letup in his church commitments, Berkeley served as a bishop, counselor to a stake president, and now mission president. He had been in the Czech Republic for two years and had a good grasp of the Czech language. He marveled that he had picked it up so quickly. He was also astonished at the needs of the people, both spiritual and physical. Now it appeared that his responsibilities extended to Americans visiting Prague. This was a new twist for an overworked president.

"I know I have intruded on your time," Anney began hesitantly, "but I do have a few questions that I feel I must ask to satisfy some information I have received about the Mormons."

"You're not intruding at all." Instead of sitting behind his desk, Berkeley drew a chair close to Anney's and sat down at the table as well.

"Where are you from, Mrs. Thorn?"

"The Bay Area of San Francisco." Long ago, Anney had stopped telling people that she was from Lafayette, California. It did no good to try and explain. No one had heard of her small community, but they all seemed to know where the Bay Area was located, so that sufficed. "I am here in Prague with my father, who is the Reverend Robert Moore. He is conducting some instructional seminars and training a group of evangelists."

"Yes," the president nodded, "I've heard of your father, and I am aware of what he is doing here in Prague."

"However, my reason for asking to meet with you has nothing to do with my father. I have come on a personal matter. It . . . well, I need some sort of clarification concerning your faith because of my special situation in relationship to my husband." Anney paused, faulting herself for stumbling over her words yet not certain how to best explain to this man who was looking at her with keen intent.

"Is your husband with you here in Prague?"

"No, he remained at home, or at least we are not together on this trip," Anney said. She now decided to go directly into the matter of asking the questions she had come to present. "President . . . um . . ."

"Berkeley," he reminded her with a smile.

"Yes, President Berkeley. I have some concerns about your faith because my husband has become involved with the Mormons." Anney took her eyes from the president and looked down at her black purse, adjusted it on her lap, and then looked back up into the face of the patient man.

With the president's quiet encouragement, Anney related as briefly as possible how Stephen had become involved with the Mormons, his former position with her father's ministry, his baptism, and that he was now working with some Mormon research program.

"Did you say your husband is now a member of the Church?"

Anney got the distinct impression when the president pronounced the word "Church" that he conveyed the feeling that it was the only church on the face of the earth. It rang with a sound of certainty.

"Oh, yes. He was baptized a few weeks ago. He wanted me to consider joining as well . . ." Anney took a deep breath and let fly with her deepest feelings. "I could not consent to such a thing, sir. I simply do not feel that this is right for either one of us. This is why I have come to talk. I would like a clearer view of what your people believe that has attracted my husband and threatened to destroy our relationship. May I go directly to the questions that are bothering me?"

President Berkeley seemed unruffled by her antagonistic tone. In fact, he grew more solicitous, if anything. "Go ahead and ask me your questions. I hope I can answer some of them."

Anney opened her purse and retrieved a folded sheet of paper on which she had made notes the evening before. "I've written them down. Is that all right?" Once again the president nodded approval.

"Someone told me that Mormons believe that you have the only true church on the earth. Is that correct?"

"Let me just say, Mrs. Thorn, before we get into a discussion of what the Mormons believe or don't believe . . . we believe that all the people of the earth are the children of our Father in Heaven. It is our responsibility to bring as many of those children back to our Father as is possible. We claim that he has given us the authority and charge to do that. In my mind, there can only be one church with that authority. To fragment the organization would be contrary to the order of heaven. Do you understand that Christ himself came into the world and established his organization with twelve apostles to carry out his will that all who would believe in him should be baptized? Were they to be baptized into any church or faith other than the one he designated?"

"No, they were to become Christians," Anney replied after a moment.

"So the church that Christ instituted while he was on earth had to be the Church of Jesus Christ."

"That's right." Anney was beginning to feel that her first hunch that this man had a legal background was accurate. She could see that he was a master at his trade.

"We, as members of Christ's Church, proclaim to the world that the same church Christ established while he was on earth has been restored to the earth in these times, beginning in the last century. This is not intended to appear egotistical to the point of saying that other churches do not have truths. After all, those truths had to filter down from Christ's original church. But over time, much was lost or changed by unscrupulous or misled men. So Christ had to restore his Church in its fullness once again. If this is offensive, I'm sorry, but the Lord—"

"I see, at least I see what you believe." Anney was not one to be put off. "Then you are confirming that what I was told is correct. You do believe that the Mormon Church is the only true church on the face of the earth." Anney shook her head from side to side. "That is quite a statement, considering all the churches there are."

President Berkeley opened his mouth to enlarge on the subject further, but before he could speak, Anney rushed on to another topic. "I glanced through a book that a member of my father's staff lent me the other evening. What I read troubles me greatly. It troubles me because of what it indicates you believe. It is about Christ having a body of flesh and blood. Do you know the book I'm referring to?"

"I know of books that attempt to refute our beliefs. But I would have to say that we have been taught that Jesus Christ was resurrected with a body of flesh and bone," the president said. Anney detected a slight edge to his reply.

"Then do your people actually believe that Christ has a body?"

The president pushed his hand to the back of his head and rubbed it for a moment. His face bore a rueful expression, and Anney had the distinct impression that he was not prepared to answer her direct question. Then he spoke, disproving her assumption.

"I can answer that question, and I will, but first let me review with you something you may find interesting. Do you read from the

King James Version of the Bible, or at least believe that version is correct?"

"My father teaches from the new standard version because the King James Bible is too old in its phrasing, but yes, we do accept the teachings of the King James Bible. I do believe it is the word of God for all Christians."

"Good." The president stepped to the bookshelf and took down the English Bible. "This is the King James Bible. I purchased it in a Christian bookstore in Washington, D.C. It is the standard version with no special comments." He handed it to Anney. She accepted it, held it in her hands for a moment, then realized he wanted her to inspect it. She thumbed through the pages and looked up.

"Turn to Luke 24:38–39. Here are a couple of scriptures that detail the appearance of Christ after his resurrection in the flesh. His disciples, who had gathered in a room, were startled when the Savior appeared to them after the resurrection. Read it, would you mind?"

Anney opened her purse, took out her reading glasses, put them on, and opened the Bible once again. She found Luke and then came to the part he asked her to read. She read: "Why are ye troubled? and why do thoughts arise in your hearts? Behold my hands and my feet, that it is I myself: handle me, and see; for a spirit hath not flesh and bone, as ye see me have. And when he had thus spoken he shewed them his hands and his feet."

Anney was silent for a moment. She had read these scriptures before. She knew about Christ's resurrection, but she also understood that her Church taught that Christ is a spirit—a Holy Spirit.

"I have been taught that Christ did not take his body into the heavens," Anney retorted. "He merely showed his body to confirm the resurrection."

"The Church of Jesus Christ of Latter-day Saints teaches that one of the most fundamental doctrines taught by the Twelve was that Jesus rose from the tomb with his glorified, resurrected body. The book of Acts, in a number of scriptures, heralds the event." The mission president spread his arms and his hands wide open and said, "Mrs. Thorn, to obtain a resurrection with a celestial, exalted body is the center point of hope in the gospel of Jesus Christ. The resurrection of Jesus is the most glorious of all messages of mankind. We believe in the reality of the resurrection of Christ and all mankind. Do you believe that you will be resurrected after you have died?"

"Yes." Anney said this without reasoning out the answer in her mind. Then she quickly followed up with, "I need to give this more thought. I don't know enough theology to refute what you are telling me. But I do have another question."

She shut the Bible on her lap as if it had let her down and took a deep breath. The next question was a big one.

"From what I have been told by a very knowledgeable person, you actually believe that you can become a god like our Father in Heaven. This is so far out of line with anything I have been taught that the very thought of such a thing is blasphemous."

"Mrs. Thorn, do you believe that you can become perfect? Not in this life necessarily, but sometime in the eternities?"

"I have never thought of myself as becoming perfect. No, I certainly don't think it is possible in this world. I doubt that man can become perfect."

"What is perfection to you?"

"I suppose it is something . . . or a state of . . . I guess it means being faultless. What are you driving at?"

"Let's apply it to you and your husband. Let's say that you both are perfect. What does that mean? Does it mean that you have achieved the highest degree of proficiency, skill, or excellence in your person?"

"I suppose. Certainly we would be without fault."

"It is very important that we establish what it means for one to be perfect. Would you say that Christ is perfect?"

"Yes, of course. Jesus Christ is perfect."

"Do you know of any other being who, in your mind, is perfect?"

"God the Father is perfect to my understanding."

"Good. It is your understanding that both Jesus Christ and God the Father are perfect. Those are at least two beings that we would agree are perfect."

"Yes."

"This means that we both agree that God the Father is perfect, meaning that He is in a state of being unqualified and absolute. He is without fault. He is whole. He is flawless. He is, therefore, perfect.

The very word perfect is an absolute. In the most technical sense, when a being is perfect, that being is complete. No flaws. So if you were to become perfect, would you, too, be without flaws? Would you also be in the same state that, at this time, we only know of two who are, God the Father and his son Jesus Christ?"

Anney stared at the president. She had no comment. Her mind was gyrating, trying to project what the man was leading up to. Was she being trapped by his keen intellect?

"Would you turn to Matthew 5:48? I want you to read to me what Christ is saying as he concludes his Sermon on the Mount. Do you recall that Jesus was instructing the people as to his whole gospel? He was exhorting them to be worthy of eternity with him. Would you agree?"

Anney looked down at the verse, then up to meet the eyes of President Berkeley. "I'm a little hesitant to answer your question. I feel like you may twist whatever I say."

President Berkeley wore a wounded expression. "Have I said something to cause you to question my intent?"

"What is your intent?"

"My intent is simply to answer your questions."

"I think your intent is to sway me to your beliefs. I suppose it is your responsibility to convert others."

"It certainly is. I wouldn't be here if it weren't." The mission president smiled with a twinkle in his eyes. He leaned forward with his hands on his knees, and his expression became earnest. His eyes held hers as he quietly said, "But, Mrs. Thorn, you came to me. You said that you wanted answers to your questions, and I am trying to answer them as clearly and truthfully as I know how."

Anney dropped her eyes, her mouth trembling with the tension of the moment. *He's right. I walked right into this myself. I'll have to see it through and then get out of here. I'm out of my league. This man is a match for my father. I don't know enough doctrine to compete with him. But how can he make such impossible beliefs seem so reasonable?*

Anney sighed with resignation. "Okay, I'll answer your question. You asked if I believe that the Sermon on the Mount is what?"

"That Christ was instructing the people in how to live on earth so that one day they could live in heaven with his Father."

"I haven't reviewed the Sermon on the Mount for some time, but I would have to say yes, that was certainly one of the reasons he gave it."

"Good." President Berkeley had his scriptures open to the same verse. "Would you please read verse 48?"

Anney's voice was barely audible. "Be ye therefore perfect, even as your Father which is in heaven is perfect."

"Did he actually command us to be perfect?"

"It seems that he did."

"Then what is perfection as we've defined it here?"

Anney saw it clearly. She had admitted that perfection would be without flaw, absolute, unconditionally whole. She didn't answer as she stared down at the verse. She had never read it quite that way. She knew what he would say next.

"Mrs. Thorn, when one is *perfect,* is not one like God the Father? I didn't say it; Jesus said it. It was commanded of us."

Anney stared at the words. They seemed to be seared into the page, imprinted by a branding iron: *Be ye therefore perfect, even as your Father which is in heaven is perfect.*

"Call it what you will. When we reach perfection, we will be as our Father in Heaven."

"A god?" Anney could not draw a breath.

"Yes. Unattainable as it may seem, that is what God wants us to be."

CHAPTER 16
Manti

Central America

"Plausibility and reason indicate that this high range of mountains was the area known to the Nephites as the narrow strip of wilderness." Dr. Polk had Stephen stop the Rover at the highest point of the rutty path that abruptly ended on a high cliff. The three stood on the very edge, five meters in front of the Rover, and shielded their eyes with their hands as they looked out on the mountain range. Its ten-thousand-foot peaks stretched from the Mexican side of the border where they stood to Guatemala in the distance. If they had been in an aircraft, they could have seen all the way across the range to the Caribbean directly east several hundred miles from the ridge. They were not, however, at such a vantage point. Still the day was clear, and much of the usual haze had lifted, and they saw sections of the range more than fifty miles away.

"This long, narrow, high range of mountains served as the barrier that kept the Nephites on the north from constant encounters with the Lamanites on the south. It isn't a wide strip. It is wilderness, though. Before I visited this area, whenever I read the term 'narrow strip of wilderness' in the Book of Mormon, I conjured up a sort of Robin Hood type forest that divided the two nations. That is not at all the case. It had to be something not easily crossed—mountain peaks. They serve the description. Here's a little trivia for you. It was the explorer John Lloyd Stephens in 1841, who when he looked out on this scene, declared that it was 'a barrier fit to separate worlds.' That's what he wrote, and I have to agree with him. What's more, there are scholars of the Book of Mormon who declare that of all geographical statements in the Book of Mormon, this is the most significant geographical statement in relation to Book of Mormon geography. In other words, nothing is so well described in the Book of Mormon as this natural boundary line. The interesting thing about the narrow strip of wilderness is the important fact that it stretches from the Pacific Ocean on the west to the Caribbean Sea or Atlantic Ocean on the east. In the book of Alma, the account says that, and I quote from memory, 'the narrow strip of wilderness that divided the Land of Nephi from the Land of Zarahemla ran from the sea east even to the sea west.'"

Polk shook his head and smiled, "It's heady stuff, eh? Think about it. Joseph Smith . . . what would he have known about this narrow range of mountains on the American frontier, when he translated the Book of Mormon in the 1820s?" Polk made a further point, as if he thought Stephen and Roy didn't catch the significance of what he was telling them. He said, "Remember, the first recorded account in English was written in the 1840s, and Joseph Smith learned of John Lloyd Stephen's explorations after his account was published some twelve years after Joseph translated the Book of Mormon."

"Why do you think this is the area where the land of Manti once stood, Dr. Polk?"

"Because everything fits. The whole area shouts land of Manti! Can't you feel it? We are standing in the very area where the great General Moroni commanded his troops." Dr. Polk moved across a shallow trench that he insisted had served the land of Manti in time of grave battle against the Lamanites who had come up from the south to conquer the Nephites in their own lands. He worked his way to the top of a ridge and stood waiting for his companions, Roy and Stephen, to catch up to him. They stood there on the ridge of the highly strategic area he referred to as the south wilderness mentioned in the book of Alma, one of the books in the Book of Mormon.

"It isn't all *feel*," Polk continued. "Some rather competent people who have researched the region agree with me." Turning to look at the right flank of the hill country, he said, "This was the primary trail between the ancient rival capitals of Nephi and Zarahemla." Polk stretched his arms out and pointed in several directions. "General

Moroni—not the same person as the Moroni who appeared to Joseph Smith—no, this general lived just prior to the birth of Christ. He was a Nephite and a skilled warrior at defense. Look along here." Polk pointed to the banks and trenches that he insisted were remains of a Nephite defensive strategy of that era. He explained that the Nephites protected the entrance to the valley, known today as the Coban valley in the highlands of Guatemala, by constructing an extensive and complex series of fortresses referred to by Mormon, the compiler of the Book of Mormon, as the "place of entrance" or pass. It was an elaborate system of trenches and palisades.

Dr. Polk had removed his ever-present Book of Mormon from its leather case and turned to the section about the fortifications that were explained in Alma 49. "Behold . . . the Nephites had dug up a ridge of earth round about them, which was so high that the Lamanites could not cast their stones and their arrows at them . . . neither could they come upon them save it was by their place of entrance. The Lamanites could not get into their forts of security by any other way save by the entrance, because of the highness of the bank which had been thrown up, and the depth of the ditch which had been dug round about, save it were by the entrance. . . . Thus, they were prepared, yea a body of their strongest men with their swords and their slings, to smite down all who should attempt to come into their place of security by the place of entrance."

Polk explained that the narrow corridor into the valley from the south was part of this elaborate setup. The enemy had to get by a well-fortified army to enter the first line of defense. The defensive line of trenches, and at one time timber palisades, extended for half a mile from the hills on either side of the center, where a long, deep corridor led an advancing foe into a trap. Because the corridor was narrow, waiting troops could hold off an army of vastly superior numbers.

"This region was discovered and explored by the archaeologist Richard Hauck in the eighties and nineties," Dr. Polk said as he began to walk the grassy ridge on the south side of the long trench. "So here we are on the very location of the massive fortification complex situated in the highlands of central Guatemala. Brethren, it is a region rich in former battles and an example of a highly developed concept of mobile defense." Dr. Polk turned about to glance down the Coban valley and said loud enough for his cohorts to hear from a distance, "We will drive through the heart of the valley and on to the lowlands of the region once known as Zarahemla."

* * *

Anney grew sentimental at the wedding. Seated with five other guests and the filming crew from Los Angeles, she began to have second thoughts about having such a small gathering. She knew her father enjoyed crowds. He knew how to conduct himself where there were many people present. Anney was aware that he had planned on a grand wedding in San Francisco, surrounded by the city's finest and most powerful. Between Katherine's circle of friends, her father's following, and civic personalities, there would have been a hundred times more guests at home.

"Simple. Keep it simple but elegant," Katherine had insisted as Anney took the lead in planning the affair. She had been elated when Anney hastened to report that her father had agreed to a Krakow wedding. "Perfect," she had sighed. "Everything will be perfect."

Krakow was a small, romantic Polish city. Set in the hills with flowing rivers and ancient buildings, it had a charm that lent itself to weddings, gaiety, and laughter. Heinrik had been helpful in arranging the wedding papers, the official documents required, and reserving the sixteenth-century cathedral. Katherine loved the interior of the old building with its baroque style. Motifs of the saints lined the forward walls, and mute sculpted angels with trumpets lent a light note to the surroundings.

The Catholic faith was the dominant religion in Krakow. The Catholic priests had acquiesced, allowing the Reverend Moore and his bride to be married by an evangelist of Bob's choosing—the Reverend Jadwig Casimir, who spoke some English. He was on hand to attend Bob's sessions in televangelism that Decker had scheduled in Krakow.

Katherine had called her attorney shortly after Bob agreed to the Krakow wedding to request that he fly to Poland and oversee the signing of a prenuptial agreement. He had advised her when she announced their engagement that she needed such an agreement. As much as she loved Bob, Katherine took the advice of her long-time attorney and executed the agreement. Bob may have been surprised and not overly happy to sign the document with Anney as witness, but he signed it without comment.

Anney had a difficult time catching the Reverend Casimir's words because he spoke softly at the altar. She guessed he was intimidated by the English-speaking wedding party. It made no difference. Who was going to challenge his pronunciation of the wedding vows?

She had steeled herself against it, but the very essence of a wedding evoked tender memories of her own special day with Stephen at her side. She was disturbingly aware that Stephen was far, far away, in more than physical distance.

Though she had been adamant with Stephen about not contacting her until he changed his mind—unless, of course, there was a serious problem in the family—she now regretted her words. She wanted Stephen to call. She longed to hear his voice. She had made vows to remain with him when she married him at the small, non-denominational chapel on the Berkeley campus. *Youth. We never figure that the realities of living will tear at our human frailness. We think our love is so strong it can endure any hardship. Maybe not.*

As quickly as her thoughts had turned to Stephen, they darted off in another direction. She mulled over what President Berkeley had said about reading the Book of Mormon. "Mrs. Thorn, please read it. You will forever be sorry if you do not at least become acquainted with its pages."

Perhaps he was right, but Anney found the request almost insurmountable—to lower herself to read something so foreign to her religious convictions. Then, too, what if it captivated her as it had Stephen? How would she handle such a possibility? Well, not to worry. It wouldn't happen. Anney knew that she was strong; nothing could sway her beliefs. She dismissed the thought.

With a start, Anney realized that she had missed those magic words, "husband and wife," that must have been pronounced by the evangelist. He must have ended the ceremony, because there they were, Dad and Katherine, kissing one another in a long and touching embrace. The cameras caught it all in the full flood of television lighting, which the priest had also allowed, for a fee.

Decker had carefully instructed the cameramen to zoom in on the two and allow no more of the chapel into the frame than necessary. It would facilitate editing the tape and would downplay the Catholic cathedral bit. The video, after all, would go out to the Bible Belt of America, and perhaps it would not set well to have the Reverend Moore standing before a Catholic altar with his bride. That could all be handled with close-ups and voice-overs to show the wedding but not the setting. They would cut to the wedding breakfast.

The ceremony was held in the morning for two vital reasons: it followed regular Mass in the chapel, and Bob and his staff needed the remainder of the day for sessions with the visiting evangelists who had streamed in from a dozen or more locations in Poland and Ukraine.

As Anney stood, it occurred to her that even if she wanted to read the Book of Mormon, she didn't have one with her. The mission president forgot to lend her one as he had offered in his office. Perhaps, she thought, this was a sign that she should not tamper with the book. The thought fled when Katherine, dressed in a pale pink silk suit, reached out and hugged her warmly. The two suddenly enjoyed an overwhelming sense of belonging to one another. "Anney, my Anney. Thank you for all you have done. I'll make it up to you someday." Anney smiled and hugged Katherine even tighter.

* * *

They had stopped for the evening at Tuxtla, where Dr. Polk had taken many tours on previous visits. The owners of the small hotel knew him well. In fact, the whole town seemed to know Dr. Polk. Tuxtla was nestled in a small valley on the incline from the mountains of highland Guatemala in the Chiapas region. The jungle encroached on the town from all sides.

The café where they had their evening meal, Polk insisted, served the most authentic Mexican/Indian cuisine in the world. They sat talking after the corn tortillas and the hot sauces had been removed. The warm, tropical air flowed freely through the barred, glassless windows. This was the land of perpetual spring; the temperature was constant. Only the rainy season brought mild change.

"You know," Dr. Polk said, satisfied with the meal—though the day before his stomach had been upset. *A little touch of Montezuma's revenge,* he thought.

"Yeah. Do we know what?" Stephen asked.

"Here it comes, Stephen, what I call the Polk mini-lectures," Roy said with the savvy of one who had been with Polk long enough to detect mood and intention. "It's kinda like attending a 'free' dinner sponsored by a land promoter. You end up paying for it when they try to sell you a piece of property on the sheer side of a cliff in the wilds of southern Colorado."

Polk ignored the barb. "What I want to explain has to do with what we've been exposed to for the past few weeks. Even Roy here will have to agree with my evaluation. It's very profound."

"Explain. We'll determine the profundity."

"Has it crossed the mind of either one of you what we have uncovered concerning the Book of Mormon as a translated document?" Polk held up his hand and waved away the cynicism of Roy, a banter he enjoyed at times and tolerated at others because Roy offered perspective. But at this moment, Polk wanted to make his point without the digs.

"If you think about it, the Book of Mormon was printed in the winter of 1830. What was the level of worldwide scholarship that year? I've given that year a great deal of thought over the past few decades. It was a pivotal point in the progress of learning. Archaeology as a recognized field of science was a half a century or more in the future. What was known up to that time among world-renowned scholars, in say the field of Biblical studies, language, and the like? On the East Coast of the United States, it was in its infancy. In Europe, it was beginning to sprout into a science.

"You know, it's easy for us to look at those fields of expertise from our vantage point and make some outstanding conclusions, but what if we were to put ourselves in western New York in say 1829, when the Book of Mormon translating process was in full swing? Think back, and try to visualize Joseph Smith and his scribe Oliver Cowdery piecing together the Book of Mormon, actually moving rapidly along with the translation. What library material was available in the entire region? Were there any colleges nearby? What was the level of scholarship?

"These are vital points when you are taking a critical look at what materials were available for Joseph Smith to research and transfer to his lengthy document. Almost nothing. We did a study of the available research material in a fifty-mile radius of Palmyra, New York, during the months of the translation of the Book of Mormon. It's interesting to note that the local library had less real material on say language, ruins, and studies of Near Eastern documents than the library in Blanding, Utah, has today.

"There were no books dealing specifically with ruins, Bible lands, Hebrew writings, Egyptian studies, archaeological books of any sort. When we made as thorough a study as possible and came up with no book or manuscript dealing remotely with subjects covered in the Book of Mormon, we shook our heads at how minor was scholarship of any type in the whole of the United States when it came to ancient worlds and understanding ancient environments. Of course, there was the King James version of the Bible. The Smiths had one. But there were no commentaries or vital studies of any sort. What's more, there is no record that Joseph Smith or Oliver Cowdery ever set foot inside either of the two local hole-in-the-wall libraries in the region. And if they had, there was little material to read.

"Don't you think it's odd that a boy with such limited education and resources could construct the kind of book he printed in Palmyra?"

"So what are you getting at?" Roy wanted to know.

"I'm asking, where did he come up with such things as the tree-of-life story? The vast civilization we are studying here in Central America? What about the unique language of the book? How could he have known about the complex study of chiasmus and the Near Eastern method of phrasing and word structuring throughout the book? And not least, what about a simple little thing like Subscriptio, where Joseph signed off with title and signature of the book not on the first page, but on the last page as was common in the Near East anciently? Oh, I could go on and on."

It was a perfect lead-in for Roy to make a wisecrack, but he refrained from the urge and listened.

"You cannot in any way categorically say that Joseph Smith wrote the Book of Mormon. It is far too complex for any single individual, even in this time of computer research and all the sophisticated methods at our fingertips, to construct such a book. Impossible.

"Why, then, do intelligent people, schooled in universities beyond anything imagined in Joseph Smith's time, look at the Book of

Mormon and say that the country boy, out on the frontier of America, wrote this very complex, far-reaching, scholarly work of scripture in the years 1828 and 1829? The days spent in actual translation numbered less than seventy.

"That is the most astounding part of all."

"What is?" Stephen probed, engrossed in Polk's comments.

"How thinking people can actually believe that the book was authored by Joseph Smith." Polk shook his head.

CHAPTER 17
Land of Bountiful

Chiapas

Stephen stood with Dr. Polk, looking out onto the magnificent beauty of the rain forest in the state of Chiapas. The mist was lifting from the valley, giving the entire vista a look of Brigadoon.

"I'm persuaded that it was in this region, somewhere around here, that the Lord came to his temple after the great destruction took place. We are in the old land of Bountiful, Stephen, my boy. It is no wonder they named this place Bountiful after the region they had once known in the southern Arabian desert. I love it here. This, to me, is as close as I may ever get to paradise on earth." Peter pointed his stubby index finger to the right and beyond two small valleys to a spot that he alone could see in his mind. "Over there. Do you see where the mist has just lifted? There is a glorious, narrow waterfall that cascades one hundred ten feet over rocky, vine-covered cliffs. I'm going to take you as close to those waters as possible. Stick with me. We'll have Roy drive us within a quarter mile of the falls."

Roy was already in the driver's seat when Stephen and Dr. Polk climbed back into the Land Rover. With instructions from Polk, Roy shifted into low and crawled over rocks and gnarled roots. The branches along the steep hillside scraped the windows, causing an eerie, whining sound. The Rover, which tipped to the side ten degrees, had traversed no more than a hundred meters when Stephen realized that the eerie sound he was hearing was not only the scraping of branches. It came from inside the car, behind him. He turned his head to glance around the head restraint at Dr. Polk in the back seat. For a moment Stephen failed to comprehend what he was observing. He strained to see the professor better.

Tears squeezed through tight lids as Polk moaned that ghostly sound of distress. His head rolled back onto the headrest then slumped to the right as if his very soul had been sucked from his body. He lay as if in a trance. His hands remained at his sides, as if he were powerless to lift them to ward off an invisible attack. His nostrils flared as he struggled mightily to inhale. He exhaled, accompanying the air with a whine. His eyes remained open though unperceiving.

Stephen, no longer confused, yanked his seat belt loose and clawed at the armrest in order to twist around and reach back to help Dr. Polk. He found his voice and shouted at Roy, "Stop! Stop this thing! Something's happened to Dr. Polk!"

Roy whirled his head around. Polk was directly behind him and difficult to see. He hit the brakes of the slow-moving vehicle and was out the door in a flash, as was Stephen on the other side. The tangled roots of trees and heavy underbrush that all but choked the path through the hills prevented them from opening the rear doors. Roy jumped back into the driver's seat, shifted into first gear, and forced the Rover to edge forward ten feet. Setting the brakes, he jumped out again as Stephen caught up to the rear door and pulled it open. In seconds, he was working over his stricken friend.

"Pull his feet to your end." Stephen knew CPR. He forced his mind to think rationally. The thought raced through his mind that he *must* remain unemotional. He had presence of mind to stretch Polk's bulky body across the seat, place his head back, and feel in his mouth for his tongue. He knew Polk had not eaten, but past training forced him to delay mouth-to-mouth procedures long enough to feel around in the cavity and check for obstructions.

Stephen then placed his mouth firmly over Polk's lips. He breathed life back into the professor. He continued his CPR efforts for the next few minutes. He stopped momentarily to check the pupils that were rolled toward the top of Dr. Polk's head. During the next pause, Roy took hold of Stephen's shoulder and pulled on him.

"Wait, man! He's breathing okay. Look at his face."

Stephen withdrew and looked down at the wide, friendly, still face. It was evident to Stephen that the entire right side of the face, from the drooping eyelids to the sagging mouth, was like melted wax.

"He's had a stroke, a massive stroke." Roy pointed at Polk's face. "I'm almost certain. My grandfather had this same appearance when I saw him in the hospital the day after he had a stroke. I tell you he has had a stroke. I mean just in the last few minutes."

Stephen felt the steady breathing of Dr. Polk and realized that Roy was right. Whatever was wrong, at least he was breathing. His heart seemed to be beating steadily, too. He had no idea that a stroke would strike this fiercely and leave its paralyzing mark so quickly. But Roy seemed to know what he was talking about. Even so, Dr. Polk surely required immediate medical attention by a qualified doctor.

Stephen hurriedly told Roy to get back in the front and pull the seats as far forward as possible. It would allow room enough for him to remain next to Dr. Polk, should he require CPR or other assistance. Roy was to rip for the nearest medical facility. Maybe someone in the little town they had passed ten miles back could help. Roy did as he was instructed, and Stephen remained pressed between the front seat and Polk's heavy body.

The village was Tenosique, situated in the lowland jungle of Chiapas. With his lower-division Spanish, Roy learned from the proprietor at the sole filling station that the village had no hospital or, for that matter, even a decent medical clinic. The man suggested that in the city of Villahermosa there was a grand hospital. He also said that Villahermosa was two, maybe three hours by auto. Opening the door to get behind the wheel of the Rover, he noticed that there were already three boys with hands cupped to the dusty side windows, peeking in to see what was happening.

Roy shooed the boys away, leaped in, and reversed the car as he reported the bad news to Stephen, who was straining every ounce of energy to help Dr. Polk breathe.

"If we go north to the main highway, we can speed. Maybe the police will pick us up and escort us with their lights to the capital," Roy said breathlessly.

"Wait, Roy. Stop! He needs help now, not two hours from now. Is that the closest hospital?"

Roy turned in his seat, white with anxiety. "He said yes, but my Spanish isn't all that great. He may not have understood me."

Stephen desperately looked around the street. Nothing he saw offered the slightest sign of help.

"Okay. Keep going," Stephen said, looking helplessly at the unconscious professor.

Roy sped out of the village on the dirt road as the Mexican boys waved and laughed, unaware of the emergency. He headed north out of town. They had gone no more than a kilometer when Roy screeched to a stop.

"What is it?" Stephen shouted.

"Look, there are two airplanes sitting over there on that grass runway." It had been a few years back, but Stephen had grown up flying a Cessna. There was an airstrip on his uncle's ranch in eastern Nevada. Flying to Ely, Las Vegas, and other cities with his uncle and older cousin was a common occurrence. By the time Stephen was fourteen, he was flying solo.

At Stephen's insistence, Roy sped to the end of the barbed wire fence that surrounded the grassy airstrip. A rock's throw from the planes stood a long, rambling house with sheds hidden by a grove of banana trees. Roy stopped in the dooryard amid a billow of dust. Chickens scattered, flapping their wings and protesting loudly. He leaped out, dashed to the front door, and began pounding. A tiny *señora* in a long dress of bright orange and blue opened the door. She stepped out onto the stoop and tilted her head up to look into Roy's face as he asked in the best Spanish he could muster if the pilot of one of those planes was around.

At first, she had no idea what Roy was saying in his broken Spanish. He pointed at the planes that were tied down with small wire cables and kept repeating "pilot . . . airplane, pilot" in Spanish.

At last, a smile of comprehension engulfed the old woman's face. She turned and shouted for someone in the house. An even older woman came to the door and stared out at the scene. Words flew between the two women as Roy tried with all the residue of Spanish that had been drilled into him as a freshman at Harvard to understand what they were saying, but he picked out only snippets of the rapid-fire conversation the old ladies spewed out. He thought he understood that one plane was operational. *"Muy vie a. El otro, si. Pero el dueño no está. El sabe la manera de andar in el nuevo avión. Pero, él no está. El está en el rancho que está muy lejos."* (The owner knows how to fly the airplane, but he is not here. He is at the ranch that is far away.) Her hands went up in a gesture of defeat.

Roy understood enough.

He rushed back to the Rover and told Stephen what he had made of the muddled conversation. Stephen eased his jacket under Polk's head and worked his way out of the rear seat to the ground. For a moment, he was unsteady and had to lean against the side of the Rover while the blood recirculated in his legs. Then he told Roy that if the keys were in the newer plane—the Cessna on the right—he would get in, see if there was enough fuel, crank it up, and test fly it for five minutes to check out the instruments.

"You mean you're going to fly that plane yourself?" Roy was aghast.

"That's exactly what I'm going to do. Stay with Dr. Polk!"

He was off and running toward the airplane at full bore. Stephen had flown his uncle's Cessna on the ranch in eastern Nevada since he was twelve. He knew all about taking off from a dirt runway. He and his cousin had flown hundreds of miles by the time they were out of high school. They had flown to Ely for rodeos and dances so many times that Stephen had learned to land on a dirt field with only the moon for lighting. It was risky, but no one on the ranch in the 1960s had bothered to instruct him otherwise. If the plane was functional, he would have Polk in the plane and be in Villahermosa in half an hour.

The keys were not in the plane, and the cockpit door was locked. The whole plane was secured. Naturally.

With a desperate groan, Stephen raced back to the old women who were still standing at the door. He shouted, "Key, por favor, key." Stephen twisted his fingers as if he were inserting a key into an ignition. They failed to understand the meaning.

"Roy, get over here. I need the keys. Ask these women where the keys are. Tell them we are not stealing the plane; we need to fly our friend to the hospital. We'll bring it back. Tell . . . tell them that. We'll even wash it before we return it. Tell 'em we'll pay. Tell 'em anything." Stephen grew more frustrated and desperate as he eyed the women.

"No, I've got a better idea," Stephen said, his face lighting up with a solution. "Get the keys out of the Rover and tell them we will swap it for the temporary use of the plane."

Roy, red-faced with frustration, shouted back, "I don't know the word in Spanish for 'swap.'"

"Just get me the keys, for crying out loud."

There was ponderous reluctance on the part of the Mexican ladies to cooperate. Roy dangled the Rover's keys in front of them and tried to come up with the words that meant they could keep the Rover if he could use the plane.

Stephen rushed to the Rover and checked Dr. Polk, placing his left ear on the professor's chest as he lay motionless in the rear seat. He guessed that Roy must have threatened the women, because the older *señora* glared at him. But she stepped back into the house and brought out a leather, wallet-like object with keys inside. Stephen was at the door in a flash, grabbed the keys, and took off running.

It took Stephen only a minute or two to orient himself to the instrument panel. In thirty years, Cessna's basic instrument panel had not changed that much. He checked out the dials and fuel gauge, and then cranked the engine. It fired up. He revved it for a moment and then hopped out and removed the blocks and cables. He repositioned himself in the cockpit and eased the craft onto the once-graded grass airstrip.

He could tell by the short grass that it must be used regularly by the owner. He noticed the position of the wind sock attached to a seven-foot pole, and then he calculated that he needed to fly east into the wind. Once on the strip, he nervously rechecked all the gauges. There was plenty of fuel, three-quarters of a tank. He strapped the seat belt across himself, sat back, took an extra deep gulp of air, and pulled back the throttle. He gained ground speed sufficient to begin lift off. When he pulled back on the wheel, the flaps engaged and the plane took flight.

As he climbed toward cumulus clouds above him, he remembered what he had learned as a boy. At five hundred feet he circled the field, making a wide turn, and lined up the plane to set her down on the grass runway. He misjudged the distance between grass and wheels, bumped three times, and then took it up again for a second try. This time he set it down smoothly and taxied to the Rover.

"Tell these ladies we'll be back," he shouted over the din of the plane. "First help me with Dr. Polk. We'll put him across the rear seats. Help me, Roy. Get with it, man." Roy was trying to gather up his camera and other items.

Villahermosa boasted a rather up-to-date airstrip that accommodated jet aircraft as well as prop. The tower was confused by the silver Cessna suddenly appearing on their radar screen.

Stephen saw one small craft land to the right of the longest runway. He surmised that the main runway was for larger prop planes and jets. He swung down to the right of the main airstrip and buzzed past the tower to get their attention. He circled the field and spotted a second plane preparing to take off from the main runway. He banked to the right to avoid the other plane's air space and circled one more time before making his final approach. He figured that all the light aircraft would now be stationary or aware of his presence. He had made his entrance, and any pilot worth his salt would know not to attempt a takeoff while so much confusion prevailed. That was basic safety in the profession.

Setting down on the asphalt strip was no problem. The problem was in the rear of the cabin, expiring by the second. When they taxied to the front entrance of the terminal, two Mexican airport officials and a security guard were waving their hands shouting "no, no, no!" Their agitated protests had no impact on Stephen. He brought the plane to within ten feet of the terminal entrance and pushed open the door, shouting for an ambulance. Roy followed his lead and began bellowing in Spanish for an ambulance. Seeing the desperate situation, one of the airport officials pivoted about and issued rapid-fire instructions, and then shouted the universal, "Okay, okay!"

* * *

It was after midnight. They lay together, she with her head on his chest. Moore sighed with satisfaction as he counted his blessings. He could hardly comprehend all that Katherine was doing to further his career. She had been so generous with funding the tour. Now she had arranged and would sponsor the prime-time video. It was the opportunity that had somehow passed him by a decade ago, when he was approached by a group of promoters to bill him big-time across gospel television land. The deal had fallen through for lack of funds. That had been a devastating blow to his career's upward thrust. The future had seemed dismal and blurred. He was approaching sixty at the time and was resigned to a mediocre end to his career. It looked like he would never become the leading light of televangelism. He finally decided that since he had a smooth-running, manageable gospel television show and many loyal followers, he would make the most of it until he was seventy and then retire. But he felt indignant at being underrated and unappreciated.

Retirement now would be unthinkable—a virtual prison to Bob. At last he could soar. Wings seemed to sprout in Krakow. He was married to a wealthy, attractive woman; he had the full backing of his staff and the funds and drive to make it to the top. The top meant national television exposure and a weekly gospel hour that would be carried into homes throughout the breadth of the land. What an exalted position for a humble little preacher from Texas to aspire to.

"Are you pleased with what the filming crew is doing to record your tour?" Katherine asked softly, interrupting his train of thought. It was barely more than twelve hours since they took their vows.

"I couldn't be happier," her new husband replied, stroking her arm. "Oh, Katherine, you have made a critical difference in my life. Are you disappointed that we have to postpone our honeymoon for a few weeks? I'm so sorry I had to dash away from this morning's wedding breakfast, but let's face it, I have to complete this tour and do an A-plus job of it, or I'm finished in the business."

"I know. I also know that you have a destiny, and now I'm part of it."

"A major part of it."

"Oh my darling, your genius, your vitality, and your experience deserve recognition by the whole country, not just the Bay Area."

"As I lie here thinking of my past, I have to say that life itself brings unexpected surprises. Don't you think so?"

"Yes. I thought the romantic side of my life had ended when my husband died. I thought I was relegated to the bleak existence of a widow, caught up in fund-raisers and endless teas. Then I saw you. You have the ability to charge others somewhat the same way you charged me, but you have to keep your life in check. As you become more and more well known, it will require discipline to maintain balance. I'll be here to help you anchor this ambition. Please, Bob, whatever you do, include me. Never leave me out of the action. Yours is a long-delayed emergence of a major talent. Make the most of it, but include me in it. Pain and pleasure have a strange way of blending together. Do you know what I'm saying?"

Suddenly Bob realized that he had as his very own, a sensitive, even slightly insecure wife. Katherine had given herself completely to him, allowing him to see her fears and frailties, sharing total intimacy, asking only to be included in his whole life. This was a new experience for Bob. Nadia was always the faithful, stay-at-home wife, who never challenged his preoccupation in his own interests.

Now he had a person who was not only rich, but also very bright and perceptive. She would demand of him body and soul. For the moment, that was suitable to Bob. He knew that she would want to pool their interests, thoughts, and energies together and act as a team. If he could view the tie as a support and not a hobble, it might prove to be a vital yoke of special talents. He had to maintain that level of commitment. He hoped that his present earnestness would not wear thin. This evening with Katherine had forced Bob to reassess the focus of his affections. He must try to care for another human being straight from the heart. Not an easy task for the popular evangelist.

CHAPTER 18
The Stroke

Salt Lake City

The doctors were guarded in their prognosis. However, they did pull Polk's family and Stephen aside and inform them that Dr. Polk had experienced a massive stroke. A cerebral hemorrhage had induced the debilitating stroke. They could not promise his full recovery. In the opinion of the senior physician, Polk might never regain full use of his motor abilities. The stroke would probably leave its mark.

The lead doctor assured Stephen that in his opinion he and his associate had done all that was humanly possible under the circumstances. It would have been helpful if they had been able to whisk him out of Mexico sooner, but the doctor knew that was hindsight.

At the hospital in Villahermosa, a concerned medical staff had monitored Polk's vital signs and given him fluids intravenously.

While Roy had made arrangements to transport Polk to Salt Lake City, Stephen flew the Cessna back to its grassy airstrip. He exchanged keys with the tiny *señora*, handing her a wad of pesos with his sincere thanks.

After chartering a small plane to take them to the Veracruz airport, Stephen and Roy had accompanied Polk from Veracruz on a special mercy flight to Salt Lake City, where an ambulance service met the jetliner and helped remove the patient for transfer to LDS Hospital. There he was placed in the intensive care unit, and two highly qualified specialists took over.

Stephen could see that it might be weeks before he could communicate with the professor. He excused himself and made a phone call to Bill Bennett's law office in Phoenix.

"I'm very sorry, Dr. Thorn." The kind voice of Bennett's receptionist sounded sincerely distressed as she explained to Stephen that Bennett was not in town. "Mr. Bennett and his wife are white-water rafting in Colombia, and at least for the next few days, they cannot be reached. But I will try to get a message through about Dr. Polk's unfortunate stroke and get back to you."

Stephen should have remembered that Bennett had mentioned his forthcoming trip the day he spent in Phoenix going over the agreement and all arrangements for the project. Stephen left the number of Roy's condo in Provo, where he would be staying for a couple of days. If Bennett's secretary heard from him, she was to call Stephen immediately. He also gave the number of the intensive care unit, in case he should be at the hospital.

Stephen knew that it was essential to get down to Provo and check with Roy, who was already in Polk's home office organizing the files for Stephen to review. He and Roy had decided to continue with whatever phases of the project they could handle without Polk's direct influence in the matter. Roy reminded Stephen that there were still a couple of presenters to be contacted and that one segment of the project was still moving forward in Provo. "I'll show you the big display that is nearly completed in a large building near Brigham Young University," Roy had informed Stephen.

Roy pulled up the notes that Dr. Polk had typed into the computer the night before he left for Mexico two weeks earlier. Stephen and Roy had been searching for the instructions that Polk had faxed to Stephen. In an effort to understand the specifics of Stephen's assignment, they reviewed all the documented material. Most of it they understood; it had already been discussed.

Among the legal documents, Roy pulled up the agreement that allowed Stephen to be a signer on the checking account. This meant that in the arrangement of things, Stephen had the legal right to dispense the three million dollars that had been earmarked for Project II in the absence of Dr. Polk, or in the event he was not capable of administering the funds, which he was not.

"In your opinion, Roy, what is my exact status in this whole chaotic affair?"

"Looking over the papers that you guys signed in Phoenix and noting what it says in the last couple of paragraphs here on the screen, you are the fair-haired boy who makes all the decisions while Dr. Polk is disabled." Roy rubbed the tip of his long, thin nose and shook his head. "I wish Bennett were around so we could talk to him, but it looks to me like you have the legal right to continue on with every part of the project and dispense funds when needed." Roy swiveled his chair around to meet Stephen's eyes. "What are you going to do?"

"Boy, I don't know. I'm uneasy about what Decker Hunt told my wife . . . You know, I told you and Dr. Polk what she said, that the project—as well as Dr. Polk and I—was under investigation for fraud. Remember?"

"Yeah, Polk didn't take it seriously at all. He said Bennett could handle that Kline fellow."

"Yeah, but Bennett will be out of the country for who knows how long. I don't know what to do. It's a tough decision, Roy."

"But there are some bills to pay and a couple of advances we promised to send out to lecturers."

"I guess . . . I guess we move forward and pray with all our might that Dr. Polk has a speedy recovery. There's not much else we can do if things are going to stay on schedule. I probably should try to reach the chairperson of the trust. It's one of Thomas Kline's daughters. I forget her name. Bennett's secretary would know how I can reach her."

Stephen leaned back in his chair, deep in thought. "It does bug me just a tad that I never received the letter of authorization you have on the screen." He pointed to the bottom of the color monitor, where a portion of the letter was displayed. Roy scrolled down the complete document, and Stephen read it again.

"It may be at my home in the stack of mail that must be there, but it wasn't there before I left to meet you guys in Mexico. Don't you think I should have that document before I sign any checks?"

"I suppose. But it's right there on the disk. We know he gave you authorization to take over the project. Surely he left a copy with Bennett. Why don't you call his secretary and ask her if she can put her hands on the original? If it's in Bennett's office, she will likely know where."

"I called her this morning," Stephen said. Even so, he pulled out his compact planner, found Bennett's number, and spoke once again to the secretary. Listening to his request, she hesitated a long moment, not remembering such an authorization. But she assured him that she would call back as soon as she had located it. It could take more than half an hour to locate it, unless it should be in Bennett's safe. In that case, since she was not authorized to open the safe, they would be forced to wait until Bennett returned.

Roy and Stephen reviewed all the projects and assignments as they waited. Bennett's secretary finally called back to say that she had been unable to locate any recent correspondence between Polk and Bennett. She would continue to look, but all such documents were probably locked in the safe.

"We know that he wrote the letter. It's here on the computer." Roy gestured at the monitor as Stephen hung up the phone.

"But did Dr. Polk sign it and mail it?" Stephen asked.

Roy summed up the situation, "I think he did. And knowing Dr. Polk, he would have sent it certified mail. But you'll have to make the decision yourself." He began a careful search of the file cabinets and drawers in the professor's office, without success.

"C'mon. While you think it over, I'll show you the project that I mentioned on the plane, the one in the old vacant supermarket."

"Duane has taken a dream that Dr. Polk has had for at least twenty years and made it a reality at last, Stephen," Roy commented as the young designer, Duane Samson, motioned for them to follow him. They had been seated for the past ten minutes while Duane oriented them to the nature of the project and enlarged on the art of making miniature land formations. At last, they ascended dimly lit, curved stairs to a platform above the floor. In the subdued light, Stephen strained to distinguish objects in what appeared to be a small amphitheater, the shape of a scaled-down football stadium with a vaulted ceiling. There were padded, bleacher-like seats arranged in clusters on both the north and south sides, with a platform and a railing surrounding the entire circumference of the bowl. Stephen could discern that the outer rim was outlined with inlaid miniature lights, but he could not identify what was displayed in the dark shadows in the center of the bowl. He stood at least twelve feet above the floor of the bowl; it reminded him of the amphitheater where elaborate cockfights were held in Puerto Rico. Except for the sounds and smells, this stadium was similar to that one.

Stephen noticed a tram with half doors next to the platform they stood on. It was oval shaped, with seating for ten to twelve passengers.

"Dr. Thorn, if you will step into the gondola with Roy, I'd like to take you for an aerial ride around our creation." Stephen was first into the gondola, followed by Roy and then Duane. Duane glanced back at the two young fellows at the lighted drafting table. "Hey, Will," he shouted, "hit the light switches and start gondola two. Okay?"

Will looked up from the table, nodded, walked ten feet to the wall at the left of the entrance, and began flipping switches. As he did so, the entire interior of the scaled-down stadium was suddenly illuminated. Lights positioned above, below, and in the corners of the building burst into a wild hue of colors. They were not ordinary lights. It was as if a Broadway interior lighting expert had magically tripped the switches of a stage setting for the musical *Cats*. Reds, greens, yellows, earth-tone browns, all in subtle array, bathed the area and brought to life the scene in the center of the bowl.

Stephen's eyes focused on the panorama spread out before him. It was like looking at a huge bas-relief map, an Alice in Wonderland view of a miniature replica of some island or country. It had Lilliputian hills, mountains, rivers, and small cities and covered a space larger than the regulation basketball courts at Berkeley.

He studied the terrain with its realistic appearance of a landmass, as if he were looking down from a plane four thousand feet above. He was reminded of the time he and Anney had flown into Hawaii and could see across Oahu from one side to the other. The lighting gave the whole scene a Disneyland appearance.

From their elevated position, Stephen could see the entire layout, across the representation of a landmass with blue ocean on either side. Small ranges of mountains were arranged in serpentine fashion, and rivers in the distance looked as if they were actually flowing. The lighting made it so. Miniature trees covered over half the countryside.

"This is it, Stephen," Roy said, beaming with pride, as if he were the creator. "This is what Dr. Polk has been anxious to show you. Do you recognize it? If you will look north," he suggested, pointing with his finger, "and let your eyes come south to the tip, you can see the places we just left, the entire area we refer to as the Book of Mormon lands." He leaned over the side of the gondola to point to a specific spot. "I'd guess we left the Land Rover right about there."

"Wow!" Stephen caught his breath. "You're right!"

"Yep. Dr. Polk hired Duane here to create this entire layout with his crew."

Duane nodded that it was so.

"As Duane told you, he is a specialist in creating miniature golf courses. He has built them all over the west for the past ten years. Right, Duane?"

"Right! Ever since I got home from my mission," he said. "Dr. Polk told me that he wanted a miniature replica of the Book of Mormon lands with all the topographical and man-made features that were present at the time of the Jaredites, Nephites, Lamanites, Mulekites, and all the others. This is what we came up with."

"Impressive," Stephen breathed as he surveyed the scene before him. *Man, what this little layout must have cost!*

Roy pointed at the center of the display. "There, you see the peaks of that mountain range? That is the narrow strip of wilderness we drove through." He laughed. "The roads don't look quite as rough from up here, do they?"

The gondola continued to inch slowly across the miniature land. "For people interested in the area where we think most of the action in the Book of Mormon took place, this little show will be a hit. Notice that all the cities are depicted. Look over there. You can see the City of Zarahemla. South of that is the City of Moroni." Roy was warming to his role as tour guide.

"Notice the River Sidon, where we got stuck last week. See how it cascades through the gorge? It's all here, Stephen. What do you think?"

"This is really something, Roy," Stephen said as he tried to take in the entire vista before him.

He turned to look at Roy's glowing face. "Why have you guys kept it a secret from me until now?"

"Not a secret, Stephen—a surprise. Dr. Polk wanted to bring you here after you had toured the actual places. He thought it would mean more to you. It was all I could do to keep from telling you about it last week while we were bouncing around those mountains."

"Actually," Duane interrupted, "we've had very skilled technicians working on this project over the past year. We even hired a couple of Disney people who happened to be on vacation and spent their spare time here, moonlighting. There isn't a geography department in the country that wouldn't love to have one of these layouts depicting parts of Europe, Asia, the United States—wherever—as part of their classroom instruction."

Duane pressed a green, illuminated button on a black plastic control unit. "Notice this slick little device," he said, holding it closer to his passengers. "It is a lot like a remote control for a television set. Let's drop down and see this thing up close." As the gondola began to inch toward the center of the bowl, swaying ever so slightly, Stephen turned from side to side to take in the changing view from his hovering position.

"We'll start here at the land of their first inheritance," Duane explained. They stopped above the seashore, looking north to a range of mountains, the plastic sea to their backs. They were above the threshold of the land.

"Okay, Dr. Thorn, if you will look directly beneath us, you will see our creation of the Pacific Ocean. The land that extends along the seashore is, as you probably know, where many authorities on the subject of the Book of Mormon lands say Lehi and his family landed."

As he spoke, a large screen lowered from the ceiling on a hydraulic rod. On the screen, six feet in front of them, computer-animated figures appeared, disembarking from a ship in the bay. Small figures depicting Lehi and his family climbed down from the ship and walked on the sandy seashore. The background appeared to be an actual shot of the water with the mountains in the distance, while the figures were caricature in design. While they moved about and set up a small encampment, a narrator's voice described the action. Time passed, and there were more small figures, some white and others dark. Lehi was laid out on a platform, dead. Then there were words with the brothers. Later, under cover of darkness, Nephi and a small band of the men, women, and children left the settlement and headed toward the mountains. All of this depicted the time when Lehi's family established themselves in the land.

After five minutes of narration, the presentation ended, the screen withdrew into the ceiling, and the gondola began to move again. Stephen noticed a large sign beyond where the screen had been lowered. In bold, yellow neon letters, accompanied by a large arrow, the sign indicated, "NORTH."

"You can always get your coordinates by looking at the sign in front of us," Duane explained. "To simplify directions, we created our layout following true compass points. The land you see toward the northwest—there, that area on our left without trees—is the heart of Mexico today. On the extreme north is Mexico City. However, it is depicted as it may have appeared in the year 200 B.C.E.

"Let your eyes wander southward and you will see the narrow area in southern Mexico called the Isthmus of Tehuantepec. It is just here to our right. Don't confuse it with the Isthmus of Panama. Panama is not depicted on this map. It is too far south to qualify as a logical location for the narrow neck of land described in the Book of Mormon. If it were depicted on this display, it would have to be beyond the wall of the building. Notice you have the Gulf of Mexico on the north side, the Yucatan, beyond that the Gulf of Honduras, and then you have the landmass of Guatemala.

"Let's move closer to the center now. This time I'm going to skip over the usual tour and go to the eastern side of the land and show you something. You'll have a chance to do the whole tour, which encompasses all three major civilizations of the Book of Mormon, but at this time, I want to give you a quick overview of the layout."

The gondola moved to the north and stopped at the narrow neck of land, above what Duane said was the continental divide between the Sea East and the Sea West.

"Off to the north, you see a hill covered with vegetation. Keep in mind that this layout is not precisely to scale. The hill you are looking at is the Hill Cumorah." Stephen nodded, remembering his recent experience there.

A second screen descended from the ceiling. The screen was instantly activated with an actual aerial video scene of the Tuxia mountain range in southeast Mexico, with many lakes and streams visible as the camera panned the area. Off in the distance, Stephen could see a large hill, or small mountain. It resembled a smaller version of Mount Shasta in Northern California, minus the snowcap. The narrator on screen said in a smooth tone: "You are now viewing what some of the leading Book of Mormon scholars agree is the famous hill which the Jaredites called Ramah, later called Cumorah by the Nephites. It is located some eighty-two miles from the central point of the Isthmus of Tehuantepec and is surrounded by smaller volcanic hills, with artesian water flowing into the land below the hill. The hill is thirty-five miles in circumference and two thousand three hundred feet in elevation.

"This is considered the hill where Mormon deposited the library of metal plates that he had removed from the Hill Shim, which may have been one of those fifty miles farther west. Look to the west, and you can observe the hill we think was the Hill Shim." It was smaller and more distant than the Hill Cumorah. "Many scholars agree that, in a cave inside the Hill Cumorah, Mormon compiled the Book of Mormon. Then he may have instructed his son, Moroni, to take only the compilation, which was a single volume, carry it from the library, and deposit it where he would be directed to do so in another hill, the present-day Hill Cumorah in upstate New York.

"The first mention of the hill Ramah/Cumorah is found in the writings of Ether in the Book of Mormon. A great battle took place here. The remainder of the entire Jaredite nation met its demise at this hill." While the narrator spoke, Computer-animated figures moved across the screen. Armies gathered, and Stephen watched as a slaughter took place on screen. Thousands were slaughtered in battle. The screen was alive with men fighting one another in an artist's animated depiction of ancient dress, armor, and swords. Stephen felt as if he were watching one of Todd's video games. Soon the battle scene was replaced by another—numberless slain bodies of warriors covered the ground. Again the scene changed. The desolate terrain was littered with the white bones of the remains of those warring men. Then onto the scene came a small group of men who walked among the bones and picked up breastplates and rusted swords. The narrator indicated that these newcomers were the troops of King Limhi who had stumbled upon the remains of the Jaredites.

At a total of nine viewing sites, the gondolas would pause for video presentations. Duane indicated that nine gondolas could be dispatched at seven-minute intervals, making the duration of the tour just over an hour.

"This display is not intended to accommodate large numbers of viewers like the Epcot Center in Orlando," Roy said to Stephen, "but it will serve very well for classes on the Book of Mormon and the community at large."

"After the conference next spring, this exposition will be open to the public," Duane added. "Of course, they will have to pay a fee. With the growth projections in the Church and the number of tourists coming into the state, our estimate is that in two years, it will begin to pay back the investment. It may never make a profit, but what a great teaching tool this can be."

Even in the face of his awe at the scope of the layout, Stephen felt a nagging concern. "How do we stand financially on this work? Have all the technicians been paid?"

"I have no idea," Roy replied. "I do know that Dr. Polk and Thomas Kline planned this over two years ago, knowing that it would be the most expensive single part of their total venture. They sanctioned it anyway." Roy shrugged. "Things that have reason to one person may seem like foolishness to another. Look at Winchester, for example. Why did he build his ever-expanding house that is such an attraction in San Jose? But this display will have great appeal to the Mormons."

* * *

"Who's running things now that Polk is laid up?" Kline asked Hadley on the telephone. He had ordered the attorney to mount a complete investigation into the matter of Polk's reported stroke and the current status of the Book of Mormon project. Hadley had secured little information yet. He wasn't sure exactly what was happening. Chet did know through his investigative services that

Stephen had sent a fax to the Hollywood film company, indicating that he had fed-exed payment by check the day before.

"That means he's signing checks on the trust account."

"That's right."

"Does he have authorization?"

"Obviously he thinks he does. But did Marj authorize him? Either Polk has left some signed, blank checks sitting around, or this Thorn is a signer on the account. Either way, he is taking over and running the operation. He may be under the impression that it is all very legal."

Kline's mouth twisted into a smirk. "No matter . . . it may be just the proof we need to get him for fraud."

"Fraud is a tough thing to prove, especially with Polk laid up, but we have an excellent case to freeze the operation. All your sisters have to do is hang tough. They have to see this thing through when Thorn has his hearing. Talk to them, Craig."

Craig flinched at the suggestion that he contact his sisters. Marjorie, yes; Delitra, no. Hadley knew nothing of the inner family feud. Craig had now committed the one cardinal sin his father had repeatedly cautioned him not to do: "Never move on a complex issue in the company without full disclosure to your attorney. If you don't trust your attorney implicitly, then get another that you do trust. Always consult with your attorney. Don't go around that key legal advisor. He can't work for your best interests if you make him work in the dark." Craig knew he was doing exactly that by keeping from Hadley the fact that his sisters had given him two weeks' notice to step down.

It had happened the day before, like a surreal nightmare. They had ganged up on him. Marj had flown over from La Jolla—at the request of Delitra, Craig was certain—and the two had stormed into his office without any pretext or appointment. They simply showed up and announced that they wanted a family meeting. Marj had remained silent throughout most of the confrontation. She would never have taken the lead in the matter of confronting her big brother. Of course, Delitra had led the assault.

Craig hated Delitra as much as he had ever hated any human being on earth. From the time they were children, she had been the boss, especially when their parents were away on trips and the three children were left with Clara, the maid and nanny. He hated her, too, though she had been dead now for fifteen years. But it was always Delitra who took charge. By the time she was ten, she was bossing Clara around and dominating Craig, who was three years younger. She once hit him with a frying pan in the game room of their parents' home when Craig called her a name and said that he didn't have to do what she said.

She merely got up, stomped into the kitchen, came back with a ten-inch cast-iron pan, and strutted up behind him while he sat on the sofa watching Hopalong Cassidy on television. He had no idea what hit him when, with all her strength, she whacked him across the shoulder and upper arm. Craig always felt that she had meant to hit him over the head but had missed.

The heavy pan dislocated and severely bruised his shoulder, bringing up serious questions concerning abuse from the emergency room staff. Clara seemed helpless to do any more than rush him to the hospital and call his parents.

Delitra was unrepentant and refused to answer her parents' probing questions about the incident. She was restricted to her room for three days, and the subject was never broached again. From that time on, Craig never crossed Delitra, not even when he grew six inches taller than her by age fifteen.

The thought of that frying pan came back as Craig sat at his father's massive desk across from his scowling, heavily made-up sisters. Delitra bluntly came to the point. She ominously informed Craig that she had carefully reviewed the financial and projected progress reports of the family copper company and found that since their father's death six months ago, the Kline company had lost three million dollars in revenues.

"What is going on here?" Delitra demanded.

Craig took ten minutes to explain how there was an adjustment period after the death of their father, that he had to fire some people and reassign others. Management that he was saddled with from his father's organization had let him down.

Delitra wanted to know why their father could make a profit with that same management and Craig couldn't. Craig explained that management did not have all that much authority to act under their father's strict administration of the company. Craig was allowing management to make more decisions while the company made the adjustment following his father's death.

"What you are saying is that you are not calling all the shots around here. Why do we have you in charge then?" She sneered with that same contempt she had always held for his opinions.

"What are you saying?"

"I'm saying you are paid $160,000 a year to run this company, and we are fed up."

"Come on, Delitra. I've only been at this for six months. There is an adjustment period in every executive turnover."

"No, Craig. I don't buy that, nor does Marj. You have worked with Dad for the past twenty years; you were the executive vice president. Don't give me that 'turnover' bit. If you haven't learned it by now, you won't learn it, period."

Marj hated these confrontations. They were personally embarrassing and reminded her that she had always accepted Delitra's management of her life. She wished that she were more assertive, but somehow the issues were never so great that she wanted to confront Delitra with an opposing view. She knew that her timid manner allowed someone like Delitra to steamroll over her. It had always been this way. Besides, it was apparent during those growing-up years that Delitra was smarter and had always maintained the respect of her father, who had, at times, praised Delitra in family gatherings for her sharp mind and her ability to get things done. After all, it was Delitra who earned the money for her own Thunderbird when she was a senior in high school. She did it through a series of stock purchases that their father had helped her set up four years earlier.

Marj never earned money of her own. She had been happy to try out for the drill team and allow her father to buy her a new car. She despised the very thought of business. Now she desperately wished that she had not come today. She should have stayed at home in her hilltop house in La Jolla with Sam, her microbiologist husband, and their one son, who was starting high school with a bad case of zits.

"Marj, how can you sit here and let Delitra call the shots?"

Unwillingly, she was dragged back into the heat of the confrontation. Was there no way to avoid this? Marj shot a sidelong glance at her sister's set face and swallowed, keeping her eyes down. "Well, Craig . . . I'm as concerned as Delitra that the company is losing money. Uh, you know . . . I depend on the income from this business to help support my own family. If the company goes broke, then I really have nothing to fall back on. Delitra feels . . . that is, Delitra and I feel that . . ."

"That you are going to wipe us out," Delitra interrupted with a sneer. "That's why we have already decided, before coming here, that you have two weeks to help us find an executive to run the company. I know a couple of people who could do a much better job than you are doing, so . . ."

"Two weeks!" Craig bounced forward in his chair and slammed both hands down on the desk in outrage. "Listen, Delitra. You have no right to do this. All I need is a little more time. What are you trying to do to me?"

"I'm trying to save this company from bankruptcy, and in the process, I'll save you from losing everything you have. That's what I'm doing," she shot back without flinching. "Marj and I, since the two of us have the controlling shares to vote you out, have decided that I should take full control of the company and make the decisions until this operation is once again in the black. Then we will rely on expert management to give it direction, though I'll never again take a back seat. You can be sure of that."

"Marj, how can you let her do this? I'm your brother. This is not fair."

Marj fumbled about in her white leather purse, searching for a Kleenex that she could use to pat her nose and mouth in case she started to cry. Then she spoke quietly. "Craig, I know you are my brother, but I also know that this is best for all of us. You will still have as much stock in the company as either Delitra or I. I know you want the added income that you are making as president, but if the company fails, you'll be out of a job and our stock will be worth nothing. This is for your own good." Marj found the tissue and pulled it from her purse. She wished it were a blanket that she could hide behind. The Kleenex would have to do. "I just wish Daddy were alive to help us all get through this financial crunch. He was so good at what he did." Tears were beginning to well up.

Delitra was far from tears. "Craig, we want you out of here in two weeks. Do I make myself clear?"

Craig came up out of his leather chair, kicking it back against the wall. His expression was pure violence. He clenched both fists and glared at his sister with poison in his eyes.

Marj stared at him with fright, not certain where this confrontation would lead or just how nasty it would get.

Delitra sat without uttering a sound for a long moment as Craig's outburst slowly abated. A small muscle along the side of her jaw twitched slightly, the only indication of tension.

Finally she could stand no more. Her voice tinged with disgust, she said, "You know, sitting in a meeting like this with the two of you convinces me that they're letting the inmates sublet the asylum." She rose with striking composure and walked serenely to the door. "I'm out of here." She tossed the words back over her shoulder. Then turning, she aimed her parting salvo, "But so are you, little brother."

CHAPTER 19
The Burden

Lafayette

Morning came suddenly and early for Stephen. He could have slept until noon. He had missed his king-size bed and the quiet comfort of the house. Stephen knew without looking, from years of living in the Bay Area, that the mist from San Francisco Bay had crept over the small hills during the night and lay in pockets about the dells of Lafayette. There was nowhere on earth as conducive to sleep, with the windows open and the night air circulating about the room.

Nevertheless, he was up, showered, and ready to meet with head-hunters and, unfortunately, the Rotary Club—or at least the president. Both contacts would take their toll on his nerves by evening. How long had it been since he had really enjoyed a good night's rest?

Stephen returned to the side of his bed after knotting his tie and lacing his shoes. He knelt down and beseeched the Lord in prayer. In every prayer, he pleaded fervently that God would bless his family and especially Anney. Her name was included in every prayer Stephen uttered. He prayed aloud, pronouncing Anney's name repeatedly, as if he felt compelled to remind his Heavenly Father that this one precious soul, this being so dear to his heart, was out in the world without the guidance of the Spirit that he enjoyed. In spite of the recent events— Anney's ultimatum, Todd's precarious future, and Dr. Polk's fragile condition—somehow Stephen felt a reassurance that things would work out. How and what the final outcomes would be, he did not know. But somewhere inside the complex nature of things, he sensed that something would surface and a solution would come. It had to.

He arose, walked purposefully downstairs to the dining room, and picked up a stack of mail from the table. He had waded through the mail the night before, placed all the bills in one pile and personal letters in another, and trashed the junk mail. No letter from Dr. Polk. No notice of certified mail. This morning, he bound the stacks with rubber bands and placed them in his briefcase, along with the family's personal checkbook. He resolved to attend to them on his flight to Salt Lake City the next morning.

Before leaving to visit his placement agent, Stephen checked his phone mail and programmed the answering machine with a new recording, giving a detailed list of locations and phone numbers where he could be reached throughout the day. He didn't want to miss a call from Anney. With the essentials covered, he breezed through the kitchen, paused in front of the fridge, and then, as he started to reach for the door handle, realized that it would do no good to open it. Anney had cleaned it out before she left for Europe. He'd grab a snack on his way.

The place was so quiet and stuffy smelling. He walked to the sliding glass door, opened it, and checked the flimsy screen door to see that it was still locked. *Some security, that door,* Stephen thought with sarcasm. With all in order, he made his way to the garage, pressing the button to engage the automatic garage door opener. Climbing into the family car, he fastened his seat belt and turned the key in the ignition, wondering if it would start after such a long rest. The powerful engine leaped instantly to life. He backed out, closed the garage door, and started toward the freeway. The neighborhood was quiet; the school kids were not yet on the move.

As he drove, Stephen considered how he could get through to Marjorie Kline and have a meaningful conversation about the course he should take with the project. He certainly hoped to get to the bottom of the rumors he had heard of pending legal action. Stephen tried to reason out his complex dealings with the trust and whether he needed to concern himself with certain individuals on the board. He reviewed the board members. *There are five members. Polk is one. He is currently out of action. The two Kline daughters make three, Bennett four, and a man I have never heard of—the director of the Southwestern Museum in Phoenix, a guy by the name of*. . . Stephen tried to recall and couldn't.

Roy had given him a thumbnail sketch of each member and whether or not that member would give Stephen a hard time. As it stood in Roy's mind, Marjorie would want to carry out whatever plans her father had made, which meant she would favor continuing the project. She, as chairperson, had had some dealings with Dr. Polk over the past month. For one thing, he had indicated that she had freed up the funds for Project II. Before that, she had been in Europe for the summer. Roy had heard from Polk that she had needed to get away after the death of her father.

Stephen remembered that during her absence, her brother Craig had tried to bypass the trust committee and halt the San Diego project with an injunction. He shook his head as he remembered the night Kline had barged into their peaceful retreat, fiercely determined to prevent Polk from paying the participants the money they had earned. According to Roy, it would be out of character for Marjorie to do anything concerning family business without consulting with either her brother or her sister.

Bennett, as a board member was, of course, a shoo-in in favor of the projects. However, Bennett was not available. Delitra, the other member, would be concerned about the money spent and might see it as some fantasy her father had dreamed up with Polk. At this point, with Dr. Polk out of commission, the possibility was there that she might attempt to side with Craig to bring the project to a halt. At least, that was the way Roy saw it. She was more like her brother than her father. And after all, she stood to gain a third of the trust should they be successful in dissolving it or pursuing legal action against it in the absence of Polk. That might appeal to her.

The only board member who was unknown was the museum director. *What is his name? . . . Quail. Yeah, Quail. Markham Quail. I've got to get to know him, but what do I care? If they fire me, so what? I just don't want them to take any kind of legal action because I've assumed the job of running the project.*

He thought again of Marjorie and how she had declined his request to speak with her. He had called her at home the night before, hoping to break the ice and get acquainted. She had refused to come to the phone. Her son had referred him to her attorney.

What Stephen didn't know was that Marjorie was feeling reclusive, a result of the hostile family powwow that had occurred in

Phoenix earlier that day. After the bloodletting and sacking of Craig, she had left his office, taken a cab directly to Sky Harbor, and flown home, leaving Delitra on the curb shaking her head at her sister's wimpy attitude.

Stephen left his telephone number and the number to Roy's condo at Shadowbrook in Provo. He had stayed with Roy for a few days prior to flying home to Lafayette the day before. He would return to Provo tomorrow, although . . . he thought seriously of resigning and letting the project work itself out or turning everything over to Roy. Without clear authorization, his actions might be construed as usurping authority that he had not been specifically granted. Oh, there was the letter on the computer authorizing Stephen to assume responsibility in the case of Polk's inability to function as administrator, but there had been no signed copy in his mail. There seemed to be nothing official, other than conversations with Polk. Stephen had an uneasy feeling. At Roy's urging, he had gone ahead and signed some checks for pressing accounts before leaving Provo the day before.

Was he getting in too deep? *Back out now while you can!* But what about the salary? More than ever, Stephen needed money for his family's sake. He knew he could not take any more funds from the project without authorization, though Roy assured him that he could. It did seem clear in the instructions on the computer that Stephen was empowered to lead the project and, since he was a signer on the bank account, to expend funds for the project, including his own pay.

Roy had made everything sound so official and acceptable. He was sure that this was the way Dr. Polk had set it up, and if Stephen wanted to please the good professor, then he should follow through. *Easy for him . . . his neck isn't on the block.* But Bennett would be back in a little over a week, Stephen reminded himself. He would do no more than required to keep all the balls in the air. Time enough to collect his own salary once he had legal advice from Bennett.

It was just as well that Rotary met on Thursday and that today was Wednesday. Stephen would have felt the pressure to attend the luncheon and speak with the president, Glen Wilson. As it was, Glen asked Stephen to meet him at his construction company office. He had even asked if Stephen had time for a round of golf. Naturally not. Stephen wondered if he would ever have time for golf again in his life. Things seemed to get more complex as he grew older. Instead, he asked to meet Glen later in the day, indicating that he had business to take care of.

The Bay Bridge was crowded with commuters as he joined their ranks, inching slowly out of San Francisco. He didn't care. He needed some extra time to unwind and reflect on the morning's job interviews. His shirt was slightly damp under his suit jacket. The interviews had been tense and stressful to say the least. Still no firm offer.

Glen's office in Concord reminded Stephen a little of Conley Wilks's Quonset hut in Tucson, with drawing boards and plans rolled up and taped to the edges of drafting tables. It was decidedly more orderly and clearly a tad better than the hut, but it had the feel of creative productions underway.

"Are you telling me that Todd got drunk and got into a brawl in Berlin? Not our A-student boy! He's the all-American kid." Glen lounged back in his Naugahyde chair. Then he grew serious, pulling his body forward to look directly at Stephen. The two men were within months of the same age. But Glen had let his appetite dominate his flesh. The flab showed through the tight shirt that stretched at the center of his gut.

Stephen nodded ruefully, that yes, in fact, it was one of those kinds of things. Todd had allowed himself to be led on by some local kids. Except that a wallet was at stake and Todd had gone after one of the guys who had stolen it. At least *he* thought so.

"You know, Stephen, I hate to have to say this, but we got a fax about this incident the next day. I wanted to hear your end of it because you happened to be in Berlin shortly after he got out of jail. I have to be frank and tell you that some of the members are . . . shall I say, disappointed with such actions. If it were just me . . ." Glen shrugged his shoulders and stuck out his lower lip. "I was eighteen once and full of vinegar, but we're not talking about some kid away at college who gets drunk and into a fight. We're talking about someone we hand-selected to go to Germany, someone who is supposed to represent the best we can send. This jail bit bothers men like Harvey

Zinger and Phil Downing. I doubt if those two were ever teenagers. I think they were born fifty years old and sour as dill pickles."

Glen fiddled with his yellow pencil, tapping it like he had taken lessons from David Letterman. "Don't worry about Phil, but Harvey is regional governor of Rotary, and he wants us to bring your boy home."

Stephen hadn't really expected such a stern resolution to Todd's problem. He was a victim of the setup in the restaurant, though admittedly he was drunk. "You've gotta be kidding, Glen. That really isn't fair. Doesn't a kid get at least a warning, probation? Then if it happens again, or anything close to it, he's sent home? Why are they so set against my boy?"

"I didn't say they were set against your son. All I said is that they feel he has set a poor example, and we need to run a tight ship for all future participants."

"I don't buy that. Something's bugging them. It's not just Todd. Do you know that Harvey is an active member of my father-in-law's congregation?"

"Oh, come on, Stephen. That has nothing to do with this. Besides, your boy happens to be the grandson of the minister Harvey admires. It doesn't wash."

"I think it does. He wants to get back at me, so he's picking on my son."

"Okay, if it makes you feel better, go ahead and think that. I don't. And what's more, if you go around here with that kind of attitude, you may find a lot of bogeymen under every table."

Glen dropped the pencil and folded his arms as he leaned back in his chair. "I know you're sensitive to what's happened with your religion, but not many of us give it the time of day. If you like being a Mormon, hey, there are four fellows in our group who are Mormons, and they are some of the best guys we have in Rotary. Come on, Stephen. Lighten up on this issue. Face it. Your son has done something that some of the members feel is an embarrassment to the group. But as I said, I'm not one of them."

Stephen stood up. He'd had enough of the conversation with Glen. "So where do I go from here with this matter?"

"You don't. My advice to you is to stay out of it. Let me help. I think I have influence with Harvey. I'll do all I can to save Todd from expulsion from the program. Okay?" Glen's hand came across the table and gripped Stephen's in a firm shake. Stephen didn't respond with his usual warmth. He was thinking of Todd and how hard it would be to tell him that he could, well, be coming home.

* * *

The two young men looked like something out of a 1960 *GQ* magazine. Their hair was well trimmed; they wore white shirts and modest ties. Their suits were dark, and their manner friendly.

"How did you ever find me?" Anney asked, a little bewildered that two Mormon missionaries, very little older than Todd, had stopped by the studio at Krakow where she was busy sorting names with the new interpreter, Mio Musky, who was spending at least twelve hours a day with the group. Heinrik had discovered her at the university and offered her a temporary job interpreting for the Americans.

Anney needed no interpreter with the two missionaries. They introduced themselves as Elder Rowley and Elder Cox, one from New York, the other from Canada. They had come at the request of the mission president in Warsaw who had received a call from the mission president in Prague, asking him to please deliver a Book of Mormon to a Mrs. Anney Thorn.

"So we have brought you the Book of Mormon in English, compliments of President Berkeley in Prague. He said that he had forgotten to give it to you while you were at the mission home. He sends his apologies for that oversight." Elder Rowley handed over the book. "We hope you will read it. Also, if you have any questions, we would be more than happy to come back and explain anything you wish, if we can."

Anney wondered if they could. They seemed so young. The book had caught up with her, and in spite of her reluctance to accept it, she thanked the young men for delivering it. The young missionaries remained for another fifteen minutes, watching with curiosity as Moore directed one would-be televangelist after another in the art of preaching with fire and drama in front of the camera. It was a lengthy process since he had to instruct through the spoken word of Heinrik, who was in his glory, knowing that he was the key man in this complex procedure.

CHAPTER 20
No End to Adversity

Bay Area

Stephen felt the pangs of disappointment when Katherine answered the phone and not Anney. He was not at all certain that Anney would speak to him. Maybe it was just as well that Katherine be the intercessor for the moment. Stephen had tried Anney's room at the hotel in Krakow with no result. When the hotel operator asked if he would like to speak to someone else in the American group, he gave her Moore's name, hoping that Anney might be in her father's room.

Katherine was friendly as she explained to Stephen that Anney was not in, but she would certainly tell her he had called when she returned from the university. Stephen wondered why she was so late. Katherine explained that sometimes Bob and the staff stayed until after midnight. They were trying to instruct as many ministers as possible in the short time they would be in Krakow. Stephen felt impressed to explain the problem he was having with Rotary about Todd's little episode in Berlin.

"Katherine, I hate to drag you into this matter, but would you tell Anney that it doesn't look good for Todd right now? Tell her I met with the president of Rotary a couple of hours ago, and he said that some of the members are not in favor of Todd remaining with the program. Tell her I'm still working on this and will get back to her tomorrow or the next day. Do you mind?"

"No, not at all. Is there anything I can do from this end to help in any way? Do you need me to call someone? I know a lot of people in the Bay Area, some out in your neck of the woods."

Stephen paused for a moment. He didn't want to ask, but his son's education was at stake. Finally, setting aside his own personal pride, he said, "Well, maybe there is something you can do. You know, Bob is a member of Rotary. He carries a lot of weight with some of those guys. Would you—"

"Would I ask Bob to give them a call? Of course. After all, he is the grandfather and is as concerned as you about Todd. Who should he call?"

"Have him get in touch with Harvey Zinger. He's the governor of Rotary. He's convinced that Todd should return home."

Stephen gave Katherine Zinger's telephone number. Then, before Stephen could hang up, Katherine divulged the news of her marriage to Bob. She bubbled as she explained how Anney had made all the arrangements and how beautiful it all was.

Stephen listened to her words, but his heart and mind were too troubled to be able to share the exhilaration Katherine expressed. When she finished her brief description of the marvelous event, Stephen extended congratulations. He wasn't exactly certain that Katherine would be so enthralled with her marriage once the *real* man she had married surfaced.

While Katherine chatted, Stephen pondered whether or not to leave a personal message for Anney.

He decided to do it.

"Katherine, I'm happy for you, and I wish you the best." He hoped his congratulations did not fall flat. Then he asked, "When Anney comes in, would you mind conveying a message to her?"

"No. Tell me what you want me to say to her."

"Uh . . . tell her, if you will . . ." Stephen stumbled over the words, embarrassed to include a stranger in their very private affairs. He hesitated and then blurted out, "Tell her that I love her dearly . . . more than anything else in the world."

"I will quote you exactly, Stephen. And she will love hearing the words. Believe me, she will."

"Thanks, Katherine. Thanks a lot."

By evening, Stephen got a response from Glen, who called to let him know that his father-in-law got through to Harvey less than an hour before and dissuaded him from voting against Todd. "He'll stay in Berlin."

When Stephen hung up, he sat for a moment staring into the mirror of the dressing table in the bedroom, convinced that he, personally, had lost his clout among his fellow Rotarians and that his father-in-law would gloat over this little triumph of influence. He also felt that Bob had already called Todd to let him know that everything was settled, that he had personally interceded on Todd's behalf, and that everything would be okay. He wouldn't say it, but Bob would be certain to leave the impression that Todd's dad could not perform like the grandfather. *Get a grip, man. Since when do you care who has the most influence? The important thing is that Todd can stay in Germany and finish his term. You ought to be grateful to Bob.*

It struck Stephen as strange that suddenly little things like who has the most power would bother him. *Where did this fragile ego come from?*

* * *

"Are you asleep? Better yet, are you studying?"

"Hey, Grandad. As a matter of fact I was in bed, but I wasn't asleep. What's up?" Todd said, holding the phone in the hallway of the Gutenbergs' flat.

"I'm just checking up on my favorite grandson. I would have called earlier, except I was in the thick of this instruction thing I have going."

"Favorite grandson, tell me about it. I'm your only grandson, and yes I am studying every night, though I may be on my way out of Berlin any day now. Grades alone won't keep me here."

"No, you won't be leaving."

"What do you mean?"

"I mean I've been in touch with a powerful fellow in Rotary back home—I do have a little pull with my own group, you know—and about five minutes ago I convinced him that it was silly to pull a kid of your abilities and good looks out of the program. Also, my good man, I put my reputation on the line when I assured him that this would never happen again."

"Grandad, I told Mom and Dad while they were here that it was behind me. I haven't been hanging around with any of those guys that I went to town with. I'm one dedicated student."

"Great. Now tell me, who's your favorite grandfather?"

"You're my only grandfather, but you really are my favorite. I love you, Grandad."

"I love you too."

Katherine smiled from across the room as she gently wiped makeup from her face using cleansing cream and a soft cloth. Katherine reached for a Kleenex and dabbed at her moist eyes. *What a touching scene.* She smiled at Bob. "You're a sweet grandfather, Bob."

Tossing the tissue into the small wastebasket under the dressing table, she thought of what Stephen had asked her to convey to Anney. Katherine had mentioned the call to Bob, though not the details, just that Stephen wanted to reach Anney and also to let Bob know that he needed to contact his friend in Rotary.

CHAPTER 21
The Book

Krakow

When Anney returned to her room at the Sienna Hotel, it was early afternoon. She had received the message that Stephen had called at midnight the night before, and she had returned the call immediately, her hands trembling on the receiver as she waited for it to go through. A stab of disappointment had rushed through her when she heard Stephen's voice on the answering machine. She had left a message and hung up. Katherine had said that it wasn't urgent, but she so wanted to have a quiet talk with her husband.

This afternoon, she had left the staff churning out schedules and arranging for the next set of seminars to be held in Warsaw beginning Monday. They would stay through the afternoon. Anney, on the other hand, was too spent to continue. After trying to reach Stephen the night before, she had slept little and desperately needed a nap.

Riding back in the taxi from the studio at Jagiellonian University, where the staff had made camp in Krakow and where awestruck ministers and students hung on every word and action made, Anney mulled over what was happening. The excitement of something energetic and new permeated the scene, yet something didn't seem quite right.

All in all, she could see that, from her father's viewpoint, the tour was a rousing success. She had never seen such a stir of publicity and outside involvement by so many zealous young and middle-aged ministers, all desiring to emulate her father. He had triumphed over anything that he had undertaken in the recent past. Anney observed his incredible energy and personal charm as he instructed the participants in how to build congregations of Christian followers through the media.

The participants were also fascinated with the omnipresent film crew from Los Angeles. Especially were they pleased to be part of the documentary. Anney noticed that the Poles wanted to be recognized and understood by Americans. It had special meaning for them to be part of the world stage, particularly in this era, when a resurgence of Christian thinking was everywhere present in these spiritually starved nations.

It was plain that her father had launched himself into a new, more dynamic role as the evangelical guru of startup TV ministries. This was especially true among the downtrodden ministers of the old communist nations. They seemed so willing to cast off the burdensome yoke of the past and launch headlong into a new era of spirituality. Starved people seeking the Lord. It certainly was exciting. Anney had to admit that.

But sometimes lately, uneasy thoughts would creep into her mind. Anney had grown up watching her father deliver his sermons Sunday after Sunday, but she had never realized that such studied effort had gone into his every movement. Now, as she watched her father coach these would-be televangelists to use their hands, arms—their whole bodies—as props and demonstrate how to manipulate the timbre of their voices, to become emotional on cue, she was disturbed. *Are the words he preaches real, or are they part of the act, too? Is his whole ministry staged? If so, for what purpose? Surely he does great good. He has thousands of followers who write that their lives are blessed by his sermons.* Again, an irritating little thought slipped into her mind: *But they also send money. And he thrives on the adulation he receives.*

Anney shook her head in an effort to dislodge the doubts that were swirling around. After all, she had grown up with her father being center stage and captivating. She stood in awe of his presence, what he stood for, of his abilities. Anney remembered that one time when she was about twelve, she told her best girlfriend, Shirley, who lived two houses away, "My father is the smartest man I know." His approach to everything was colored by overwhelming intensity. He was considered a spiritual giant by many. He could take a very ordinary story, even one a bit hackneyed, and give it a brilliant spin. He spoke of common, everyday things—such as a child reaching for a father's hand in a crowd—and made such a mundane happening sound gripping, so essential to love and security. Anney had been part of this from her childhood up.

What was so different now? Maybe it was the strain of the tour and all of her personal problems that caused these negative feelings. Nothing seems right when you're so tired. *Get hold of yourself girl. You'll be a nutcase if you don't, and soon!*

Perhaps a shower and a half-hour nap would soothe her thoughts and make the remainder of the day more tolerable. She remembered that there was a dinner planned this evening by local dignitaries to honor her father. Anney was beginning to hate the dinners, especially here in Krakow. They were so proud of their rich, almost greasy, foods. She would simply taste them and leave most of the highly spiced meats and fried vegetables on her plate. She wished they would not pile the plates full and expect her to consume the entire four thousand calories she calculated were part of one celebration dinner. She knew Katherine felt the same way, except Katherine, with her charming manner, as she sat and talked with everyone near her—no matter the language barrier—was able to ignore the food in front of her. They didn't seem to pressure her to eat as they did Anney. It must have something to do with Katherine's years of experience with social affairs. She certainly knew how to manipulate the scene. Quite a talent she possessed.

When Anney finished her hot shower, she wrapped a terry-cloth robe about her and collapsed onto the bed with a sigh. She noticed the Book of Mormon, which she had tossed onto the nightstand. Casually, she reached over and picked up the book, recalling what the mission president had counseled her to do: "Read it, Mrs. Thorn. What can it hurt? You owe it to your relationship with your husband. At least see if you can detect what it was about the book that led him off in this new direction. Simply pick it up and read it. It will take you a few days, but what is that compared to the loss of your marriage?"

Katherine had advised the same thing the night before in the hotel hallway when she said good night to Anney and delivered Stephen's message. Bob had already disappeared into their bedroom to plead Todd's case with his Rotary friend.

From the rosy color that had crept into Anney's face, Katherine could see that she was pleased with Stephen's words. Taking a quick breath, Katherine burst forth with words of counsel she had been thinking about since she had talked to Stephen.

"You know what I would do if I had your special problem?"

"No, what?"

"I'd read that book . . . you know, the Book of Mormon. You know why?"

"No, why?"

"Because it was the thing that caused Stephen to change. It probably won't have the same effect on you, but at least maybe you can figure out what pulled him to the Mormons. To me, that would be an important little tidbit to know. Think about it, Anney. Read the book, then make your case."

Katherine had put up her hand to suppress the protest she could see in Anney's expression. "I don't get into personal religious views. All I know, honey, is that Stephen seems to be coming more than halfway in this quandary, and I think you need to give him a little space." She had leaned over and pecked Anney on the cheek, then wiggled her little finger good night and stepped back into her suite.

Anney touched the small, black-covered book, reluctant to open the pages. Stephen popped into her mind. *How had he first opened the book? Easy, he had read it because he was paid to read it.* Suddenly she felt ashamed of her attitude. She glanced up at her reflection in the mirror beside the bed and touched her drawn face. How hard and mean she had become. Her thoughts, even her conversations, especially where Stephen was concerned, were negative. Anney groaned silently. She hated the change that was creeping into her very personality. She *had* to harness the ugliness that drove her lately.

Why did she fear reading the Book of Mormon? Was she afraid that by taking the plunge she would only measure the depth of her abyss? But how could reading the book make things worse? Weren't they as bad as they could be already? *Yes, they're right. I should read this book.* She vacillated. *But I'm not ready yet. I need to take a nap first.* She pushed the book away and laid her head on the heavenly goose-down pillow. The drapes were drawn, though linear shafts of afternoon light slipped in on either side of the drapes, casting a soft, ethereal glow.

Noticing the halo effect, Anney pondered her actions, wondering if, at this very moment, they were not blocking out the full light she could enjoy. Why did such a thought inch into her mind? It startled her wide-awake. Try as she might, she could not mute the voice in her head, urging her to follow its promptings. Over and over the thought kept recurring—pick up the book, pick up the book. *Okay, okay! I will at least look at it now.*

With a sigh of resignation, Anney reached above the nightstand and switched on the lamp. She repositioned the pillow and scooted her back up against the headboard. Then she retrieved her reading glasses from the stand and solemnly picked up the Book of Mormon. Resolve replaced hesitancy. Anney opened the book and began reading.

She did not nap as she had intended when she took the afternoon off. She spent three hours reading the Book of Mormon, and was startled when she heard a faint knock on the door. On the heels of the knock, Katherine's quiet voice called her name, asking if she were awake. Anney set aside her reading glasses, then the Book of Mormon, face down, so as not to lose her place, got up, and started for the door. Then she turned, picked up her pillow, and laid it over the Book of Mormon, hiding it from view.

Katherine came in, apologizing for the intrusion. "Are you okay, honey? Bob told me you left the university early to get some rest. I thought I'd come in and see how you are."

"That's thoughtful of you, Katherine." Anney ran her hands through her tousled hair self-consciously. "You know, I don't think I'm up to dinner this evening, not with all those people and the pork in sauerkraut that is sure to be served. Do you mind awfully, Katherine?"

"Not at all," Katherine laughed. "I wish I had the good fortune not to feel well this evening. I would beg off, too."

"Oh, it's not so much that I don't feel well; it's just that, well, I would appreciate it if you and Dad would go without me this evening."

Katherine was sure she could read the situation. Anney was such a conscientious person. She was pretending to be well for the sake of her responsibilities. This afternoon was the first that Anney had taken off early. "I completely understand, dear. Would you like me to call room service for a light dinner?"

"No. I'm really not at all hungry."

Katherine was not the sort who pushed food onto anyone. "Okay, we'll be back around ten. Can I peek in and say goodnight?"

"Sure."

Anney resumed her place in 2 Nephi 14 as soon as Katherine left. She stopped a moment to adjust her pillow and then proceeded. She couldn't get over how sort of innocent the book seemed to her . . . So far, it was just the story of a family who left Jerusalem because it was destined to be destroyed. She noticed that the book had a good deal of religious doctrine interspersed with the account of the family's travels in the desert. It was not easy to comprehend; nevertheless, she was able to glean insights into some of the Mormon beliefs. The precepts taught by Christ and the prophets were powerful and clear. The book was not merely a collection of excerpts from the Old and New Testaments, tossed together with minimal thought and effort as Decker had said it was. It was emotionally rich reading, certainly different than she had expected it to be. *What did you think this book was about, anyway? The language sounds a lot like the Bible, but the feeling, the people are different.*

She read until after midnight. By that time, sleep overcame her ability to concentrate. She had been interrupted by Katherine at 10:45 when she came in for a moment to learn that, yes, Anney was feeling fine. As soon as Katherine left, it was back to the book. She had finished all of First and Second Nephi by the time she turned off the lamp and fell asleep.

Anney woke up four hours later with a start. She stepped into the bathroom and then returned to the bed wide awake. Once again she fluffed her pillow behind her back and began reading the Book of Mormon where she had left off at midnight.

She realized with surprise that a feeling of serenity had replaced the troubling thoughts she had endured for days, even weeks. Although she began the book with hostility, she had to admit that there was something captivating about the account she was reading. It had none of the schmaltzy writings she had envisioned. It was a logical account of a family's dispute and the rise of religion in the new environment where Nephi had taken his family after a falling-out with his brothers. She identified with Nephi and his tribulation. He was very spiritual, at least by his own account. But he, too, had not been at peace with his family, and he was too sensitive not to let it disturb his thoughts.

Anney no longer sensed a foreboding about reading this Mormon Bible. Nor was there an ominous spirit hovering over her thoughts as she turned the pages. It all seemed so refreshing. It was warm and direct, and she found it interesting. How could that be? Was she being subjected to the same spirit of persuasion that Stephen had experienced? Was she allowing her mind to be captured in the same way? *This book is not about to change my beliefs. But to think, I was once convinced that it was evil. Unwieldy, yes. Sinister, no.*

* * *

Anney had secured a first-class sleeper compartment on the late Friday night train from Krakow back to Prague. She was glad that her father had purchased European East Rail passes for all the members of his entourage. It was early morning when she hailed a taxi and drove to her aunt Elena's apartment.

The day before, she had spent the entire day in her room reading. First her father had visited her and ordered her a continental breakfast that she ate after he left for the university. Then Katherine came in again to inquire about Anney's health. Anney frankly told Katherine that she wanted to spend the day in her room reading. No, she was not ill.

Katherine had pursed her lips in concern. "You know, Anney, I think I can find a good doctor somewhere in this city. Shall I have Heinrik help me?" When Anney insisted that she just needed time alone, it had occurred to Katherine that she might be reading the Book of Mormon, so she backed off.

Now at Aunt Elena's apartment in Prague, Anney wanted to talk. They had spent most of the day poring over family photos and letters that Elena had saved from Anney's mother. Anney had never really learned to read Ukrainian. Elena read parts of the many letters Nadia had written from San Francisco before she became ill. The words and phrasing flooded Anney's mind with tender memories.

She had planned to tell her aunt that she was reading the Book of Mormon, but so far she had avoided the subject. She did call the mission president from Elena's neighbor's phone to thank him for the Book of Mormon and for taking so much time with her.

The president was with a group of missionaries, the receptionist informed her. She remembered Anney and reminded her that she was Sister Brighton, the sister missionary who was in the office the day she came in with her aunt. She said that the president would be out of the city until sometime next week, but that she would slip him a note asking if he could take a minute to speak to her. Anney protested that it was not that important, but in three minutes President Berkeley came on the line.

Anney asked if he had time to visit with her again late this afternoon, while she was still in Prague. She even offered to stay over until the next day if he could see her in the morning. The president hesitated, genuinely sorry that he was in the process of preparing to leave his office. He would be gone until the following Thursday, visiting with his missionaries and some of their contacts in other communities.

"Why don't you let me make arrangements for a couple of very knowledgeable, English-speaking missionaries to meet with you?"

"Well . . . I really do need to go on to Warsaw. And then we will only be there a week before we travel to St. Petersburg."

"And when do you plan to return to California?"

"We'll be home in four weeks."

"Well, if our missionaries don't catch up with you before you get home, there is another mission in the Bay Area. Their missionaries are just as fine, and they'll be glad to answer all of your questions. Would you like me to write to the president of the San Francisco area mission to tell him of your concerns?"

With a trace of disappointment, Anney thanked him for his kindness and concern but declined his offer. She really didn't want to involve herself that deeply in the study of Mormonism.

"Before you hang up," Anney interjected, "would you mind answering one quick question?"

"Of course."

"Angels," Anney said abruptly. "I keep hearing about how Joseph Smith had an angel visit him and give him the record from which he claimed to have written the Book of Mormon. I can't accept the idea that an angel would come down and visit Joseph Smith. It is too far-fetched for me to buy. How do you explain this angel?"

"That is a fair question," Berkeley answered patiently. "Do you accept the fact that angels came to the earth and met with the ancient prophets, such as Jacob, who became Israel?"

"Yes," Anney answered. "But that was anciently and things were different then."

"Do you accept the fact that angels came to earth at the birth of Christ? Do you also believe that the shepherds in the fields the night of Christ's birth saw the angels they claimed to have seen?"

"Yes. It is very clear in the New Testament." *Here we go again. He loves to play these mind games.*

"One more thing. Do you think an angel was present when Mary came to the tomb early that Sunday morning when Christ resurrected?"

"Certainly. But that was during a very special time, and those incidents deal with the time Christ was upon the earth. I can't see where this line of thought has anything to do with an angel appearing to Joseph Smith in the last century."

"But you do accept the fact that angels did appear and administer to Christ and others. What about *those* angels who appeared to Peter and the other apostles on the Mount of Transfiguration? Remember? Christ took them up on top of the mount, and hosts of angels appeared. Do you accept that as an actual event that took place in the time of Christ?"

Anney simply remained quiet. She knew she believed in *those* angels.

"Then, Mrs. Thorn, since you do believe that angels appeared to Christ and others in times past, you must accept the fact that angels do exist. You believe that they appeared at times in both the Old and New Testaments for some special purpose." The mission president paused for a moment, then continued. "I also believe that angels appeared throughout the times of the Bible. But your question is, was it possible for an angel to appear to Joseph Smith? Is that right?"

"Exactly."

"Do you feel that God could send angels to the earth again in our time, if he truly felt that he needed to? Has God disappeared from all the dealings of man in our time? *Can* God send down angels?"

"Of course he can, but I don't believe he has done that in our time."

"Why? Are we not in need of direction as much as Peter and the others in their time?"

"We have all of his teachings in the New Testament. We don't need God to send us angels."

"But you believe that if God *felt* that we needed direction in our era, as they did in times past, that he could? I honestly believe that God, in our time, in the last century, during the life of Joseph Smith, sent an angel." The president was quiet.

"I see," Anney said finally. "Well, thank you again for your time and for sending the book." She said good-bye and ended the conversation.

Back in her aunt's apartment, she invited Elena to a late lunch or an early dinner. "You decide which," Anney had offered.

The two enjoyed their stroll to nearby Old Town. Elena walked with a new spring in her step. She felt very fashionable in the soft, gray knit dress and warm, camelhair coat that had once belonged to her sister, Nadia. She had been thrilled when Anney struggled up her stairway with two large suitcases full of Nadia's clothes, which the Reverend Moore had brought back with him. Though the clothes were more than twenty years old, they were beautiful to Elena. She had lovingly caressed each garment, tears streaming down her face. When it came time to dress, however, she had put aside the bright colors, opting for the muted shades. Noticing her choices, Anney reflected that she had seen few brightly colored clothes in all the time they had been traveling in Eastern Europe. Glancing down at her own royal blue coat and floral scarf, she wondered what the European people must think of Americans in their flashy clothes.

Elena led the way to a tired, dark restaurant. It was the one that she had visited through the years with her neighbors, the one she could afford. They did have a savory red beet soup called *barszcz* that Anney enjoyed. The bread was tasty also, but the entrée of the day was another of those fatty meat dishes of pork and beef. It was expensive, too. Anney poked around with her fork and ate little.

"So your father has remarried," Elena declared, more as a statement than a question, after Anney described the wedding scene in detail. "But my sweet Nadia has only been dead . . . what? Two months, maybe?"

"You'll have to take that up with Daddy. I think his new wife is perfect for him. Remember, Aunt Elena, Daddy lost a wife many years ago when she could no longer communicate or understand anything. She simply lived on in body alone." Anney had not been so frank with Elena about Nadia's condition on her earlier visits. "She just sat there in that rest home, without communicating with us. She remained there all my married life."

Anney put down her knife and fork, looked down for a moment, and then looked up with a smile. "I think it is time for Daddy to have a normal marriage relationship again. I'm happy for them. If you knew Katherine better—you met her while she was here in Prague— you would love her as I do. She is a very kind and giving person. She is also very rich."

"Ah, maybe that is why your father rushed into this marriage business. Money makes a man do things quickly. But who am I to judge? I only think of my Nadia."

"I know, and I often think of her too, though I think she would approve of Katherine. She's good for Daddy."

Both women were silent for a moment. Anney sat with her hands folded in her lap, not able to eat another bite. Elena was keenly aware that her niece had hardly touched the main course, and her traditional values surfaced. She was the elder, the one who gave advice to the children.

"My sweetheart, don't waste food," Elena admonished.

For a moment, Anney felt certain that she would be lectured by this proud and modest lady who had already told her twice how she nearly starved during the Russian invasion of Berlin in 1945.

There was nothing more said, however. It then occurred to Anney that her aunt Elena gave counsel sparingly. She reminded Anney of an absolute monarch who made decrees only once, and her subjects had best remember what she said.

Anney decided against sharing with her aunt the fact that she was reading the Book of Mormon. She was not up to whatever response would be forthcoming from Elena.

At the apartment as a taxi waited, Anney promised to visit Aunt Elena one more time before returning to the United States. "Bring your father next time. You know, he must not like me. I'm just an old lady who has no influence with such a grand man who was seen by the whole world on television."

Anney protested that her father wasn't all that famous but he was a busy man. She reassured her aunt that her father had told her while they were on the train from Prague to Krakow the other day that he was sorry he had failed to visit with Elena, but that he would come as soon as the tour was completed.

"Fine. I will expect him."

CHAPTER 22
Roy

Salt Lake City

They stood in the intensive care waiting room. Stephen had never met Peter Polk's large family of children and grandchildren. His daughters all took the time to shake hands with Stephen and express appreciation for the way he had whisked their father out of Mexico. The oldest daughter, Susan, with tears streaming down her cheeks, thanked Stephen and then reached out and pulled him into a quick embrace. "I know Daddy likes you very much. He mentioned your name repeatedly when he had dinner with us before leaving for Mexico."

"I'm sorry there is little improvement in his condition," Stephen commented. "You know we are praying for him."

Roy leaned against his car and watched from a distance as Stephen made his way across the parking lot to the car. He had decided not to go up to meet Dr. Polk's family. He had said that Stephen's presence was enough. Stephen wondered if there was more to it than that. Something was bothering Roy.

The two got into Roy's car and slowly made their way to Fifth South, merged onto I-15 and sped towards Provo. Neither man spoke for the first few miles. Stephen finally broke the silence. "Things can change so quickly. I can hardly believe that just last week we were tramping around the ruins with Dr. Polk. And now . . . how fast this all happened."

He had intended to discuss the project with Dr. Polk's adult children, hoping to get some direction, and then realized through conversation with them that they had not been included in any of Dr. Polk's business. They had busy lives of their own, and though they were interested in their father's work, they had little comprehension of how far-flung the projects were or how much money had been spent on Project II.

Stephen knew that the key to moving forward was not centered in the Polk family; rather, it was with the Kline family in Arizona. He *had* to reach Kline's daughter, Marjorie Biddle.

Stephen knew that he could never replace Dr. Polk in directing the project. He had candidly admitted to Roy that he was nowhere nearly as proficient in such matters as the man who had spent a lifetime pursuing this dream. It would take someone with a broader vision and a greater depth of understanding of the Book of Mormon and all of its complex evidences to ultimately bring this project to fruition. It would be up to the board to rearrange affairs and appoint an administrator to handle all the matters at hand. In the meantime, however, as Roy had reminded him once again the night before when they were reviewing all the loose ends and experts involved, "You are the man in charge for the time being."

A few miles past the Point of the Mountain, heading south to his leased condo, Roy said softly, "Stephen . . . I decided last night that there is really nothing in this for me now. Without Dr. Polk . . . well, I guess I've lost interest in the project."

Stephen's face registered shock. He tried to fathom what Roy had said. He hadn't expected this from him. Not Roy, the man who expressed enthusiasm and commitment without complaint, the man he desperately needed at his elbow if he were to walk through this maze called Book of Mormon Project II. *This can't be happening, not on top of everything else.* Of all people, Roy did not seem to be the type to jump ship. He had been so loyal to Dr. Polk throughout the project.

"Roy! C'mon. You can't be serious."

Roy nodded his head that he was.

"Why? Why are you leaving right now when I need you so badly? You know I need your help. This doesn't make sense to me." Roy knew that Stephen felt abandoned. The pangs of unloading everything onto a single person, a man who had only been in on the project for a few weeks, had tormented Roy for several days now. He knew that Stephen would be upset with his decision, but he had mustered the courage to reveal his thoughts and get this behind him.

Roy instinctively responded with a rationalization of his position when he said, "Look, man, this has nothing to do with you, and certainly nothing to do with Dr. Polk. I really love that guy with all my heart. It has to do with me."

"What do you mean by that?"

"I mean . . . it's the way I see things now. Meaning *now*. I have to say to myself that without Dr. Polk, the project means very little to me. I don't have the inner resources, the faith, or commitment to press on like you do. When I was in Missouri the other day with that bigot of a professor . . ."

"Johnson?"

"Yeah, I guess I have a mental block preventing me from remembering his name. But I won't forget his ugly face," Roy remembered with scorn. "Somehow, though, he caused me to reevaluate what I was doing. He got to me. He wanted nothing to do with the project and rejected the offer outright. Oh, I've had a couple of others turn me down, but this was different. In some ways, I had to agree with him. He wanted nothing to do with a Mormon-biased project about a subject he has spent his entire career developing and lecturing about." Roy pulled the car into his garage. He turned to meet Stephen's troubled eyes.

"I think what I want to say . . . and I certainly didn't have the courage to confide this to Dr. Polk because I never wanted to hurt him, is that I lack . . . well, I guess it's courage. I don't want to have my future clouded by this project. In other words, I have my life ahead of me. People are going to ask me about my background and experience. I don't want to remain here and be dragged into court or be involved in some kind of scandal over this project."

"Are you saying that you don't think we did the right thing? You're the guy who encouraged me to continue spending money. Are you thinking now that what I did was illegal? Do you think I'm going to be charged with some kind of fraud? What are you getting at, Roy?"

Roy crossed his arms over the top of the steering wheel, and slowly lowered his forehead onto his arms. He took a labored breath and raised back up. "I don't honestly know how it will all turn out.

All I'm saying is . . . I want out. I have an opportunity to return home for the next few weeks, then enter USC in January." Roy sighed, rubbed his hands nervously around the steering wheel and said, "I'm going to take it." He shook his head and pushed back the long strand of hair that had fallen forward. He looked like a defeated man.

Stephen remained silent for a moment longer, stunned by Roy's defection. He couldn't begin to comprehend all the managing it would take to handle the whole mess by himself. But he would not beg Roy to stay with the project. He looked over at his young friend with disappointment tempered by understanding; he was a father, after all.

He knew that he could probably intimidate this young scholar. Roy had never been an aggressive person, yet here he was demonstrating an ability to assert himself for his own good by confronting Stephen about leaving. On one hand, he saw this as a plus in Roy's development. But this backing out, this turning away when Stephen needed an ally. He wished Roy had a stronger sense of responsibility.

Stephen sighed under the heavy awareness that he was now on his own. What could he do but let Roy go his way? He knew he had to hold back, that to bombard Roy with angry accusations would only destroy their relationship and mar all future contact. He could see the relief in Roy's eyes when he slowly smiled, shook his hand, and wished him well.

* * *

"Decker, I'm dropping this thing with Kline. I can't do it. It could get nasty." Bob took Decker aside in the lobby. He had asked Katherine if she would mind going up to their room ahead of him. He needed to tie down a couple things with Decker. The two men moved to the side of the ornate lobby and sat down on a settee next to a gilded pillar.

"I spoke with Kline on the phone last night, and he told me that there is a warrant out for Stephen's arrest. He's in deep trouble with the Klines. Craig informed me that his family is pressing charges for fraud. It seems that Stephen has authorized projects, signed checks, and who knows what all. All of this since that Polk fellow had his stroke. Stephen's in big trouble."

Decker tried to evaluate what he was hearing. "How do we fit into all of this?"

"We don't. I believe the information we have passed on to him more than satisfies the ten thousand he advanced me before this tour. I don't need the balance he would pay for the information that would establish his case. The problem is the current object of his charges—my son-in-law. I can't be a party to such things. I have my daughter to consider. It was one thing when Kline was after Polk. Stephen was just a means to the end. But it's different now. If my son-in-law were to end up in jail and I helped put him there, you can imagine the stress and heartache it would bring into our family."

Bob stood up and paced back and forth for a few minutes. Sitting back down, he resumed the discussion. "Also, I have to look out for my own image. It would do none of us any good to see Stephen in jail. Here I am, ready to make my move nationally, and my son-in-law hits the local front page, charged with fraud and embezzlement. I've got to work this thing out and keep my son-in-law out of jail. I mean, he's the father of my grandchildren. How would it look to have their father in jail? What if they ever found out that I'm the one who helped put him there? I can't do that. No, it would be terribly wrong."

Decker listened without comment. His mind was churning. There must be a way he could get into this action and help Kline get the evidence he needed to nail Stephen. Bob would never know. And Kline wouldn't care that Bob was out of the loop. His eyes narrowed as his plan took shape.

* * *

Night had almost enveloped the city. The overcast haze hung low over the pine-covered foothills in the town of Krynicka. Anney learned from her small guidebook that this had been a popular place with artists over the last century. They had discovered the spa with its reputed healing properties and flocked to it over the years. It was also the starting point for summer hikers who trekked through the Jaworzyna Krynicka mountains to the southeast. The cable car that carried passengers to the top of the mountains was based three blocks from the station. Anney, through gestures and the help of a student from the University at Lublin who spoke some English, managed to locate a taxi to take her to the castle up Poprad Road that had been converted into a bed-and-breakfast inn of sorts. The key reason Anney had selected the old castle was its low rates, which she heard about in Warsaw. They offered their rooms for half price during the off-season.

A small, battered Citroen taxi drove her the three kilometers up Poprad Road and delivered her to the front entrance of the ancient castle that stood on a small knoll surrounded by a forest. It was too dark to discern the higher mountains and peaks that daylight would reveal. The young driver opened the back door and took Anney's sole bag that she had packed with essentials and a change of clothes before she left to go to Aunt Elena's apartment. She had expected to return from Elena's to Krakow and move on to Warsaw with the rest of her father's staff. But she would be fine. What did it take to survive for a couple of days? A little cash and a change of clothes. Little else, really.

* * *

Stephen dejectedly contacted his phone mail service after Roy turned in for the night. One of the messages was devastating. Officer Crandall of the Phoenix police department left a number for Stephen to call, stating that the matter was urgent. Stephen sensed that much. He picked up Roy's phone again and dialed Phoenix. As he nervously waited for someone to answer the phone, he doubted that he would tell Roy anything about the problem, whatever it turned out to be. He wanted Roy to leave in peace.

Besides, it could have something to do with the plane they had borrowed in Mexico. If so, the responsibility was all his, anyway. Perhaps the Mexican officials had contacted Phoenix because that was home to the Mormon Project. Maybe he had violated some air traffic law, like flying without a license. Stephen's heart was cold with fear. *Or it could be . . .*

"Police Department."

Stephen identified himself and indicated that Officer Crandall had left a message for him on his phone mail.

"Mr. Thorn, yes, would you please hold while I retrieve the information?"

Stephen held the phone, unable to think of another thing until the officer came back on the line. "Yes, Mr. Thorn, a warrant has been issued for your arrest."

Arrest! The word conjured up images of jail, criminals, and a few other loathsome impressions. The worst had happened! *How can this be? A warrant for my arrest!*

"Mr. Thorn, I would suggest that you voluntarily surrender yourself. Are you calling from Lafayette?" The officer was polite but insistent.

"What? Uh . . . no. I'm at a friend's in Provo, Utah."

"Then you can either go to the Provo police station and they will handle this matter with us, or you can come directly here to Phoenix and turn yourself in. What do you want to do?"

"Just a moment." Stephen begged for time while his mind tried to process the crushing news. "Are those my only options?"

"I'm afraid so."

"What am I being charged with?"

"It looks like fraud and embezzlement. Please inform me of your intentions so we can avoid picking you up."

"Wait . . . who made the charges?"

"A Ms. Marjorie Biddle's name is listed here."

Stephen couldn't think clearly. He knew that he needed legal counsel. He wished Bennett were in Phoenix. He guessed he could call someone in the Bay Area. He knew a few lawyers, but they were all connected to Moore's ministry. What to do?

"What about having an attorney with me?"

"That's fine, but we will only question you and run you through the arresting procedure; then you will have a chance to speak to an attorney. Please, would you tell me your intentions?"

"I'll come in. I'll be in Phoenix Monday morning. Can I turn myself in at that time?"

"If you come in by 11:00 Monday morning, that will be okay. I'll note that on the computer. Be sure you are here by that time. I warn you not to evade arrest. That's a very serious matter. Good night."

Good night. What a joke!

* * *

It was Sunday afternoon. Bob and Katherine sat together in their first-class compartment on the train from Krakow to Warsaw. He pondered how to broach his involvement with Kline. He had no choice. If Katherine were to learn what had gone on from some other source, it could prove difficult.

Bob Moore had never before renounced his past wrongdoings. He had pushed ahead with deals most of his life. He had learned long ago, while tramping about with the tent preachers, that you never admit fault and you always cover yourself with local officials by making side payments to hoist a tent near town. A little money always made those lawmen deaf and blind. It worked the same way in the big time: cover yourself on any arrangements, and avoid less-than-honest deals with family and close friends. He had broken with this when he agreed to help Kline nail Polk and Stephen. Now he had backed off and was uneasy about Katherine. If she learned from someone else that he had been doing some underhanded dealing with Kline, who knew how she would take it?

Katherine rested her head on Bob's shoulder as they sat in silence while the countryside rushed by outside the compartment window. The trains in Europe were much smoother and quieter than the ones he remembered riding while growing up in Texas; but then, maybe trains had improved even in America. He hadn't traveled on one in years. It felt comfortable to relax this way and to remember that there were modes of travel other than by air.

Decker and Heinrik shared the compartment with Bob and Katherine, but at the moment they were in the dining car.

"Katherine."

"Humm?"

"Sweetheart, I have something to discuss with you." The moment seemed right. "I . . . I need to get something out in the open so we have no secrets between us. This is the counsel I give to the young marrieds in my congregation who meet with me from time to time for spiritual strength. I always advise them to lay everything on the table in their relationship."

Katherine turned her face slightly and nodded that she agreed.

"I need to tell you something that I may have done to Stephen that has come about by circumstance and not intentionally."

"What?" Katherine pulled her head up and met Bob's eyes.

"I was approached by this Kline fellow in Phoenix who has been trying to disrupt the Mormon project that Stephen has been involved in. Anyway, he asked me to help him destroy the project by finding some kind of dirt about the administrator of the project, Polk. You've heard Anney mention his name. Well, I felt I would be doing a service by helping out, and Kline mentioned that he would like to cover my time and expenses, plus make a donation to the ministry. He advanced me money . . . and I got involved." Bob could see by the expression on Katherine's face that she was interested in what he had to say and troubled that it might be serious.

"I did as I agreed to do. Nothing hurtful, merely informative for Kline's attorney. Then what happens? Polk has a stroke and is out of commission. I broke this thing off abruptly when that happened. However, the residual effect has been, well, an arrest warrant for Stephen."

"Oh, dear! I had heard that there were some legal problems, but . . . a warrant for his arrest? That's terrible!"

"I'm sad to say that it's true. A warrant has been issued."

"And you are telling me that you helped cause this whole mess that Stephen is going through?" Katherine was incredulous.

"No. That is not so. I said that up to the time Polk had his stroke, I was involved with Kline. I have dropped all involvement. I have had nothing to do with anything since. My sorrow, and the reason I'm telling you this, has to do with Stephen. I feel somewhat responsible for the situation he is in right now. All I want is for things to work out for him. I need to clear this up somehow, so I've started with you."

"Does Anney know about your involvement?"

"No."

"If she finds out . . . she may . . . I don't even want to imagine how she will feel about you."

"Listen, honey, Anney doesn't need to find out. She may be going through a divorce. She doesn't need to worry about some side issue right now."

"Is that how you view this? Is it a side issue when a person may go to jail?"

"I don't mean to minimize my involvement." This was not totally true. Bob was hoping in every way to explain what had happened without looking bad.

"I only took part when Polk was the target. I was helping Kline stop Polk. Frankly, I don't think I was in the wrong by exposing some goings-on among the Mormons. They are so pushy in the world and it's my Christian responsibility to help put the damper on them. Look how far-flung these people are. You didn't see those two young fellows in white shirts that showed up at the university studio the other day and spoke with Anney. They were Mormon missionaries, sent over here to convert the people in Poland to Mormonism. I tell you they are everywhere. I can't just sit by and let that group run over the rest of us without doing my part to stop the spread of their doctrine." Bob had not realized that he had slipped into his accustomed preaching voice.

Katherine noticed. "Calm down, Bob. I'm right here. You don't have to convince me of anything. But I have no axe to grind with any religious group. I don't think it matters a whole lot who does what when it comes to preaching love and respect. The Mormons are not bad people. They just have their own spin on the gospel as far as I'm concerned. What I am worried about is your daughter and her husband finding common ground and piecing together their lives." Katherine lifted herself off the plush, navy-blue seat and ran her open palms along her legs to smooth out her red wool skirt. Then she repositioned herself and stared across the compartment in deep thought.

"I'm glad you told me about your involvement in this thing," she responded at length. "Whatever you've done, Bob, I'm sure it was not meant to hurt Stephen, but I'm sorry you were involved. I just hope Anney and Stephen can work this out. I feel so helpless. Also, I wish Anney would call me. I don't even know where she is."

Bob chuckled quietly at her comment.

"What? What did I say?" Katherine gave Bob a puzzled grin. "I said something that you think is funny. What?"

Bob gently touched Katherine's cheek. "You have become the mother," he said. "You show more concern than I do for Anney, which means you have achieved this mother-hen role much sooner than I ever guessed you would. And thank you for your under-standing. You are something, Katherine. You amaze me." Bob reached over and pulled Katherine to him and kissed her, relieved that she had been so reasonable.

Katherine responded lovingly to Bob's embrace, but her thoughts were flying. *How could Bob do such a thing? Well, you didn't think he was perfect, did you? I wonder if he has manipulated other situations in this way. But just confessing to me shows that he wants to be a better person . . . doesn't it? Heaven knows good men are pretty scarce at my age, and he is such a prize. Just the same . . .*

Katherine drew away from Bob and smiled amiably. "Bob, I love you so much . . . You do know that, don't you?"

Bob opened his mouth to declare his own affections, when Katherine touched his lips lightly with one elegantly manicured finger. "I'm sure that you would never, never want to upset our relationship. I certainly will try to be the kind of person you can respect. I want the same from you, too. Is that asking too much?"

Bob slowly shook his head, fully realizing that the brief honeymoon was over and real life had begun.

* * *

Decker made the call to Craig Kline in the late afternoon from Warsaw. He persuaded Kline to allow him to be the conduit for information that he could extract from the family and sources he had learned about on his last trip to Provo. He mentioned to Kline that Stephen's wife, Anney, had left the group and was off somewhere, probably deciding to leave her husband. He had learned that much from talking with her father.

"Then you're saying that ol' Moore has bowed out on me? He kinda left things up to you anyway, didn't he?"

"Pretty much."

"Well, let me tell you, I need all the information I can get on Thorn. I made a financial deal with Moore, and he has my money. If you can get me hard facts in the next couple of weeks that I can use in court about the trust money Thorn is pouring into these projects, I'll spring for another five thousand and pay it directly to you."

"I think the amount you were willing to pay Moore was more than twice that, if I recall."

Kline came back with, "Take it or leave it. I'm not paying a dime more. When you deliver the information with names and facts, I'll cut you a check for five thousand. Okay?"

Decker had no choice. Five was better than nothing. He conceded to the new terms.

CHAPTER 23
Crisis

Phoenix

Stephen had checked into his hotel room at the Holiday Inn in Phoenix by early afternoon. The place was comfortable and less expensive than the Sheraton or Hilton. He was spending his own money now. He would pay no more than he had to on lodging and travel. Boy, had things changed since Dr. Polk's illness.

Concerned beyond anything he had known in recent years, he had started fasting the evening before. In an effort to get help beyond his own abilities, he went down on his knees, pleading with the Lord to hear his prayer. Never had he prayed like this.

Dr. Polk had told Stephen, while he instructed him in the gospel, mainly on their trip to Mexico, that prayers of faith are always answered in one way or the other. "Stephen, the Lord is aware of our needs and is eager to help us if we will humble ourselves and fast and pray."

Well, he desperately needed help. Every part of his life was in disarray, but right now, this moment, the aim of his fast and prayer was that the trust's attorney, William Bennett, would somehow know that Stephen needed his help.

He thought of the lively discussion that had taken place in elders quorum meeting earlier in the day. Stephen had attended Sunday services in the Edgewood Ward, the home ward of Roy's neighbors in Shadowbrook, before flying to Phoenix.

The lesson had centered on prayer. More than one of the men had admitted that all too often their prayers were perfunctory—a result of habit, rather than sincere communication with their Father in Heaven.

Touching experiences of prayers being answered in surprising ways had also been shared.

Stephen had been overwhelmed with gratitude once again that he had found the gospel of Jesus Christ, that he was privileged to be part of an organized body of sincere, intelligent people who instructed and encouraged each other without a paid clergy. He had left the meeting uplifted, his faith strengthened. His Father in Heaven knew of his needs. Surely he would reach out and help.

Stephen had certainly tried to find Bennett on his own. After exhausting all leads from Bennett's office staff, he had consulted every rafting outfit in the country around Bogota. What Stephen didn't know was that the headquarters for the agency that booked the Bennetts' tour was in Panama.

Now, all Stephen had was fervent, sincere prayer to help him get through to Bennett. In all his years working with Moore in the ministry, he had never learned the meaning of real prayer. Now he knew his Heavenly Father better. God had promised that if he prayed sincerely, his prayer would be answered. Stephen's prayer today was piercingly focused, and he was oblivious to any other actions around him. He wanted an answer. He needed Bennett.

He would take time later in the evening to plead for spiritual assistance with Marjorie—for some way to get her to listen to him. And underlying his stream of thoughts were prayers for his precious Anney, for Todd and Brenda. Also he was concerned about Dr. Polk. But above all, his supplication to the Lord was to open a way for the Spirit to reach Bill Bennett. Bennett knew so much about the entire trust and projects. *Where are you, Bennett?*

* * *

A thousand gallons of white water slapped Bill Bennett like the force of a two-inch fire hose turned directly on his upper body. The impact caused him to slide backward in the twenty-foot rubber raft. He grabbed the side handles to keep from slipping off the craft. Water cascaded all about his muscle-tight body. Somehow he managed to pull himself back into the bottom of the boat and brace for the next deluge. It would surely come in these rapids, the most challenging rough waters he had ever endured.

Karen, Bill's wife, had both hands on the grippers attached to the top of the inflated portion of the bright orange raft. Elation was imprinted across her face. Enduring the tortuous fifty kilometers of whitecaps and surging water was all by choice. After the latest fray, splashing water continued to dash across the bow of the raft, though not so forcefully as the one that had nearly swept Bill from the boat.

To Karen, it was the ultimate experience—woman and man encountering the wilds of nature with all her pent-up fury. No wonder her friends, knowing her penchant for the challenge, had insisted that she and Bill try the Cauca River rapids of Colombia's raw interior. Nothing she had ever attempted compared to these perilous white-water rapids. Only daredevils attempted this river. The torrent of white, dashing foam continued for another half hour, the boat masterfully navigated by its thirty-year-old captain.

They emerged from the canyon, where the caps subsided, and floated into a wide clearing of jungle edged by a narrow white beach. The river in this location was swift, though wide and glassy. On shore was a tropical Shangrila, where bright blue, yellow, and red tents and tables were already set up, and refreshments were waiting. It was all part of the charter package.

The white-water rafting tour had promised to be in primitive lands, geared for rafters of means who, after the daring clash with tons of water, wanted the luxury of a mini-resort in the jungle. Bill Bennett had to hand it to them; these guys came through with their promise. There would be five more days of sheer excitement before the Bennetts would have to catch a flight out of Bogota for home.

The trip had done wonders for Bill and Karen. Isolated from all outside communication, they had enjoyed the rapids and the primitive, wondrous jungle offered up with impeccable service, both on land and water.

The evenings after rafting were spent in large tents, complete with mosquito netting, tables set with linen, and cooks and their scullery maids scurrying about under colorful fringed canopies. At night, the stars seemed closer than anywhere on earth.

Karen and Bill Bennett, seated at the small table, dined by candlelight on crab and lobster plus sautéed mushrooms dripping with creamy butter. Bill leaned forward and reminded his vibrant wife that all this grandeur—eating and sleeping as if they were at the Ritz Carlton—came via the magic of helicopters.

The tour agency that made all the lavish accommodations in the wilds was careful not to disturb the rafters as they descended the narrows in a torrent of fresh river water, with sheer rock cliffs rising like skyscrapers above their heads and leaping waves of water pouring across the rafts that never sank. Excitement and relaxation. After challenging the rapids, they lounged in the sun on the quieter waters near lagoons and fabulous fishing holes. Bennett was most in his element when the rafters took two or three hours to enjoy the wonders of nature in the still waters, casting for fish to their hearts' content.

When the Bennetts finished dessert, they strolled along the quiet but fast-flowing river and watched the frogs and fish snap up the insects that hovered close to the water's surface. Karen noticed that Bill had been unusually pensive since leaving the river. She had asked him at least three times what was bothering him. She figured he didn't know, so she had let it be until now. Finally, unable to ignore it longer, she put her arm around his waist and asked, "I know something is eating at you. Why not get it out, Bill?"

He shook his head in bewilderment, "Darling, I hate to tell you, but I have experienced the craziest, most uneasy feeling for the past few hours," Bill said hesitantly. "I can't seem to shake it. I get the distinct impression that some urgent thing has happened at home and I should be there."

"Oh, come on, Bill." Karen let go of his waist and spun around in front of him. "Of course you get those feelings. You left a bustling office full of attorneys and paralegals that you have to pay, day in and day out, whether they do any good or not."

She swept back her long hair and said, "You have irons in the fire at home. Your thoughts are naturally there. No sane person could escape for a couple of weeks out of contact with the outside world without conjuring up images of imminent disasters at home. It goes with your kind of work. I knew that your mind would never be able to shut off your sense of responsibility. It is nearly impossible for a person with your makeup to do such a thing." She rubbed his face soothingly. "You just have to say to yourself, 'I'm here. They know I require a vacation after so many months in the salt mines.'" She studied his face. "Leave it alone, honey. Your staff will manage somehow. Enjoy, Bill!"

Bill moved his head from side to side. "That isn't it. For the entire trip, up until this afternoon, I have been as relaxed as a hippo in warm water. Really I have. This thing has swept over me, as I said, just this afternoon. That's why I know I have to check in."

"Bill, you're really serious." Karen's pretty lips turned down in a pout.

"Yeah, I am. Dead serious. I would like to ride into Bogota tomorrow morning when the big chopper makes its daily pickup and delivery."

"Honeeey, if there really was a major problem, your secretary would have called the agency and one of the helicopter pilots would have delivered you a message."

Bill stood looking at Karen, shaking his head. "Not really. I told no one exactly where we are. I said zip. Now, maybe you left word, but I didn't."

"Hmmm. I guess not. I didn't even tell my mother our exact location. I figured you would take care of it with your secretary."

Bennett, as he did so often in court, cut to the core and said, "Do you want to fly in with me or remain on the raft?"

Karen considered it for a moment, but really, there was no question in her mind. "I'll stay on the river. You go if you have to, but I'm sure you will fly back out on the next helicopter, and you will have missed the best narrows of all and the funneled water passage they have been warning us about. We go through them an hour after we start out tomorrow. You'll hate yourself for this."

"If I have to go home, the helicopter pilots will get the message to you. If so, I'll make certain your flight out of Bogota is booked and ready. I'll talk to the Richards over there before I go and have them look out for you. You could fly home with them. They are landing in Phoenix and making a connecting flight to Vegas. They told me on the raft."

"Oh, Bill, *try* to get back." Karen took Bill's strong arm and snuggled up to him as they retraced their steps to base camp and luxury.

* * *

Anney had spent all day Sunday reading through the book of Mosiah; Monday morning, early, she was into Alma. She was making progress. The momentum built, but she still wondered about the book and its place in her life. She understood much of what it expressed, yet it failed to move her to the spiritual reaction that Stephen maintained he had undergone. Book or not, she was still the same Anney she had always been. Or was she? Was it possible that she was looking at the religion from Stephen's point of view? *Nonsense! . . . But I have to admit that I can see where someone might be impressed by the doctrines in it. And Stephen did say that his group of scholars heard experts validate many facets of the book. I guess I can see how it might happen.*

Anney had called Katherine from Krynica Monday evening and told her she was taking time off to relax and to get a better perspective on her life and her future. She was in seclusion, but her motives were different than they appeared. She wanted to finish the Book of Mormon.

"Honey, Stephen called," Katherine told her.

"Did he?" Anney said, her heart beating more rapidly.

"Yes, he did. Anney, he's your husband, after all."

"Katherine, I know you have our best interests in mind, but I still need time to think. I've tried to call him several times. We keep missing each other."

"I know, sweetheart. I think of the misery you are going through, and all I do is nag you. Sorry. Still, Stephen left a couple of messages for you."

"Did he?"

"Yes, he said that this Dr. Polk is still unable to speak. Stephen seemed a little down. I guess they were good friends."

"Dr. Polk isn't able to run things?" Anney hated herself for not feeling deeply sorry about his condition. Polk was part of her misery after all. She wouldn't have wished him ill. A flicker of hope surfaced as Anney thought that, just perhaps, the whole Mormon project would fold with Dr. Polk out of the picture. Her delight was dashed when a second thought entered her head. *If it folds that means Stephen is out of a job . . . Well, I don't care. I really don't care if he will only come home to us . . . He can find a another job closer to home.*

Katherine conveyed the second message, "Did you get that? Are you there?"

"Oh, I'm sorry, what did you say?"

"I said that Stephen has a special request. He seemed almost embarrassed to convey it to me."

"What is it?"

"He asked that I tell you that he wants you to remember to pray. Not just to pray, but to pray out loud. I suppose you know what he means."

"No, I don't know what he means. I guess he wants me to pray for a miracle. I don't know."

"Okay, you can toss it off lightly if you want, but I still think it was kinda sweet the way he gave me the message for you. He's trying, I tell you, honey. He's trying to let you know something."

"Well, I'm not sure I get his meaning."

"When will I hear from you again? Do you have a phone where I can call if I need to reach you?"

"No . . . please don't call . . . that is, not just you. I need to be left alone. I'll call you again. How's that?"

"Fine, I guess."

"Katherine, I'm sorry to be so uncooperative. I'm trying to get this whole awful situation back in place, and I need to be alone to do it. It has nothing to do with you. Since we've been together these last few weeks, I've come to appreciate you very much. You really are a dear person to me. I promise to be in better spirits next time. I will, believe me, Katherine."

* * *

Sleep wouldn't come. With his hands under the back of his head, Stephen lay awake staring at two dots of light that reflected on the ceiling from a streetlight outside his hotel room. Over and over, he reviewed the facets of his crumbling life. Every few minutes his mind would revert to the warrant out for his arrest.

Once he had stolen a Hershey bar at a drugstore in Ely, Nevada, when he and his cousin were in town. He couldn't have been more than twelve or thirteen. He got caught. The druggist threatened to call the police. He didn't, but that was as close as Stephen had ever come to facing official justice.

In a state of half-sleep, he played and rewound and played again a mental video, the scenario that would culminate his legal nightmare: a judge with a long, serious face peered over the black rims of his half-glasses, pronouncing his sentence. All the legal minds had come together—Bennett was there, Anney was not—she would have no more to do with a criminal. But the defense could not come up with a convincing case. The computer document authorizing Stephen's actions, which Roy had assured him was valid, was not. There were no smiles in the courtroom. Solemnity prevailed. The judge held up his index finger and moved it back and forth as Stephen had often seen his aunt do. "Mr. Thorn, you have violated the law. You have disgraced your family, and not even the influence of your famous father-in-law will have any effect on the judgment of this court. You are hereby sentenced to . . ."

A loud siren outside his hotel room window stirred. Stephen from his restless sleep and forced him to return to reality. Reality was a nightmare as well. Would morning never come?

* * *

All his adult life, Markham Quail, curator and director of the Southwestern Museum in Phoenix, or more exactly in Scottsdale, a suburb of the desert city, had been dealing in western art. He had been at it for forty years and over time had established a reputation for acquisitions that rivaled some of the large museums on the east and west coasts of America.

Quail had been a good friend of the late Thomas Kline. It was he who graciously accepted the Remington painting that Thomas donated to the museum; the one Thomas had dearly loved and hung on the south wall in his high-rise office.

The donation of the valuable painting had been a controversial matter with Craig Kline when he had been forced to turn over the piece to the Southwestern Museum the month before. Craig had contested the validity of the donation of such an expensive work. He maintained that it belonged to the family. He, in fact, had no grounds to keep the painting. When this was explicitly explained to him by his own attorney, as well as the museum's legal counsel, he had conceded the issue and reluctantly surrendered the painting, which he had stored for several months in a bank vault at First Security in Phoenix.

Quail had been disappointed that Craig had acted with such immaturity regarding a gift his father intended for the enjoyment of the public. It was also a rather prized gift for the museum, and of course, Quail took full credit for the procurement of the art piece.

Because Thomas Kline admired Markham Quail's professional status and acquisition skills in the world of art, he requested the year before that Quail serve as a board member of the foundation Thomas created to promote intense study of the Book of Mormon. Quail was not a Mormon, but he gladly accepted the position, though up to this time, he had maintained little contact with the foundation. As he recalled, he had attended but one board meeting, and that was before the death of his friend Thomas Kline. For the most part, especially since the death of Thomas, he gave his membership on the board little thought. Now, he listened by telephone to this Stephen Thorn, who was handling pressing matters for the foundation because of the sudden illness of the director, Dr. Polk, whom he had met only twice.

Stephen had called Quail to inquire about his own status insofar as the board was concerned. Quail pleaded ignorant to any information or direction that he may have been given as to the current situation as it impacted the foundation. He advised Stephen to contact other members of the board, principally Thomas Kline's oldest daughter, Delitra, who would perhaps be Stephen's best ally in these matters, though her sister Marjorie was the chairperson.

"I have a question to ask you, Mr. Quail," Stephen interjected before ending the call. "It appears that Delitra's brother, Craig Kline, is seeking criminal charges against me through his sister Marjorie on grounds that I have illegally usurped authority in the administration of the Book of Mormon Project trust. The trust attorney, Bob Bennett, is in South America, and I am unable to reach him at this time to have him clarify the legal aspects of what is happening. I'm frankly troubled about this whole matter. What do you know about all this?"

Quail replied that he had no information except the notice he had received from Stephen that Dr. Peter Polk was ill and that

Stephen would be contacting foundation board members. Quail then told Stephen that he had been in New York when the fax came in. He had read it for the first time when he arrived at his office this morning.

"How else can I help you in this matter?"

"I'm not sure. All I really know is that the Phoenix police have asked me to turn myself in by 11:00 this morning."

Apparently Quail had heard nothing of the troubling issues surrounding the board. He responded by saying, "Let me look into this matter a little further. Do you know Craig Kline?"

"I've met him."

"Craig is an impetuous person. I've known him for a number of years. His father was a close friend of mine. Are you aware that the rumors around town are that Craig is having real financial trouble with his father's company?"

"No."

"Actually, it is more than rumor. I'm concerned that the company may go under and we will lose the annual sustaining funds to house and properly care for the art pieces that Thomas has donated to our museum. One of my museum board members is a banker here in Phoenix, and he has informed me of some serious reverses in the Kline company. I suspect that Kline's motives are to get hold of some badly needed funds."

"I understand from a conversation I had with Dr. Polk," Stephen interjected, "while we were together in Mexico, that you had a devil of a time wresting an expensive painting from Craig. Is that true?"

"Yes, but I would rather not get into that." The acrid tone to Quail's voice came through clearly, but immediately his voice became cordial once again. "One other thing you may be interested in knowing, however. I have it on good authority that Craig's two sisters have asked for his resignation from the firm. And I also understand it is to take place in a matter of days."

"I may need to contact you again on this funding matter. Things are coming at me rather fast. May I call you if I need your help, since you are one of the five board members of the Book of Mormon Project Foundation? I may need some advice on where I stand."

"I will say this. Up to now, I have not been fully apprised of exactly what is happening in this organization. I should like to look into the matter before making any type of commitment to be of assistance to you. I hope this is not too difficult for you to accept, but you must understand my position and how I must handle this matter as a board member. Marjorie Biddle is chairperson, and she ought to be the person you discuss these matters with."

"I know. I have tried to contact her, but she has not returned my calls."

"Then go see her. Perhaps you would get further with her and resolve this problem if you confronted her in person."

"How?"

"Go to her home in La Jolla and talk with her. She is not a forceful person. If you were to show up on her doorstep, I'm quite certain she would speak with you. Give it a try, but please don't mention that I suggested this approach. I have had enough problems in my dealings with some of the family. By the way, if I were you, I would seek counsel from a respected attorney here in Phoenix, and soon."

"I know . . . I know I need a lawyer, but I have to report to the authorities in half an hour."

The arrest process was a totally new experience of the most degrading kind. Never had Stephen been plunged into such depths of personal embarrassment.

He had entered the Phoenix police station, where he sat outside the cluster of offices in a small waiting room without windows. It was strictly utilitarian: two plastic-covered, brown sofas, an end table, some government documents in a small rack—that was it.

Five minutes later, Detective Crandall, a man with a wide, friendly face and businesslike manner, walked into the waiting room and introduced himself. Stephen guessed he was nearing sixty years of age. He thanked Stephen for voluntarily coming in and asked him to please step into his office. Crandall pressed a series of buttons on an electronic lock; the door clicked, and he opened it. He led Stephen down a narrow hall to an enclosed room about eight by ten feet in size, with bright overhead lighting. Crandall's niche was one of a covey of offices in the locked sector of the building. They entered, and the formal arrest process began.

A lengthy form detailing all past arrests, violations, and other personal information had to be filled out. Stephen had no criminal record, had never been fingerprinted, photographed, questioned, or had experience with any one of dozens of circumstances that Crandall asked about and noted.

After the forms were completed, the detective began to question Stephen in greater depth about his involvement with the project and those associated with it.

"I would rather discuss the details in the presence of an attorney," Stephen answered.

"Do you have an attorney?"

"I do, but he is in South America. I intend to call one here in Phoenix today."

Crandall folded his notebook and escorted Stephen to another area of the complex, where a young female police officer in a uniform too tight to conceal her bulges received Stephen for fingerprinting and photos. At that point Crandall disappeared. The entire process took another hour, much of it spent sitting in a hard chair, waiting. With all the paperwork completed, Stephen was turned over to a third police officer, who permitted him to call Bill Bennett's office.

Apprehension mounted when Bennett's secretary told him that she had no way to reach her employer. She was certainly sorry about his arrest and promised to send one of the firm's attorneys to the jail to give him some legal counsel.

The police officer escorted him to a crowded cell. The heavy steel doors clanged shut behind him, and Stephen was enveloped with a feeling of doom. He was relieved, as he moved further into the cell, that he had not worn a suit and tie. As it was, Stephen could see the hard, suspicious stares of his fellow inmates. He realized with panic that he should have sought legal counsel before surrendering to the police, since he was not at all certain of his legal options now. *How could I have been so trusting . . . so stupid? Why are those guys staring at me? Man, I've got to get out of here.* It occurred to Stephen that he was the second Thorn to be jailed in less than a month. *Poor Todd, what a frightening experience for him . . . and he couldn't even speak the language.* How would he explain this whole mess to Todd? Worse yet, to Anney?

* * *

Bennett took a taxi from the airport, where the helicopter had dropped him, to the Sheraton in downtown Bogota. The rainy season was over, and dust swirled about him. The late morning heat was oppressive as he emerged from the taxi. He headed straight for the telephones in the lobby and asked the hotel operator to help him put a call through to his office in the United States.

His secretary picked up the phone in Phoenix. "Oh, Mr. Bennett, thank goodness it's you! It's great to hear your voice. I have a long list of people wanting to talk with you."

She paused a second and then told Bennett about Dr. Polk's stroke. It was alarming and sad for Bill. He had built a strong friendship with the aging professor. How could so much happen in such a short span of time?

"Most of the people who want to talk to you can wait until you return next week. However, this Thorn fellow, the one who was working with Dr. Polk . . . he's in deep trouble. He was arrested this morning. Harvey is going down to the jail to see what he can do . . . I have more, but I can hold it until you get here, or I can send you a fax."

"Hold the fax, Jolinda. I'm coming home. I had a premonition out in the jungle that something serious had happened. It looks like Stephen Thorn needs our help. Why was he arrested?"

"It has to do with that, that . . . you know . . . that Book of Mormon project. They have charged him with misuse of funds and fraud. I don't recall all that he's facing."

"Do they have a strong case against him? How does it look?"

"He hasn't been arraigned yet. That comes this afternoon. I'm no judge in these matters. I guess he wrote checks to pay some project accounts. They claim he had no authority. You have seen enough cases to know that these things can go either way. He really needs you, though. He called here and asked to have an attorney go over to the jail and talk with him. As I said, Harvey Dotson's on his way."

"Is Harvey still there?"

"Yes, but he's on the phone right now."

Bennett took a minute to let the information compute and come up with a plan before directing Jolinda in how she should handle things. Then, with Jolinda scribbling as fast as her pen would write, he instructed her to tell Harvey Dotson to get Stephen before a magistrate, post bail, and get him out of there. He indicated that he would call Valley Bank from Bogota and have his good friend Bradford Scott release the funds needed for bail. Dotson was to call the bank in thirty minutes to confirm that the money was available. Bennett asked Jolinda to stay at the office until he called her during his one-hour connection in Mexico City to see how things were progressing. "Just tell Dotson to get that man out of jail; he shouldn't be there in the first place. I'll arrive in Phoenix late tonight. Get Thorn to meet me in my office at six o'clock in the morning."

* * *

It was late afternoon by the time Stephen emerged from the police station to be escorted to the courthouse. In the courtroom, he found Bill Bennett's associate, Harvey Dotson. Dotson shook hands with Stephen cordially and reaffirmed that he would assist him through the process of arraignment and get him released on bail. Stephen was mightily relieved to learn that Bennett was on his way.

The process consumed another two hours; most of it spent waiting their turn to appear before the judge. Because of the amount of money involved in the criminal charges, the judge, a young man of Japanese descent, set bail at one hundred thousand dollars. He scheduled a court date two weeks hence and moved on to the next prisoner. An hour later, after Harvey Dotson and an assistant scurried to Valley Bank to pick up a certified check; bail was duly posted and Stephen set free.

While he waited for his appearance before the judge, Stephen had outlined in detail a possible strategy to clear up his personal disaster. He would need Bennett's approval and legal counsel to set the plan in motion. If Bennett agreed, he would start with Marjorie Kline Biddle who lived in La Jolla, California. He knew that by flying here and there he was using up personal funds that his family couldn't spare, but it was essential that he speak in person with Marjorie. She was the key.

Stephen silently gave thanks for the little cushion he and Anney had in the bank in Lafayette—the remainder of his share of the money he received from last summer's San Diego Book of Mormon study.

Bennett's eyes were red-rimmed from long hours of travel and little sleep, but his mind zeroed in on the issue at hand—Stephen. He shook Stephen's hand, gripping him around the shoulder with the other arm, and smiled. "I hear you've been rounding out your education. What do you think of our fair city's complimentary lodgings?"

"Listen, man, I'll never again take freedom for granted," Stephen replied. Standing next to this confident ally boosted his spirits beyond belief. After all the body blows he had taken, maybe he could now begin to score some points.

Bennett motioned Stephen to a chair, while he sat on the edge of his desk and scooped up a manila file. "Let's get to work!"

* * *

Stephen caught an America West flight that put him in San Diego in an hour. Despite his current emergency, the dominating thoughts rolling over and over again in his mind were of Anney. The worst part of the whole situation was that he needed her support. What's more, he knew that he had to communicate with her immediately. If she were to learn about his arrest from some other source, it would crush her. It would anyway, but at least he would be the one to tell her. *Oh, Anney, Anney. Please don't tear yourself out of my life. I can't handle it alone.*

Marjorie's hillside home had a panoramic view of the coastline of La Jolla. The ocean spread out before Stephen in one of those radiant San Diego mornings that brought retired naval officers back to its shores to live out their lives. The rock-front house appeared to be one story, but from the winding street below, there was a lower-story walkout to the pool and tennis court. The three doors of the front-facing garage were shut tight. Stephen noticed when he glanced at his watch for the fourth time in ten minutes that it was 10:40 A.M.

He stood for a moment on the opposite side of the tree-lined road with a concrete reinforced wall to his back and then crossed the street and rang the doorbell. For the wealthy, it was early, but he had to catch a 12:30 P.M. flight back to Phoenix. If Marjorie was inclined to speak with him, she would do so as willingly at this hour as later.

He heard the faint tinkle of chimes from within the entrance hall. He was about to depress the doorbell a second time when a young Mexican woman in a bright blue dress and white apron opened one of the solid oak double doors.

"Yes? May I help you?" She spoke with the lyrical accent typical of those from south of the border who speak marginal English.

Stephen stood in the doorway for several minutes. Finally, he heard a woman's voice coming from a hallway off the entryway. "Did you want something?" He turned to see a thin, angular woman with small features. She weighed perhaps a hundred and ten pounds, Stephen guessed. She looked at him uncertainly, fingering the fringe on her lounging caftan.

Stephen introduced himself. "I work with Dr. Peter Polk," he said, watching the woman carefully. Marjorie Kline Biddle frowned apprehensively at him. Surprised but able to be civil, she made an awkward gesture that he come into the living room.

Stephen sat down opposite Marjorie on one of the luxurious sofas. After apologizing for his intrusion into her home, he did a full-court press and went directly to the issue of his arrest. He refused to shy away from stepping on toes. "I'm concerned about the Book of Mormon project. I am frankly puzzled by your charges, since I have done nothing illegal. I am here to request that you and your brother stop the legal action you have filed against me. Are you aware that I was arrested and charged with fraud, and have been released on bail?"

Marjorie's head throbbed. She wished that she had hidden in her room. How could she know that this man would be so persistent? Why, oh, why had she gone along with Craig? She really knew nothing of dishonest behavior on the part of anyone connected with the Book of Mormon trust. When was she ever going to make her own decisions? She sighed and spoke in a timid voice.

"My brother . . . that is, we have taken legal action to protect the trust. I'm not clear on the details. He is handling all of it for me. I didn't know anyone would be arrested."

"But you are the chair of the board. Your name was on the complaint."

Marjorie fidgeted, trying to remain composed without success. "Yes, however . . . you see, I let Craig handle the entire affair. He was quite insistent, you see. All I did was sign the papers he brought to me."

Marjorie haltingly explained to Stephen that she had not taken an active part in directing the trust. Yes, she was chairperson but in name only. She had left with her son for Switzerland shortly after her father's funeral in late May and had not returned until school started in September. She had given Craig full authority to handle all matters pertaining to the trust. Oh, he had faxed her legal documents and letters that she had signed.

"If the truth be known, I never looked at the documents Craig sent me. I simply signed them and rushed them back to him. So you see, I have had little direct involvement in this trust thing."

She further explained, "I did meet with Dr. Polk at his request in September. Craig was in the Orient on business the second week in September. I tried to reach him, but he was not available. Dr. Polk needed me to transfer funds—three million dollars, I think—from the trust account and place it in the account he operated from. I did that simply because I knew that what he was asking for had already been planned by my father prior to his death. When Craig learned of the transfer he screamed at me over the phone. He . . . well, I won't go into the language and tone he used."

Stephen was astounded that anyone could be as cowed by another as this shadow of a person was by her brother.

In the simplest of terms, he outlined precisely what actions he had taken after Dr. Polk suffered his stroke. He stated that his was one of the authorized signatures on the project checking account and that Dr. Polk had drafted a document giving him the right to administer the project should he not be able to carry out the responsibilities. Stephen explained that it was in the form of a letter to him that was on Dr. Polk's computer. Granted, it had not been printed or signed, but that was clearly his intent.

"In all fairness, Mrs. Biddle, I have been trying to reach you for days to get your approval. You refused to speak to me."

"I was only following Craig's instructions." Marjorie spoke barely above a whisper. "He can get so angry."

Stephen tried another approach. "Why did Dr. Polk not hold board meetings with you present? That was one of the complaints in the warrant."

"I don't know. He was involved, and I'm sure he intended to hold them when things settled down and we were all in the area once again."

"By we, you mean the five board members that govern the trust?"

"Yes, my sister Delitra, Dr. Polk, Mr. Quail, Mr. Bennett, and myself."

Stephen already knew the makeup of the board. He was ready to discuss a solution. For the following ten minutes he explained his plan to clear up what he chose to term a misunderstanding.

Marjorie listened, but she was shaking visibly. Stephen wondered uneasily if she was about to have a seizure. At the very least, he judged, she had some severe emotional problems. He knew he must get what he came for and get out.

Marjorie walked with Stephen to the front door. She was about to shake his hand when she abruptly pulled her hand back and blurted out, "I know my brother has been a burden to you, first here in San Diego, and now in Phoenix. I want to tell you that he is still my brother and I love him. I may sound a little hard . . . and Delitra is very harsh on him, but we really think that he needs to step down from the company for his good as well as ours. I know my brother's ambitions have led him to break a few codes of honor, but he is under great strain."

Marjorie looked down at the brass door handle she was holding. "Craig is going through a very difficult time. He called me last evening and told me that if he loses his annual income as president of the family firm, he will have little money to maintain his family. I understand he is in debt, seriously in debt."

Her apology for her scumbag brother brought no tears to Stephen's eyes. He knew that Craig treated people as disposable, including his own sisters. The information she had just revealed only confirmed what he had suspected after listening to the museum curator. Rumors usually come from some form of the truth—Craig needed money. Just what Stephen wanted to know. He had what he came for—Marjorie had signed the papers—now Stephen had a plane to catch.

CHAPTER 24
Kline

Phoenix

Three hours later, Stephen called Delitra from Bill Bennett's office. She would not see him. She was brusque on the telephone. No, she was not interested in the matter of her father's contribution to the Book of Mormon project. She thought he had been ill advised by his personal attorney to give away so much money to his pet project, but that was her father's business. Stephen would have to take the matter up with legal counsel and her sister, who was chairperson. Delitra had her hands full simply taking over the family firm and getting it back in the black.

Stephen wasn't all that disappointed in Delitra's abruptness. She, like her sister, had revealed that Craig was on his way out. Bill Bennett had assured him that he had ways of getting around her if Stephen couldn't get past her crust.

If Marjorie stood up to her sister for once, as she promised, she might even help his case. Somehow, Stephen would make it through this maze. He had never before gone around the clock in serious negotiations. It was a new and disconcerting undertaking that he wished would soon end.

Consulting with Bennett, Stephen decided to let him handle the Delitra hurdle. Bennett said he would take care of it within the hour. Since Stephen had just talked to her, they knew that Delitra was in her office. Good. He would make no appointment—merely drop in. She would see him.

While he waited in Bennett's office, Stephen called Anney, using his phone card. A room was reserved for her at the hotel where the Moore group was registered, but she had not yet checked in. This puzzled Stephen, because he knew that it was late evening in Warsaw. He asked for the Moores' room. They were out. He left a message requesting that someone in the Moore family return his call and gave Bennett's number as well as his room number at the Holiday Inn.

He called again a half-hour later and got Katherine. She told him that Bob was still at the studio. How could she help him?

"Katherine, the operator at the hotel told me that Anney has not yet checked in. Where is she?"

"She didn't come to Warsaw with us when we left Krakow. She returned to Prague to visit her aunt, then she called me the next day from the mountains south of Krakow and said that she wanted to spend a few days in seclusion." Katherine cleared her throat. "She didn't tell me where. Really, Stephen, she doesn't want any one to disturb her; she said she needed time for thought."

"Well . . . uh . . . did she tell you what she is hoping to accomplish, going off by herself?"

"She didn't confide that to me or, to my knowledge, to anyone else."

Stephen wasn't sure he was reading Katherine right. He really didn't know her. She sounded evasive, as if she was not sure how much she could tell him. He wondered if she was trying to distance herself from him. Then Katherine's tone changed entirely.

"Oh, Stephen," she said gently, "surely you know that she has things to sort out, things that are extremely troubling to her. I have advised her to work this out with you and get on with your lives together. I don't personally care about religion in this matter, and I wish it weren't so important to the two of you. I'm now part of this family, and all in heaven I want is to see two unhappy people start rebuilding their lives."

"Thank you, Katherine," Stephen replied with a low voice. "I appreciate that spirit; believe me, I do. Would you please tell Anney for me that it is urgent that she call me, that is, if she should contact you in a day or so?"

"Oh, I expect Anney to call or come up here to Warsaw tomorrow or the next day. She promised me that she would call again. For all I know, she will show up here tomorrow. Either way, I will give her your message and urge her to call. I so want to have harmony in the family. Really I do."

Stephen argued with himself and then decided to reveal his circumstances to Katherine. He told her that he had been arrested and was currently out on bail, but that he and his attorney had worked out a war plan and that he expected to have all charges against him dropped by late afternoon Phoenix time. Katherine listened. She said nothing about her previous knowledge of his possible arrest.

"Stephen, thank heavens this will be behind you! What will you do after this is over?"

"I may be the temporary director of the Book of Mormon project . . . that is, if we are successful today with the Klines. If so, I will get back to work. I only wish that I were scheduled to interview another expert in Europe and could meet with Anney to resolve this dilemma."

For a moment there was silence on Katherine's end, then she said, "I'm thinking . . . would you be offended if I were to arrange for a round-trip ticket for you? I really think you two could work things out if you could be alone together for a little while. Anney seems . . . well . . . perhaps a little more reasonable."

Stephen listened, his heart pumping double time, incredulous that she would offer to fly him to meet with Anney. He had misjudged Katherine's intentions. She really did want them back together. *What did she say . . . Anney is more reasonable? I've got to get to her, soon.* Stephen gulped. "If you think there might be a chance, I will come. But I'll buy my own ticket. We're not quite flat broke yet. I'll never forget you for offering, though. Katherine, you're great."

* * *

After seeing Delitra, Bennett rejoined Stephen in his law office. They had both spent every available minute securing the documentation and letters required for the meeting in the morning with Craig and his attorney. For the next hour, they compared notes and planned the details of their strategy. All the paperwork had been processed in the computer and printed before Jolinda shut off her equipment for the night. She had left when Stephen and Bennett went into their closed session. At least they had done their homework. Now, whether they could pull it off in the morning was yet to be seen.

Bennett was exhausted. He propped his feet up on his desk and leaned back in his black leather chair in wind-down mode. "Now, I need you to bring me up to date on where things stand with this Book of Mormon project."

"Gladly," Stephen replied, seated across from Bennett. He, too, was more relaxed. After the day's frenetic activity, he was more hopeful that his legal problems would be resolved in his favor. "Yesterday, I made a list and checked off all of the proposed lecturers; then I did a summary of who we have lined up, who still needs to be contacted, and what yet remains to be done."

Stephen reached inside his leather bag and pulled out a file folder stuffed with notes, letters, and the complete working plan that Dr. Polk had printed up for him before they had departed for their Central American trip. He covered all of the topics: from the land Bountiful to the gold plates, the Urim and Thummim, and so on.

"All of these are pretty sure except the bird-god presentation and the Book of Mormon Exposition, or whatever Dr. Polk named it, in Provo. There is another recognized English-speaking authority on Quetzalcoatl at the University of Texas. I'll contact him in the next week or so. Roy didn't have much luck with that guy, Johnson, at the University of Missouri.

"Now," Stephen continued, "we are ahead of schedule in lining up presenters for the conference. Of course, if I'm not in jail, I'll follow up on all of these presenters for the next two months and have everything set by the first of March."

"Oh, that reminds me. You said earlier that you were going to discuss the status of Roy Carver. What's happened with that guy?"

Stephen explained that Roy had lost heart in the project and wanted out. "It was beginning to get a little complex for his blood."

"Hmmm. I would have staked money on that kid. He was such a great help to Peter. Okay, what about that thing in Provo . . . what did you call it?"

"Exposition? To tell the truth, I don't know what Dr. Polk planned to call it."

"Yeah. Let me tell you, I was not for that from the start. I think it was the thing that got us into this quagmire in the first place. It's expensive as all get-out to do all that construction and animation and what have you. I warned Peter and Thomas when they were planning this whole venture that this exhibition veered from our objective. Why, to construct and maintain a facility like that . . . I think it was the very thing that got you arrested. Kline took a look at that money drain and said, 'Whoa!' What do you think of that project in Provo?"

"I was absolutely impressed with the layout and concept of having a miniature Book of Mormon land right in the heart of Provo." Stephen felt at ease with Bennett. His confident manner of speaking reflected his renewed hope in the future.

"I agree it's expensive," Stephen went on, "but I think that after the conference next spring we can turn that over to Brigham Young University to maintain and even charge admission, or sell it off to some commercial group. People are going to pay money to see it. Now, this doesn't mean that we will make back our investment, but that was not the original intent."

Stephen was unaware that he had slipped comfortably into the role of chief honcho of the project, though he was closely following Bennett's suggestions for making the plan of action work, at least until Polk regained his ability to direct. He clasped his hands behind his head and began to relax slightly, "It will be finished in about six weeks, and then they are going to allow classes to use it—BYU, seminaries, institutes—until the conference next spring, then turn it over to the public to view. It is a great tool to teach the concepts and locations of the Book of Mormon."

Bennett began chuckling.

"What's so amusing?" Stephen failed to see any humor in what they were discussing.

"You. You didn't know the first thing about the Mormons six months ago, and now you reel off things like seminaries and institutes as if you had been a Mormon all your life. You've really picked up the Mormonese. Good for you."

Stephen was quiet for a minute. Then he asked a question that had been on his mind all day. "Bill, weren't you intending to stay another week in Colombia?"

Bennett's eyes met Stephen's. "Yeah, actually about five days more. Why?"

"What made you come home sooner?"

Ever the lawyer, Bennett mulled over the question. He could see where Stephen was going, but he hated to reveal that he might be the least bit sensitive.

"Aw, I'd swallowed so much of that river, I had a yen for this bone-dry climate."

Bennett's eyes narrowed. He thought he saw disappointment in Stephen's face. Heaving a sigh, he said, "Listen, Thorn, if you can keep a secret, I'll tell you what happened. I was having the time of my life. I was dreading the very minute I would have to come back to the grind. Then the craziest thing happened. All of a sudden, I had a feeling . . . no, I knew, that something was wrong. Karen couldn't believe that I would give up the best part of the trip on a hunch. Something pushed me all the way onto the helicopter and into Bogota, where I called Jolinda. She told me about Peter's stroke and that you were being jerked around, so here I am."

Stephen slowly let out a long breath, a smile covering his face. *Thank you, Heavenly Father. You did it. You answered my prayer. I knew you would!* "Bill, you're a good man," he said aloud. "Did you know I was praying that you would come back? Thanks more than I can say."

* * *

Stephen marveled at Bill Bennett's ability to remain calm and in control. He needed to practice this art of confrontation without getting emotional. He knew one thing. This encounter with Kline had to be done with dead-on detail. This was real life, and he had to make it stick. Up until yesterday, he had felt like Alice falling down a deepening hole. Meeting with Marjorie was one of the more encouraging signs of regaining control of his life.

To be sure, Craig Kline was a slippery devil, a crazy quilter who could go in any one of a thousand unpredictable directions. He would have no mercy on Stephen. Bennett had forewarned him in the car coming over that Kline was a lunatic. "Watch him and his henchman, Hadley," he had said. Now Stephen was determined to nail Kline, even though he lacked Bennett's experience in conflict.

"Bill Bennett to see Mr. Kline. He's expecting me."

The receptionist called Craig's office to verify the appointment. Smiling, she said, "Mr. Kline's office is Suite One at the end of the corridor on your left." Bennett knew from the directions that Craig was roosting in his father's office. He escorted Stephen to the executive suite, having taken this carpeted, well-appointed path frequently in the past.

In an attempt at high fashion, Craig's fortyish private secretary wore do-it-too-much makeup and a hairstyle straight out of *Cosmopolitan*. Her earrings hung down to her shoulders. The only problem was that her mirror had failed to convince her that she was twenty years older than the models she was trying to emulate. Her smile had been practiced over a decade of greeting important people. She did it well. "Mr. Kline is in a meeting at the moment," she said. "Won't you have a seat? I'm sure he won't be long."

In front of them were the white double doors that Stephen supposed led to Kline's office. The doors were shut as tight as a bank vault. He had wondered last summer when Kline had given them such fits over the remaining monies to be paid to him and his fellow conference participants what kind of quarters Kline was encamped in. The corporate best, naturally.

One minute after the smiling secretary buzzed the interior of Craig's office, the double doors swung open and a man about Stephen's age emerged. He sized them up for a long moment. "Well, Bennett, you're on time . . . Who's your friend?"

"Stephen Thorn," Bennett said smoothly, "I'd like you to meet Craig Kline's counsel, Chet Hadley. Chet, I think you recognize the name."

Hadley stood blocking the door, considering the implication of Thorn's presence. Finally, he stepped back to let the men enter the office.

Craig did not stand. He remained slumped behind his massive desk. It was his way of letting them know that, as far as he was concerned, they were scum. There was no evidence of work in progress. If his desk ever had papers or files cluttering its polished white surface, visitors never knew. If Kline was anything, he was neat.

He had inherited the office from his father last summer but had changed more than he had retained of the original decor. It still reflected the eclectic notions his father enjoyed, but the walls had been stripped of their original paintings, some western, some contemporary. They were all contemporary now, and none were originals.

Stephen had never been in Kline's office, but Bennett had been the older Kline's attorney for twenty years. He could feel Craig's influence on the decor; it was strange to him. Nothing about Craig impressed Bennett, least of all his futile attempt to personalize the office. However, he had no interest in the appearance of the place. His good friend Thomas Kline had fled this life, and none of his earthly trappings could bring him back. It was just as well, thought Bennett, that Craig had changed everything. It made it less troubling to recall whose place this had once been. Besides, he and Stephen were not here to look at furniture. They had come to settle a score.

"I'd like to speak to you alone, Mr. Kline," Stephen said, according to plan. A commanding officer giving orders to a private first class.

"Oh, you would?" Kline snapped. "My attorney stays."

Stephen's legs felt like jelly. It was a totally new experience to be so confrontational. But he met Craig eye to eye. "Would you gentlemen excuse us, please?" Stephen asked politely, focusing on Kline as if the two attorneys had already left the room.

Hadley shot a glance at Kline, seeking his cue. Kline stared back at Stephen, not uttering a word. Hadley didn't know what to do.

"I suggest you instruct your attorney to leave the office with Mr. Bennett," Stephen persisted, with no visible trembling from the waist up, glad the desk covered his shaking knees, which he attempted to steady. Still no response from Craig.

"So help me, Kline, if your attorney remains in this office, I get up and walk out, and you'll see me in court a year or two from now. Are you prepared to spend that amount of time getting this suit to trial? Can you afford to?"

Craig dropped his eyes from Stephen's, crossed his legs, and brushed an imaginary fleck from his gray pant cuff. "Okay, Chet, we'll humor this intruder for about ten minutes. Then get yourself back in here."

Hadley began to sputter an objection. Kline tossed a loose hand in his direction, indicating he was to leave. Bennett was already holding the door open for Hadley, and the two left the office together.

* * *

The woods cast long shadows across the open spaces. Anney had no idea how long she had been out walking, walking and sometimes climbing. She did have the presence of mind to keep the castle in view whenever she rounded a curve as she climbed higher and higher. The approaching dusk warned her that it was time to turn back. Yet the struggle inside her intensified. No relief. She had been troubled for the past what, half-hour? She had finished reading the Book of Mormon by late afternoon.

Mentally, she had set aside her conflict with Stephen for the moment. She could now see how powerful the book really was. She realized that the Book of Mormon was far more wide-reaching in its doctrine than she had ever dreamed. The writings were nothing like Decker had led her to believe. Whoever actually wrote the Book of Mormon was much more skilled than Decker gave him credit. Whether it was valid scripture or something fabricated by a man she was not yet certain. Anney knew that lately she had sharpened her extraordinary sense of selective vision. She saw what she wanted to see. Yet this book compelled her to ponder its contents. It was not a simple read, nor was it anything like she had thought before she picked it up.

Stephen said that he experienced an immediate confirmation of its truth when he studied the Book of Mormon. Why? Who could have invented such a detailed book? But the audacity of the Mormons! They claim to be the only true church. That means they as much as disregard all other churches. Was the book designed just to con people into believing it? Or is it really the word of God? Why now do I sense a strange linkage with Stephen? I wonder if he had thoughts like mine in the beginning. The book seemed to have a dimension beyond her faculties of discernment.

Because of her Christian training, the book's theme of obedience to the commandments of God was compelling. She wanted to make no mental assertion, no judgment—one way or the other—about the book. She had to reconcile in her mind the fact that the tenets presented in the Book of Mormon were consistent with the teachings in the Bible. Strangely, this insight caused a repeated struggle with her inner self. She had been led to believe that the Mormons had unorthodox beliefs, and yet they had a familiar sound. Despite what Decker had told her, the Jesus Christ of the Book of Mormon seemed to be the same person she had envisioned all of her life. *And as to the Savior having a body . . . well, I don't know why, but he has always been a physical person in my mind.*

She stopped abruptly beside the trail and let her body slump to a rock lightly brushed with snow. She was not cold. Her heavy down jacket and leather gloves did their job. What she felt was somehow not physical. It was all inside her head. The canyons inside her mind that divided decision from indecision kept shifting, as if she were in some sort of mental earthquake.

She had never in her life gone on a quest for religion. Her father's religion was just part of her existence. Regardless of what the old Anney found acceptable, something new inside her wanted to surface.

She lowered her head and let her hair fall across her cheeks and forehead as she pondered this soul-searching encounter that she had brought upon herself. What to do? Prayer flashed into her mind. She remembered that someone, maybe those young missionaries, had underlined a passage close to the end of the Book of Mormon. Moroni . . . wasn't that the name of the angel who supposedly loaned the gold plates to Joseph Smith? . . . had suggested—no, *exhorted*—any reader of the book to ask God if the things written in the book were true. He promised that if the reader prayed with real intent and had faith in Christ, the Holy Ghost would reveal whether or not it was true. *That's right! Stephen asked me to pray. Only he said to pray aloud.*

Anney had never prayed aloud. In all her life, she had never uttered an audible supplication to God. She had prayed, of course. But her prayers had always been silent. Her father prayed aloud every Sunday while opening and closing his sermons. She had understood all of her life that only the minister—the man or woman of God— offered prayers aloud.

Had not her aunt Elena, on her last visit, begged her to pray to the Lord? "Pray, my darling," her aunt had urged before they said good-bye. She had encouraged her to gain the spirit of understanding "You must pray to your Father in Heaven with pureness. With pure intent. Don't be frightened, my child. If you pray, the Lord will hear you. Don't ask me to explain how it happens, but He will fill your heart so that you will hardly be able to withstand the love. I promise you."

Her aunt's voice echoed, "He will hear you . . . He will . . ."

Anney threw back her head, her hair flying in a swirl from her crown to her shoulders, as she thrust her face directly into the late afternoon sky. It was a fresh breaking of the vessels when she whispered, "Dear God in heaven, hear me then. Aunt Elena says you will hear me."

It startled Anney to hear herself speak the words in the narrow canyon with woods all about. "I want to know. Dear God . . . I need to know that you are listening. Can you hear me? Please let me know. I can't bear things as they are. I want to settle this matter." Tears flowed unnoticed down her face. "I will give up anything to know that you are listening and that you approve of me reading the Book of Mormon. I no longer feel that it is wrong . . . but I don't know that it is right. Please help me. Help me. Help me."

A peace gradually enveloped Anney's thoughts. The stupor, the darkness that had haunted her mind, lifted. The troubled canyons of her mind sealed together, easing her pain. A gradual feeling of quiet contentment enfolded her. She was aware of being physically warm, as if she were home in her own kitchen and Stephen had just slipped up from behind and embraced her with one of his enveloping bear hugs. What joy, what peace!

Is this the way I'm to know that it's true? Are you telling me that what Stephen has been trying to tell me and what my aunt Elena believes is true? Is this the very gospel of Jesus Christ?

The warmth continued to spread throughout her body. All she could think was how tender and sweet this feeling was. It seemed to encompass her entire body. Love. Yes, it seemed like love. *I must talk to Stephen.*

Still . . . how could I ever turn away from my father's ministry?

* * *

When the door to Kline's office shut quietly, Stephen began to remove papers from his leather bag. He arranged them in order, telling Kline that if he would be patient, he would proceed with what he wanted him to hear. Kline snorted his contempt. He stood up from behind his desk and walked to the windows that looked out on downtown Phoenix. He wished he had a drink to wash down the unpleasant vibes he was getting. He had a hunch, judging from Thorn's determined attitude, that whatever he had to discuss, it would hardly be good news. He hated to face it without a stiff drink to dull the edges.

At last Stephen was set. He cleared his throat and said briskly, "I'm ready, Mr. Kline, if you would care to take a look." He wanted Kline to turn around, but he refused to move. It appeared that he was not going to give Stephen the courtesy of looking him in the eye. Stephen decided to speak anyway. He had come to set things in order and set them he would, even if it meant staring at a fat back.

"Mr. Kline, I have here papers drawn up by my attorney, Mr. Bennett. After speaking to Mr. Bennett and getting his approval on this very serious matter, I've come to make some kind of peace with you."

Stephen cleared his throat and said, "Mr. Bennett and I have consulted with each member of the board of directors for the Book of Mormon project that was originally endowed with fifteen million dollars, according to your father's wishes. The money has been applied to projects completed, ongoing, and future that your father approved of and participated in. In other words, he planned them before his death."

Craig whirled about. "You don't have to explain to me what my father did. I already know."

"That's true; you probably do. Still, what you don't know is what the board has decided."

"Who do you think you are?" Kline glared at Stephen with the same sneer on his wide lips that Stephen remembered the night he came storming into the estate in San Diego and declared to everyone that the project had just been canceled, that there would be no funds to pay the participants. He could see that it was an oft-used expression.

Stephen refused to let this bully intimidate him. He stood erect at the side of the desk and then calmly pushed four documents nearer to the edge, positioning them so that Craig could read them if he stepped a few feet closer. "I have here four signed papers authorizing me as the board-approved, new director of the Book of Mormon project to disperse funds from the trust to certain persons. In this case, they have authorized me to pay you a sum of money."

"What are you talking about?"

Stephen could see that he had piqued the irate man's curiosity. Craig twisted his head sideways in an effort to read the first document from where he was standing. Stephen unobtrusively turned the sheets so that Craig would not have to strain his neck to read.

"I'll summarize what they say, so as not to linger here any longer than I have to. The documents say that the board has allowed me to cut a check for you—a check in the amount of two million dollars. The proposal before board members yesterday was that Thomas Kline's children receive one-half of the remaining funds in the trust, amounting to six million dollars, as part of an agreement to allow the Book of Mormon project to be completed using the remaining half of the funds, or six million dollars. In this way, each of Thomas Kline's children—and that includes you—receives one-third of six million dollars. So you get two million as your share." Stephen glanced up at Kline to see how this offer was registering on his brain.

"Out of my office. Out!" Veins bulged at Craig's temples and his face was purple with rage. "You have the nerve to stand there and rob my family of millions of dollars! You mean to tell me that you seriously think I would accept your measly offer? Well, you've come to the wrong guy. I'm going after you with everything I can muster, and believe me, I have some good sources—your father-in-law for one." Craig smirked as he saw the shock on Stephen's face.

"Oh yes, the reverend has kept me abreast of your comings and goings . . . for a hefty 'donation' to his ministry. Before I'm through, I'll have you busted for fraud and anything else I can get on you. You're not kidding anyone. We both know that you are out on bail right now. Man, you just stepped into a bear trap. I am going to bury you."

For a moment, Stephen was too stunned to think. *So I was right! Bob, how could you sink so low? Surely . . . I can't believe Anney was aware . . .*

Stephen's jaw hardened. Anger and disappointment rekindled his resolve. He had come to wipe out this maze of cunning schemes. He had already made up his mind to settle with this tormentor once and for all.

"Before you get your shovel, Kline, I suggest you think again."

"I don't have to agree to this," Craig screamed, "not when there is twelve million in that fund that belongs to the Kline family."

"No one has asked you to agree to anything. I am the temporary director, and the board has asked me to deliver the check to you. Really, Mr. Kline, you don't have to take it, but I do have a cashier's check in my bag written to you for two million dollars, which I happen to think is fair."

Craig fingered the papers on the desk and edged an inch closer. "Show me the check," he snarled.

Stephen's right palm went up in a signal for Kline to hold on. "In a minute. I think you ought to know that when the board voted, your sisters decided that since this was a project that your father wanted very much to see come about, and whether they are in sympathy with it or not, they wish to honor his intentions. Therefore, they opted to leave their share of the money in the trust.

"Your sister Delitra sat on the fence when it came to voting. At the outset she, too, wanted the full twelve million to revert back to the family if there was to be some sort of dividing of the funds. However, her accountant worked out an arrangement whereby her share of the money will remain in the trust until such a time that she feels she needs it. In the meantime, we are free to use the interest on her share.

"According to Mr. Bennett, her CPA told her that if she were to receive her two million right now, her increase in taxes would total more than half the amount she would receive."

Stephen tapped the black leather business bag on his lap. His knees felt steady now, and his mind was clear. "You may want to look into how much the government will take from your two million before you grab it."

Craig's mind was in a turmoil. *That Delitra! And Marjorie, too! She is so spineless! I thought I had her in control. They'll pay for this. Two million won't begin to be enough but maybe this agreement can work both ways. I've got to get Hadley in here.*

"I've got to talk with my attorney before I accept anything."

"Well, he's right outside. You had better talk fast, because I have an agreement attached to the check that Mr. Bennett has drawn up and which you will be required to sign, to the effect that you will not seek any further legal action once you accept the two million."

Stephen pressed his hands together with a sense of satisfaction that Craig had mellowed. "I don't wish to intrude on your personal life, but I happen to know from several sources that if you don't accept the check, you may end up in bankruptcy."

"Who told you that?" Craig's face was distorted with hatred.

"Your sisters, for a starter, and I don't care to reveal the others." Stephen didn't intend to reveal any others. He couldn't; he had no other names in mind. Only rumors. It was all rumors. No matter. Craig didn't ask.

Stephen stood up, pulled out the document attached to the bank check, removed the paper clip binding the two, handed Craig the paper, and replaced the check in his black leather bag. Then he declared, "I plan to leave Phoenix in one hour. It will take me time to drive to Sky Harbor and check in. I'll give you fifteen minutes with your attorney to sign the document that is attached to the check. If you choose not to sign, I'm authorized to take the check with me and inform you that you are powerless to bring any further legal action against me. Your sister Marjorie, through her attorney, is in the process of dropping all civil and criminal charges against me."

Stephen held tightly to his bag and headed for the door.

Craig was visibly perspiring now. "Look, Thorn . . . let's talk. This is sudden for me. I need more time."

Stephen, his hand gripping the brass knob, turned and looked at Craig and then his watch, and said, "You have ten minutes to make up your mind." He stepped out and spoke to Bennett.

* * *

"Thanks for all your help," said Stephen. "Tell your wife that if you people are game, I'd like to compensate you for the days you gave up on the river by inviting you to go with me down the Kern River above Bakersfield in California. I know it's not as exotic as the white water in Colombia, but in spots it's rated a five."

"Thank you. I'll bet Karen would like it." Then Bennett said warmly, "I hope all goes well with you in Warsaw. I don't know exactly what the problem is, but I wish you well anyway."

Stephen nodded at Bill Bennett as he opened the door of Bennett's car, minutes before his flight to Atlanta, connecting to Warsaw.

Leaning in the open window on the passenger side, Stephen admitted, "I couldn't have bullied ol' Craig without your expert coaching. I thought it was interesting that it only took him and his attorney five minutes to emerge from their little session, sign the document, and grab the check."

Bennett shrugged his shoulders and adjusted the shoulder restraint. Then he said, "Remember one thing about Craig. He has a cowardly way of backing off when he can see a wall too high to climb. After all, he is the Kline family's treasured looney. What else can I tell you?"

With a wide grin, Bennett added, "Good luck, Stephen. I think you have a great future ahead of you. You know why? Because you possess an insurgent spirit when it comes to facing what is."

Stephen chuckled and moved away from the curb as Bennett inched his Mercedes into the mainstream of Sky Harbor traffic.

* * *

Stephen made his way to the wall telephone bank after receiving his boarding pass for his flight to Atlanta. He inserted his calling card and punched in the number for LDS Hospital in Salt Lake City. He was anxious to check in with Dr. Polk's family or, failing that, the nursing staff to determine his friend's condition before leaving.

As he waited for his call to reach the intensive care station, he felt as if he had been out of touch with Polk's medical progress for weeks. It had only been four days. Abruptly a high-pitched, friendly voice on the other end identified the ICU location and asked how she could help.

"Yes, this is Stephen Thorn, I'm an associate of Dr. Peter Polk. He is a patient there in intensive care. Are there any members of his family nearby who can speak with me?"

"Just a moment."

Stephen waited impatiently. He heard the first boarding call for his flight. People who had been seated in rows facing the windows began to scramble to their feet and move to the queue that was forming at gate nine. Stephen knew that he had at least another five minutes before he needed to board.

"Mr. Thorn?" The voice said.

"Yes?"

"Checking our records, I see that Peter Polk was moved this morning to room 435. He is no longer in intensive care."

Stephen quickly asked, "Is he better?"

"I'm sorry. I have no information on him. I will be happy to transfer you to that section of the hospital. Please wait."

Another minute and Stephen had the nursing station on Polk's new floor. He quickly asked if he could get a report on Dr. Polk or speak to a family member. He was put on hold a second time. He turned around to check the activity at gate nine. The wait for someone to pick up the telephone seemed interminable.

"Hello?"

The voice was familiar. Roy! It was Roy.

"Roy, I thought you were in the East. How is Dr. Polk? They said he's out of intensive care."

"Stephen?"

"Yeah."

"Did you get my message? I called Bennett's office a couple of hours ago."

"No, but I'm rushing to catch a plane. How is he?"

"He's coming around. Last night he began mumbling words, and this morning his eyes were open and he could nod his head when his family spoke to him. He's coming around, Stephen. He's going to make it." Roy could not keep his relief and joy out of his voice.

Stephen felt elation sweep over him. "Oh, Roy, that's great news. Would you tell him, if he is able to comprehend what you say, that I have left for Warsaw and will be back in a couple of days? Tell him the projects are moving forward."

"Sure, I'll tell him. How are things going in Phoenix for you?"

"I've got the whole thing under wraps. I had to do some horse-trading. I don't have time to explain, but at least this terrible ordeal is behind me. I'll let you know in detail when I get back. I have a lot of explaining to do to Dr. Polk, but I think he will understand. I hope he doesn't hold it against me . . . what I did today. I had to give up some of the funds to get square with the board. I'll explain later, if you are anywhere I can reach you."

Stephen glanced over his shoulder again at the line of passengers filing past the airline agent and disappearing through the gate. He knew he had to go. "One more thing, Roy. Why didn't you go home as you said you would last Saturday?"

"Stephen." The pause lasted an eternity. "I hope you can overlook my actions this past week. I know I'm a wimp and I dropped the ball when you needed me most, but I couldn't leave, after all. I know too much about . . . uh . . . things relating to the Book of Mormon to ever put this thing away. I'm staying with you guys, at least until the conference is over in the spring. Then I'll decide. Is that okay? I mean, if you want me to or rather if Dr. Polk wants me to."

"Roy, that's the best thing in the world! Of course I want you to stay. Dr. Polk will never know anything about your decision to leave last week unless you tell him."

Stephen could see that the line had disappeared beyond the boarding gate. He had to leave. "Roy, I hate to cut you off, but I have to catch this flight. They are getting ready to close the doors. All I can say is hang in there, man."

CHAPTER 25
Stephen and Anney

Warsaw

The morning had turned cold and damp. Stephen caught a grimy black taxi. He knew Anney could never live out her life in Eastern Europe, where the clouds hung a misty ceiling above the steeples of the numerous cathedrals the cab whizzed past on its way to the hotel. He longed for the Bay Area, for home and family. Never had he been away from home for such a protracted period. Lafayette was sunny much of the time. San Francisco, twenty miles to the west, was often shrouded in fog or low clouds, and at times, they penetrated all the way to Lafayette—but not often. The weather most of the year was temperate and balmy—neither hot nor cold—just the way Stephen liked it. Anney loved California, too. Warsaw in late fall, on the other hand, was gray and definitely uninviting as the city moved into winter.

In the morning bleakness, Stephen wondered for the hundredth time how Anney would receive him. He was impatient to see her, to hold her. How would she respond?

Oh, was he ever tired of traveling. He had logged countless hours trying to make all the threads come together in his life. He reflected on the turn of events in Phoenix. At least he had one major hurdle behind him. Yet in this entire marathon, the obstacle ahead could be the highest and most difficult to leap.

Reaching to open the window to let much-needed air into the cab, Stephen caught sight of the thumbnail he had smashed in Phoenix. He had been so busy and preoccupied with his struggles that he hadn't been aware that it was gradually healing. The black had almost totally disappeared. Slowly he closed his eyes. *Father, please help us heal our marriage, too.*

He knocked at the door of the Moores' suite. Katherine answered it in her robe. She had done her face and hair; that was always preeminent. Stephen had called her before he left Phoenix but hadn't given her the particulars of his schedule.

She swung the door wide and opened her arms, beaming with pleasure. "So, you are Stephen. Yes, I remember you."

"Hello."

Katherine made the first move, pulling Stephen to her in a quick embrace of friendship and affection. She stepped back. "No wonder Anney is attracted to you. I forgot what an impressive man you really are. Come in. Please, come in."

Stephen moved into the living room of the suite. It was baroque and ornate. As he moved toward one of two facing sofas which were close to the fireplace, he saw Bob come from the bedroom. He was dressed in a dark suit and bright tie. His mane was well brushed, every hair in place. He, too, paused when he saw Stephen's startled look. Stephen knew he would meet Bob, but the moment was disquieting and abrupt. He nodded uncertainly. What else could he do? Bob returned the nod.

Katherine moved around Stephen to Bob's side and took his arm. "Stephen, I'm Mrs. Robert Moore, and the name suits me fine." She let the announcement hang in the scented air of the suite. With the courage of a true diplomat, she continued, "As Mrs. Moore, I would like to have a complete and loving family. It would be the most precious wedding gift I could possibly imagine." There was still no movement on the part of either man.

"Please. I know I may seem a little feathery about this, but it is not an inconsequential matter to me. I want you two to be friends again. This can't go on."

"Katherine," Stephen said, shaking his head, "I came to see Anney. I . . ."

"I know that, Stephen. She called to say that she is coming by train from the south and is due to arrive about 5:00 P.M."

"She called you?" Bob queried.

"Yes, while you were in the shower. I haven't had time to tell you; you've been dressing." Katherine let go of Bob's upper arm and extended her left hand, her thin well-manicured fingers almost touching Stephen's, in a gesture of reconciliation—acting as a bridge between the two men. "I know that both of you have been hurt in some way. Haven't we all been wounded to one extent or another? Life is too short for this kind of behavior. I want you two as dear friends of mine, but I can't have it that way if you can't come together and work this out."

Stephen looked over at Moore, holding the older man's eyes with his own. Choosing his words carefully, he said, "Bob, I just came from a meeting with Craig Kline."

The minister's expression sagged. Suddenly, he seemed old and tired, ineffectual and defeated.

For so many years, this man was my mentor, my father figure, the symbol of spiritual strength for my family. But his feet are made of clay. He has compromised his integrity for money again and again . . . and at my expense. Can it be that he doesn't really understand right from wrong? Is manipulation his Achilles heel? I thought I hated him. But what good would it do me to expose and humiliate him? It would only bring me down to his level. Pity and forgiveness for the weak man standing before him replaced the anger and resentment that had seethed in Stephen's mind throughout his flight to Warsaw.

"You'll be pleased to know," Stephen continued quietly, "that we have reached an agreement and that he no longer seeks to charge me with fraud."

Moore stood mute with gravity. Stephen knew that he was a proud man, that he would have to make the move if a reconciliation were to happen. He moved closer to his father-in-law and slowly extended his hand.

Stephen's approach was tempered by realism. If he did not lead out and offer the olive branch, the problem would be an increasingly troublesome issue in the family. Katherine was right. Amends were imperative.

"Bob, I know that you were probably ashamed of me when I left the ministry to join the Mormon faith. We have never taken the time to talk about it, have we? It's just been a series of frustrating fits and starts that has to be resolved. I can't hope to explain my spiritual awakening to you, and I surely wouldn't attempt to convert you to my beliefs, but perhaps you can bring yourself to respect my right to worship as I choose. I love your daughter. I'm still the same guy, only trying to be a better man, a better husband. I want to take her home with me and care for her with all the tenderness a man is capable of expressing."

As Bob hesitantly moved his hand forward, Stephen suddenly grinned and hugged him, pounding him on the back like old times. "Hey, Dad," he said huskily, "you're my kids' grandfather. We've got some great days ahead of us!"

Stephen's eyes were moist. Lately, whenever he encountered emotional situations, he came close to tears. This was such a moment. By reaching out, by being forgiving, he felt his soul enlarge. He was grateful that tears did not begin to trickle down his cheeks.

Similarly, Bob held onto Stephen, unable to formulate the words he now longed to articulate. They were hard to get out. This was a strange and unusual occurrence for a man who made his living speaking words and counseling people on human relationships. He struggled even as the two of them moved apart and Stephen turned and smiled at Katherine. Neither felt they could add any more to the sincere appeal.

At last, words began to come forth. The first sound was a sigh. Then Moore said haltingly, "You are being big about this, Stephen. What can I say? I'm not pleased with my part in all of this, naturally, but you have to understand that I've been in a sort of a state of shock by your joining the Mormons. It has not been an easy adjustment."

"Dad, I understand."

Katherine chimed in, "And I'm as thrilled right now as I will ever be!" Her lovely face beamed with delight. All three knew that Bob had come as close to an apology as he ever would.

Bob and Katherine did not offer to accompany Stephen to the depot in downtown Warsaw but invited him to lunch before Anney's arrival time. Stephen was too restless to eat a bite. The Moores, on the other hand, were starved and ordered the full course. As she ate her salad daintily, Katherine kept up the conversation. She did not expect—and the men did not deliver—instant reconciliation to the point that they were once again buddies. It would come. Time heals most wounds. She was not concerned.

Stephen took leave of Bob and Katherine in Warsaw's restored war circle monument, telling them that he wanted to walk the three kilometers to the station. He wrapped his black overcoat tightly about his body. The brisk breeze felt more like spring to Stephen than fall. It awakened in him a sense of revival and awareness. He had hoped that the walk would relieve his nervousness at meeting Anney and learning of their status, but dodging aggressive vendors of everything from cassette recorders to full-blown portable television sets through the bustling streets of Warsaw seemed not to ease the tension much. He still felt prickly with the uncertainty of what awaited him at the station. He rounded the wrought-iron fence that separated taxis from the sidewalk leading into the train station and moved into the great hall that had been restored after the Nazis had made their devastating mark on it.

He walked along the corridor leading to the arrival platforms. The coach doors would be level with the concrete platforms that lined the tracks. He paced impatiently as he waited.

* * *

Would the train ever arrive in Warsaw? Anney could hardly remain seated. She arose and walked to the passageway adjacent to her compartment. She could see the browning countryside and marveled at the changing leaves on the trees that graced the fields and small villages. Passengers made their way around Anney; they too seemed restless, but she was certain that their reasons were different. She was meeting her husband. Hers was a new life that held such promise. Never could she recall such an exciting moment.

Anney had called the Moores again during her connection at the station in Katowice and learned that Stephen was meeting her at the train. She wasn't certain of the time she would arrive, having been informed that the train could be as much as half an hour late getting into Warsaw. She had required help with the telephone. Long-distance service remained a less-than-satisfying venture with the fledgling technology of Poland. It didn't surprise or trouble Anney. It was life in Poland. When the call did go through to the Moores' suite, Bob answered it. He and Katherine had arrived back in their suite ten minutes earlier from their lunch with Stephen.

* * *

That morning, Bob had canceled appointments with a delegation of three ministers from Kiev. He mentioned to Decker at the studio that he would have to squeeze them in first thing in the morning. He intended to spend time with his family.

"Did Anney arrive?"

"Not yet. But she will be coming in later this afternoon." Bob did not tell Decker about Stephen's sudden arrival in Warsaw. He simply didn't want to share that information with him. He was weary of Decker. There was something about the man that failed to lift Bob's spirits. He was certainly efficient, punctual, and organized, but he was so lacking in warmth and congeniality. He wasn't sorry he had hired him, he just had a nagging feeling of doubt about his assistant. It didn't make sense, but what subjective feeling did?

* * *

Anney rehearsed repeatedly how she would meet Stephen at the station and what she would tell him about her changing heart. "Stephen, I have had a personal encounter with the Spirit. The Book of Mormon may be true after all . . . Honey, you may have been right all along . . . I love you. I now know what you know about prayer."

She looked at her watch and then at the countryside once more. *Why was it taking so long? Move, train. Move!*

Stephen did not understand the announcement over the public address system that told of a twenty-minute delay of the passenger train from Katowice on track ten, which was Anney's. When it was ten minutes past her arrival time, he wondered if he had followed the directions he had received at the information counter. He decided to return to the main lobby and ask the woman, who spoke very poor English, if track ten was correct.

* * *

"It's for you, Bob." Katherine held her hand over the telephone as she nodded to Bob, who was watching CNN. It still amazed him how technology brought the news from America instantly to Eastern Europe. "I think it's that guy from Phoenix." Katherine handed the receiver to Bob.

Bob listened to Craig explain that he no longer needed his assistance. He would handle his own affairs from now on. The problem had resolved itself in his family's favor. What Craig didn't know was that during lunch, Stephen had already explained some of the details of what had happened in Phoenix. Bob had to smile to himself. But he was puzzled. He was sure Craig had understood that he had cut off their arrangement.

"Oh, by the way," Craig said as an afterthought. "Tell your man Decker that I don't need his services now, either. Maybe I should call him, though, since he insisted, when he called yesterday, that all contacts and money should go directly to him."

This bit of information troubled Bob. Craig was brief, and Bob soon hung up the telephone. He picked it up immediately and asked the hotel operator for Walinsky studio. Decker came on the line. Bob was direct. "Decker, I need you to meet me early tomorrow. We have a problem. No, I'll tell you tomorrow. Just meet me—7:00 A.M. in the lobby." Bob hung up.

Katherine, overhearing the conversation, raised her eyebrows in surprise. "That was short," she commented.

"He's out. He went behind my back with this Kline thing."

"Bob," Katherine said in that voice of patience that Bob had come to understand. "We all have to give a little. Work with the man. He's not a real threat to you. Not at all. Remember, others are doing the same with you. I personally think you ought to confront him with the matter and explain your feelings and why you are very concerned that he would do something behind your back. Then put him on notice that if anything like this happens again, he's out. What do you think?"

Bob knew there was wisdom in Katherine's approach. Why make an issue of this? His own behavior needed some shoring up.

* * *

Stephen rushed back to the platform. By the time he got to the concrete strip that stretched out to the far end of the train, the electrically powered engine was creeping to a stop. As soon as the couplings jarred together between cars, doors slid back and passengers streamed out. Stephen spotted Anney six cars back, one of the first to emerge.

He threw up his arms and waved. A radiant smile covered his whole face as he dodged hurrying passengers headed in the opposite direction. He kept his eyes on Anney.

Anney saw Stephen the second she stepped from the coach door. She too rushed along the platform, lugging her bag and waving her handbag in the air to signal to Stephen. When she got within a few feet of Stephen, she dropped her bag and leaped forward into his arms, laughing out loud with excitement and joy. With tears of elation, they kissed, hugged, and ignored passengers rapidly moving around them on the platform.

When Anney regained her composure, she whispered in Stephen's ear, "Stephen, oh, Stephen. I love you."

Stephen's heart pounded. She really did seem happy to see him. Had anything changed? He pushed her back, still holding her with both hands. "You know I love you, too."

"I've had a wonderful experience," she said in a rush. "I can't wait to tell you everything."

Stephen picked up her bag, with one hand still holding tightly to her. The two moved with the crowd toward the main concourse.

"I can't wait any longer, Stephen. I have to explain some things." Anney pulled him over to one side of the passenger flow. Inside the station was a small snack shop with tiny round tables. Seeing that one was empty, Anney pointed to it. "Can we sit down over there for a minute?"

"Sure."

Stephen pulled out one of the scratched, brown chairs for Anney, then sat down in the one next to it. His thoughts were anything but settled. What did she have to tell him? Was she going into another one of her tirades against the Mormons? No, Anney would not be so excited if she were. He had known her too long to misread her mood. He took a deep breath, eyebrows raised—ready for anything.

"Darling, I escaped to the mountains south of Krakow these last few days because I absolutely *had* to know what you experienced in San Diego. Really, though, I started the Book of Mormon while I was still in Krakow. Well—"

"You read the Book of Mormon?" Stephen was scarcely breathing.

"Yes . . . uh, yes, I did. Oh, Stephen, I misjudged that book. When I got into it I started seeing things I had believed all my life, but more so. Much more. At first I thought it was just what some people had told me, a jumbled account of sorts, using the Old Testament and some of the New, making up doctrine as it went along." Anney shook her head. "It's not. I got so wrapped up in my reading that I didn't have time to think of anything else. Somewhere in the reading—I think it came when Christ appeared to those poor people who had suffered in that great destruction—I began to feel like it was written just for me. Am I making sense?"

Anney's words echoed again and again in Stephen's mind. He could hardly grasp the import of what she had said. Peering closely into her eyes, he could see that she was sincere. As if moving in slow motion, Stephen rose to his feet, unaware that his chair had fallen over onto the floor. In one sweeping motion, he pulled Anney into his arms. *Oh, thank you, thank you, thank you, Father.* "Sweetheart, my Anney." He whispered over and over. "You are making wonderful sense. Oh, Anney, you have no idea how I have prayed that you would read it and feel what I did. But I wasn't sure that my faith was strong enough for both of us."

Anney laid her cheek against Stephen's and felt it wet with tears. She gently touched his face with her hands, tears stinging her own eyes. "Stephen, I have been such a trial to you. Will you ever forgive me? I didn't know. Really, really my mind . . ."

"Forgive *you?* I guess I've put you through the ordeal of your life. Will you forgive me? But can you begin to see why I couldn't just walk away from this church after I had learned the truth?"

"Yes, I can understand now. I sort of think maybe we had to go through a little stress . . . to appreciate each other and this wonderful book."

"Oh, my dearest, you are the center of my life. Just thinking that you might walk away forever has been pure torture."

Anney pulled back a few inches and ducked her head in sorrow. "Stephen, I'm so sorry for hurting you. I could never have left you, or divorced you. I mean, Katherine helped me see things more clearly. She is a wonderful person, you know. Daddy is luckier than he knows."

Stephen gradually became aware of the smiles and snickers coming from the people at the other tables. He flushed with embarrassment, picked up his chair, and grinned at Anney, and they sat down again. But he still clung to Anney's hand, as though she might slip away if he let go.

A slight frown crept over Anney's face when she said, "Speaking of Daddy, how are we going to tell him about our feelings?"

Stephen shrugged. What Bob thought had very little significance to him, but he was aware of Anney's concern.

"Don't get me wrong," Anney hurried on. "I know nothing else about your church, except a lot of incorrect stuff Decker told me. Judging from his mistakes about the Book of Mormon, it's probably all wrong. I have a bagful of questions." She put her hand to Stephen's chest and patted it softly. "Do you think I could have two of those young guys—are there any girls? Girls would be fine—who wear the white shirts and ties? I don't mean the girls do . . . Anyway, you know . . ."

"You mean the missionaries?" Stephen was beaming.

"Yes, I've been told that they can answer my questions. Though I think you could tell me a whole lot before I ever talk to them."

Stephen had heard all he needed to hear. He looked long and steadily into Anney's excited face, his deep love mirrored in her eyes. Then, not caring about their absorbed audience, he tenderly cupped her face with his hands and kissed her. It felt like the first time.

ABOUT THE AUTHOR

Keith Terry is a popular and prolific writer who has authored a number of fiction and nonfiction books for the LDS market. *Out of Darkness* and *Into the Light* are his first novels to be published by Covenant.

A perpetual scholar and researcher, Keith has earned bachelor's and master's degrees from Brigham Young University. He has also pursued graduate studies at the University of California. Along with his busy writing schedule, he enjoys scuba diving, jogging, and family history research.

Keith and his wife, Ann, live in Provo, Utah. They are the parents of nine children.

Excerpt from Seventh Seal

The three earthquakes hit simultaneously. Incredible pressure building along tectonic fault lines all over the world suddenly released as millions of tons of rock shuddered, groaned, and slipped far underground. The seismic shift discharged massive waves of energy, rippling through the earth's crust and warping the surface of the land. Compression waves spread outward from the epicenters of the quakes, contracting and expanding solid ground like ripples in a still pond.

The ripples rushed through actual water, too. With the first massive shockwave rising from the deep-hidden seafloor, the ocean suddenly sucked away from the beaches on the easternmost Philippine islands. Inland, the crowds jostling through the city streets—haggling, bargaining, jockeying for position—came to a standstill after the first shudder whispered through the ground beneath their feet. They had just enough time to realize that something had gone very wrong indeed when the full force of the quake hit. The ground bucked and heaved, throwing people from their feet and buildings from their foundations. Palm trees shivered and lashed in the still air. Sidewalks and roads cracked, chunks of concrete tossed upward, meeting their cousins falling from the buildings above. Multistory apartment buildings, hurriedly thrown up to house the immigrants pouring into the cities, collapsed in on themselves, story after story compressed into concrete, wood, and blood laminate. Geysers of water plumed into the air as underground water mains exploded under the twisting pressure. Geysers of flame followed as pipelines ripped and power lines fell, their sparks igniting volatile fumes. The inhabitants fled, screaming, crying, begging for mercy, praying, as the earth heaved beneath them. Some paused to help others as they stumbled; many shoved the unlucky out of their way; all struggled to escape the terrible avalanches of brick, wood, and cement cascading down man-made cliffs.

Those closer to the shoreline abandoned their hovels or hotels for the beach, where a vast expanse of wet sand greeted their astonished gazes. The first series of shocks faded, the sounds of destruction gradually dying into the howls of the wounded and bereft, the thunder of explosions—and a dim, distant roaring that began at the very edge of hearing, then grew. Sunlight, slightly dimmed by smoke and dust, glittered from a distant whitecap, glinted from the foaming crest of a gigantic wave. It swept over the tide pools the water had abruptly deserted before, then hit the beach, sweeping the earthquake's survivors back into the broken buildings they had abandoned, uprooting trees, and dousing the fires glowing in the ruins under a frothing, hissing tide.

The tide in Central China needed no mighty whitecaps or curling crests of waves. The earthquakes ripping through the deep mountain faults spread into the deep topsoil of the plains and weakened and crumbled the mighty dams and dikes that held the Yellow River in its enforced course. Millions of acre-feet of water spilled out, the floodwaters inexorably fanning out in all directions. Fields, factories, villages, and roads all fell under the rolling, tumbling currents spreading through the countryside. Peasants lucky enough to have some warning of the watery doom rapidly converging on them jammed the roads; others, closer to the dikes and dams, lost their lives as well as their farms in the ochre-colored floods. Their cries merged with those of city dwellers lost in a nightmare of crashing masonry, twisted girders, and yawning pits where subway tunnels had run.

Pits yawned through downtown San Francisco as well, cracks raggedly bisecting streets, parks, and buildings. The taller skyscrapers swayed, the ground twisting and shifting under their massive foundations. Some, built to withstand only lesser quakes—or built with substandard materials—groaned, shivered, and finally tumbled, smashing into the smaller buildings surrounding them. Glass exploded outward in glittering cascades, showering the streets below with lethal shards. Freeways slithered like snakes on their supports and then crashed down, one, two, six layers deep, overpasses meeting the underpasses in catastrophic embraces. Subway tunnels collapsed under avalanches of dirt, rocks, and substandard materials. Power lines writhed and snapped, sending hissing sparks arcing into the night air. Beach houses built like cliff dwellings tumbled, rolling into the ravenous ocean below. Nightmare darkness crashed into the city on a wave of extinguished lights, subsonic rumbles replaced with the din of sirens, screams, and car alarms.

* * *

In the cramped, plastic-smelling confines of the International Space Station, another alarm rang, its persistent buzzing finally driving the nighttime crew to action.

"Jim. Jim. James. Hey, Hideyoshi! Wake up!" Ivana poked the tectonic specialist sleeping in the hammock, then poked him again when all she got was a half-conscious grunt in response. "Rise and shine, sleeping beauty. Your infernal buzzers are beeping."

"Buzzers beeping?" Hideyoshi stirred, the words filtering through his uneasy dreams of falling through seemingly solid ground. He sat up abruptly, the motion setting the hammock thumping against its supports in the weightless environment of the space station. "The alarm on the geologic lasers? Why didn't you tell me?"

"I did," Ivana pointed out, watching her crewmate struggle with the zipper and straps that snugged him into the sleeping cocoon. She grinned. "Hate to say it, Jimbo, but it doesn't take a rocket scientist to figure out a slumber bag."

Hideyoshi finally gave up on the zipper and simply unhooked the bag from its wall fastenings. He launched himself down the round corridor toward the laser-detection module, wearing the slumber bag like a half-shed skin. "Obviously, it doesn't take a tectonic specialist, either," he shot back over his shoulder.

Ivana grinned and glided after him. "So, what's up with all the alarms? The sonar detectors catch something big going on?"

"No, not the sonar. It's the InSAR system alert," Hideyoshi said, his fingers dancing over the console controls. "Remember? I told you about it last week."

Ivana rolled her eyes. "Right. Like I remember all the acronyms you throw at me. I'll stick with my own bag of tricks for trying to calculate the butterfly effect." She glanced at the readouts. "Still, this looks interesting, now that it's screaming. Which experiment is this again?"

"This one's satellite-borne radar imaging. We're using it to keep an eye on the Three Sisters in Oregon. Got Becker down there, running surface tests for outgassing and salinity levels in the lakes around the volcanic sites." Data scrolled down the screens, and topographical maps zoomed in to show a definite rise in the low dome between the taller, more sharply defined cones of the mountains around it. "Crust deformation, terrain rise—wow, 27 inches! What the heck is going on . . ." His voice trailed off.

"Outgassing? Sounds like something Captain Nakima would be involved in," Ivana observed. "What are you chasing with training lasers at the ground between a bunch of volcanoes? What does 27 inches mean?"

"It means incipient volcanic activity," Hideyoshi said, after his crewmate smacked his shoulder to get his attention. His eyes remained glued on the readouts, a deep frown line growing between his straight, black brows. "InSAR keeps track of the rising ground over a big magma chamber. They detected a buildup of pressure underground back in the '90s, higher levels of carbon dioxide in the air, more dissolved minerals in the water. All signs of incipient volcanic activity—"

"Whoa!" Ivana exclaimed, staring at another screen across the tiny room that housed the terrestrial-science module. (The astronomers and physicists got the comparatively large, luxurious suites near the station's powerful telescopes; the biologists had more room, too, but it was full of rats, monkeys, and for one very long mission, vocalizing bullfrogs.)

"Whoa is right," Hideyoshi agreed. "We thought we had a baby volcano back then, but with these readings—Ivana, what's wrong?"

"James!" she exclaimed at the same time, her voice higher and more frightened than his. "Not your baby volcano—something else. Look!"

Hideyoshi dragged his eyes away from his readouts to follow Ivana's pointing finger. The scene on the TV monitor tuned to the news channels chilled them both: screaming crowds running from onrushing water, walls collapsing in aftershocks, fires roaring through ruins, graphics showing the spreading waves of destruction around the earthquakes' epicenters.

"Dear Heaven," Ivana whispered, the words she used so casually on other occasions taking on the tones of prayer.

The images of catastrophe reflected in their eyes, blue and brown irises around ebony pools of horror. The InSAR alarm sounded again, its urgent tones cutting through the muted sound from the satellite-news broadcast.

Hideyoshi looked at it vaguely, then gasped. He launched himself across the room, grabbing a handhold to keep himself from bouncing off the wall. Activation lights blossomed on the sat-phone's face as he ripped it out of its cradle and stabbed at its buttons. "Becker, answer, answer, answer," he chanted tightly. "Answer, answer—Becker!"

"Jim? What—it's nearly1:00 A.M.! I know there's no nighttime in space, but some of us need our sleep."

"Becker, get off that mountain," Hideyoshi ordered.

"What? Why?" The geologist's voice sounded less upset than excited.

"Get in your truck, turn on the radio, and listen to the news—as you drive as fast as you can off that mountain!" Hideyoshi repeated. "InSAR's going nuts. The dome's risen nearly *three feet* in the last three hours, and there's been an earthquake along at least two Northern California faults. Becker, our baby volcano's about to be born—"

"And I'm standing right in the delivery room!" Becker finished the thought. Thuds, crashes, and whispered grunts came through the open connection, followed by the sound of rushing air abruptly cut off with the slam of a truck door. "Jim, you still there?" Becker asked as the engine roared to life.

"Still here, Andre, costing the taxpayers thousands of dollars in connect fees while you skip around camp wasting valuable time," Hideyoshi reminded him.

"Wind's kicked up," the geologist informed him. "Trees are shaking like crazy." Static, then the professionally unruffled voice of a news announcer filled the spaces between his words. "Had a crazy dream about sleeping on a mother-lode pile of JELL-O—but that's more along your line, isn't it?"

"What?" Hideyoshi asked, his gaze fixed on InSAR's readouts. The topographical representation changed abruptly from burnt orange to glowing red as the lasers detected another ground surge.

"JELL-O, Mormons, you know, Jim, that's what you folks are famous for," Becker informed him. "You haven't—Cripes!"

"What?" Ivana and Hideyoshi both yelped.

"Steam," Becker shouted. "Ground's shaking. Road's bucking like a trawler deck."

The geologist kept up a running commentary for about twenty minutes, objective observations interspersed with decidedly subjective yelps. He raced his truck down the mountain road, dodging falling tree limbs, dislodged boulders, and terrified wildlife.

Far behind him, Becker's seismograph registered each successive shock, its sensitive needle swinging in wider and wider arcs across the blue-lined paper. Suddenly, it stopped, then quivered slightly. The tent Becker had abandoned shivered, then went still as the wind abruptly died. The night seemed to hold its breath, then a sigh rippled through the dark woods. The sky having said its piece, the ground took over. The sound began too low for anything but giants to hear, then gradually rose into the audible range as the magma and gasses beneath the dome reached critical pressure and erupted into the night, spewing a million tons of glowing molten rock, superheated steam, and suffocating cinders.

The InSAR console went silent as the lasers lost their lock on the now-vanished ground. Becker's satellite phone caught one last, "Whoa!" and fell silent as well. The dust cloud rolled upward and outward in great billowing gouts, smashing through the lowest layer of clouds and spreading across the thinner layers of the sky in a huge plateau of choking talc, lit from beneath like the roof of the Inferno. The superheated dust cloud flowed horizontally as well, blasting through the trees, vaporizing the tender needles and spring buds, laying flat the trunks of forest giants. Steam erupted from meadows, and boiling water bubbled through streams and ponds, killing plants and animals alike. Flows of molten rock followed, glowing ebony scarlet as it oozed in ever-widening streams out of the rents ripped deep in the ground, gouts of it spattering in sluggish fountains as the flows piled and mounted in the deep pit.

A shoulder of a hill shielded the main access road from the first blast wave, but it couldn't dampen the vibration through the ground. As the explosion hit, Becker's truck bounded off the road, careened through the trees, and landed hard in the creek below. The geologist tumbled out of the vehicle, kicking the door open and falling into the frighteningly warm and muddy water. He pushed toward the shore through the chest-high water, keeping his feet until another explosion threw him into the stream. He surfaced, spluttering—until the surface of the water bloomed into red-gold highlights. Chunks of half-melted rock crashed out of the sky, annihilating the disabled truck and lighting fires through the still-standing trees and underbrush. He dove and surfaced once again, considered the flames blossoming along the creek's shoreline, and swam as quickly as he could downstream, riding the increasingly turbulent, debris-choked flow.

The creek widened into a ford about the same time that the water became too wild—and too hot—for comfort. Becker pulled himself up and waded toward the moving lights on the shore, stumbling over the rocks barely submerged in the roiling flood. Hands reached down to help him climb the steep bank. He looked up to see Bob Fox, the owner of the bait shop/general store beside the ford, and two rangers. A small group of other people huddled behind them, frightened, dirty, and sporting temporary bandages.

"Glad you got out, Becker," Fox said. "You were up there pretty far."

"You're the geologist?" one of the rangers asked. When Becker said yes, he checked off an entry on his clipboard. "Still twenty-six missing," he informed his colleague, stepping away to bark an update into his radio. The reply was buried in static from the electrical charges in the dust.

"Thought you were keeping an eye on that volcano." The ranger looked at Becker.

"We were," Becker said, beginning to shake as the real danger he'd so narrowly escaped sank in, replacing the mixture of scientific interest and blind panic that had carried him through his mad flight down the mountain. Good thing he hadn't set up camp right on top of the dome!

"Didn't get a lot of warning," Fox commented.

Becker took a deep breath. "As my Mormon colleague on the ISS would say, Bob, nobody knows the time or season for an act of God. Even if we keep trying to figure it out."

A light dusting of ash fell from the sky, thickening into drifting, feather-sized flakes. The full moon had vanished behind a curtain of ash-filled clouds.

* * *

In the week before the earthquake hit, two hundred and twenty-two LDS missionaries left the Mission Training Center in Provo, Utah, for their mission assignments in the Orient. The quake knocked out transmission stations in many areas, including those in Taiwan. The missionaries' parents anxiously waited for word of their children's well-being. Among them were Chinedu Ojukwu, an administrator in the Church Educational System in Salt Lake City, and his wife, Adaure. Their youngest son, Chisom, was assigned to the Taiwan Taipei West Mission. Unable to sleep, Chinedu stepped out onto his back porch, glancing up as the silvery full moon slid behind a bank of clouds.

* * *

The moon electronically reappeared over the shoulder of a shaken reporter in San Francisco. Above the glow of the fires burning throughout the city, the moon hung like a rusty coin, its silver brightness dimmed into bloody shadow. "Casualty reports are still coming in; estimates from FEMA put the death toll at 7,000 and rising, just five hours after the earthquakes. Aftershocks still rock this area, terrifying the traumatized survivors of what many insurance-investment specialists are calling the most destructive and expensive natural disaster in human history." Crawls along the bottom and sides of the screen augmented the news with cold, hard statistics: damages, deaths, injuries, hotline numbers to call to check on survivors, and promos for private investigation and tracking businesses, hospitals, and ambulance services.